AUG 0 7 2018

LLER

IRRATIONAL FEARS

LEE LINDAUER

STORY MERCHANT BOOKS
LOS ANGELES
2018

STORY MERCHANT BOOKS

Story Merchant Books
400 S. Burnside Avenue #11B
Los Angeles, CA 90036

www.storymerchantbooks.com

ISBN: 978-0-9991621-6-3

This is a work of fiction. Names, characters, businesses, places, events and incidents are either the products of the author's imagination or used in a fictitious manner. Any resemblance to actual persons, living or dead, or actual events is purely coincidental.

Interior format & cover design by IndieDesignz.com

I dedicate this novel to my wife, Teri, for her keen insight and incredible editing skills, a woman who can proofread a page and turn it into a bloody mess of red ink. For that I am forever grateful. I thank you with love.

And a sincere thanks to my good friend and partner in crime Bryan Sims for his talent with a pencil in bringing to life his rendition of Angels Landing.

CHAPTER 1

Angels Landing
Zion National Park, Utah

ACROPHOBIA BE DAMNED.

Professor Mallory Lowe knew the notorious Knife-Ridge was all that separated her from the haven of the valley and the summit of Angels Landing. Any of her analytical geometry students could easily graph her journey on the X-Y plane, beginning with her morning coffee at the hotel and culminating exactly where she now stood. The curve would be gentle at first, sloping slightly, then rise sharply, correlating flawlessly with her increasing heart rate. Now, if she was to fall off the ridge to her death, the curve would suddenly become a vertical line, something mathematicians call a discontinuity.

Acrophobia be damned, who was she kidding?

But the text she had received two days earlier provided the incentive she needed to again attempt one of the most intimidating hikes in any national park. She recalled it verbatim:

Mallory, I'll be hiking Angels Landing on Wednesday. I understand you're in the area. How about reminiscing old times with a view? I know you'll succeed this time.

Tom Haley

Tom, what a treat that would be. She hadn't seen him in years. A quick text back confirmed she would meet him there.

She felt the warming sun on her cheeks, not to mention an accelerating apprehension as she gazed upon the ridgeline bisecting the sheer twelve hundred foot cliffs on each side. Any miscalculation would certainly be fatal. Refocusing, she took little time to consider that point. Firmly clutching the safety chain hanging between pipes embedded into the sandstone, she forced her impetuous nature to dissolve and drift into a meditative state. Her mind swiftly calculated the hyperbolic equation describing the chain's curve, a series of graceful catenaries blazing in the sun.

It was now or never.

One foot over the other she inched along, her New Balance sneakers securely gripping the cross-bedded rock. The equation kept repeating itself, recalculating in her head as she slid her hand along each section of chain—*arc length...curvature...tangential angle...arc length*—her thoughts a million miles away from the drop-offs on each side. After thirty feet, the ridge widened enough to grant a small sense of security. Releasing her vise-like grip, she bent over and kissed the chain. The strong, euphoric mood coursing through her body wouldn't last forever—yet, at this moment, nothing could silence it.

She pulled a water bottle from her pack, drew a long, wet drink, and continued up the trail punctuated by a few gnarled pinyon pines rooted in rocky crevices. Arriving at the summit, she saw daredevil chipmunks beg for handouts from lounging hikers. A fat lizard scurried across her path, then disappeared over the edge. A light breeze blew across her face.

Taking a deep breath, she mopped the sweat off her brow. Overhead, the hot midday sun polished the surrounding canyon walls with brilliant hues of crimson and chocolate, a far cry from the rounded promontories of the Wichita Mountains rising above the plains of Oklahoma. On rare occasions she would escape her family's struggling cotton farm and explore those rocky crags, imagining what life could be away from the hard times her family endured. Zion, like other remarkable places, was an awe-inspiring, one-of-a-kind seductive magnificence, a place where hardship never reared its ugly head.

Watching the Virgin River meander down the Zion Valley far below, she had totally forgotten about Tom's text until she noticed a man wearing a wide-brim hat walking her way. The familiarity of his lopsided gait and lean build made her smile. He approached with the eagerness of a long-lost friend.

"Tom, my God, it really is you," she said, wrapping him in a hug.

"Mallory, after all this time, I—" he fumbled to complete the sentence.

"When was it, six, seven years? You tried to coax me across the Knife-Ridge. I froze; couldn't budge. Me and heights, remember?"

"I never doubted you'd finally conquer it. Congratulations."

"Your text was a surprise. It challenged me, and you know I never turn down a challenge."

"I can vouch for that. I thought it would be fun to try this again."

She saw the trace of a smile. "You still at UNLV?"

"Still living at Mountain Springs; retired four years ago." He took off his hat and combed his hand through his thinning gray hair. "It's good to see you, Mallory." He sat down on a sandstone pedestal. "I called your math department. They had your vacation itinerary and were gracious enough to share it. Timing was perfect, so I sent you the text."

"But why not meet in town? We could have a drink or two?" She slid next to him.

"I kinda like it up here. It's like, you know…a *sanctuary*."

"Tom, what's going on?" She stared at his troubled eyes. "Something's on your mind. For an engineer, you don't hide it well."

"…Katie and I not seeing eye-to-eye. You know the difficulty we've had communicating. She won't return my calls. I'm concerned."

Tom's adopted daughter was her best friend. When was the last time they talked? Katie had been in Switzerland—one of her many stops rambling through Europe after her Peace Corps stint. What else had she mentioned? She had a boyfriend—a Turk—might even move to Turkey, live the ex-pat life. True love, didn't she say?

"I talked to her a few weeks ago," Mallory said. "When did you last hear from her?"

"I've been calling forever. She won't answer. Something's wrong, I just know it. It's my fault—"

"Tom, what are you talking about?"

"She might be killed if the dam is blown up." He blinked erratically and threw up his hands. "For God's sake—any day now!"

The words caused a wave of emotion as the weight of the world came crashing down. "Killed, what do you mean? What dam?"

He stood up quickly, his eyes darting along the summit from one hiker to the next as if he was looking for someone, somebody. He turned, faced Mallory. "I didn't know at first what was going on. I learned *too much*—way too much."

"What's this all about, Tom, in English, please?"

"If they find me, they'll—" He fidgeted, pacing erratically in a circle. He removed his bandana, swiping at his face with a jittery hand.

She got to her feet. Twelve hundred feet in the air on a narrow isthmus of rock wasn't the place for this conversation. "Listen, why don't we head on down and talk about it out of the hot sun. I'll give her a call. My cell phone is in the car."

Tom wasn't listening, bouncing back and forth like a pinball. "I begged her to leave. I'd get her myself, but they're after me. I need to disappear until this is over, but the dam—"

"Talk sense, Tom, what's going on?"

"I pleaded with her to come home, told her I'd make things right. Mallory, you're the only one she'll listen to."

"We'll get ahold of her, I promise. She'll answer my call." *Crap, this isn't good —way... up... here.*

He reached into his back pocket, searching. "Damn, I must have left it at home. It's a photograph of Katie and—"

The whine of a motor broke the conversation. Steadily it grew louder, the raucous sound of rotor blades. Mallory flicked her head to the south, glimpsing an object reflecting the strong rays of the late morning sun. The helicopter drew closer, the low-pitched *thwap-thwap* rising in decibels. She was aware of park regulations that banned aircraft from operating within its boundaries. The helicopter swooped lower into the depth of the canyon. The air echoed in a deafening roar. The rock beneath her feet vibrated. She turned and stared at Tom. His face said it all—a look of absolute terror.

The blue and white chopper displayed no identifying markings, hovering level with Angels Landing, not more than one hundred feet out. The other hikers took notice, clustering away from the uproar. She tried to make sense of what was happening. Slowly, it climbed over the summit barely five feet above the rim. Backing away from the tail rotor, she covered her ears. The helicopter maneuvered closer, the skids swinging back and forth above the rock.

"No way!" Tom yelled, turning to run and stumbling on the uneven surface. The helicopter swung his way; the right skid slammed him in the back, knocking him within inches of the edge.

She stood helpless; the chopper swerved back and forth, the rotor keeping her at bay. She was pinned, couldn't move, teetering a couple of feet from the edge. Her heart thumped wildly. She glanced at Tom, the skid bearing down on him, but the unevenness of the rock surface kept him from being crushed. Tom rolled away, pushing himself up. The helicopter powered forward, catching him square in the midsection as he let out a scream and slumped over the steel skid. Abruptly, the chopper lifted and floated over the cliff. Tom held on for dear life.

She watched in shock. The door of the helicopter opened. A man moved out of shadow, his face dull, displaying no sign of emotion. He held a rifle by the barrel, jabbing at Tom's head. Tom held tight. She could see his face—a face so pained it made her weep.

"Please, Tom—" Mallory cried out. "Hang on!"

The man hammered the rifle butt into Tom's fingers, mashing skin and bone.

Agony and unimaginable terror clouded his face. "Find Katie! Tell her I love her," he cried in agony.

And then he fell into the blue nothingness.

Horrified screams echoed down the valley. Mallory clasped her hands over her mouth. Her thoughts froze, her mind paralyzed. My God, what had she just witnessed? She stared out where Tom had vanished. Her eyes swept back to the helicopter, its incessant rotors churning an aggressive tenor. It pivoted ninety degrees.

The rifle pointed at her.

In a split second, she dove behind the sandstone pedestal just as the weapon ripped, bullets mowing over the rock. Chips flew in every direction. She remained down, knowing full well if the helicopter flew over her position she wouldn't have a chance. Then the sound of retreating rotors. Something must have spooked it. She stood up cautiously and watched it swoop over the western cliffs and into the vast wilderness of Zion.

CHAPTER 2

After the helicopter disappeared, Mallory raced down the trail. Slipping on the sandstone, she thought of one thing and one thing only: lose altitude fast! The harrowing Knife-Ridge passed in a blur. Everyone was anxious to get off the summit. There was little conversation between hikers, only the message in their eyes—pure panic. From her viewpoint along the West End Trail, she observed hikers and park personnel crowded in a chaotic scene below. She had a decision to make. If she admitted to authorities that she knew Tom Haley, she might be tied into an investigation for a long time.

Time was one commodity she didn't have. She had known Tom Haley for close to twenty years; met him working on her doctorate in mathematics at the University of Oklahoma. The image of him being murdered kept flashing. She wanted to scream. *Damn, I'm losing my mind!* She stopped at the side of the trail, unsure of her sanity, unsure of anything. Two hikers hurried past, nothing said. Another helicopter hovered above. Looked like law enforcement. It must have spooked the one that killed Tom.

Her ears rang with a clang of clashing tower bells—intolerable, crazy, a frenzied clamor. She cupped her ears. She had to get control. Taking several deep breaths, she scolded herself. *Get it together!*

And the photograph—a photograph of Katie and what? She'd better check it out. Knowing Tom, he was not one to stretch the truth. *Any day now, a dam will be destroyed—any day—and Katie killed.* Where was this dam? Something Tom worked on? And if he said Katie was in trouble, he meant it. As far as the authorities, hiding information would not sit well, but she had neither time nor patience for analyzing the pros and the cons. She had to take the bull by the horns and let the chips fall where they may.

She stayed off the main trail, slinking through the trees and bushes and bypassing the parking lot. Hiking down the valley another half a mile, she reached Zion Lodge. Five minutes later, she caught a shuttle back to the park entrance. Within fifteen minutes, she was out of Zion without raising suspicion.

The drive to Mountain Springs was nothing but a breakneck journey of ninety-five miles per hour speeding down I-15, flying by excited Vegas bound tourists and sleepy truck drivers. Her mind was pumping as fast as her foot on the accelerator. More than once, she tried to reach Katie on her cell phone. No answer. Each time she left a message. Had Katie lost her phone, or was she avoiding everyone? Where was she, someplace in Europe without cell service? It was no secret she was alienated from Tom, a tit for tat that had been going on for years. The flip side of the coin was unnerving. What if the worst had happened already: the dam destroyed, Katie already dead? Something Mallory didn't want to imagine.

She noticed the needle edge to one hundred. Backing off the accelerator, the speedometer leveled at an even ninety. Never once did she think about getting pulled over by a state trooper. Never once did she think her speed was endangering others. Never...once...never. There was no time. She slowed to eighty when she reached Vegas. Slowed even more as she wound through the city paralleling the strip: past Palace Station, past the Rio, Caesar's Palace, past the Aria, past Mandalay Bay. *Damn rush hour.* Who would live in this glitzy foolishness?

It was close to sunset when Mallory arrived in the small hamlet of Mountain Springs, twenty-five miles southwest of Las Vegas. As she drove, her mind spinning, she tried to make sense of what she witnessed. Tom said he shouldn't have gotten involved. Involved in what?

A quick search of his house and she would be gone. She knew Tom wouldn't have objected. Still, she felt uneasy—almost criminal; but more than that, she remembered Tom saying he couldn't go back or they would kill him. *Who and why?*

Finding Tom's house wasn't difficult. She'd been here when Katie had graduated college a few years earlier. Easing off Highway 160, the dirt road careened away from the few houses in the hamlet and looped around a juniper-covered hillside. It took two minutes to locate the mailbox with the name Haley stenciled on the side. Turning down a lane studded with expanses of blackbrush, she pulled next to the adobe rancher hoping not to be seen. Several desert willows graced the perimeter of the residence—the deep burgundy of the blooms catching the last bit of the day's rays. *Red as blood*, she couldn't help but think.

She stepped out of the rental car. It was twilight; her eyes darted back and forth on the lookout. A dreadful sensation of being watched hung like a dark cloud. Her nerves felt like an inescapable inferno. *Shake it off. Stay strong*, she admonished. Dusk was descending, and she needed to complete her task as quickly as possible. She came here for a reason: to find the photograph, hoping it would give her a clue as to where Katie may be. Soon it would be night and lights in the house would only invite scrutiny. Once Tom's body was recovered and his identity confirmed, it would only be a matter of time before the police swarmed the place.

She pulled herself together and approached the front door, then pushed the latch. Surprised, the door snapped open. Entering the long Southwest foyer, she moved quickly into the living room. She froze.

The room was trashed—a hurricane of destruction: smashed table lamps, sofa cushions shredded. Her heart was lashing in her chest. She entered the double doors off to her left, Tom's study. More devastation. Desk drawers littered the floor, papers scattered, a bookshelf emptied of its contents. She wiped the sweat dripping into her eyes. Who did this? Were they still here? Her guts constricted into knots.

She had to find the strength to search for the photograph. She must! She flicked the light switch on. A desk lamp on the floor illuminated a scratch pad of paper. She picked both up. She placed the lamp upright, righted an overturned chair, then sat down and stared at the pad.

The first thing that caught her eye: the phone number of the mathematics department at CU. Tom was right when he said he called the department for her vacation schedule; it too was jotted down. At the bottom was her cell phone number.

Taking up most of the space on the pad, he'd drawn a good representation of Angels Landing, since one of his passions was sketching in pencil. She'd recognize it anywhere. Staring at the intricacy of the drawing, she suddenly blinked. Did she see something other than fissures and rock layers on the promontory? She squinted again. Were her eyes playing tricks— was that the symbol for pi (π) embedded in the cliff near the top? Then below was that an e—and to the right, the square root of two? Pi (π)...3.1416, e, the base of natural logarithms...2.7183, and the square root of 2 ($\sqrt{2}$), or 1.4142, all slightly discernible in the rock face. Then her eyes took a double take, another irrational, the odd $\pi^2/6$, seen flowing over a small waterfall in the Virgin River below the promontory. What was so special about these four irrational numbers? But it was the $\pi^2/6$, the lone irrational that caught her attention. Of course, she had seen this number many times. *The Basel Problem,* the beautiful mathematical summation from the eighteenth-century. She knew it well. First proposed by Italian mathematician Pietro Mengoli in 1644, it wasn't solved until 1734 by Leonhard Euler. The equation easily scrolled across her mind, a subliminal relationship of inverse squares to circles.

$$1 + 1/2^2 + 1/3^2 + 1/4^2 + 1/5^2 + 1/6^2 + \ldots + 1/k^2 + \ldots = \pi^2/6$$

Tom had made a distinction on the scratch pad with these irrational numbers scribbled on the face of Angels Landing. The exception—$\pi^2/6$ by itself, floating away. Was Katie associated with *The Basel Problem* in some manner? Could mean something or nothing—she was here to find a photograph.

She bent down and picked through the mass of books and papers strewn over the floor. Cluttered about were professional journals and papers on hydrology of the upper Mesopotamia. She began to thumb through the journals, frantically looking for the photograph or some other clue. Several worn textbooks were interspersed with the journals on the floor. She picked them up one at a time and flipped through them. Nothing. She read the title of a dark-brown hardback. It was a textbook written by Tom himself: *The Influence of Dams on Water Basin Hydrology.* If she was lucky, maybe she could find something here on the dam that was to be destroyed. Tom was a world expert on hydrology, specializing in Eurasia. Even while a member of the UNLV faculty he had consulted on dam projects around the world. Flicking through the pages, a folded sheet of paper flew out. She unfolded it—a picture of Katie and a man other than Tom—older, graying hair pulled back in a ponytail. They were standing in front of a stone archway. She flipped the photo over and on the back was scrawled in pencil, barely legible: *Basel Museum.* She stuffed it into her pocket. Looking again at the scribbles of math constants on the pad, she ripped the sheet off and stuffed it into her pocket as well.

Lane McKenzie had not anticipated seeing a car parked in front of Tom Haley's house. He had driven the Suburban onto a gravel road that skirted a low hill paralleling Haley's driveway and parked in a group of junipers out of sight of any snoopy neighbors. Here, he had an unobstructed view of the adobe rancher and the vehicle. It was deathly quiet, except for the downshifting of a tractor-trailer coming down the main highway. He picked up the night-vision goggles lying on the passenger seat and stepped out of the Suburban. Dusk was beginning to dim his view. He walked thirty yards down a rocky path until he came to a clearing. Stretching his stiff neck, he adjusted the view finder on the goggles. He scanned the house and surroundings. The car was a Hyundai sedan with a Nevada license plate.

Lowering the goggles, he arched his aching back. Zion seemed like weeks ago, but it had only been a few hours—hours from hell. Christ sakes, how did he fuck up so bad? They had Haley in their control for two years and in their sights all last week. How on earth could they have let him slip them? Locating him at Zion was sheer luck, but it was too late—way too late.

There were days like this when McKenzie wondered why he stayed in the agency, and there were times he wished he'd never met Haley. What had gone smoothly the last two years had suddenly taken a nosedive. Winners and losers was all the goddamn business was about, and lately it seemed that the losers were winning. "Ironic," he mumbled.

He had been in this situation before. The dead ends, the lack of information that would send a covert operation straight to the grave. He'd also remembered the out of the blue infusion of luck that would carry him to the finish line, all because of credible information which had a life of its own, moving from one participant to another. Despite not knowing whom the woman with Haley was, his only option was to investigate the house before local authorities swarmed it. Hopefully something useful would be found to help him identify her and her connection.

Now it looked like someone had beaten him to the punch. Completing a secondary scan with the goggles, the dry scrub around Haley's house took on a greenish mask as ambient daylight slowly disappeared. He zoomed into the window on the west side of the house. An interior light suddenly lit. He could not see anyone distinctly, although a shadow flittered back and forth.

Raising the power level on the goggles, his gaze spotted a flutter of bushes lining an arroyo to the left. Abruptly, a man stepped out of the streambed.

Stooped over, he waddled over to the vehicle. Now on high alert, McKenzie watched as he opened the passenger door and reached in. Seconds later, he retrieved a paper packet from the glove box. After skimming through them, he stuffed it into his shirt pocket. The man straightened up and pulled a gun from his waistband. Out of his back pocket, he retrieved a stub barrel and attached it onto the muzzle of the gun. McKenzie took a double take. It was eccentric with flat side walls and angled edges. An Osprey multi-caliber silencer if he wasn't mistaken. The man hastened to the house.

A voice echoed down the foyer startling Mallory.

"Ms. Lowe; Mallory Lowe," the voice called out evenly. "I'm with the police."

How would the police know her name? And how could they be here so quickly? No way Tom's identity could have been determined so fast. Her stomach churned. She flicked the desk lamp off. A faint stream of light funneled into the room. A murky shadow appeared on the wall. The front door was open.

"Ms. Lowe," the voice repeated. "The killers in the helicopter have been captured. You are safe."

The shadow began to undulate. Someone was moving her direction.

"Ms. Lowe." The voice was getting closer.

She crouched low and crawled across the room. Ducking through the opening into the kitchen, she reached the back door and paused. What if others were outside, waiting? Spinning, she saw the door to the garage and slipped inside. A small window to her right provided a meager amount of light. With uneasy gulps, she focused on the door and listened.

A sound intensified coming from the kitchen. A click of heels on the tile floor, leaden in step…silence…the snap of a latch, a door opening, and the clink of it closing…silence.

"*Ms. Looooo*—" The voice hissed right outside the garage door. Too close.

She clasped her mouth to muffle her scream. She held her breath afraid to inhale. What she needed was a weapon, at least a fighting chance. Her eye caught a rack of tools, shovels, rakes, loppers—an axe. She grabbed the axe and retreated into shadows. She waited, the axe shaking in her hands.

The door opened. The silhouette of a man stood in the doorway—tall, broad shoulders. His sweeping eyes were black—hollow sockets on an ashen face, scanning, searching. He sniffed the air. She watched him move slowly, click-clack of heels across the garage floor.

Mallory let out an unexpected gasp. His dark eyes darted in her direction. She imagined a rabid smile on his face as he methodically moved past a row of storage units. Closer. She remained motionless, crunched tight behind a water heater, the axe raised in defense.

The man took another step into the diffused light.

The long barrel of a gun materialized—then his crazed face. "Fucking bitch!" he snarled, taking aim. In anticipation, Mallory slammed the cutting edge of the axe down hard. A hideous shriek followed by the man's body stumbling backwards. The gun flew. His injured hand hung limp, blood spurting. Mallory sprinted past him without looking back. Oblivious to anyone else who might be waiting, she rushed out the back door to her car and sped away, her heart hammering fiercely against her rib cage.

McKenzie raced up the trail back to the Suburban when he saw the man enter the house with the fixed silencer. What if the person in the house was the woman he was hunting? As he flung open the Suburban door, he swore he heard a vehicle peel out on the gravel road below. He hopped in, made a U-turn and raced back to the highway. The Hyundai he had seen earlier hit the road heading east. Before he could pursue, another pair of headlights emerged out of the brush on the south side and gunned after the vehicle.

Mallory swallowed hard trying to rid the puke rising inside, the vision of the man still fresh—the hand hanging grotesquely, barely attached. Barreling down Highway 160, she headed back to Las Vegas. The tops of the hillsides drifted from pink to gray.

A pair of headlights came her way. She turned her own lights on. Dammit, her mind was not functioning on all cylinders. If finding Katie was high-priority, the police might have a clue after their investigation...*after.* That man was no cop. What she needed now were the police, the *real* ones. Let them do their job. She should have stopped and talked to them at Zion before coming to Tom's house. Now she had probably contaminated any evidence left by the killers. And her fingerprints were everywhere. *What a fool!* It was time to cut her losses and let the authorities in on what Tom had told her. It was the right thing to do—or was it? If she talked to the authorities, Katie's fate would be sealed. *Could I live through another period of inaction in my life?* A resounding *no* escaped from her lips.

As she relived the horrors of the day, another pair of headlights came out of nowhere, this time from behind. She slowed, hoping the vehicle would pass. The headlights turned bright, coming within inches of her bumper. A sickening feeling emerged—no way.

The vehicle rammed her.

She engaged, floored the gas, and rocketed down the highway. The headlights kept up, blinding her rearview mirror. The road straightened and the vehicle steered into the other lane, coming up fast beside her. She took a quick peek. It was a dark SUV, two men in front, maybe a third in the back. She returned her attention to the road.

The SUV swerved, this time smashing into the side of the Hyundai. Her hands tightened on the wheel. To her right, the shoulder disappeared; a steep embankment hugged the edge. She hit the brakes, and the SUV shot past in a blur. Tires screeched. Losing control of the vehicle, Mallory braced herself as she rode down the steep slope, plowing through a patch of creosote. Tossed like a beanbag, she stared at headlight-illuminated shrubs flying over the hood like the internal workings of a tornado. Abruptly, the rental came to a stop, inertia throwing her forward and deploying the airbag. She screamed in response as her head snapped. Then all was calm. She took a deep breath, allowing her fogged mind to clear. Undoing the seatbelt, she struggled against the deflating airbag and fumbled for the door handle. Finding it, she pushed it open, freeing herself from the wrecked car.

She heard shouting. "Over here."

She ran away from the voices. Dark as it was, her eyes adjusted. Another shout in the distance. Maybe this had nothing to do with Tom, but common sense told her different.

Her tired legs tripped over a large rock in the drainage, causing her to fall. She pushed herself up, spitting blood and grit from her mouth. Looking around, she noticed a steel culvert roughly ten feet high. She could see a haze of light at the far end.

The shouting loomed closer. They were following her in the ravine. She dashed into the culvert stumbling over debris, even a splash of water. Exiting, she turned in time to see a man running towards her. She spotted a trail climbing out of the arroyo, winding itself up to the highway.

She dragged up the path, steep at first. Pausing halfway to catch her breath, she heard footfall echoing below, getting closer. She found a large rock, picked it up, ten pounds at best. Eyes glued, she waited, her heartbeat pounding like a tin drum. A man's head appeared, an arm outstretched, gun pointed. She released her grip and the rock fell, hitting him squarely in the back. He went down with a thud, the gun coughing from his hand.

She clawed the remaining distance to the highway. Breathing hard, she neared the top. And then her worst fears as a hand seized her arm, and yanked her onto the pavement. She hit the road hard.

"Stay down," the man demanded.

Without warning, he aimed a gun into the ravine and triggered off three shots.

"This way," he said, pushing her toward a vehicle across the highway.

She jumped into the passenger side of a Suburban realizing this man saved her life. He keyed the engine and threw it into gear. The dashboard glow swathed his face, his dark irises trained on the road as he barreled towards Las Vegas. Lean and muscular, his fingers gripped the wheel firmly with a sense of command. She thought about his gun and then she saw it was docked in a shoulder holster below his left arm.

"Are you all right?" he asked.

Her spinning head nodded. "Who are you?"

Ignoring the question, he said, "We've still got trouble."

She turned her head and saw headlights coming fast. It was the same SUV that had pursued her. He accelerated but then slowed as they approached a curve veering sharply to the left. The SUV didn't brake. It rammed into them with a fury, and her head slammed hard against the headrest. Her teeth chattered. The Suburban fishtailed across the center stripe as the stranger kept a tight grip. "Hang on," he said, stepping on the accelerator after gaining control. He reached across his chest and took out his gun and handed it to her, butt first.

"It's chambered, so be careful. Ever shoot a Beretta?"

"Old Colt revolver, but if it has a trigger—" Mallory grasped it with both hands, her mind buzzing. She remembered more than one occasion killing rattlesnakes in Oklahoma. Shooting was easy, steady grip—front sight on target —press the trigger—*piece of cake.*

"Roll your window down and wait until they're on us. Put the sight on the driver and shoot. That baby will do the rest of the work for you."

She stared at the weapon, her hands beginning to shake. Visions of police action movies played across her mind, especially the part where the bad guys shot back. She swallowed hard, knowing her choices were limited.

The SUV caught up and positioned itself. Her benefactor waited patiently, watching headlights come from behind. "Get ready." The advancing vehicle prepared for another ramming. He jerked the wheel to the left, crossed the double-yellow line and stepped on the brakes. The tailing SUV shot ahead in the opposite lane. The Suburban sped up, coming alongside. "Now," he yelled. "Let the driver have it."

Her face flush with anger, she aimed the Beretta with both hands and pressed the trigger in quick succession. The gun bucked wildly, glass exploded. Swerving, the SUV couldn't hold its position and careened down an embankment, plowing through a forest of Joshua trees, then flipping and landing on its roof. The Suburban eased back into the right lane.

Mallory yanked the pistol back in. Teeth still clenched, she stared straight ahead. After a moment, her heart rate moderated. She handed the gun back.

He holstered it, his eyes reassuring her that they were again safe. "Someone wants you dead."

CHAPTER 3

Lane McKenzie tossed the keys of the Chevy Suburban to the young Airman First Class and trudged into the supply hanger. The heat from the day remained, sharpened and intensified with the noisy barrage of F-22A Raptors conducting nighttime maneuvers. A couple of hundred feet away on the tarmac, a C-17 transport was being loaded with cargo and pre-checked for a late-night flight. In one hour he would board the plane and shuttle across country to Langley Air Force Base in Virginia.

He entered the small office and found the woman he'd rescued on the highway west of Vegas staring at the walls. He studied her features. Now beneath the fluorescents, she didn't look as bedeviled as when he first encountered her. Her dark-chestnut locks hung shy of her shoulders and there was wildness in her deep-set green eyes. She exhibited a survivalist mentality, a surprising ferocity when she triggered the Beretta. He was good at pegging a person's character, and he liked what he saw. She didn't take shit from anyone, proven by her coolness shooting at the SUV and her story about the axe affair at Haley's place. Though she had been through hell and back—as displayed by the bruises on her face, split lip, and torn T-shirt—she showed a dogged determination.

He straddled an oaken chair and leaned over the back. "Can't remember if I introduced myself. Lane McKenzie."

She hesitated, and then grasped his outstretched hand. "Thanks again." She flicked a curly strand from her eyes. "Mallory Lowe, vacationing college professor," she mocked.

"A professor?"

"Mathematics, University of Colorado, Boulder."

"Why mathematics?"

"A love of the Greek alphabet, and I didn't have to join a sorority," she said sarcastically.

"Why were you at Haley's place?"

She avoided the question. "What's this, an interrogation?"

"Didn't mean to pry, just curious. Is he family?"

"I have no immediate family."

"What brings you here?"

"Visiting friends in San Diego. Thought I'd spend a couple of relaxing days at Zion before heading back home—or so I thought they'd be relaxing." She picked up a water bottle and took a swig. "On the drive here you said you were CIA. If I'm not mistaken, this is an Air Force base."

"I work closely with the fly boys."

Mallory twisted her head sideways. "Are you going to tell me it was just a coincidence you were out cruising Highway 160?"

"No. The truth? I've been tailing you since Zion. Unfortunately, I got there a little too late."

Mallory stared at the CIA man. "You were at Zion? A friend of mine was murdered there."

"I know."

"You know?" she repeated, dumfounded.

He brushed aside the question. "How are you and Tom Haley connected?"

"From my graduate days. He was an advisor."

"Why did you meet him on that crazy precipice?"

"He sent me a text; said he'd be there."

"Why'd he want to meet up there?"

"Old times' sake, I thought. He was always kind of cryptic like that, even back at OU. Then he told me his daughter Katie was missing." Her eyes misted as they bore into McKenzie. "Why was he murdered?"

"He was working for us. I'm not at liberty to tell you more than that." He watched her reaction, her anger growing.

"So, you're saying he was an operative?"

McKenzie nodded.

"And now he's dead? Whose fault is that?"

"It's the business."

"You're in a crappy business."

"Well, it saved your sweet ass this evening."

"All right, dammit! But how could a helicopter penetrate Zion and end up killing Tom?"

"If we knew that, this wouldn't have happened, don't you think?"

Mallory slunk back in her chair. "Something's rotten."

"The whole world is. Now, how'd he act up there?"

Mallory reflected. "Something drove him to desperation. I could see it in his eyes…and then the helicopter."

"Anything else?"

"He said something about a dam that was to be destroyed—blown-up. Does that mean anything?"

McKenzie felt strangely helpless, as if he was caught with his pants down. *Haley told her about the dam.* "What exactly did he say?"

"He said Katie will die if the dam blows."

He knew he couldn't discuss the dam. It might compromise their present operation. "Haley was a hydrological consultant. He never talked to us about any specific dam. Why were you at Haley's house?"

"Curiosity. Maybe something there would lead me to Katie to warn her."

McKenzie combed through his unruly hair and shifted his near six-foot frame in the rock-hard chair. He had reason to suspect she knew more than she was sharing, as he was also. "You know they still want you dead."

She raised her brow.

"Curiosity killed the cat."

She looked at him with a renewed vigor. "I'm not a cat, but I do have one, and he's fine, thank you."

"What are you going to do?"

"Listen, I'm just a nerdy, overly cautious, professor. I like to stick to my business— teaching, writing, research, picking cat hair off the sofa. Guns and killing make me nervous. You tell me, what should I do?"

"If I were you, I'd stay out of trouble."

Her expression hardened. "I have no choice. I have to find Katie."

"Where would you start?"

"Switzerland. That's where she was last time we talked."

"By yourself?"

"If that's what it takes," she shot back. "I'm not teaching this summer. I have the time."

She's damn independent, that could be good. "Why would Haley ask you to search for his daughter?"

Mallory sat motionless. "You wouldn't understand."

He left it at that. Why not see where this would lead. Believing there still could be a way to keep the investigation on track, he pointed to the tarmac. "That C-17 out there is going to leave within the hour for Washington D.C. I think I have enough pull to have them divert to Denver. It would be wise to rethink your vacation plans. Would you care for a ride?"

Her mood lightened. "Yes, thanks."

CHAPTER 4

Istanbul, Turkey

Katie Haley moved briskly along the pier past the berths of dilapidated trawlers and derelict fishing boats, past the pungent smell of salt air and reeking fish. Above, a lone cumulus cloud blocked the morning sun, reinforcing the chill created by the unseasonably cool temperatures over the Bosporus. She looked to her left towards the Galata Bridge spanning the Golden Horn inlet, connecting the sun-drenched Fatih district to the south. Oddly, the cloud was positioned to allow sunshine to strike the old walled city of Istanbul. Maybe that's where she should be.

She had deep-set brown eyes, a straight nose and dark brown hair. At first glance, she didn't look out of the ordinary. Modern Turkish women in the cities were no different than their European and American counterparts. Headscarves and conservative clothing were hardly the norm in secular, urban Turkey, even rare in the working class neighborhoods and the many docks and piers that encircled the megalopolis. At twenty-eight years old and six months removed from her assignment in the Peace Corps, she relished her ex-pat status. In the last month, she was able to completely accept the separation from her father. It was her decision, a form of therapy and survival.

Today, she was nervous and excited at the same time. Her mission: find the *Harem Kayip*. It didn't take long. Directly ahead, she spotted the rusted red-and-white-hulled fishing boat with the paint-peeled aft bridge splitting the double trawling booms. In faded letters, *Harem Kayip* was stenciled on the side. A little over sixty-five feet long, the trawler had seen better days when fishing for tuna provided a decent living. Now, with the fisheries of the Marmara Sea increasingly depleted, the owner found other ways to meet expenses.

As Katie approached, she recognized the wiry gray beard and Greek fisherman cap of the captain, Selim. His eyebrows rose as he looked up from splicing the ends of a rope together.

"Come, hurry please," he said in stilted English. He dropped the rope and pointed to the ramp, pivoted and knocked briskly on the door to the cabin, and then rushed up the stairs to the bridge.

She stepped onto the deck just as Ismet Firat appeared in the doorway. Her eyes sparkled. She hadn't seen him in two weeks. He was her age and handsome, with a short black beard, square jaw, and a Sig Sauer stuffed in his waistband. Turning, he disappeared into the shadow of the cabin. Katie followed. Ismet shut the door behind her and placed the gun down on a small wooden table. The only light came from a small porthole, the sun's rays streaking across the table and climbing the near wall.

He faced her, his intense expression softening. Every time she saw him, a jolt streaked through her veins. This was a new stage of her life with freedom to see where it would lead. He was her alibi, her excuse to stay away from her father. She moved closer, reached up, and touched his cheek. Yearning, he wrapped his arms around her and kissed her hard on the lips, holding her close for a moment.

"We have to move fast," he said. "We only have a few more days."

Deep concern clouded his face. He was not one to overstate difficulties or believe in half-truths. This was his territory. He understood the obstacles they faced, and he knew when to adjust.

"Is it the military?"

He shook his head. "The military we can deal with, the police, too." He moved over to the porthole and looked out. "It's *them*."

A flash of apprehension darted across her face as she watched Ismet stuff the Sig back in his waistband. She did love him, didn't she? She had thought long and hard on this. Yes, she did love Ismet. Her father, even though he had deep ties to the dam, was no longer involved and had no say on her relationship.

"What do we do?" she asked, frightened.

"It is too risky to stay here. Selim will get us down the coast. Near Canakkale, we will take a small plane back to Diyarbakir. There, we will regroup."

Katie didn't like the change. "What about remaining logistics? How can we procure all that we need in eastern Anatolia? Isn't Istanbul the only supermarket around?"

"Everything is set. What we don't get, we can live without. There are other connections. We must move fast."

Ismet opened the door and yelled up to the captain to push off. A few moments later, the *Harem Kayip* was motoring under the bridge. The Bosporus Strait opened in front, the narrow waterway separating the European from the Asiatic side of the city. She remembered before the Peace Corps, falling in love with Turkey and its people the first time she laid eyes on its beauty. That time, she had taken a ferry down the Bosporus from the Black Sea to the Sea of Marmara and eventually into the Mediterranean, retracing the ancient route of Jason and the Argonauts—a very quixotic journey interspersed with salt, sea and sun.

Out on the deck taking in the sights, Katie was startled when Ismet rushed down from the bridge. "Quick, to shore," he yelled at Selim.

"What's wrong?" she asked.

"We are being followed." Ismet raced toward the stern and raised binoculars to his eyes. "They are closing fast."

He tossed the binoculars to Katie and disappeared around the bridge. She steadied herself, peering through the lenses. A speedboat came into view, full throttle, heading right at them. She squinted for a better look.

"Selim, cut across their bow," Ismet demanded, pointing at a barge that was steaming their direction.

The captain's eyes flared. "We will be hit; no time."

"Do it now!"

Face frozen, Selim twirled the wheel, redirecting the trawler towards the oncoming barge. If they made it, the barge would offer a screen and give them time to get lost in boat traffic on the other side. With any luck, they would be able to escape.

Her eyes flashed to the barge. The air reverberated with five blasts of a horn, an ominous warning. Her lips tightened as she attempted to gauge the chance of being hit. Now, they were dead center with the oncoming barge, a vessel of bone-crushing steel just shy of three thousand tons. The odds were not good. The flat-headed nautical freight train was one hundred and fifty feet away and closing fast.

She closed her eyes and prayed.

The end never came. Voices from the passing behemoth yelled words in Turkish, words that sounded as offensive in another language as they did in four-letter English. She opened her eyes to see it steam on by; the voices subsided as the *Harem Kayip* continued.

Ismet joined Selim on the bridge and directed him to a wharf not far away. Katie remained motionless as the captain piloted the boat along the nearest dock.

"We will leave here," Ismet said. "We can't afford to have them catch up."

Selim came up alongside an empty berth and stabilized the trawler. Ismet haphazardly tied up the mooring lines. Reaching over the rail, he helped Katie.

Looking at Selim he advised, "Tell them you were just ferrying us across. They have no gripe with you."

Selim nodded.

"Hurry," Ismet said, taking off at a fast clip.

"Where to?" she panted, trying to keep up.

"Anywhere but here. We have to outrun them."

Glancing back, Katie could see the speedboat edge next to the trawler. They couldn't lose the ground they had gained. Instinctively, Ismet flagged down a passing *taksi*. He directed the driver to the Grand Bazaar. He told Katie that if they couldn't lose their assailants in the huge covered shopping mecca housing thousands of stores, shoppers, and tourists, they deserved to be caught.

Ten minutes later, they arrived at the Nuruosmaniye Gate. Ismet paid the driver. Another *taksi* stopped across the street. Two men got out, a tall one in a tan jacket and a short one dressed in black leather. He seemed to be in charge.

"Quick, inside, they've found us," Ismet ordered.

Seeing the men dodge the afternoon traffic, her instincts for self-preservation pulsed through her body. They meant business. She hurried after Ismet under the gate. Entering the bazaar, they found it difficult to maneuver. They pushed through the crowds with Katie constantly looking over her shoulder. The heat overwhelmed her, rising fifteen degrees, courtesy of the thousands of electric lights and packed bodies. She found herself on a narrow street covered by an arched roof structure. Shops lined both sides, crammed with meats, produce, and Turkish wares of all types.

"We need to lose them," Ismet yelled above the din, as they pushed through the frenzy.

Katie kept up.

Nevzat Sari slowed his pace as he neared the gate. This was not what he had in mind, but then the hordes of shoppers and stifling crowds could make it easier to finish the job. He pulled a silencer out of his back pocket and attached it to his Makarov, keeping it hidden beneath his leather jacket. His number one objective was to take them alive, but if the opportunity arose, he would not hesitate to kill Ismet Firat. He wasn't surprised to see the woman with him; it had to be the American, the Haley girl. A heavy envy spread.

"Do not kill them yet," he commanded Mehmet, his partner. "Take them alive."

They rushed under the gate. Sari was short and agile, with neatly trimmed black hair and intense brown eyes. The sideburns and pencil-thin mustache seemed odd on his baby-smooth face, a sharp contrast to his physical abilities.

"Move ahead," he instructed Mehmet. He could see Ismet's head bobbing through the crowd. The woman was close behind. Mehmet had almost caught up with them. This may be easier than he thought. He picked up his pace ever so slightly. He had them in his sight.

Katie and Ismet moved ahead along Kalpakcilar Caddesi, aware they were still being followed. The crowd bunched, and the sound of Turkish music exploded off to their right. Jostled from behind, shoppers stumbled into one another as the rhythmic gyrations of several folk dancers in embroidered trousers and colorful shirts stormed in from an intersecting street, forcing the shoppers to retreat to the side.

Street dancers performing in a crowded marketplace didn't make much sense. Constricted and separated by the swarm, she panicked when she lost sight of Ismet,

And then her worst fear—a sharp pain in her back. Hot breath singed her ear. "Move!" the heavily accented voice hissed.

Katie twisted her head. It was the tall one with the curved nose; the one wearing the tan jacket. He didn't look happy, and she didn't want to imagine what was pressed to her back.

"I can't move through here."

The gun barrel thrust deeper.

The music grew louder.

"Move, now!"

Feeling the pressure, she pushed against those in front, causing a few nasty stares, as if being squeezed to death wasn't scary enough. She was frightened beyond anything she had known before. The incident with the trawler was a distant memory. She had to get away…somehow.

The gunman kept her advancing, forcing her to take the next cross street. The crowds were still heavy, but nothing compared to where the dancers and the music blared. She kept her pace, afraid to turn around. She couldn't feel the gun barrel anymore; maybe he had it hidden under his jacket to avoid making a scene.

A scene was what she needed.

Sari pushed through the throngs. A street event with dancers was not what he expected. He tried to find Mehmet in the crowds, angling his head in all directions. He could only hope his partner had the two subjects in sight.

The music slowed; clapping erupted.

Still scanning the crowds, he saw Ismet, his head weaving above the masses.

Sari tightened the grip on his reliable Makarov. *Take him alive,* he kept telling himself. Killing can come later. He charged through the bystanders rushing after him.

Katie's senses were heightened, overpowered by the smell of fine leather from the endless shops lining the corridor packed with purses, belts, jackets, everything imaginable. She sized up a display of leather jackets four rows high. It was not attached to the wall. It was now or never.

"Keep moving!" the gunman ordered.

In an instant of desperation, she grabbed the end of a rack and yanked it with all the strength she could muster. The heavy metal frame tumbled into the corridor, burying her assailant and several other shoppers under an avalanche of leather. Shouts erupted in the ensuing madness. A clerk came running out, a look of dismay on his face. But Katie was long gone, zigzagging around tourists and shoppers like an Olympic slalom gold medalist. After a few minutes she paused to catch her breath, exhausted and shaking. No sign of the gunman, she pressed on, turning right at the next intersection.

She moved quickly down the covered street, passing shop after shop. She reached the Cevahir Bedesten, the fifteenth-century domed-roof market. Stepping inside, she gaped at the glut of bright lights and jewelry shops, a treasure chest of gold, pearls, and precious gems.

Her eyes darted up and down the corridor. She spotted a policeman strolling along the aisle watching the crowds, which were still rather thick. She wanted to feel secure, but fear remained. What if he was alerted to her deed back in the leather section? Maybe that would be good. An arrest may save her life. She turned toward a jewelry case with a glittering array of gold bracelets. She stared at the case, but her eyes didn't register anything. She should move on while she had the chance.

"May I help you?" a voice in acceptable English said.

Startled, Katie turned. The proprietor smiled at her, a balding middle-aged man with white shirt and black slacks.

"Would you care to see something?" he continued, unlocking the case.

"Well, I…" She gazed back at the bracelets and pointed at one. While he was removing it, she twisted her head to look around. No sign of Ismet, or the gunman.

"I give you good price," the proprietor said, handing the bracelet to Katie.

She slipped it on and admired it. "How much?"

"Three hundred dollars."

"What—that's robbery."

The proprietor didn't let up. "For you, two-fifty. My best."

Looking up from the counter, a chill ran along her spine. The man in the tan jacket was at the far end of the aisle, hurrying her way. He was not smiling, a leather coat draped over his arm. The gun must be hidden underneath.

The proprietor became restless. "Two-twenty-five, a steal."

Katie shook her head. "Fifty." She looked back the other way. The policeman was no longer there.

"Fifty dollars. You insult me." He grabbed the bracelet back.

She moved slightly to her left, putting the proprietor in the way of the gunman. "Okay," she said. "One-fifty."

The proprietor smiled. "Two hundred, best price. Fourteen carat, fine gold."

She glanced back at the gunman. His jaw dropped slightly and his eyes wavered.

Katie heard a voice say, "Backup slowly."

It was Ismet. The Sig was pointed at the man. The surprised proprietor stumbled into the case. She moved just as the gunman raised the leather jacket.

Ismet didn't hesitate. He fired, and the gunman buckled, red oozing from a chest wound. The proprietor fell to his knees as chaos ensued.

Ismet slammed the Sig into a nearby fire alarm box, breaking the glass. He pushed the button. The alarm screeched loudly—fire sprinklers erupted.

"Quick, this way," he yelled, pushing Katie through the confusion.

The policeman Katie saw earlier ran their direction. Ismet pleaded something in Turkish, pointing towards the jewelry shop. The policeman's eyes bulged, and he raced toward the shop, one hand reaching for his gun, the other talking into his collar radio.

Katie sprinted after Ismet, disappearing into the crowd.

Sari heard the gunshot. Shoppers were running toward him, terrified expressions etched on their faces. He reached the Bedesten and plowed through the masses into the large domed structure. A crowd had gathered around one of the jewelry stores. They were being held back by several policemen. The jewelry store in a state of bedlam, water rained down from the ceiling, the alarm still screeching. And on the floor, he glimpsed the body of a man face down. Blood pooled beneath, mixing with the water, rose-colored.

It was Mehmet.

CHAPTER 5

Lane McKenzie sat in his office waiting for a driver to take him to Andrews Air Force Base. It was late evening. Three hours earlier, he learned Mallory Lowe had boarded a flight to Basel, Switzerland. No surprise there. Whatever her shortcomings, lack of guts wasn't one of them.

He had graduated in international affairs from Northwestern University with a degree but no career. Puttering along from job to job—bartender, financial planner, and broker assistant—he worked everything and anything that kept the rent paid. He met a woman at Milo's, near Michigan and E. Huron in Chicago where he tended the late afternoon bar shift. Her name was Jennifer Reilly—a Chicago police detective with short caramel hair, silky skin, an alluring smile, and a hidden toughness. She had frequented the bar off-duty, and the relationship was steady; nothing too serious, just two people satisfying each other's needs with occasional talk of marriage. He quit bartending and found a decent job selling securities. She stayed on the police force, stressful as it was, working drug rings, murders, and illegal firearm sales. Off hours she studied the CIA recruitment manual. She always wanted to be an agent. The week before the test, he got word—Jennifer was shot dead, a drug deal gone awry. He didn't allow himself to grieve; what good would it have done? Looking back, he realized now how much he loved her. Jennifer had dreams and ambitions, snuffed out in the blink of an eye. If she had lived, would they have fulfilled them together? Not knowing, he decided to finish what she had started, taking and passing the CIA entrance exam.

The sharp beep of his phone startled him. He picked the receiver up and identified himself.

"Wanted to catch you before you left," Lou Amistad, his case officer barked.

"I thought you'd call."

"Damn right—and we all know why."

"It's tough to straddle the fence, you know that Lou."

"Cut the bullshit, Lane, we know your abilities. Losing Tom Haley was tough, but it wasn't a failure. He was recruited, he agreed to the task, but now you've got this university professor to deal with."

"I'm not interfering. She's making all her own decisions."

"That's my point; you know she's out of her league. Any ethics board would bury you in a second if they found out the CIA is involved, and that right there will get you tossed from the agency."

McKenzie took a deep breath.

Amistad continued. "You've got one job and one job only. If I understand, this professor is trying to track down Haley's daughter. That may be her business, but it's your responsibility to keep her safe. I know you, so don't try to interject anything into her agenda."

McKenzie exhaled a deep breath. "COMPLETELY understood."

"This is a national security issue as high as any on our radar. You know the fallout if we find out the IFC has been compromised. We could have a major international problem, a real world crisis. Developing countries linked to the World Bank could turn to economic blackmail, their currencies could fail, destabilization. The list goes on and on and on."

McKenzie could picture Amistad pacing in front of his desk, still preaching. How many times had he heard this same tired old lecture about the International Finance Corporation?

Amistad's voice was crisp. "Accountability, that's all I'm asking."

"In regards to—"

"Letting her rush into our problem is pretty cut and dry and goes against every department rule. If she gets into trouble, get her out. No more dead Americans on my watch."

"You've made yourself clear, Lou."

"Have a safe trip." Amistad hung up.

McKenzie slunk back in his chair. Amistad was right. They fucked up; Haley was killed. His thoughts swirled through the tough talk from Amistad to the woman, Mallory Lowe. He knew he needed all the recon he could muster. She was intelligent and driven—and she knew something he didn't. What it was he wasn't sure, yet.

Conflicted, damn right he was. Let her go and further his cause, or let her go and she gets killed. What the fuck, the agency does it all the time. McKenzie's mind was made. The good news: his agents in Basel would have Mallory Lowe tailed the minute she landed. The hell with any ethics boards.

His driver interrupted his thoughts. He checked his watch. In a couple of hours, he too would be jetting across the Atlantic.

CHAPTER 6

Somewhere over the Atlantic

allory checked the map on the seat-mounted screen and realized she was halfway to Frankfurt, on time for an early morning arrival. The garbled voice of the Airbus A340 pilot informed the passengers of their location south of Greenland. Her mathematical brain always churning, great circles popped into her mind. To prove that the shortest path between two points on a sphere is a great circle, one had to apply a bit of calculus. Denver to Frankfurt, just like two other points on the globe, followed such a path.

There she went again, preoccupying her mind with number manipulation, any and everything from zero to infinity. It was something she had done most of her life. She remembered working magic square puzzles with her father back on the farm in Oklahoma. From those humble beginnings, it was as if an irresistible door had opened to the realm of numbers and logical analysis. From simple beginnings to complex subjects such as advanced linear algebra and differential topology, mathematics was the only refuge that provided her comfort. When her father died from a heart attack, she had to relinquish her mathematical passions to help with the foreclosed farm and her younger sister, Britt.

Analyzing the doodles of the irrational numbers, π, e, and $\sqrt{2}$, she wondered what was with the $\pi^2/6$ and how Katie was involved. There had to be some importance here. Surely these famous irrationals were one of the reasons she was headed to Switzerland.

She was grateful Lane McKenzie offered her airlift to Denver. What the heck; why not let the government pick up the tab? Still, it felt like he might have been too accommodating. Even if she had reason to question his motives, she didn't have the energy to question him about Tom's involvement with the CIA.

It took her less than two days to wrap things up in Boulder, apologize to Kato, her male, gray tiger-striped tabby, for taking another leave of absence. The cat was not amused. The shredding of the armrest of her sofa was sign enough to Mallory that she was again walking on thin ice.

She booked a Lufthansa flight to Frankfurt connecting onto Basel, Switzerland. It was the Basel Museum that was scrawled on the back of the photograph and the $\pi^2/6$ kept swimming in her head, the infamous *Basel Problem*. A Basel trifecta, for Christ sake.

Tom Haley was *murdered*. She saw it with her own two eyes. The deep blue sky, the warming sun on her cheeks, the helicopter from hell—the noise, the fear, the savage murder of an old friend. If only she could erase the vision. But she couldn't. The vision was now clouded with that of a further crisis—an apparent danger to Katie; now her life on the line. *She'll be killed if the dam is blown up. For God's sake—any day now.* Really? In her confused mind, there was no waffling. She had to act, like a blind man in a maze.

She herself was targeted. Her mind drifted back to what McKenzie had said. He warned her in explicit language: SOMEONE WANTS YOU DEAD. Not a comforting thought. She was stumped as to how her life had taken such a U-turn. Now she was jetting across the Atlantic on what may be a fool's errand. So be it. She was the fool. Sitting idly by would be the worst of decisions.

She shifted in her seat, not wishing to analyze her impulsiveness. Doing so would only give her a headache. Putting her earplugs on, she switched through the onboard music stations, desperate to find something relaxing—easy listening—something to help her sleep. Finding a new age channel, she dialed it in and reclined in her seat. *Flying Condor* by *Cusco* swelled in her ears, followed by *Malaga Sunset* by *Incendio*. *This may work*, she hoped. A few more minutes passed, but her eyes remained wide open. She gave it another couple of songs. The music didn't release her built-up tension. She felt restless, impatient. Maybe she needed something that stirred her. Flipping through the backseat video screen, she checked the inflight movies. Looks like *Steven Spielberg Honors Month*, a host of movies he directed were available. She scanned the listings: Raiders of the Lost Ark, Poltergeist, Jaws, Saving Private Ryan…on and on. Jaws, when did she last see it, as a kid? It scared her to death. Maybe now the horror of a flesh-eating sea monster, a no-brainer, would keep her mind away from reality. Without hesitation, she selected it.

Several minutes into the film, Mallory turned the screen off with shaky fingers. This wasn't working either. She stopped at the part where the mother of the latest shark victim confronted Police Chief Brody for not closing the beaches. Chief Brody's guilt was now front and center for his inaction. Wasn't that the real reason she was rushing off to find Katie—guilt, the kind that wears you down year after year. The gnarl of tension that had overwhelmed her the last few days was not letting up.

Promises made, promises broken.

For God's sake, would the haunting words of her dying mother ever cease to bring her to tears? *Be there for Britt. You know she needs you. She's your sister; she looks up to you...and loves you, you know.* Mallory wiped the lone tear rolling down her cheek. No time for that. And Britt, such a long, long time ago.

A bit of turbulence bounced Mallory from her untimely thoughts. She pulled at her seatbelt, checked the clasp, tilted her seat back and closed her eyes. Her body relaxed, coaxing her heart to slow to a mesmerizing beat. Irrational numbers floated across her mind, like sheep jumping over a fence.

CHAPTER 7

Diyarbakir Province, Turkey

K atie looked through the binoculars at the sleek face of the dam glistening in the midday sun. At this distance, the thin-shelled concrete arch looked incapable of holding back the tremendous pressure of the Tepecik River. Behind the soaring concave structure, the once violent river had been tamed and buried under a placid artificial lake, a crooked finger clawing its way into the ever-deepening gorge. The blue-green waters of the reservoir appeared as if at any moment they would rise higher and swallow the dam, returning the river to its treacherous self again. She lowered the binoculars and proceeded to the ruins, knowing that day was near.

Devoid of any archeological significance, the Roman ruins were situated high on an indistinct and desolate hilltop that had been excavated forty years earlier, catalogued as an unimportant fortress that was never completed. Behind one of the crumbling walls, a small stone hut had been constructed by another culture a century later. Used as a refuge by locals herding goats, it was now abandoned. Simple and solid, the mud and stone structure blended well with the ruinous Roman walls. For the time being, it served as a staging area.

A dry, hot breeze buffeted her face. She hoped someday she could return to enjoy the history from the isolated hilltop. With one last nostalgic look, she slid back into the beat up Nissan truck, sucked down the last swallow from a warm bottle of Coca-Cola, and tossed the empty onto the passenger seat. She drove down the hillside turning onto a rutted cart path, half a kilometer from the center of Eshai. The path wound down into a gulley for a hundred yards before it snaked up the other side squeezed between a wheat field and a low hill. At the end of the field she studied her surroundings, parked behind a grouping of stone and mud structures, and waited a few minutes. Ismet had warned her to be observant always, even in full daylight.

The village of Eshai was a small community where questions were not asked. It was old, the houses and buildings lacking any modern conveniences except for satellite dishes curiously located on the roofs of a few mud huts. Any semblance of municipal services was still rare in the Eastern Anatolia region.

She approached the third mud hut on her right and knocked on the wooden door with three staccato hits followed by two slow thumps. From the opposite side, five staccato knocks answered. With relief, she entered. Behind the door, a man stepped out; his submachine gun pointed at her.

A piercing emptiness burst within. Where was Ismet? Another man appeared, shorter than Katie. She had seen him before, the short, baby-faced man in the bazaar.

CHAPTER 8

Basel, Switzerland

allory admired Münster Cathedral, its twin sandstone towers puncturing a hazy blue sky. The black-lettered plaque identified the landmark as a twelfth-century Catholic cathedral, now a reformed Protestant church. Built on a hill, it commanded an unmatched view of the Rhine and the barges, ferries and pleasure boats plying the wide expanse of Switzerland's only navigational conduit to the sea. She passed the Romanesque structure hurrying down the Münsterplatz. There was no time to be a tourist.

Der Basel Museum Für Mathematik Und Wissenschaft, the Basel Museum of Mathematics and Science, sat south of the Rhine. This was where she would begin her day. An online search on museums in Basel revealed one museum devoted entirely to the mathematical brilliance that sprang from Switzerland's oldest university town.

She found the museum, a well-maintained two-story Renaissance structure on Freiestrasse. She walked up a short flight of stairs, stepped under the shallow-arched entry framed by Romanesque columns, and entered. The anteroom contained a small counter in the center and a rack of tourist brochures off to her right. On the desk, she noticed a sign indicating a twelve euro entrance fee. She paid the woman attendant who directed her to the guest registry. Signing her real name would be a mistake. She picked up the pen, scribbled Susan Smith from the United States and then hustled to the main exhibition hall.

Moving through a double door, a large map of Europe eclipsed the open exhibit space highlighting the *Age of Enlightenment*, considered by many to be the golden age of mathematics. Basel was featured prominently. Some of the most famous mathematicians called the university town home. It was here an abundance of mathematical concepts were developed.

She looked at the exhibit for a few moments, and then followed the path through an arched opening into the second exhibit space. Pausing, she pulled the photograph from her pocket and saw it was the same arch in the background with Katie and the older man. Damn, the exact same spot. She continued to the next exhibit, passing under another arched opening. The exhibits were separated by these faux stone arched openings in a parabolic shape, *keeping with the mathematical theme*, she thought.

She was anxious to find mention of *The Basel Problem*. For what reason, she didn't know, other than its importance. The rooms were trapezoidal separated by high partition walls ending with the arches. She imagined walking through the narrow streets of Basel, a journey of mathematical history, each exhibit devoted to a segment of mathematical and scientific interest that had transpired in Basel. In one room, the Bernoulli family tree was displayed. She recalled the two most celebrated Bernoulli's, Jakob and his younger brother Johann, bitter rivals throughout their careers, both leaving an indelible mark on the mathematics of today.

There were two other visitors in the display area, a man and a woman. The woman seemed bored to the core, only here to satisfy the man's interest. Theory proposed: *he is a single-minded husband with his subservient wife*, Mallory mused. She caught the eye of the woman who turned for a moment before following the man as he slowly meandered through an archway into the next exhibit.

In the following room, a diorama displayed two life-like figures of the Bernoulli brothers—wax creations of some sort. Beyond, in the next exhibit, she saw a maintenance man working on a light fixture. Her attention returned to the exhibit placard explaining the Bernoulli brother's history and their contribution to mathematics, even commenting on their competitive nature. She scrutinized the wax figure of the older Bernoulli, Jakob, sitting at a desk. Standing behind, Johann grinned boastfully, having bettered his brother by solving a stubborn problem. Decked out in seventeenth century clothing—lace-edged jabots, white linen shirts, and satin knee breeches—they even sported fashionable powdered wigs. Period furniture filled the space: a carved oaken desk with a host of items, quills and ink holder, pieces of paper with mathematical scribbling, and candleholders with half-dripped candles. In the background a large bookshelf covered the wall, filled with faded folios, calfskins, and books of the period.

As she walked to the next life-like diorama, she noticed the maintenance man had finished his work. He gave her a passing glance, folded his ladder, and left. At this exhibit, a wax figure looked out at museum goers with only his left eye; the right eye weak and lethargic. *This isn't working*, she thought. Not only did she have the scrutiny of real flesh and blood eyes, now this inanimate figure seemed to be staring as well. She tried to concentrate on the placard describing Leonhard Euler, one of the most prolific and gifted mathematicians ever, his accomplishments unsurpassed in all the history of mathematics. With quill and paper, Euler's wax facsimile sat at his desk working through some undoubtedly complex mathematical equations with two young children playing at his feet.

She moved over to the right-hand side of the Euler exhibit and found what she had been looking for, the placard for *The Basel Problem*, one of the most well-known infinite series.

THE BASEL PROBLEM

First posed to European mathematicians in 1644, it withstood various attempts by mathematicians of the day to come up with a solution. Even the bitter rivalry of Basel brothers Jakob and Johann Bernoulli failed. They worked individually on the problem for years without success in a fierce competition to be first. Not until 1735 did 28 year old Leonhard Euler solve the problem in a stroke of mathematical genius that even to this day is looked upon with wonderment.

$$1 + 1/2^2 + 1/3^2 + 1/4^2 + 1/5^2 + 1/6^2 + \ldots + 1/k^2 + \ldots = \pi^2/6$$

She ambled through the next archway to another exhibit. A well-dressed man entered from the opposite end, stopping to chat with the man and woman. Oddly, his eyes kept roaming her direction. Mallory examined the placard in front, explaining Infinite Series and their importance in real world applications. She brushed over the verbiage of Power to Fourier and Trigonometric Series. She hastily read the discussion on the Harmonic Series, the one infinite summation that had the closest relationship with the Bernoulli brothers and Basel.

When she looked up, the well-dressed man who had been eyeing her strolled her direction. He had stately silver hair and wore a sleek gray suit. He was taller than she imagined and now she felt vulnerable as he neared.

"Enjoying our exhibits?" he asked in faultless English.

"Very interesting. It's exciting to see Euler in the flesh."

"You are a mathematician, yes."

"I hold a professorship in mathematics at the University of Indiana in the United States," she lied.

"I could see it in your manner, your eyes."

"Really?"

"Very inquisitive, like all logical-thinking creatures."

"That's very flattering.

"My manners are lacking. I am David Wyss, curator for this humble little institution."

Mallory took his extended hand. "Susan Smith. Pleased to meet you."

"We are visited quite often by professionals from academia, mainly from Europe. On occasion, an American will stumble in having just found out about the museum by accident. We had two Canadians here just last week. Refreshing."

"The descriptions are straight forward, very easily understood by a layman. I commend you."

"Thank you."

"And *The Basel Problem* made your fair city famous." She pointed at the placard.

"Yes, yes! It was wondrously solved by Leonhard Euler in 1735. Euler was a native of Basel."

"And he was a student of Johann Bernoulli, if I am not mistaken," Mallory added.

Wyss smiled. "You know your history."

"One of the classes I teach is history of mathematics." She thought it was time for a little fib. "To be honest, I occasionally write articles for mathematical magazines and understand that there is a gentleman living in Basel who is quite knowledgeable on infinite series, his specialty *The Basel Problem*. You wouldn't by chance know of someone that would fit that description?"

Wyss scratched his chin. "I can't say that there is anyone. There are those that could be considered experts, but experts of what? These mathematical problems were popular three hundred years ago. Today they are topics of historical interest only. That is why we have established this museum."

"What about a young woman named Katie Haley? Does that name mean anything? I heard she may be in Basel and possibly had connections to this museum."

Mallory sensed a change in Wyss' demeanor. The mention of Katie's name initiated a reaction—a connection was there.

"No, I do not know that name." Wyss pulled on the knot of his tie. It was obvious he was uncomfortable. "Why do you ask?"

Mallory continued her lie. "I'm a friend. I can't remember who, but someone said she was in Basel and the name of this museum came up in the conversation."

"Sorry that I cannot be of any further help. Now, if you will excuse me."

He turned and rushed away. No doubt David Wyss knew something about Katie.

CHAPTER 9

The sun hung low in the western sky stretching an orange blaze across the Rhine. Mallory joined the large group of tourists mulling about at the end of Feldergstrassse. Earlier, she had returned to her hotel and was handed a note by the clerk. It was not signed, a white piece of paper stuffed inside a smudged and stained envelope, overpowered with the smell of cigarettes. She opened it and read: *Meet me at 7:00 at Ferdi's, north side of Johanniterbrücke. About Katie Haley.*

The note could provide *two outcomes*. One, she could follow a request from someone she didn't know, setting herself up to get killed. Sheer lunacy. Or two, whoever sent it had information she needed. She was baffled they knew her name and where she was staying. There had already been two attempts on her life. The museum was the only place she had shown her face, so everyone associated with it now was suspect. Only David Wyss knew she was looking for Katie. The curator acted strange when he heard the name. Had he changed his mind?

She was hoping for the *second outcome*.

Finding Ferdi's, an outdoor bar nestled next to the Rhine, she looked over the patrons. On the far side she saw a man smoking a cigarette. He glanced up and waved her over. She knew this man; maybe it was the coveralls he wore. She neared and remembered; the maintenance man from the museum. She threaded her way between the tables.

The man started to stand, inadvertently kicking the table behind him. "*Verzeihung bitte,*" he muttered to the couple sitting there. He turned back around and nodded awkwardly at Mallory. He sat down and smashed the stump of cigarette he had remaining in an ashtray overflowing with butts. "Please, sit," he said in German accented English. He was a thin man, eyes sunken, tired, late-forties. Years of self-inflicted abuse was likely responsible for the rawness of his features and the wrinkles that radiated from the drooping corners of his eyes.She pulled out a chair and sat down.

"This is one of the few establishments that let one light up." He lit another cigarette and registered disgust as he blew a halo of smoke in the air. "Buy you a beer?"

"I'm fine."

"I am Franz Zellweger. I saw you…at my museum." He took a drink from a large mug on the table.

"Your museum?"

He tapped the cigarette on the ashtray and paused. "Not really. I just work there."

She looked at him squarely. "How'd you find me?"

"I followed you when you left. Your hotel was close by. The clerk told me your name. It's not Susan Smith." He smiled proudly.

Mallory swallowed hard. "Your note says you know Katie Haley."

"I know of her." He leaned close, the smell of beer and cigarettes heavy on his breath. "And so does Mr. Wyss."

"He told me he didn't."

"He lied." Franz cocked his head suspiciously. "I don't know who you are, or why you are looking for this Katie, so maybe I tell you nothing." He settled back in his chair. The cigarette smoldered in his hand, the ash growing uncomfortably long.

Mallory showed her frustration. "Why did you send me the note, Mr. Zellweger? Dammit man, lives are in danger, mine included."

He paused. "Why do you search for this Katie?"

Mallory fixated on him. "Her father, Tom Haley asked me."

Franz's eyes softened. "It is a small museum. Any day I am mopping or shining the display cases. One day, outside *Herr* Wyss' office. The door was open. He was talking on the phone."

"Who with?"

Franz shrugged and flicked the ash.

"What did you hear?"

"They argue—about an exhibit."

"Go on."

"They argue, maybe take it away, make it less…*important*."

Mallory gave him a riveted look. "Did Mr. Wyss say which exhibit?"

A devilish grin spread on Franz's face. "The exhibit you spent most time visiting—*The Basel Problem*, of course."

Mallory blinked with excitement. "*The Basel Problem?*"

"Yes—yes, they argue in French. They don't think I understand; I keep mopping. I speak French well. I speak English. I speak German too. I am German. This is Basel, *Fräulein!*" He smiled triumphantly.

She had another question. "Did you hear any talk about a dam?"

"A dam…I don't understand?"

"You know. A dam holds back water in a reservoir, a large lake."

"Oh—no, no, never."

"I see. What else?"

"More arguing. *Herr* Wyss talks of Tom Haley. He visited often."

"Why?"

Franz shrugged. Maybe he enjoyed the exhibits."

"Was there anyone else ever here with Mr. Haley?"

"Once I remember. Two, three months ago, he came with Katie and another man."

"Who was he?"

He shook his head. "I was busy working on a display case. I have seen him before, but don't recollect his name."

The photograph of Katie and the unknown man standing in front of one of the exhibit arches flittered through her mind. "Anything else?"

Franz took a long drag on his cigarette and exhaled. "Look at me; do I look like a man of brains?"

"You look like someone who has more information." She saw his mug was empty. "Let me buy you a beer."

Franz smiled and raised the empty mug. A server came over with a fresh liter.

"So, Tom Haley had been to the museum several times? Did you ever talk with him?"

"The last time I saw him, several days ago. We talked."

"About what."

"He said someone may ask about his daughter."

"Where is she now?"

He shook his head, gave a spidery smile exposing tobacco-stained teeth, and snuffed out the cigarette.

"Talk to me Franz. You must know something?"

Franz fumbled for another cigarette. The pack was empty. His face grew weary.

Her eyes focused on the janitor. Could she trust him? She remembered the mathematical constants Tom had scribbled down. "As you have pointed out, I spent time viewing the display on *The Basel Problem.* What about other mathematical constants, like *pi*—do you know anything about them?"

Veins popped out on Franz's temple. "They treat them like *God symbols!*" His face suddenly went pale. He stiffened. The effect of alcohol had vanished. He stared across the bar courtyard towards Feldergstrassse. What was he looking at—something, somebody?

"I must go," he said. Rising from the table, there was apprehension on his fearful face. He wrote an address on a napkin. "Meet me in Degenfelden, eighteen kilometers from here, across the border, *Deutschland.*" He left the café in a rush.

It was growing dark and without the directions from people at a local grocery store, Mallory wouldn't have found it. One kilometer east on the E54, she found the paved road that ended at a hillside. She was now on the German side of the Rhine. The address, Reisberg 43, was painted on a weathered piece of wood bolted to a stone fence post. She drove her rental car onto the gravel drive, dusk shrouding the residence. It was a ramshackle cottage, cracked stucco walls and a slate roof, some split, others missing. Set back from the road, the closest adjacent house was at least two hundred yards away, separated by a large meadow. Did Franz live here? The way he left the café in such a hurry startled her. It was as if something or someone had frightened him. She felt a shiver. Should she have even come here with darkness settling in?

She shut the car door and approached the cottage. This was beginning to feel like a trap. Why had she thrown caution to the wind—and with night approaching, the opportune time to get hurt…or killed?

The front door was open—inside, darkness. Fortunately, she had bought a flashlight at the grocery store and now beamed it across the threshold. The room was tiny, sparse, heavy wooden furniture. She stepped inside, the flashlight unsteady in her hand.

"Turn it off and shut the door," a voice came from the corner.

Startled, Mallory fumbled, lowering the beam while trying to switch it off. Allowing her eyes to adjust to the dim room, she caught a shadowy figure reclining in a chair next to a lone window.

"Sorry for the German drama," Franz blurted. She saw him strike a match and light a cigarette. "I am more relaxed here. Please, sit down."

Mallory located a heavy wooden chair, and took an uncomfortable seat. "Is this your house?"

He shook his head. "My cousin's. He farms the fields. No one lives here."

They talked small talk for a few minutes. Then she asked the question that had brought her here. "Why did you leave the bar so fast?"

His hands waved in the dusky room. "Did I recognize someone staring at us? Was my mind playing tricks? We are in danger." He nervously puffed on the cigarette.

She studied the janitor. He looked fearful. "Franz, tell me, where's Katie?"

Franz remained silent.

"Listen, I have to find her. Her father, Tom Haley was killed."

"*Schweine*," he shrieked. Pigs. "They mean what they say. Let them rot in hell."

"Where is she, Franz?"

"No longer in Basel. That, I know."

The sound of scraping came from outside the front door. Franz jumped up and opened a drawer on a desk next to his chair. He removed a handgun. "Quick, back door," he ordered, waving her over.

Mallory held her breath and then she whispered, "Could it have been the wind?"

His voice was tense. "No wind."

The door crashed open, as if it had been kicked.

In the doorway, the silhouette of a man holding a military-looking weapon appeared. Franz dropped behind a table and pumped off a shot. Through the dark, she saw him leap, fully exposed to the gunman. A flurry of bullets came from the doorway. Franz moved awkwardly, arched his back, his head snapping sideways. Mallory caught the petrified look on his face. He dropped the gun and fell backward on the floor.

Terrified, Mallory reached down in the dark and felt around for the gun. Just as she located it, she saw the shaded profile coming her way. She raised the pistol rapidly, pressed the trigger several times until the last casing ejected. A man cried out, then the sound of something crashing.

Terrified, she peered around the corner and saw the gunman face down. Her body contorted into shock when she saw Franz. She heard a raspy sound. He was still alive. She rushed over to help. His eyes rolled back, a placid expression in the dimness. Dark circles of blood seeped from his chest. He gurgled again, drowning in his own blood. He gagged, unable to get a breath. She found his hand and squeezed it. Then he was gone.

"*Gunnar, es dir gut?*" A voice from outside yelled.

Frantic, she dashed to the backdoor and flung it open. The voice had come from the front. It was now dusk, the lights of Degenfelden flickering in the distance. She could hear the rustle of someone at the front of the house. Crouched low, she sidled toward a wooded area in the direction of town. If she could reach the trees without being seen, she might have a chance.

After a minute she disappeared into the woods. She stumbled about blindly, tripping over exposed tree roots, thorns scraping her face and arms. Somewhere there had to be a path, but where?

A sound came from behind. She tried to react, but a stump caught her toe, sending her face first to the ground, the taste of aging undergrowth coating her tongue. Spitting out the humus, she pushed herself up. She whirled around to see a black form charge, arms flaying. Defensively, she thrust her hands out in front and caught the brunt of the man's body.

"Hündin," he shouted. Bitch.

They both slammed into the ground. Even in the twilight, she saw murderous eyes glaring at her. And then the glint of metal in his right hand. He stabbed at her. She caught the blow with her outstretched hand, but not before the end of the knife nicked the side of her neck.

Mallory rolled to her left and thrust a knee into the man's crotch. He coughed a hideous cough, but kept pressure on his knife hand, driving the blade closer to her throat. Her strength began to wane, muscles starting to lose control. They trundled again as one and found themselves precariously close to the edge of a steep slope. Unsteady, both bodies spun downhill several yards. Halfway down, the assailant's hand collided against a rock and the knife popped out. The momentum carried her further until she could gain her footing. Not looking back, feet slipping, she scrambled up with enough traction to reach the top.

She spotted a path through the trees and ran like hell.

Off to her left, breaking twigs exploded—a commotion heard through the undergrowth, something moving…someone racing towards her. The muzzled pop of a gun: one, two shots fired. The aria of terror took grip, a shadow in the dark…closing in!

Panic blurred her senses.

She scurried around like a rat in a maze trying to find an exit, spinning around, frantic. Out of the blackness, the shadow grabbed her.

She screamed.

The touch of cold hands made her heart race to infinity.

Lane McKenzie released his grip. "Are you all right?

CHAPTER 10

*CIA Operations
Basel*

n the dark, Mallory heard the scraping of metal as McKenzie worked a key into a lock. They were at a five-story building across the Rhine from Münster Cathedral. Mallory's mind overplayed the possibilities as she trailed after McKenzie to the back of the building and down a set of cobblestone stairs.

Opening the door, he led her up four poorly lit flights. At the top, they followed a short hallway to a lone door. He punched in a code on a keypad inset in the wall, and a metal panel slid open. He stepped closer and stared at a dark retinal glass scanner inset in the wall. A red infrared dot flashed. After several seconds, he stepped back and the door swung open to an abrupt brightness that forced her eyes to blink and squint. No sofas, recliners, televisions, nor wall decorations, the room contained a spectral of surveillance apparatus and sophisticated electronic equipment—communication and encryption devices, a sea of computers—a virtual alpha display of spy wares.

She touched the newly placed Band-Aid on her neck as she took in the room. "So, this is your spy headquarters?'

"Welcome to *Operations.*"

Her eyes kept wandering. "Pretty impressive, all this electronic gadgetry, but tell me, where's the real magic?"

McKenzie raised an eyebrow. "Magic?"

"Yea, you know; the hocus pocus stuff. How is it you have the wizardry to appear every time I'm about to make an unplanned departure from this world?"

In the bright light, Mallory watched McKenzie's eyes narrow. "I'd laugh if that wasn't a serious question. You do have a sense of humor, and an uncanny ability to survive."

"Speaking of survival, what about the man in the farmhouse?"

"He did have a few bullet holes in him."

She took a deep breath and exhaled.

"You had no choice. If it will make you feel part of the group, I shot the other one that was intent on spearing you with that toad-stabber."

"He dead, too?"

"Deader than a doornail."

"And you knew this was all going to happen?"

"I didn't think you would create this much attention. I should have known better. You came close to killing those in the SUV in Nevada, and the guy this evening, he's history. Hell, you're a woman to be reckoned with," he said with admiration. "We should hire you as an assassin."

Mallory didn't look amused.

"Seriously, we've got a lot to discuss."

She looked back at the man with the habit of being in the right place at the right time, taking note of his features for the first time: soft blue eyes and sandy-brown hair. Aside from his *white knight* appeal, he had an opposite pedigree than one would associate with a CIA agent—blunt, but with a gentle coating. She'd seen it back in Nevada, and it seemed to shine the same here. But there was one problem—she felt toyed with, manipulated like Tom Haley.

"So, why didn't you demand I stay home?" she snapped. "Why is it I have this feeling I've been used like a worm on a hook. You left me in the dark, refusing to tell me why you recruited Tom Haley. Dammit, if I'd known the facts, maybe I would have made better decisions."

McKenzie disregarded her rant. He pointed to a coffee pot in the corner. "Care for a cup of day old coffee?"

She stared at him, jaw tightened.

Pouring himself a cup, he motioned to a couple of padded bistro chairs placed around a small wooden table near a bay window. The view of Münster cathedral was illuminated by well-placed floodlights. He pulled out a chair. "You're absolutely right. I allowed you to put yourself in danger."

"Why didn't you come clean back in Nevada, dammit?"

A hesitation. "Because I'm a sonofabitch who has a job to do."

"Lead the lamb to slaughter, is that it?"

"Not intentionally. We had our eyes on you. Unfortunately, things moved faster than anticipated."

Mallory sat down and stared across at McKenzie. "Just like you had eyes on Tom Haley."

McKenzie stretched his jaw. She could see she had hit a nerve. "How in the hell could we know you'd be traipsing right under their noses. Hell, by now they've probably figured out you're the woman in Nevada."

Her thoughts turned to signing the museum guestbook. Susan Smith, not Mallory Lowe. She was betting they hadn't made the connection to Nevada.

"*These people* are sophisticated," McKenzie continued. "They have a million ways to get information. You were with Tom Haley, you were at his house, and you had a rental car. They know your real name."

"What about that poor man, Franz Zellweger? Were *they* after him or me?"

McKenzie took a gulp of cold coffee. "We think it was him. We've known for some time that they had him marked; in fact, we've approached him a time or two. To them, he's a snoop, but not until tonight did they figure his time had run out. At that sidewalk *biergarten* they spotted him talking to someone, and that someone was you."

"Were you tailing him—or me?"

"Now, why would we be interested in a drunken old janitor?" He leaned on the table and stared at her. "Truce. Give me a rundown of your day up to the excitement tonight."

Mallory wiped her forehead and calmed. "Franz saw me at the museum. He found out where I was staying and left a note asking to meet." She shifted uncomfortably in the chair. "He told me Tom had visited the museum before. Then he saw someone, and he got scared. Before he left, he asked me to meet him across the river. I took a risk meeting him, I won't deny it, but at this point I had no alternatives."

"That's all?"

Mallory's expression hardened. "Don't you think you owe me a full explanation as to what the hell is going on? It's your turn goddammit."

"I like a woman who says what's on her mind, and please, call me Lane."

"Well, then talk *Lane*. Who are *these people*?"

"*These people* are a large multinational corporation named Möbius, offices all over the world, headquartered here in Basel. Mostly invested in private water utilities. We've had them under surveillance for the last two years. It's a collaboration between the CIA and FIS, the Swiss Federal Intelligence Service. There's concern that they have taken control of some of the big wheels in the IFC, the International Finance Corp, an arm of the World Bank. The IFC encourages private development of projects in developing nations, especially water projects."

"Water projects like a dam? Talk to me, *Lane!*"

McKenzie nodded slowly. "A dam, yes, a dam in Turkey. I did lie to you, but at that moment I couldn't risk our operation."

"How could you? Tom was convinced Katie might die if it were *blown up*—and it could happen any minute, if it hasn't already. Where's your sense of urgency?"

McKenzie shook his head. "Highly unlikely. Tepecik Dam has impeccable security; it's hard to access. If we really felt Katie's life hinged on the viability of the dam, we would move pronto."

She was sick of the lying. Of course, hadn't she done the same? "But what's Katie's involvement?"

"How the hell would I know? We only knew Haley had a daughter in the Peace Corps, nothing more. Let's concentrate on what we do know. Möbius built the dam and generating station with financing provided by the IFC. A lot of strings were pulled to make that happen. It's not a longshot to think that the IFC has been corrupted in approving the deal. Möbius has their fingers in everything that has to do with water—dams, utilities, bottled water. The list goes on."

"Wars have started over water."

"That's why we're keeping an eye on Coulomb and friends."

"Coulomb, who's that?"

"Paul Coulomb, president of the board."

"What about him?"

"There's plenty. Incidentally, he was the founder of the museum you visited. Möbius essentially funds it. Mathematics is one of his passions. You've been there; it's not exactly a money-making establishment."

"Now I understand why the curator had a sudden change in attitude when I mentioned Katie's name."

McKenzie shrugged. "Oh hell, why not. I've already got the ethics board sniffing up my ass," he muttered.

"You what?"

McKenzie rose, walked over to a file and took out a folder, searched for a paper and tossed it on the table. "His mini dossier. It's declassified, so maybe I won't get too fried by the boss."

She gave him a peculiar look and began to read.

ABBREVIATED *DOSSIER: Paul Coulomb*

Born in Chambéry, France, French national, age 57, only child. Father, Pierre, a regional banker, mother, Josette, a lawyer. Both deceased. Graduated from the École Polytechnique with an engineering degree in applied mathematics. Admitted to the University of California at Berkeley, received his PhD in mathematics, doctoral thesis in number theory titled: The Rationale of Irrational Numbers. *After obtaining doctorate, employed by Automaton International as an applied mathematician. He started Möbius several years later with funding from his family trust. The corporation grew steadily with the help of two Americans, Harry Meadowlark, whom he met at Berkeley, and Shelby Wallace, systems engineer at Automaton in Palo Alto.*

Sidebar: Coulomb continues his fascination with mathematics. He parades this passion in private and public life, even to the point of naming the corporation, Möbius, after the famed two-dimensional, one-sided mathematical peculiarity called The Möbius Strip. *The topics of irrational and transcendental numbers infatuate him. They are an obsession and a trademark of the company.*

In an odd way, she could identify with this Paul Coulomb. Both had parents that were deceased; both had PhD's in mathematics and a passion for the beauty of the calculating world.

"What about these other two characters, Meadowlark and Wallace?" she asked.

"Meadowlark's no longer there, disappeared, gone a few months. From what we gather, he was half the brains of Möbius' success, but kind of a loner. Never really seemed to fit with the organization. Probably left with a lot of money and decided to disappear for his own sanity. Wallace is still part of his inner circle."

She handed the dossier back to McKenzie and stared at the reflection of Münster Cathedral shimmering in the Rhine. "So, this Möbius is into private water utilities. That's scary. Fresh water should be a fundamental right, like fresh air, like that pleasant flowing river down there."

"The world doesn't operate that way."

She nodded, reflecting on Colorado and the arid West. "There have always been water wars. Sooner rather than later, the water runs out. I read a statistic that in the last forty years, domestic water use has doubled. And now, you're telling me about corporate takeover."

He nodded. "That makes it worse."

"There's an adage: water flows uphill to money."

"That's Möbius. They're intent on making huge profits and will kill anyone that gets in the way." McKenzie leaned back. "Tell me, what motivates you? Not many people would put their lives on the line for something this risky."

"Tom Haley served as one of my advisors during my dissertation. I got to know him well. Katie and I became very close; still are. Not that it matters, but Katie was adopted."

"How old was she when you got to know her?"

"Thirteen, I was twenty-four." Mallory took a deep, hesitant breath. "I remember it like it was yesterday. I was in Tom's office; Katie was there in the corner reading a book. Out of earshot, Tom told me that his wife had died recently from a brain aneurism, and Katie was having a hard time. I was surprised, since Tom had kept her death private. Before I left, I remember Katie coming up to me, and I'll never forget; with those deep-set brown eyes she said in the very candid voice of a teen, 'My mother died. Would you be my friend?' After that, she depended on me. We're as close to best friends as you can be, keeping close contact ever since; although, I think through the years she resented my friendship with her dad."

"In what respect?" he asked, puzzled.

Mallory shook her head. "She may have thought I was taking his side over hers in the father-daughter squabbles."

"Why the estrangement?"

"Teenage growing pains; Tom tended to be distant. He didn't mean to. I just think he withdrew after his wife died. It was hard on him."

"I can't blame you for wanting to find Katie. Hell, I feel responsible for her myself, but these people want you dead. Why don't you go home; let us do our job. We'll find Katie."

She shook her head. "I can't go home now and wait for the phone to ring. I want no regrets."

"Believe me, I understand, but you've already burned through three lives. Don't press your luck. These folks are deadly serious about stopping you. Heed my advice—go home."

She knew he was right. But her stubbornness wouldn't back down. "Sorry, can't do that."

Exasperated, he asked, "For God's sake, what do you think you can do?"

"Möbius, I'll give them a visit."

McKenzie jumped up, flinging his arms emphatically. "You can't do that, go roaring in on their territory. Like I said, they'll make the connection to Nevada, if they haven't already. You hurry in to see them, they'll have you skewered before you ask, 'at what temperature.'"

"It's a chance I have to take. You can't stop me, can you?"

"If it interferes with our investigation and surveillance, you bet your ass I can."

Mallory felt a tightening of the noose. "But will you?"

McKenzie snorted, pacing the room. She could imagine his thoughts racing, a man weighing every option, every avenue of reason.

Abruptly, he sat back down. "Tell you what," he said. "We have concurrent goals here. You need to find Katie; we need to tie Möbius with the IFC. Let's work together."

CHAPTER 11

Near Chambéry, France

Paul Coulomb sat down on the plush sofa in his private rail car and split the blinds with his fingers. He saw the lights of Chambéry flickering in the distance as the train sped westward. Beyond, the rosy peaks of the Chartreuse Mountains shone in the lingering twilight, the mountains of his youth. He took one last look, cursed in disgust, and closed the blinds.

He drummed his fingers on the desk to no recognizable rhythm. The slight jolt of his rail car reminded him that travelling by train gave him ample time to put his mind at ease and reflect on future endeavors. He could hear the naysayers whispering in quiet circles that the man from France was naïve, a dreamer, full of unrealistic fantasies. French visionaries were long dead, crushed since the days of the Napoleonic crusades. Yet, dreams were meant to be fulfilled, the more grandiose the better. Soon, his adversaries and competitors would be begging at his feet, pleading for a piece of the action.

He walked over to the bar and poured himself another finger of Van Winkle Special Reserve. Quite unusual for a Frenchman, but he acquired the taste for good old American bourbon during his time spent in the States. French wines didn't appeal, as they implied weakness—an unfair identity that had branded the French. He smirked as he lifted the glass to his nose and sniffed the signature aroma, took a sip, and let the throat burn settle his mind as he explored the realm of soon-to-be successes. He checked his watch. They would arrive in Monte Carlo in another seven hours.

The swish of a sliding door broke the spell. Shelby Wallace entered, walked over to a table, and unrolled a map he carried. Thirty-five years ago, Coulomb met the six-foot-three Alabaman when both were employed at Automaton, a robotics company. Little did he know at that time, but Wallace was being closely watched for selling trade secrets to a company in Korea. He was fired, but there was never enough evidence to convict him of industrial espionage. After Coulomb left to start Möbius, he called Wallace and offered him a job. He had been impressed with the way the Southerner was able to manipulate the criminal investigation and deflect evidence of his involvement. It was truly enlightening. Wallace had skills that could be useful. He had shown a propensity to take risks—and stay out of jail.

The door swished open again. Standing on the other side was a tall woman, fine-boned as a super model, thick brows, dark eyes, and light-olive skin. She was dressed in a knee-length charcoal skirt and sleeveless coral blouse that accented her black hair. Esra Sahin was brought into the fold because of her Turkish citizenship, invaluable to the construction and operation of one of Möbius' prime projects, Tepecik Dam in the Eastern Anatolia region. She served as Coulomb's personal secretary and confidant.

Coulomb waved her in.

Wallace finally spoke in his finest Alabaman drawl, stretching out his words. "Harry's in the Kelebak Valley." He took a red marker and commenced to sketch a circle on the map. "I'd like to think he's within ten miles of the dam."

Anger rippled across Coulomb's face. Why had he missed the signs that Harry Meadowlark was bailing from Möbius and going into hiding? Whatever his intention, it left a gaping hole in Möbius' plans. "Do we have the resources to track him down?"

"He's movin' about a bit. We know he has a secondary microchip built-in his SAT phone that scrambles his location. We can't locate it exactly but we know he's in Turkey with the rest of them. We've decoded enough information to pinpoint the area I've circled." He looked at Coulomb with alarm. "The dam could be at risk."

"My dear, do you see anything in the Kelebak Valley that would attract Harry?" Coulomb asked Esra.

"Southeastern Anatolia has many Assyrian and Roman ruins and man-made caves." She pointed to the map. "There are several; two in the general vicinity. Harry visited them during the dam's construction." She uttered his name with revulsion. "I believe he's drawn to them like a bee to nectar."

"Then we concentrate on those first." Coulomb tossed down the whiskey and eyed Wallace. "The dam security—has it been increased?"

"Guarded twenty-four-seven," Wallace assured. "Personnel equipped with automatic weapons, even shoulder-launched SAM's. Everything's under control."

"The security must be on high-alert," Coulomb insisted. "When we start building the pipeline, people will revolt."

"What about the Haley woman?" Esra asked Wallace.

"We've got her under lock and key at the dam."

"After our visit to Monte Carlo, I will let Harry know we have her if he hasn't already figured it out. I doubt he would like to see her hurt. This may convince him," Coulomb responded.

The swish of the door brought Valencia García Melendez into view. Posed in the doorway, the Spanish harlot smiled at Coulomb, then left.

Esra's mouth twitched open, her teeth slightly exposed. Coulomb swore he heard her growl. He placed his glass on the bar. "After tomorrow, we will regroup. We should have the final permits from the IFC and the Turkish government soon. Once the pipeline is under construction, it will take the devil himself to stop us."

Coulomb bid everyone goodnight. As he exited, he could feel Esra's lonely eyes stab him in the back.

CHAPTER 12

Basel

A nd what's the price?" Mallory asked, suspiciously. "It's past midnight; way past my bedtime, you know."

McKenzie leaned in. His voice was calm and irresistible. "Just give us a few days, and then, if you're hell bent on dropping in on Möbius, at that point it's out of my hands. Until then, you may be able to help us out."

"In what way?"

"It has to do with mathematics."

Her eyes shone with interest.

"You read the dossier. He likes numbers."

"Some people do."

"Come with me; I want you to meet someone."

She followed McKenzie into the next room. A man was sitting at a computer monitor working a keyboard. He turned as they entered, removing his earbuds.

"Neal, this is Mallory Lowe. Mallory, Neal Richardson."

Neal stood. He was younger than Mallory—early thirties, mid-height, medium length flaxen hair. Stubble of beard peppered his pinkish face. "Glad to see you made it out of Degenfelden."

"Me too." She shook his offered hand.

"Neal wears two hats," McKenzie explained. "He's our top cyber-surveillance man as well as one of our best field agents."

"I don't mind office work," Neal said, "but one can't sit around all day and get rusty." He cracked his knuckles.

"Neal has hacked into the Möbius computers and has a good handle on a number of things. We've learned a lot, but not enough to put the screws to them yet. Some of the things we've learned are quite unique. Neal, give Mallory a tour of their pride and joy."

Neal's fingers flew over the keyboard, and after a moment an image appeared. Mallory stared at what appeared to be a large circular pool of water centered in the lobby of a building. Another camera zeroed in on the water feature.

"What you're looking at is a daytime recording of a large publicity water feature at Möbius headquarters," Neal said. "A prototype of this was developed in Japan. A kind of dynamic logo. This device creates shapes and letters on the water surface through wave generators that encircle the pool. This water feature is controlled by their mainframe computer. We had success hacking into it, and we want to thank the Russians for their expertise." He grinned.

Thinking her eyes were playing tricks, she blinked in disbelief at what she saw. In the middle of the pool, several letters amazingly appeared and disappeared on the surface of the water, as if by magic. Recognizable, the letters, formed by wave crests, cycled in order: M-Ö-B-I-U-S. "What the—"

"Keep watching," Neal said with a grin. "This video was recorded from web cams that can be accessed by anyone on the Internet."

After the S dissolved the symbol π appeared, followed by e and $\sqrt{2}$.

"Now, I'm impressed."

"We thought you'd be," McKenzie said. "We've had our analysts work on this, but they haven't been able to tell us why Coulomb would showcase these math symbols, other than he's fascinated with them."

"They're three very famous irrational numbers, no question about that," Mallory said.

"That's our conclusion. Any thoughts as to why?" McKenzie asked.

"Nothing that stands out, except there's one constant missing," she said.

McKenzie peered at her curiously.

"When I was at Tom's house, I saw a notepad with four irrational numbers on it, those three and a $\pi^2/6$."

"Shit and you didn't tell me about it?" he said. "What else haven't you told me?"

"Sorry. To be honest, they are what got me to visit the museum." Mallory's eyes bore into him. "Hey, we both seem to be hiding information."

"The fourth number used to be with the others on the water feature," Neal added. "The $\pi^2/6$ followed π originally and then was removed a couple of months ago."

Mallory thought about the $\pi^2/6$ floating down the Virgin River on the notepad. "Could that be a software glitch?"

"No software glitch." Neal said. "They removed several lines of code from the program. Their website never explained why it was removed, only that they had to refine the wave generators for better superposition. I respectively disagree. I thought the waves produced a very striking representation for all the symbols and letters."

Was it stuffy in here, or was she beginning to see the unknowns stack higher? She needed more time to let it all soak in. "Would it be possible to add back that fourth constant?"

Neal smiled. "That would be kinky."

McKenzie gazed at Mallory with skepticism. "I see some mischievous gears churning in there."

"Think about it. What do these mathematical constants have to do with anything other than Coulomb's passion for numbers? If you were to add back the fourth constant, what kind of reaction would that get?"

"They may go ballistic," Neal replied.

"Or, their curiosity may reveal something else." McKenzie said thoughtfully. "We could gage how long it would take for them to discover the hack, maybe we could learn a little bit more about their information systems."

"Or divulge their security protocols," Neal said. "That would be awesome."

"Can you do it, Neal?" McKenzie asked.

"Give me twenty-four hours."

Mallory's cool eyes switched between the two men. What truly made her blood run ice-cold was the thought Möbius would kill Katie if they found her. Looking back at the computer monitor and the wave pond, her mind was spinning in a different direction. *Why the missing $\pi^2/6$?*

After Mallory left, McKenzie turned to Neal.

"Amistad would drop-kick my ass off the highest bridge if he knew we were going to do what she suggested," McKenzie commented.

"It's a good idea," Neal said. "Besides, we've arranged for her to stay somewhere else. She should be out of danger for the time being."

"Yea, but your computer hacking is part of this fucking scheme. We're involved. If this backfires, we're toast."

Neal cocked his head. "I guess if you go down, I go with you."

McKenzie leaned back, squirming in his chair. How did one ever get to where they were—the career path, the choices, the luck of the draw? Did that path always flow the way one wanted? "Did you ever think back to your training?" he finally commented.

"I try not to. It was brutal."

McKenzie thought for a moment. "They expected every recruit to follow the book. Really, in a tense situation, are you going to stop the action, take out the manual, find page four hundred and twenty-seven, and at the same time yell over to your adversary, 'Don't shoot, I'm busy at the moment.'"

"I get it."

"The powers to be keep hammering the idea to evaluate every situation copiously. I don't disagree, but there are times *raw instincts* need to come into play."

"I kept a low profile during my training. I just went with the flow. No sense upsetting the applecart, man"

"I envy you," McKenzie sighed. "You know how to let things go. I should learn from you; I take this *fucking* job too serious."

"Someone has to, and you're good at it."

"Thanks a million, but since I'm burdened with that reality, we still have those that are risk adverse and those that accept the risk. Which way are we headed with this woman professor?"

Neal answered quickly. "From what is happening now, I'd say we are on a risk-taking binge."

"I hope it's more balance—knowing when to access the situation, understanding the objective, and make the decision. A little bit of risk with a little bit of conservative decision making."

"Do you think our approach has that balance?"

McKenzie shook his head. "During my training my success rate was average, but I did argue on occasion that when I did jump into the fire, the situation was diffused quicker than by standing back and analyzing options." He rolled his eyes. "Somehow, I graduated."

"Congratulations boss."

McKenzie stared straight ahead. It was a lifetime ago. He could have been selling securities, and Jennifer would have been the bread-winner. That alternate universe never happened. Now, there was another woman involved—another course correction—another possible loss he didn't need. He really liked having her around.

"You still there?' Neal asked. Your eyes have that glazed-over look."

McKenzie straightened up, smiled for the first time in a long while. "I have the most ungodly, far-fetched, through-the-roof feeling if Professor Lowe ever got her way, she might be able to agitate them long enough to force them to make a mistake."

Neal cocked his head. "Without getting killed?"

"I don't want to hear that Neal, so don't bring it up again."

CHAPTER 13

Hotel Hermitage
Monte Carlo, Monaco

P aul Coulomb took the glass of whiskey from the bartender and turned his attention to Valencia Garcia Melendez. "Will you excuse me, my dear?" he asked after a gentle peck on her cheek. "I have a little business to attend to." She frowned with disappointment.

It was early afternoon, and he wound his way through the sea of international movers and shakers. There were more millionaires, billionaires, and celebrities inhabiting the hotel's Eiffel mezzanine than anywhere else in the world. Below the turn of the century steel and glass dome designed by Gustave Eiffel himself, the early afternoon gala celebrated nothing in particular except worldly excess and constant greed.

Coulomb relished this venue. He loved using other people's money to further his own causes. That was one of the reasons for his success. Leverage, isn't that what it was called? And now, he had more money than God and a desirous urge to have more. It had to be something in his genes. His father had it, but murderous business partners... Coulomb banished the same fate from his conscious.

He moved toward Jim Romano, who was conversing with a couple of Saudi businessmen decked out in traditional Saudi garb. As Coulomb neared, Romano greeted him.

"The usual suspects are in attendance," Romano said.

"I am anxious to meet them, as I have already met their money." He raised his whiskey glass with a salutary gesture and took a sip. "I must commend your management team. The IFC has moved with exceptional speed." He grinned at the asset manager from the IFC, who had become a trusted ally and gave Möbius legitimate international cover.

"We're pleased your project has fulfilled the requirements in a timely fashion. Land acquisition, environmental mitigation, archeological and cultural preservation, all facets addressed. Now, it's a straight-forward process to secure the shareholders. These water projects are a major draw."

"Understandably, seventy-percent of this planet is covered by water, yet only one-percent is drinkable. Increased pollution, climate change, aquifer depletion, those are rapidly making that less than one percent, but I doubt our investors want to save the world."

"They have their reasons."

"Money is their reason," Coulomb said with a devilish grin as he polished the side of the glass with naked pleasure. "I must admit, the eagerness on their faces is heartwarming."

"The Saudis, the Sokolovskii consortium, the Bromely brothers from New York, Ying Construction from China, they're all here, and a great deal of their money is already sunk into the project. There is strong enthusiasm to be part of Phase Two."

"Visions of billions floating in their heads."

Romano nodded in agreement.

"It's as much an international affair as we could have hoped for. Möbius is a company that works for the good of the world." He winked. "Jim, you have selected wisely."

Romano blushed. "You've made all the right moves, Mr. Coulomb."

Glancing over the man's shoulder, Coulomb watched Shelby Wallace work his way across the floor. He caught up with the American, picking a piece of lint off the sleeve of his black pin-stripe suit and flicking it onto the floor.

"Have you found the woman?" Coulomb asked.

"We're working on that."

"If Haley squealed, that could blow everything sky high." He placed his glass on a passing server's tray. "Find her. We leave for Basel immediately after this affair."

"We're on it."

Coulomb was unnerved. Möbius' plans must not be compromised. Even with the IFC on their side, it wouldn't take much to raise a few eyebrows.

Wallace looked at his watch. "I need to make a few phone calls. I'll keep ya'll informed." He headed for the veranda.

Coulomb turned as Jim Romano approached. "Mr. Coulomb, would this be a good time for introductions?"

The Frenchman smiled. "I would be honored to meet our shareholders." Out of the corner of his eye, he caught the young Spanish beauty looking his way. He waved her over. "Valencia, my dear, care to meet a few of our partners?"

Her alluring smile said it all, as she locked arms with Coulomb.

"We're all yours, Jim."

CHAPTER 14

Mallory entered the sleek structure, a dazzling double curvature of glass and gray granite. She sauntered across the lobby's lustrous marble floor reflecting the copper-clad curtainwalls along one side. *A perfect display for the mega-egos of Möbius,* she thought, *huge and extravagant.* Her eyes fell on the water feature, prominently placed in the center of the lobby, directly below a massive glass dome eight-stories high.

Two women staffed an information desk to the right of the fountain. To her left, a self-standing, glass-enclosed, circular elevator core fed each floor with a small bridge. She remembered McKenzie telling her that the entire eighth floor encompassed the offices of the all-powerful Paul Coulomb.

The fountain itself was a Basel attraction. Nowhere else in the world did water write such complicated symbols. Besides tourists, business professionals zipped across the lobby. Canali oxfords, Dansko clogs, and an assortment of other expensive footwear tapped out a midday rhythm on the Italian marble inlaid with floral medallions in blue and golden brown. Mallory looked around, trying to locate where the web cameras were placed. Impossible to tell; the space was too large, and the interior design lavish enough to hide a peeping Tom. Six shimmering crystal chandeliers hung around the perimeter of the high dome, supported by stainless-steel rods several stories long. For all she knew, the cameras were hidden in those fancy lighting fixtures or buried in the mixture of architectural transoms and futuristic molding. Once her appearance was noted on camera, the shit would hit the fan. If Möbius personnel didn't recognize her and cause alarm, McKenzie would certainly kill her the next time they met. She looked at her watch. She had ten minutes until Neal's hack commenced.

She shifted her gaze. Four or five people stood on the raised tier surrounding the circular pool, staring intently. Dressed casually, she assumed they were visitors. She strolled over; *now or never*. Had she been identified because of her visit to the museum? McKenzie was convinced she was in their sights. It was something that gnawed at her after she left CIA *Operations*. It took all her willpower to not look up and smile at the cameras and wave.

Roughly forty feet in diameter, the water feature was rimmed with a railing that followed the circumference. She joined the group and examined the shallow pool of water, which was at least a foot deep. Small waves emanated from around the perimeter, travelling ever so gently towards the center of the pool. Even though she'd studied the feature several times via the web cam, she still couldn't believe her eyes. As the waves approached the center in a circular pattern, they overlapped and collided with one another in what seemed like a chaotic fashion. And what she saw in person sent a sensation of awe and amazement spiraling down her spine. In the center, letters of the alphabet materialized on the surface, incredibly spelling out— M-Ö-B-I-U-S—one letter after another. Each filled a five-foot square area and lasted at least three seconds before the next letter formed miraculously.

"Oh my God!" Neal exclaimed. "You won't believe this."

McKenzie rushed over and stared at the computer monitor. "What's the problem?"

"Woman on the upper tier, third from the left. Look familiar?"

McKenzie stared at the monitor speechless. "Shit, what the hell is she doing there?"

Neal shook his head. "She's a piece of work, that one."

"Can we stop the hack?" McKenzie demanded.

"Too late for that."

McKenzie squinted at the screen. Maybe this wasn't as bad as he thought. Kill two birds with one stone. If they realize who Mallory Lowe was, that will tell them something. After a couple of minutes, he wasn't disappointed. If he was not mistaken, it was Esra Sahin who had entered the picture and approached

Mallory. He could only hope they recognized her from the museum and were curious, otherwise he had a feeling Amistad would flush his career down the toilet if things went bad. Maybe that wasn't as bad as losing her. The more he dealt with her, the more he felt an attraction. He could only pray he wouldn't experience another lost allure all over again.

"Do you like our pool?" a voice from behind said in English, her accent indistinguishable.

Mallory spun and stared at the woman. She was tall, impeccably dressed in an emerald pants suit, the visage of a woman of importance. Her presence was inviting, her eyes stunning, yet—shrewd, diminished somewhat by her smile.

"This is quite the thing," Mallory exclaimed portending excitement.

"It was installed a year ago. The technology is the latest, created by advanced wave generators you see around the perimeter."

Mallory looked closely and saw what appeared to be six-inch square metal plates attached around the perimeter a couple of inches below the surface. They were all in a state of individual movement, pushing out from the wall at different speeds and angles of rotation, creating water movement, generating waves.

"There are three hundred of them; each one can independently create a wave as you can see. By sophisticated computer software, we are able to spell out individual letters and symbols in the center of the pool."

"Fascinating. Superposition of waves combine to form the shapes of the characters that we see."

"Correct. The waves interact, cancel and subtract, resulting in the formation of letters."

"Can they spell out full words yet instead of individual letters and symbols?"

"Not quite, the wave generating devices and the software are not sophisticated enough, but we are working towards that goal." The woman glanced at the water and then back at Mallory. "Look again, the sequence is programmed to spell out Möbius three times then a series of symbols. It should be happening about now."

Mallory returned her gaze to the center and saw the I-U-S come and go. She glanced at her watch. It was two o'clock. Now was the time the fourth constant would be added via Neal's hacking. Her heart began to beat in overdrive as the next characters appeared in succession

$$\pi\ldots\ldots\pi^2/6\ldots\ldots e\ldots\ldots\sqrt{2}$$

She turned and stared at the woman whose reaction didn't disappoint. There was an expression of shock, followed by teeth exposed anger. The woman glared at Mallory, her face a study in evil. She felt exposed.

"Your name?" the woman asked coldly.

Mallory kept calm and under control, "Susan Smith, I'm a mathematics professor on a business vacation.

The woman's demeanor relaxed, the head-hunting stare transforming to an eye-pleasing gaze. "Esra Sahin with Möbius."

Mallory extended her hand. "Pleased to meet you. I must be honest. I came here today because I am writing an article on the history of mathematics in the Basel area. Somewhere I read that Möbius' Paul Coulomb is a mathematician. This water writing must surely be his idea. Do you think it would be possible to interview him?"

Esra contrived a smile. "I work closely with Mr. Coulomb. I am sure he would grant you an interview. Would you be available to join us this evening for dinner?"

Mallory smiled. "That would be wonderful."

CHAPTER 15

Lake Lucerne, Switzerland

Paul Coulomb walked down the garden pathway, admiring the snow-capped peak of Mt. Pilatus high above the green slopes rising from the lake. It was pleasant to be back from Monte Carlo. This was where he was the happiest, especially on glorious days like this. He analyzed the way the afternoon sun bounced off the lake and reflected a medley of passing cumulus, his world in full view, magnified in wealth and abundance, class and power, and the obsessive drive to dominate.

He admitted he was a product of privilege, but that never stopped him from wanting more. Hours skiing, hiking, dreaming—living, learning, and taking advantage of his parents' positions and wealth. Both long gone, killed in what the gendarmes claimed was an automobile accident. Coulomb insisted it was no accident, evidence suppressed by Chambéry authorities. His father had become the fall guy in a citywide corruption scandal; his mother, unfortunately, was collateral damage. Until his last days, the memory of their flower-draped coffins would never leave his consciousness.

Lake Lucerne brought blissful recollections. He remembered his parents bringing him on vacations here as a youth. Now, he had the best of both worlds: the leverage of a multi-faceted international corporation with obscene profits, and the beauty and serenity of his lakeside estate, increasingly vital to him as each day passed. He had it built ten years ago when Möbius was just beginning to control the European bottled water market.

He stepped down onto the middle terrace, his favorite part of the garden. The path wound under a vine-covered arbor and circled a majestic fountain, dismantled stone by stone and brought all the way from Provence. Rows of colorful perennials bordered the cobblestone, enhancing the scene as if he had stepped into an Impressionist Oil. His nose took in the fragrance of lavender, still blooming vigorously.

Continuing down a flight of stone steps, he viewed a small man sitting on a bench looking out across the lake. Unlike Coulomb—who was dressed in beige slacks and a custom embroidered polo shirt—Nevzat Sari wore jeans, an open-neck shirt, and sneakers.

Coulomb had known Sari for a little over four years. The Turk had proven himself during the dam's construction by confronting the hordes of protestors bent on seeing the project halted. Like many of those responsible for safeguarding Möbius' interests, it was best to motivate those that had a personal stake, or in Sari's case, a personal vendetta.

"Congratulations on finding the Haley woman," Coulomb said. "It's vital that we use her wisely."

"And the others?"

"They must be located, but my concern is the dam. If Harry has retreated to Eshai, they must be ready to strike the dam." Coulomb looked firmly at the Turk. "Remember, Harry has to be taken alive. I do not care what you do with the Assyrian. Once Harry has been located, you can do as you wish with him …and her."

Coulomb understood Sari's lack of skills when communicating with women. He had none—but on the other hand, he had no problem killing them. He continued. "I know Harry very well. He is resourceful and clear thinking. He will not be found easily."

Sari nodded. "I will find him."

Coulomb watched him move up the path through the gardens.

His mind turned back to Harry Meadowlark. It was Berkeley where they met. Like Coulomb, he was working on a PhD in mathematics, having already attained one in computer science. At that time, California had endured several years of drought. This triggered Harry's obsession with the computer management of water resources. Coulomb admired Harry's visions—control of freshwater would be the new frontier. Political and environmental pressures would boil over as population growth created nightmares.

Coulomb ambled up the path to his private office on the third level of his mansion. He sat down in front of his computer and punched a few keys on the keyboard. A private e-mail account popped up, only accessible by himself and Harry. Reaching into the draft folder, he opened a file.

Brilliant, Paul! Four fucking keys embedded with signal detection software. It was your idea to ensure the ultimate security. It would have worked if it wasn't for a defector, that being me of course. So sorry for that. But don't disappoint me now. I've given you every opportunity to find my key. This is child's play. It's right under your ever-loving egotistical ass. Here's another hint: take a close look at all your associates, maybe it's under their asses (not mine of course, I'm a former associate, eh, eh.) Hell, it could be anywhere. It's you and me bro, so fucking think. You ask, why do I make a game of this? Simple, it's for my amusement.

He had received this email only a few hours ago. He knew Harry was trying to bait him. That had always been Harry's modus operandi. If there was a subtle logical idea, Harry would use it to his advantage.

The e-mail had clues. He would begin with his outside associates. Several could be suspect, but one of Möbius' attorneys, Vincent Marotte, scored high on the list. Coulomb had kept his law firm on retainer for one simple reason—they were not averse to practicing jurisprudence in an unsavory manner. Through another contact in the law firm, Shelby had determined Marotte had been in communication with Meadowlark within the last two weeks. That raised the largest red flag of them all—did Marotte know the location of Meadowlark's key?

There was a limit to Harry's brilliance. He was endowed with what psychologists labeled *intrinsic motivation*—the thrill of the game. A sense of accomplishment was gained by proposing clues and basking in the glory when the clues could not be deciphered. If Coulomb was to succeed, it was imperative he have patience. Soon, Harry would learn they had the Haley woman. Then, he would negotiate.

CHAPTER 16

The picture-postcard views of Lake Lucerne were not lost on Mallory as she navigated the twisting road along the northern shore in her rental VW. She had to stay focused; try not to let the impressive rise of the Alps across the lake divert her attention.

She'd settled her nerves, but now that she was close to her destination, they flared. The goal: *Find Katie*. Her gut told her that the road to Katie went through Paul Coulomb. There was no escape, no alternate route to take. She kept reminding herself that she was doing the right thing, even if it meant putting her life at risk. She was convinced Katie would do the same if the roles were reversed. And there was that *hypothesis* she had kept in the back of her mind for so many years. Why not go for broke?

The gentle rise and fall of the road allowed her to think about the evening ahead and the unknown. Dinner at Coulomb's estate, a little over an hour drive from Basel. Esra had insisted this was the only way the head of Möbius would find the time to grant the interview.

She slowed the rental as it approached a rise in the road. Coming down the other side, her cell phone buzzed. Her heart thumped hard. She could only guess who it was.

"Hello," she answered.

"That was quite the stunt, showing up on camera just as the hack was to occur." McKenzie said. "Just curious, are you trying to destroy our surveillance?"

"No, I'm trying to find Katie."

"Where are you now?"

She swallowed hard, knowing he would be livid with what she was about to say. "I'm headed to Coulomb's estate."

"*Whaaat?* Didn't we discuss—no, didn't I order you not to get involved? Do you not have a brain in that disruptive head of yours?"

"This has nothing to do with your CIA. I've been invited to dinner, that's all."

"Dinner, fuck, are you deaf to orders? For Christ sakes, those folks won't stop until you're dead. Look at their body count already."

There was a silence, and there was a tone in McKenzie's voice that she had not heard before. "I'll be fine. They don't know I was with Tom. They think I'm a naïve math professor doing an interview with another mathematician, that's all."

"We've got a lot invested in surveillance of this group and if you screw it up—"

That touched a raw nerve. "How? They already know you have them under watch; remember Tom Haley, my friend, *your* operative?"

The line went silent. Then McKenzie warned, "If you get yourself in trouble, we may not be able to help this time." He paused, letting his next sentence soak in. "I'd like to not see you get killed."

She hesitated. "Thank you, I'll be fine." She hung up. She could sense a real concern, a kind of sincerity and caring in his last sentence. He was right, and she knew it. She felt an ache and a stabbing loneliness in her heart. Would she survive to see him or Katie again?

Her foot held steady on the gas pedal. The blurred profile of a red Aston Martin whizzing by in the opposite direction brought her attention back to the winding road. Readdressing the wheel with a tighter grip, Mallory continued over a short wooden bridge spanning a small stream. On her right, she found a stone pedestal at an intersection. Turning off the main road she ascended through a series of heavily wooded switchbacks. Coming out of the thick stand of trees, the road swung sharply to her left on a ninety-degree curve. With a gasp, she slammed on her brakes. Taking a deep breath, she maneuvered ever so slowly along the road, single lane at this spot. Cut into the face of a vertical escarpment, the road defied engineering saneness, narrow and not for the weak of heart. A very inadequate guardrail ran along her right side. She estimated the cliff was several hundred feet of dizzy verticality. She took another frenzied breath as she cleared the drop-off and entered a short tunnel that led back into the trees, safely away from the unexpected gorge. She sighed with relief.

The road descended a few more switchbacks, then leveled off in a clearing. The lake came into view—an inland sea of blue that seemed to extend for miles, contrasting sharply with the wooded slopes of the mighty Alps soaring steeply from the passive waters. After another sharp corner, the mansion materialized—four stories, native stone, with the architectural flavor of Tuscany. She was now entering the arena of a very wealthy and powerful man.

She shivered.

She gaped at the multi-level terrace below the home, meandering towards the water where a private marina extended out into the lake. Along one side, she saw the largest yacht she had ever seen. The long, sleek beauty was double decked, overwhelming the dock. The rich and famous, there was no denying their excesses. Even among the filthy overabundance on display, there had to be information on Katie.

Mallory parked the rental in an open area to the left of the entrance. What if they found the hotel where she was staying, and discovered Susan Smith was not her real name? It certainly wouldn't take a genius to connect the dots, maybe even link her to Nevada. Her only saving grace—McKenzie? Dammit, but what the hell could he do? She had made her decision, made her own bed, as ratty as it was. She knew her one major fault was impatience, so what was the point? She sat immobile, feeling her pulse race, that awkward, foolish sensation that she had stepped into the lion's den.

She exited the car with her satchel hanging from her shoulder. The massive face of conglomerate rock beyond the mansion grabbed her attention. Rising sharply from the green hills was The Wall, or as the locals called it, *Die Wandung*, the thousand foot near-vertical cliff face posed formidably. She cringed, gaping at the sheer exposure. Perched on the top, like a spaceship ready for flight, was the upper terminal to Coulomb's private tramway jutting out over the edge of the cliff. She remembered Neal mentioning the aerial attraction. She caught a glimpse of the cables stretching far down the mountain and threading into the lower terminal situated not far from the house.

She walked up the steps to the entry. She thought it odd that there was no one here to meet her, nor any outside staff, gardeners, or such. It was as if the place was deserted. An eerie sensation swept over her. She was being watched, there was no doubt about it. She couldn't brush this inkling aside; her instincts always embodied some visage of truth. Her eyes darted around, careful not to alert anyone that her nerves were on edge. For the time being, she needed to wave off her insecurity and relax.

She reached for the large brass knocker on the oversized wooden door. It immediately swung open.

Esra Sahin stood in the entryway.

"Ms. Smith, we are so happy you could make it. Please, come in."

"Oh, thank you." Mallory said, sucking in a deep breath. She stepped inside.

"This way."

She followed Esra through the foyer and into a massive reception hall, the extravagance of a painted barrel vault above, an imposing iconographic representation of Michelangelo's famous ceiling, *a la Sistine chapel*. Overhead, transom lights illuminated the frescoes with a soft touch of drama. The extravagance was now beginning to grate on her nerves. Impressive, it felt like a prison.

"Your drive was pleasant, I hope?"

Mallory stood there in a watchful pose. Why was it she felt more fearful of this woman than she did driving along the edge of the cliff? "The lake is absolutely gorgeous."

"Yes, it is."

As they neared the large curved stairway, a woman entered through a door to the right.

"Ana, will you please show Ms. Smith to the guest room where she can freshen up?"

Ana took Mallory's satchel. "Follow me, please," she said in accented English.

"Take your time," Esra said. "Mr. Coulomb is busy finishing some tasks and will be able to meet with you shortly. In the meantime, make yourself comfortable; wander the grounds and enjoy the gardens. Mr. Coulomb's estate is yours, and if you need anything, I'll be nearby."

"Thank you for your hospitality." Mallory followed Ana up the stairs.

The guest room was located on the south side, with a dramatic view of the Alps and the lake. She slid the door open to the balcony and stepped outside. Halfway across the lake, a ferry plied eastward, and a few sailboats dotted the horizon.

A rush of iciness spread over her. She stepped back into the room and took a controlled breath—*do not act nervous; do not talk with yourself. Be wary…all the time.* The reasons were quite simple. It was in her interest to act natural, play the part—a composed mathematics professor charged with the task of interviewing a very wealthy man with a mathematical mind—albeit a very dangerous mind.

She knew the water feature would come up. But she had a plan for that. And Katie, she had that covered. For now, she needed to keep her guard up—especially when dealing with Esra. The woman was shrewd and cold, someone to avoid.

CHAPTER 17

The gardens around Coulomb's estate were stunning. Mallory followed the stone walkway as it snaked its way down to the boat dock from the upper level of the terrace. After a view of the stately yacht, she returned, winding her way along the curved path surrounded by a plethora of colorful flowers, the delectable fragrance of lavender overpowering. She contemplated the purpose of her visit. With the magnificence of this estate, her feeling of insecurity diminished. How could Paul Coulomb be as dangerous as the CIA says? She caught herself. Was she suddenly letting her guard down? Möbius killed Tom Haley and Franz Zellweger. They had her in their sights three times. Don't be a fool.

Out of the corner of her eye, she caught movement coming down the walkway. It was Esra Sahin, dressed in a casual pair of jeans and open-tailed chambray shirt, unlike her business-like attire earlier. She strode towards Mallory.

Approaching, she inquired, "Enjoying the grounds?"

Mallory smiled. "I've never seen such a stunning setting; reminds me of some of our national parks." She pointed at *Die Wandung*.

"That used to be a mountain climber's paradise. Unfortunately, there were too many deaths. After Mr. Coulomb bought it, climbing became prohibited. That did not sit well with the climbing community, but the local authorities at the village of Vetsch have been supportive. So many deaths looked bad for the village." Esra pointed at an outdoor table and chairs. "Care to join me?"

"I'd love to."

Esra's dark eyes were an exotic blend of secrets and mystery. The secrets—and her background—stirred Mallory's interest. Didn't McKenzie mention she was Turkish? And the dam in Turkey, there had to be a connection.

"How long have you been with Möbius?" she asked.

"Eight years. I met Mr. Coulomb when I was a resource director for the Southeast Anatolia Project. We oversaw planning and permitting the many water storage projects that have been built. A year after meeting, he offered me a job."

"And Turkey is your home?"

Her thin lips creased into a frown. "It was. Tell me, Ms. Smith, are you really on vacation?"

The woman wasted no time getting to the point. "Well, sort of. I am on the faculty at the University of Indiana. I also write articles for mathematical journals and magazines. I admit, this idea of an interview with Mr. Coulomb wasn't on my agenda, so you could say it's a working vacation."

"But, you had no idea that you would be able to see Mr. Coulomb. Wasn't that a little presumptuous on your part?"

"Not at all. I have an appointment with the director of CERN to interview him about the complexity of the mathematics embedded in their nuclear physics research." The lie was straightforward but not without peril. If Coulomb checked on the validity, she surely would be flushed out. But now, in her topsy-turvy world, it was worth the risk.

"A detour here from Geneva, just in hopes of seeing Mr. Coulomb?" she said with a hollow smile.

"I'd seen Möbius' website and learned of Mr. Coulomb's mathematical passions. I decided to fly into here first. It would give me the opportunity to check out the Museum of Mathematics and Science, such a fascinating place honoring those Basel-bred mathematicians from the fifteenth and sixteenth-centuries."

"We are pleased with our involvement in the museum. I am quite sure Mr. Coulomb will enjoy his conversation with you. You both seem to have a lot in common."

She kept her eyes framed on Esra, endeavoring to read the woman's thoughts. Questions were asked in a subtle way, attempting to get Mallory to stumble, make a mistake. To trust this woman would be like throwing oneself to the wolves. And she hadn't even met Coulomb yet. It might get worse.

"Forgive me. Mr. Coulomb said he is available in an hour. He is looking forward to the interview and having dinner with you. In the meantime, relax."

"That will be easy; it's such a magnificent place."
"Please feel at home. May we offer you some refreshment in the meantime?"
"I'm fine. The beautiful surroundings are all I need."

CHAPTER 18

P aul Coulomb admired the colorful plethora of visual wavelengths.

In his office, the sun filtered through the large Romanesque window, striking the icosahedron paperweight on the oaken desk and flooding the far wall with a spectral rainbow. That was the beauty of mathematics; numbers designed into the very fabric of the universe—the essence of mathematics in all things *natural* and *divine*, yet his definition of *divine* had a whole different meaning. He could have easily seen himself happy as a career mathematician, a professorship at some major university or working in industry in applied mathematics, doing complicated things with numbers. Appealing, very appealing, but his addiction to money, influence, and domination were stronger.

He had no regrets.

He gazed out the window at the lake's gentle lapping waters, a delicate contrast in which to frame the lush green and white-capped Alps in the distance. His eyes momentarily averted from the picture-frame view to the parked rental car below. Who was this woman who had visited the museum and asked about Katie Haley?

As he pondered her further, the door opened.

The professor walked in, followed by Esra Sahin.

Mallory approached the desk as he rose. His blue-gray eyes were riveting, nothing Napoleonic in his stature. He was tall, straight-edged nose, firm lips, overtly handsome. She kept her eyes locked on him as he gently took her hand in a welcoming handshake.

"Susan Smith, is it? It is a pleasure to meet you."

"The pleasure's all mine."

As soon as Mallory and Esra sat, Coulomb began to speak comically. "When Esra told me about our water feature malfunction, I was quite amused, thinking one of our former associates had overridden the computer program that controls the formation of water characters—sort of a parting shot."

Mallory smiled. "I confess that was all my doing."

Coulomb raised a brow. "Oh?"

"I felt it would be a sure-fire way to get this interview. I know how busy you are and all—"

He broke out laughing. "Absolutely devious. I give you credit for your knowledge and passion."

Esra did not laugh.

Mallory couldn't get over her derisive glare. "My intent was not to cause alarm. I'm just a foolhardy attention getter."

"It certainly worked," he said, smiling. "But, how did you do it?"

"I think it was six months ago, I saw an article in the newspaper on Möbius. Its focus was on your prowess as a CEO of a major international corporation and, of course, on your mathematical background. I checked your website and that is where I saw the water feature and the staging of the four irrational constants. Two weeks ago, I took another look at the site and found one of the constants had been removed. Since I was coming to Switzerland, it gave me an idea for an article I proposed for the journal of The American Mathematical Society. I have a friend who is a computer whiz. He hacked into your network and we reprogrammed the sequence. I had no right to do that. I do apologize."

Coulomb turned and caught Esra's eye. "I guess that means we'll have to upgrade our cybersecurity. I'm impressed. What do you think, Esra?"

"We could have her arrested."

"I suppose we could, but I prefer to reward innovation. I commend you Ms. Smith. Maybe you should come to work for me."

Mallory feigned shyness. "You're way too kind. If there is anything I can do to make up for this mischievous prank—"

Coulomb nodded Esra's direction.

"If you will excuse me," Esra said.

"Of course, my dear; we will meet up later." He turned all his attention back to Mallory as Esra left the room.

Alone with the lion. Mallory shifted in her chair. "She seems to be a very valuable member of your organization."

"Yes, indispensable. We as a corporation are very fortunate. She speaks honestly, as you have probably seen. She listens, she questions, she analyzes; she never bends. Part of her upbringing I would imagine."

"Her upbringing?"

Coulomb's eyes blinked. "Mathematics. Isn't that the real reason you're here?"

"Oh, absolutely," she said, trying to regroup her thoughts. "I think the readers would be fascinated to learn about Möbius. Such an intriguing name for a large multinational. Would you elaborate on that choice?" Mallory reached into her purse for her iPhone and turned on the voice memo. "Do you mind?"

Coulomb smiled. "Not at all. Ah, yes, Möbius. What a wonderful gift the German mathematician August Ferdinand Möbius has given us. As a mathematician, you can surely appreciate the grand subject of topology?"

"I do! In fact, I touch on it in a graduate course I teach. But from a practical standpoint, I remember as a kid taking a paper strip, giving it a half-twist, and gluing the ends together. That's the Möbius strip that most people know. Does that fall within your definition?"

"Of course. From a philosophical point of view, we like to imagine ourselves on a journey where we transform our challenges into solutions. Like an ant crawling along one surface of your paper strip, the ant traverses both surfaces during its journey. There is only one solution, but our journey has taken both sides of the argument to get there."

"That's a fascinating bit of logic applied to the corporate structure."

His smile relaxed. "A topological ideology."

She gazed around the room, decorated in an analytical, geeky style. Behind Coulomb's desk, a large framed reproduction of Leonardo da Vinci's Vitruvian Man hung from the wall. "I can see that you surround yourself with all things mathematical. If I'm not mistaken, Da Vinci was obsessed with the study of proportions, so elegantly depicted on that famous sketch behind you."

Coulomb nodded. "There is no question about the mathematical relationships of the human body, especially as visualized by Leonardo. The circle and square scribed over the body give it proportion."

Mallory stared at the famous drawing depicted in two different formations. She pretended it held her interest. "The first body with outstretched arms is inscribed in the square, and the second with raised arms and outspread feet is inscribed in the circle where I believe the navel represents the center. Question, what is the relationship to the two geometries?" She couldn't help but think of *The Basel problem*, squares and circles.

"It comes down to the age old question, can you square the circle?"

She feigned ignorance. "Start with a circle and produce a square of the same area. Mathematically impossible, and has been proven such."

"Precisely. The reason it is impossible: the number *pi*, an irrational number."

"And that's a whole other subject."

"Imagine if pi was not irrational; what kind of universe would we all be living in? But, that was not da Vinci's prime objective. His was just an anthropometry study, the perfectly proportioned male body and how it relates to mathematics, particularly geometry, and to science in general."

"Interesting, although my understanding is today's male body does not possess Vitruvian Man dimensions."

Coulomb offered a sweet smile. "I must have missed that."

"Oh, don't blame yourself. It was a lesser known study by a Scotsman named Kilgore, if I recall. He compared the dimensions of the average Renaissance man to today's modern man, a good five hundred years difference. Men today are taller, average height somewhere around four or five inches more. It would be hard pressed to get the average modern man to fit the circle and square geometries."

"Fascinating."

"I suppose you could attribute the findings to evolution. The human body is always adapting to its environment." She couldn't escape his gaze. It would be best to shift his attention to something else. "May I," she said, pointing to the glass case opposite the desk.

"Please." He stood and walked over to the case. Mallory followed.

"This is one of the few cuneiform tablets ever found in northern Mesopotamia."

Mallory bent down and studied the tan-colored clay object in the case. A multitude of stamped wedge-shaped marking covered it, like the ones she had seen on Babylonian tablets.

"I'm certainly no expert, but I would guess this is similar to the famous tablets found in Iraq, a depiction of sexagesimal mathematics."

"I'm impressed with your knowledge. It is base sixty. The Babylonians were more advanced than the Egyptians, but this is not Babylonian."

"Then what is it?" she asked.

"Let's just say it's very rare."

His answer was blunt. There would be no discussing the tablet any further. He probably acquired it illegally. Let it be.

He looked at his watch. "I have a few things to clear up before our dinner cruise. We'll continue our enlightening visit then."

"Cruise?" Mallory asked.

Coulomb looked out the window. "You cannot leave without a mystical voyage aboard the *Lune Corbeau*."

CHAPTER 19

Mallory stared out the window across the grounds to the pier. She could make out Paul Coulomb talking to another man next to a cruiser that had recently docked. Directly below on the terrace, she could see Esra Sahin walking down the path. A rush of adrenalin coursed through her. She was alone in the mansion.

It was now or never, except for one thing. The housekeeper, Ana—wasn't that her name? She hoped Ana kept to the lower level in the kitchen area. She took another glance out the window. Esra had joined the others on the dock, all three deep in conversation. Mallory had no doubt she was the topic of discussion.

She rushed over to the door and stepped out into the hallway. Keeping an observant bearing, she moved swiftly to the stairs. She looked to see if there were any security cameras— although if there was, they may well be hidden. This made her uneasy. Brushing aside the idea that she was being watched, she darted up the stairs.

She was on the third floor, where she had been earlier. She had to move cautiously. The door to Coulomb's office was closed. Gently, she turned the latch. Closed, but unlocked. She darted into the office, all the while feeling the ragged thumping of her heart. She ambled over to the window and gazed down at the dock. A feeling of relief swept over her. They were all there, still conversing. Prancing back to the desk, she rifled through the drawers, quickly examining anything that might scream out Katie. Flipping through files, papers, a desk tray filled with an assortment of pens and pencils, paper clips and rubber bands. Nothing jumped out at her—nothing that would point to Katie's whereabouts.

She closed the drawers and took another peek out the window. All three were still on the dock, still talking. Looking back around the office, she remembered the cuneiform tablet she had seen earlier. Something unusual about it suddenly sprang into her mind. She moved over to the cabinet and peered at the clay tablet. Coulomb admitted it was rare but didn't say where it was from, only that it was not Babylonian. She examined it closely. On one corner of the tablet a circle was scribed with three-quarters of it shaded by a series of closely-spaced parallel lines. The remaining quadrant in the circle was scribed with a row of cuneiform wedge-shaped symbols. She was convinced these were numbers and not Sumerian or Babylonian letters. Recalling what she knew about Sumerian script, the shaded portion of circle made sense, representing 270 degrees, three-quarters of 360 degrees. Assyrians were the first to invent the 360 degree circle.

Now she knew why Coulomb didn't admit where it came from. Assyrian mathematical tablets were rare, more so than Babylonian and other Sumerian clay writings. This one likely originated in Syria or Turkey. Turkey would be her first choice. And Esra Sahin was Turkish. Weren't these reasons enough to believe that was where Katie was?

Perspiration dotted her forehead. She rushed over to the window. Her heart rose in her throat.

They were no longer on the pier.

It was time to leave, if it wasn't already too late.

She rushed over to the door and listened. Stone quiet. She darted into the hallway and down the stairs. The house still appeared deserted. Feeling confident, she entered her room, closed the door and collapsed on the bed. Her breathing began to return to normal.

She was safe.

CHAPTER 20

There was hardly a murmur coming from the twin diesel-electric engines as the *Lune Corbeau* glided effortlessly on the lake's glass-like surface. Mallory sipped at her glass of Pinot Noir ever so slowly as she listened closely to the man standing next to her. He introduced himself as Shelby Wallace.

His still recognizable drawl came off strange sounding on the multimillion-dollar yacht. "So miss the pleasure of talkin' with someone from back home, especially another Southerner. Oklahoma, I understand." he twanged.

"Born and bred there. I'm in Indiana now. But still, it's hard to believe they have such large boats on this lake," she said.

"Yachts," he corrected. He was tall, muscular with sandy hair and a good ol' boy gaze.

She shook off a shiver. She'd seen these types in Oklahoma, knowing he was analyzing her every move.

"It's the largest yacht allowed on the lake at one hundred and fifty feet in length. Truthfully now, they *ain't* many ocean-going pleasure vessels as large as this. Lucerne here now is big, plenty ah room to maneuver." His eyes kept her caged. "So, tell me, ya'll here to interview Paul? For what publication?"

"The AMS, American Mathematical Society."

"I don't think ya'll be disappointed.

"Have you been with Möbius long?"

"Close to twenty-five years."

She took another sip from her glass when a short stub of a man approached dressed in a flowery Hawaiian shirt, white jeans, and rose-colored sunglasses. He was middle-aged, wavy brown hair and a plump face. He carried a glass of wine, which he kept spilling.

"Susan Smith, this is Vincent Marotte. Vincent's an attorney with one of the largest law firms in Switzerland."

"It is a pleasure, *Mademoiselle*," he said, taking her hand and giving it a kiss.

"Nice to meet you."

"If ya'll excuse me." Wallace patted Marotte on the back and gave them both a smile. Before she could respond, he disappeared down a stairway to the lower deck.

Her eyes fell back on the lascivious face of the man standing next to her. She detested the way his eyes flicked up and down her body.

"I must say, Paul does find the most beautiful women to invite to dinner."

She needed to get away from this creep—the way he looked at her, the dribble of red wine on his lips. If Coulomb and his crew were not to be trusted, this ass was just as dangerous in a whole different way.

"You're too kind."

"What part of the states are you from?" he said, rubbing the wine off his chin.

"Originally from Oklahoma."

He threw her a stupid grin. "Oklahoma, *oui*, is that in Texas?"

"Almost."

"Everything is big in Texas." His eyes grew into silver dollars.

"If you excuse me, I think I'll go freshen up before dinner," she said.

"Of course." He bowed as she slipped away towards the restroom on the starboard side. All the while, she cringed knowing his ravenous eyes were tattooing her the whole way.

The setting sun floated on the horizon, slowly dipping beneath the black waters of the lake. The *Lune Corbeau* slowed to a mellow cruising speed, the air temperature a comfortable 75F. Dinner was on the upper covered deck, replete with a linen tablecloth, sterling silverware, and fine white china. Thankfully, Esra sat between her and the lusty Vincent Marotte, who by now appeared fully intoxicated. Shelby Wallace was at the far end of the table. Next to him, a man named Bruno Metzier and his wife, Pauline. Across from Mallory sat the young and beautiful Valencia García Melendez. Coulomb sat at the head of the table. He introduced Valencia as a dear friend, but it was obvious she was beyond the friend stage. Shy, she hardly said three words the whole evening.

"You are a professor of mathematics," Bruno said, directing his attention at Mallory. "Are you as interesting as Paul? He is one of the most interesting mathematicians I have ever met, as if I know a lot of mathematicians." He laughed whole-heartedly.

"We seem to have that in common." Mallory studied the fiftyish, rotund man wearing an open-collar pink shirt. "Tell me, what do you do for a living?"

"Drug dealer," he said with a dopey smile. "Our company is one of many pharmaceuticals that call Basel home."

"Bruno and I have been friends for some time," Coulomb interjected. "Bruno just loves to cruise the lake so when he sees the opportunity, he finds a way to invite himself." Complimentary smiles exchanged between the two men.

Mallory's gaze drifted to Pauline, who seemed indifferent to the gathering.

"I provide the eye candy, so he drags me along," she said, answering Mallory's eye contact.

Mallory could tell she was a fake blond, with other fake parts.

"But you enjoy every minute," Bruno protested. "Every minute."

"Do I have a choice?" She looked at him blankly, turned to Mallory with a smile, tossed her napkin on the plate in an act of defiance. It was obvious she was bored stiff.

"Drugs, drugs, how about just some plain old wine," Vincent complained, raising his glass. A server rushed over and refilled it.

Bruno ignored the boozed-up attorney. "Tell me, Ms. Smith, since I can't seem to get an answer out of my friend Paul here, what is it about mathematics that so fascinates you?"

"Well, it underlies everything we humans touch, usually in a subtle way. It—is the language of the universe."

"I would concur," Coulomb affirmed. "The universe and all its laws are easily described by numbers. It is an essential tool that is used in every human endeavor, even pharmaceuticals."

"Oh, now Paul, I'm not that naïve," Bruno said. Why don't you explain to the lovely lady here your reasoning for being so aroused with those crazy symbols that keep bubbling up on your fountain."

Mallory took the opening. "Yes, I'd like to know. We never touched on the subject of the irrationals."

"Numbers, numbers…floating on water, like magic, but one is missing— gone, *disparu*." Marotte's inflamed eyes drifted effortlessly. "*J'ai une question*, a question—where do you have it hidden?" He broke into a laugh.

Coulomb took notice of Marotte's intoxication. How easy it was for the attorney to open his mouth and spout things indiscriminately.

"Well, what is a number?" Coulomb said. "We have rational, irrational, real, imaginary, even, odd, prime and so on. Irrationals are dear to me. One must understand the definition of an irrational number in the first place. It cannot be expressed as a fraction, nor can it be expressed as a repeating decimal. It continues on indefinitely."

Mallory questioned, "Why the three irrational numbers that we see in the fountain. Is there some special meaning to them?"

Coulomb leaned back in his chair. "We both know the amazing utility of both *pi* and *e*. They show up in so many places in mathematics. *Pi*, the ratio of the circumference of a circle to its diameter but there is much more. And *e* occurs in so many areas, compound interest, radioactive decay, population growth, and so forth."

"The one true exponential number," Mallory added.

"True, very true." Coulomb smiled down the table at Shelby. "Exponential, like profits, huh, Shelby?"

Shelby smiled back. "Larger and larger."

Coulomb continued, "Möbius has adopted these universal constants as the bedrock of the company. They are never ending, always rushing to infinity. They will never change, and they have value in so many ways. He leaned forward. "They are almost...*immortal*."

Mallory went along. "That's an interesting philosophy for your company. Tell me then, what about the square root of two? What meaning does that have?"

"It has a special meaning, wouldn't you agree, Esra?"

Esra raised an eyebrow at Mallory. "As a mathematician, you should recognize that it is likely the first irrational number ever discovered. It is embedded in history."

Mallory didn't miss a beat. "Yes, you're right. It was the Pythagoreans who realized that the diagonal of a square with the sides all one unit long, was the square root of two or a number that wasn't a whole number or a fraction composed of whole numbers. I believe poor Hippasus was tossed overboard a ship for suggesting this. Irrational numbers were beyond the Greek's reasoning."

"Is it not ironic," Esra mocked. "I do believe we are on a vessel in the *middle* of the water talking mathematics."

Mallory's raised brow was not lost on Coulomb.

McKenzie was furious as he maneuvered the cabin cruiser within a mile of the *Lune Corbeau*. He should never have trusted Mallory Lowe to stay put? It would be a miracle if she got out of Coulomb's grasp alive. Now, he would have to report to Amistad that he had screwed up and should have kept a tighter rein on her. He could see himself standing in front of the ethics board, getting the book thrown at him—fired; and later, served with an unlawful death lawsuit. He would be disgraced, finished.

All his tormented thoughts led to unwelcome scenarios. Did they know she was the woman in Nevada? Did they think she was CIA? My God, had they killed her already? From what he knew of Möbius and their *modus operandi*, it would be easy for them to conclude Mallory Lowe was better off out of the picture. And now they were on water. It would be easy to throw her body overboard.

Tight as a drum, McKenzie piloted the cruiser near the northern shore as Neal kept the luxury yacht *Lune Corbeau* in focus through the binoculars. The sun had set fifteen minutes ago, and soon it would be dark.

"I'm starting to lose detail, but it appears they have finished dinner on the deck," Neal said.

"Can you still see Mallory?"

"So far. In another ten minutes, it will be too dark. The good news; the yacht is turning, heading back."

McKenzie wrestled with *what ifs*. Would they kill Mallory in the middle of the Lake, with her rental car at Coulomb's estate? If they were to kill her, wouldn't they want it to appear as an accident? After all, they would want an alibi.

For now, he would maintain their distance. There was no need to raise suspicion that Coulomb and his group were being tailed.

After dinner, Coulomb and Wallace excused themselves and went below deck, explaining they had some minor Möbius business.

"I haven't heard back from the *bastard*," Coulomb said. "I emailed him before dinner to let him know we had the *Haley woman*. It's not like him to not respond promptly."

"He's a bit shell-shocked," Wallace said with satisfaction. "GPS still locates his SAT phone, his padded location bounces around, but he's there, no doubt. Sari moved her from one of the mechanical rooms at the dam to the electrical gallery. Better security and all."

Coulomb looked at Wallace, impressed. "You have a rare smile, Shelby. Do you have more to share?"

"Our guest ain't Susan Smith."

"You certain?"

"Positive."

"Well, well." He turned on an overhead television screen. "One more thing our professor needs to explain." He punched a remote and a video of the woman appeared opening the door to his office and entering.

Wallace shook his head as the professor was seen pilfering through desk drawers and nosing about. "Well now, she's as dumb as a sack of hammers."

Coulomb turned the television off. "I think it is time to have a very intimate talk with our guest."

Mallory wasn't surprised when Coulomb and Wallace excused themselves. She was left to listen to the conversation between Bruno and Marotte, arguing passionately over the role of the Swiss government in not intervening to keep the Swiss franc from edging down against the euro. Esra and Valencia were in a private conversation between themselves, one that Esra seemed to be controlling. Pauline had left the table, walking the deck smoking a cigarette. After a few minutes, Mallory excused herself, noting Esra's cold gaze.

She walked along the main deck passing a dual set of tenders in an attempt to clear her mind. The sun had set, and darkness was beginning to dissolve the lake into obscurity. A few clouds hovered on the horizon, a patch of altocumulus catching the last streaks of crimson. Mallory estimated they should arrive back within the next fifteen or twenty minutes. In the meantime, she swiftly reviewed the dinner conversation in her mind, the essence of the irrationals. Originally on the fountain, the irrationals came in the order of π, $\pi^2/6$, e and $\sqrt{2}$. Later, the $\pi^2/6$ was dropped. The question lingered—why?

Pauline Metzier appeared around the corner, a cigarette dangling between her fingers. She eyed Mallory, moved next to the rail and flung it into the lake.

"Enjoying the cruise?" she asked.

"Quite the treat."

"Don't get overly comfortable. This can be a rough crowd." She smiled impatiently and sauntered on down the deck.

Mallory thought a moment of what Pauline meant, brushed it aside, and continued her walk towards the aft. A stairway appeared off to her right. Why not check where this went? Nobody said there were any places off-limits on the yacht. It was not as if she was snooping, just enjoying the enormity of the *Lune Corbeau*. Stepping down two risers, she stopped for a moment. She heard voices. She stepped down another riser and leaned towards a wall vent. Sure enough, she recognized them.

Coulomb and Wallace were deep in conversation.

Near the bottom of the stair, a corridor ran to her left. She kept two steps above, not wanting to be seen by whoever could be at the other end. She noticed light flooding her way, possibly from the room where the conversation was occurring. Bending her ear closer to the vent, she could make out the exchange between the two men. And then three words fell on her ears like an anvil on her foot.

The Haley woman!

Did she hear correctly? *Katie Haley caught and held at the dam, hidden in the electrical gallery* and *something about e-mailing the bastard, GPS and SAT phone.* She turned and looked around, her pulse had quickened with excitement and fear. If she was found snooping, how would she explain that she wasn't eavesdropping, just out and about exploring the magnificent yacht? She knew that would not go over well. Feeling vulnerable, she abruptly turned to leave but was stopped in her tracks.

Esra Sahin stood at the top of the stairs.

Mallory's heart stuck in her throat. The peace and tranquility she'd felt had taken a hike. Why was she stupid enough to think she was safe?

Another sound along the deck drew both women's attention. Vincent weaved his way toward them. He smiled at Esra, then gazed down at Mallory.

"Very difficult... to hide on this vessel, you know?" he babbled, gushing at Mallory.

"I wasn't hiding, just enjoying the fresh air."

He stumbled down a riser, forcing Mallory to retreat. He hiccupped. "Oh, I know; I've probably…had a little bit too much wine, but…"

Esra grabbed a hold of Vincent's arm and helped him back up to the deck. "We'll be docking in a few minutes. Everyone should be on the main deck when we arrive. Vincent, your ride will be waiting when we return. I'm sure you will enjoy a nice nap in the backseat on your way back to Basel?"

Marotte's puffy cheeks and rosy nose shone in the deck lights. "I would be…delighted…for the ride." He turned, swaying towards the main stairs.

Esra turned her attention back to Mallory. "What are your intentions, Ms. Smith?"

"I'll be driving back to Basel tonight." She took a step up.

"No, I think not. Your plans have changed." She blocked Mallory's way, a gun in her hand.

CHAPTER 21

Tepecik Dam

I t was less than eight hours since Nevzat Sari had left Coulomb, a feat made possible by one of Möbius' private jets. Back in familiar surroundings, he leaned over the parapet of the high dam and stared down at the generator complex four hundred feet below. The late evening air was sweet and warm. A few clouds streamed by, reflecting the light of a crescent moon still hidden by the high edge of the gorge. He heard the wailing howls of jackals in the distance tracking their prey.

He enjoyed nights like this. It gave him time to think clearly and prepare for Ismet's next move. Imagining himself in the bastard's shoes would allow him to achieve his goals. By thinking like the man he despised, he would find and crush him.

Just like the jackals in the distance, he was on the hunt.

Before the dam was built, he and Ismet Firat were friends, a coveted bond that defied the conflicted relationship between Turks and Assyrians. In their view, there was no glory in religious wars and genocides. They were the future, not the past.

It was a matter of philosophy that created differing views on the construction of Tepecik Dam that brought their friendship to an end. Nevzat Sari supported the dam. Ismet Firat opposed it, as its construction would bring displacement of his people and their Assyrian villages in Southeastern Anatolia.

Sari paused and reflected. His former friend had led the group protesting the construction of the dam because of ethnic, cultural, and environmental concerns. They blocked the main access into the inner gorge. To get to the site, Sari's father, one of the laborers, had to traverse a primitive and dangerous trail to bypass the demonstrators. One night returning home, he slipped and fell to his death. His beloved father, gone, for the simple act of trying to feed his family. This altered Sari's life forever, his heart forever stuck in his throat. From that moment forward, he had a personal stake in the dam's completion—and a personal crusade. He would find Ismet and kill him—an eye for an eye.

Sari pulled back from the parapet and walked along the crest toward the west end. Several guards patrolled the top of the dam carrying AK-47s. A lone guard passed by, acknowledging him with a pleasant nod. It would be very difficult to sabotage the dam. There were lookouts stationed on both access roads from top to bottom, and the dam itself was heavily fortified.

Gazing at the south side of the gorge, he saw the remnants of the primitive trail that crisscrossed the cliffs—the same trail that his father was forced to use. He groaned in pain. He shook off the memory, knowing the trail would never be used again; it had been dynamited— destroyed by his command.

Reaching the end of the dam, he entered a rectangular concrete core and stepped into an elevator. A minute later, he exited out into a cavernous room. The ceiling soared high above with space for an overhead crane that could travel the full length. The walls, floor, and roof were all concrete; scores of halogen lights illuminated the tunnel-like chamber. Catwalks extended along each wall below the crane rails.

He walked along the floor passing two of the six generators humming along in a monotonous shrill. A door opened from the main control room, and a man approached. There was a smile on his face.

"You look pleased, Ozan."

"And so should you," the man replied.

"What do you mean?"

"Deha just checked in. In her drugged state, the Haley woman garbled about an old Roman ruin on a hill. We have it in our sights. Ismet was just there."

"Deha sure?"

"Yes."

Sari exhaled slowly, keeping a strong gaze on Ozan. A sliver of excitement erupted inside, growing with each passing second. He could not let this opportunity elude him.

"Have it watched twenty-four-seven."

Ozan nodded, then offered a bawdy grin. "Why not celebrate with Deha and me. He has a cousin who lives in Eshai. She has two friends visiting from Ankara, both card-carrying ladies. Would you like to join us for a little fun and relaxation?"

Sari felt weak, as if his strength had been syphoned away. Women for pleasure, the thought—a bead of sweat popped on his forehead—ice cold. He turned away from Ozan not wanting to let him see his panic.

Regrouping, he wheeled back around. "How dare you think of fun and games at a time like this? There will be no free time. Do not take your eyes off that ruin!"

CHAPTER 22

Lake Lucerne

Mallory watched Paul Coulomb pace back and forth in his berth, undoubtedly contemplating her fate. If life was to be lived on the edge, she certainly was teetering on it. Would they kill her here, shoot her and throw her overboard, or take her back to shore and dispose of her in some faraway landfill? The methods were endless, her future for a long-life very much in doubt.

Esra still pointed the gun at her. Shelby Wallace had left to take control of the docking and to arrange to disembark the other guests.

"So it comes to this," Coulomb said, abruptly turning in her direction.

"I was just wandering the lower deck. I apologize, I didn't know those stairs were off limits."

"That is a very feeble excuse, especially coming from a woman who has a knack for nosing around."

"Did you search her?" he asked Esra.

Esra handed an iPhone over. "This is all we found."

Coulomb took and pocketed it. Mallory kept her composure although inside she felt panic taking control.

Coulomb picked up the television remote and punched a button. The video of Mallory intruding in his office appeared on the screen. No words were exchanged. After a minute, he turned it off. His voice rose. "You, my dear professor, owe us an explanation."

Her throat tightened further. She felt as if she was heading towards extinction. "The door was open, and I fought the temptation to enter. I had no right going into your office. I was intrigued by the cuneiform tablet, the mathematics and all."

Coulomb's voice came across direct. "If I may use an expression I acquired while I lived in the States. Bullshit!" He continued his pacing. "Honesty is the best policy. You looked at more than an old clay tablet. Your best option is to come clean. University professors don't go around riffling through private offices. Who do you work for?"

"Nobody sent me."

Esra handed the gun to Coulomb. She meandered over, reached down, and twirled a lock of Mallory's hair, smiling bitterly. "We should shoot her here and dump the body. Then it won't matter who she works for."

Mallory stiffened.

"I will give you one chance," Coulomb said. "You are a professor, but your name is not Susan Smith. It is Mallory Lowe, from the University of Colorado, not Indiana—and you were the woman in Nevada, last seen with a man named Tom Haley."

She felt her heart suck into the hollows of a tar pit. She couldn't breathe.

Coulomb continued, his voice remained calm. "What did Tom Haley tell you before he fell to his death?"

She felt her control softening. "It wasn't an accident. He was murdered."

Esra quickly clamped a hand on her shoulder, bore down, twisting her left arm up behind her.

"Tell us what he told you, or she will snap it in two," Coulomb said.

"You're hurting me," Mallory screamed, feeling the pain torch her tendons.

"Did he mention anything about the IFC?" Coulomb continued.

Esra pressured her arm higher.

"Nothing," she writhed in pain. "He never said anything." Tears streaked down her cheeks.

Esra looked back at Coulomb. He nodded. She released Mallory's arm and backed away.

Breathing erratically, Mallory pulled her arm in front and massaged it.

"You were asking about Haley's daughter. Why?"

The question of Katie's fate made Mallory forget her own. "She's a friend. What have you done to her?"

He ignored the question. "You may survive this ordeal if you explain why you are looking for her."

"Her father asked me."

"Why would he do that?"

"Is she okay?" She wiped the tears from her face.

"You do not ask the questions, I do," he ordered, as Wallace reentered the cabin.

"We'll be docked in five minutes," informed the Southerner.

Coulomb handed the gun to Wallace and started for the door. He turned. "You start to explain everything now—or your beloved Katie Haley suffers the consequences. I'll be in my office. Bring her out in fifteen minutes."

McKenzie radioed for his men to station themselves above Coulomb's house. There was no time to lose, and now they had no clue as to Mallory's whereabouts. After the *Lune Corbeau* turned and started back to the mansion, McKenzie and Neal kept their distance, not wanting to raise suspicion. Even in the dark, they navigated to shore without running lights. A momentary coolness rushed over them as they neared, the aroma of moss and conifers filling their nostrils. Pulling into a small cove several hundred yards west of the compound, they beached the cruiser, the bow scraping gravel. They tossed an anchor and waded ashore.

McKenzie scanned the rocky slope above them. Enough residual light remained, enabling him to make out a worn path. He made quick contact with his men using an ear mic. The *Lune Corbeau* had just arrived at the dock. They still had time to position themselves before it was moored.

"Let's go," he said to Neal. They scurried off the beach, their boots crunching on gravel. The sky had turned black except for a glow coming from the village of Vetsch to the west.

There was no time to waste.

The path made a switchback up the face of the slope. Keeping their flashlight beams low to the ground, they wound between tall tufts of grass. It was an arduous and demanding climb, but it was the only way they could safely get away from the lakeshore without being spotted from the dock. Ten minutes later and out of breath, they reached the top, a few yards below the road that careened away from the compound. Fortunately, his agents were already waiting for them, hidden off the road behind a line of trees. Neal took one of the agents and raced down the road, along the cliff, and through the tunnel, stationing above the mansion.

McKenzie peered through night-vision binoculars across the ravine towards Coulomb's mansion. Except for the dock lights, the blinking of fireflies, and a cloud-covered crescent moon, darkness ruled. Several dock hands scurried about, securing anchor lines. At any moment, he expected Coulomb and his guests to exit. He looked at his watch. He'd already been on high alert for five minutes. What if they'd missed seeing Mallory? The thought that she wouldn't be getting off did not sit well.

Rubbing the sweat from his eyes, he resumed his surveillance. A moment later four people exited the yacht. He recognized the American, Shelby Wallace. He was talking to three others as they walked to a waiting limousine in the parking lot. One of the three was having a hard time staying upright, as if he was drunk. Wallace helped him climb inside the limo before shaking hands with the other two and bidding them good evening. The door closed and the limo started up the road.

"Top control, tail the limo," McKenzie communicated through the ear mic. "It's leaving the compound."

The limo climbed the driveway and circled the edge of the ridge, looping up towards his position. Unseen above the road, he ducked behind a rock outcropping as the headlights sprayed the hillside then passed into the short tunnel. Once through, it traversed the cliff and passed his position. He stood up and watched it disappear into the trees. Not a good place to miss a turn, he pondered, thinking about the vertical drop-off where the road was cut dramatically into the cliff.

He turned his attention back in time to see Coulomb leave the yacht. A moment later, he entered the mansion. Soon, a light came on in one of the third-level windows.

Where was Mallory? God, how he hoped they were not too late.

A voice came over the earpiece. "Coulomb has armed sentries posted all around the compound," Neal informed. "They're all carrying automatic rifles. We can't get much closer than two hundred yards."

He suspected as much. They had known for some time that Coulomb always took extraordinary precautions. "Don't move until absolutely necessary. I'll feel better once I see the professor."

"Roger."

"We'll wait until she comes off the yacht—assuming she does."

"Understood," said Neal.

McKenzie cursed himself for not having a tail on Mallory. He should have known better. She was a determined woman, fearless, even a little cocky—enough to get in deep shit. Even though he knew her only a short time, she handled unexpected situations better than some of the men he'd trained. He hoped that worked in her favor for staying alive. Still, that didn't absolve his lack of judgment.

To hell with what would happen with Amistad. If she was killed, he would never forgive himself.

CHAPTER 23

Coulomb looked down on the pier from his office and watched as his guests were taken to their waiting limousine. The woman professor was smart, but very bad at espionage. What was her connection, the reason to put her life on the line in Nevada and now?

"I am inclined to think Haley may not have told her about the IFC, but I don't think we can take a chance."

Esra agreed. "It is best to be on the safe side."

"I do like your idea about an accident."

Esra toyed with the paper weight on Coulomb's desk. "We would be fools to think nobody knows she's here."

Coulomb smiled at her with admiration. Could anyone be tougher than Esra? One look at her would never convey her past. Beautiful on the exterior, but tough as nails on the inside. She never knew her father; chastised and abandoned by her mother, she spent her youth in an orphanage. From those rough beginnings she hardened; became educated and took advantage of other's weaknesses. She was dangerous—a perfect fit for Möbius.

Esra smiled back. "I will be downstairs.

Coulomb sat down at his desk and began to type:

The wise thing to do is concede. We have Katie Haley. Her life is in your hands. Think quickly. We will act within the next two hours and it will not be pretty.

He placed the letter in the draft folder. He knew he would get a quick reply, as Harry was always punctual.

The woman professor was a liability, with or without information. They had the Haley girl, and they would break her. As to the safety of the dam, there was no compromise on the security. He couldn't imagine a scenario where Harry and his group of misfits could infiltrate its perimeter and put it out of commission. He would wait for Sari's call.

Mallory walked slowly down the ramp, her left arm drooping. It hurt like hell.

Wallace trailed, gun pointed. "No false moves, professor. I can hit a 'possum from a hundred yards."

She could feel the noose tighten. Every step along the dock took her one step closer to the gallows. What a damn fool she'd been. Why hadn't she obeyed Lane? There was no way she was getting out of this alive. Even if she was able to give Coulomb the information he wanted, she would still die. These people were killers, and now she was about to experience that truth. If there was an escape option, she certainly didn't see it.

Esra was waiting next to the curb.

"Our guests have gone, but I see we have one left," Wallace said.

Esra smirked. "She'll be gone soon. I think she has worn out her welcome."

"I hope ya'll got what ya'll come for?" he said directing his question to Mallory.

"What are you going to do to me?" she asked, cradling her left arm. It was crazy to think this would turn out in her favor. Her mind was spinning in fear.

"We have no use for you," Esra said. "You came in a rental car; you will leave in a rental car."

Wallace displayed his best Southern smile and cooed. "After a granddaddy time with friends, a wonderful cruise, lil' wine—maybe a lil' bit too much wine—you had one damn nice time, I'd say." His smile turned vile as he waved towards the parking lot and her VW was brought over.

What did they mean by *a little bit too much wine*? They certainly weren't going to let her drive out of here. If she was going to die, what was their plan? If she could somehow make a break for the mansion, she could disappear around the side and possibly escape into the forest behind. But that was a big *if*. By the time she reached the house, Wallace would probably have emptied the entire magazine into her back.

Coulomb read the e-mail response from Harry:

Release Katie Haley. She is nothing to you. Kill her and you are finished. You had more brains at Berkeley.

He strode out of the front door with a cell phone glued to his ear. After a minute he placed it back in his pocket. Sari had responded. The Haley girl hadn't divulged anything yet. They would have to use other means to squeeze information from her.

When Harry was found, he would take great pleasure in watching Esra cut his balls off. She would probably like that. But first, he must bid the professor goodnight. What an unfortunate waste.

"Professor, are you ready to explain the real reason you are here?" he asked, approaching.

"I told you, the magazine article."

"You are a sneak and a liar."

"Call the university. They will vouch for me. As for entering your office, yes, I made a terrible mistake, but it was for me and no one else."

"That's not the only mistake you have made, professor. Using an alias is another." He reached into his pocket, withdrew her iPhone, and tossed it to Mallory. "I always return what is not mine." She instinctively reached up to grab it. "Your last phone call was untraceable, but I guess at this point it doesn't matter." he said.

Coulomb signaled. Before she understood, a powerful arm flew around her head, clasping her mouth in a vise. She struggled, clawing for air. She let out a gasp as something stung the back of her neck. She clutched her neck and spun around. Wallace stood behind her, a nasty grin on his face. He held a hypodermic needle in his right hand.

Her eyes floated from Wallace to Esra to Coulomb. A thick, oily film of fog systematically rolled across her vision. Coulomb's face distorted, twisted and vibrated until it eroded away. She reached out for anything to hold onto, but her knees buckled. She fell to the ground, her outstretched arms trying to soften the fall. Her head snapped forward, hitting the pavement. The pain was quick and sharp. She tried pushing herself up, her arms rubbery. Her eyes spun out of focus; voices flew past, a jumble of incomprehensible gibberish.

McKenzie felt a huge weight lift off him when he saw Mallory walk down the ramp onto the pier. But it was short lived. He pulled his Beretta out and started to run down the road, but after a few feet, he halted. He had to think.

Why did Mallory rush into situations without a full understanding of the risk? The answer came easy. *Dammit, she's just like me.* Wasn't he the same way, always jumping into the fray before careful analysis? *CIA training, remember?* He decided he couldn't blame her entirely.

He sunk back behind a bush and glassed the scene. Mallory was still moving, slowly crawling on the ground. He could hear voices but from this distance, indistinguishable. A moment passed. Wallace reached down and helped her up, guiding her into the backseat of the VW. From what McKenzie could tell, she was as unresponsive as a ragdoll.

CHAPTER 24

Coulomb watched Wallace place Mallory into the back seat of the VW and pour a half-bottle of Château Gruaud Larose down her throat. She gasped and choked, most dripping from her slack lips, soaking her blouse red. Coulomb hoped she'd swallow a good portion. Once the body was found by authorities, it would be a simple deduction as to what had happened.

One should never drink and drive.

Considering the events, he couldn't have asked for a more enjoyable evening. The weather cooperated with a warming breeze drifting down the mountains and the crescent moon adding a tranquil glow to the lake. It was amazing how things had fallen in place. The professor was close to being history, and Harry—yes, Harry, who loved to gamble, loved to take risks—now, his luck was running out.

Coulomb instructed the driver, "Stop at the tunnel and wait for me."

Wallace tossed the empty wine bottle into the backseat. The rental sped away.

Coulomb pulled Wallace to the side. "I can't imagine the CIA or others sending an untrained woman to do their work. But if they did, she's so ill prepared. Stay alert in any case."

Wallace nodded.

Coulomb reached under his jacket and checked for the Glock 23, secured in a shoulder holster. There was no sense being unarmed. It gave him comfort. He turned to Esra, who had remained quiet during this time. "Shall we watch the fun?"

A wicked smile filled her face. "I wouldn't miss it for the world."

A black Mercedes pulled up beside them. They climbed inside and followed the VW.

McKenzie spoke; the ear bone mic vibrated. "Top control. Two vehicles headed your way—a light-colored Volkswagen followed by a black Mercedes. Don't tail until I give the order. We don't want the professor in the crossfire."

He waited for the two vehicles to exit the tunnel. Focusing the night-vision binoculars, McKenzie saw a pair of headlights light up the tunnel. In another minute, the VW would be past his position.

Abruptly, the headlights came to a standstill. He caught the fanning of the Mercedes' headlights working around the last switchback. It, too, entered the tunnel and came to a standstill.

The hush of darkness took over the once roar of motors—now…silence. What the hell was happening? Had Coulomb discovered their presence? He readied his men to close in their perimeter when the VW slowly emerged, the motor purring softly. The driver edged it toward the cliff face, stopped then backed up. Both the driver and Wallace were seen dragging Mallory out, her wobbly frame barely able to stand. McKenzie could envision what was about to happen next.

This was all planned, a setup—her death an accident.

Tossing the night-vision goggles aside, he rushed back into the trees where a parked SUV waited. "Keep me covered," he blurted.

Coulomb and Esra calmly walked out of the tunnel. Wallace was buckling Mallory into the driver's seat. "When will they learn not to drink and drive?" He chuckled.

"I'm afraid it's a human failing." Coulomb moved to the open car door. He gazed at the glassy-eyed professor, trying to fathom what must be going through her anesthetized brain. Did she have any inkling she was about to die? He turned toward Esra; a look of exultation covered her face, along with a mask of satisfaction. She seemed to be enjoying herself, but then, didn't all women find a deep satisfaction when triumphing over other women? It was the same when she looked at Valencia, a case study in jealousy. Such feminine battles warmed his heart.

Coulomb backed away and nodded to Wallace.

The Southerner reached down and placed Mallory's foot on the brake, then shifted the Volkswagen into drive. In her drugged state, her foot could not maintain pressure and over the cliff she would go.

Coulomb's smile broadened, watching the VW crawl towards the edge.

Panicked, McKenzie slid the SUV into gear and barreled onto the road. His mind kept overplaying the scenario that was unfolding just a hundred yards away. God, he prayed he would get there in time.

The last stand of trees disappeared, and his headlights swept out over space. He braked as he spun the wheel to his left, tires skidding on the asphalt. The tight ninety-degree turn came fast, as the road sliced into the face of the vertical granite. He raced along the narrow roadway, disregarding the right-side drop-offs. The VW was rolling faster now.

McKenzie floored the SUV. A string of gunshots ripped through the night, echoing down the chasm. Bullet holes mushroomed on the windshield. He ducked, lost his vision, scraping the guardrail.

There was no stopping the advancing SUV. Coulomb moved quickly, tripping over a rock jutting out in his path. The SUV plowed into the VW, spinning it halfway around. The crush of metal added to the cacophony of gunfire. The front of the VW spun towards him, unobstructed. He waited for the impact, but it never came. The VW stopped a mere hand-width away. Metal crunched, and glass flew as the impact spun the rear end of the SUV through the railing, wobbling on the edge. Coulomb sprinted back into the tunnel where he spotted

Esra on one knee, triggering her gun with precision.

McKenzie felt his life spin out of control, waiting for gravity to continue his long plunge to the bottom. The blow jarred his senses. He ripped at his seatbelt, unable to find the clasp. The SUV wobbled on the brink.

A thunderous roar of gunfire peppered the rocks nearby. The SUV rocked backwards, creaking on its fulcrum. Finding the clasp, he popped it open. He flung the door wide just as the SUV lost its balance and plunged over the cliff. He dove out the door hoping to find something solid to grab.

In the pitiless dark, he found only air.

Coulomb turned in time to see the SUV succumbing to gravity, sliding over the side, crashing down the near vertical cliff in a ball of fire on its way to the rocky inlet below.

It looked as if her hero had come up short.

Bon voyage.

Mallory's eyes fluttered. Her mind drifted with an aimless stream of useless thoughts and her head felt as if it would explode. Where was she? There were sounds, loud pops that did nothing but confuse an already jumbled mind. She reached for her neck; there was a searing pain that seized her foggy attention. Another shot rang out.

Boom! The back windshield blew out.

McKenzie felt his left ankle, the throbbing rocketing up his leg. Reaching out, his hands searching like a blind man. He felt around the sharp conglomerate niche, barely three feet wide. He must have landed on the small ledge when he jumped. He struggled up into a standing position, allowing his eyes to adjust to the dark. His arms and hands were bleeding.

He was alive.

Peering above the edge, a shot rang out, the bullet smashing into the rock above his head. He quickly ducked. A trio of shots ripped as he palmed the Beretta. A volley of gunfire erupted from high above. It was Neal and the other agents, giving him cover.

Sucking in a deep breath, he scrambled onto the roadway and crawled to safety behind the VW. He gave a sign he was okay, aware the agents could see him with their night-vision goggles. Then, he remembered Mallory. He whirled around and opened the car door. Several rounds from the tunnel slammed into the VW, dotting the body. Abandoning any protection, he leaned in and unhooked her seatbelt, just as a bullet pinged into the dashboard. Pulling her free, he dragged her like a grain sack onto the ground. He checked her breathing and pulse. Both were erratic. He pulled his hand away and felt stickiness on his fingers. Her wrist had blood on it. He had to find the source. Then he saw his shirt sleeve was soaked. It wasn't her, it was him. He drew a heavy breath and exhaled.

He turned his attention back to Mallory. Her eyes fluttered open; a gurgle escaped from her mouth.

"Mallory—Mallory, can you hear me?"

She rolled her eyes, rubbing her forehead.

To his left, a stand of trees ran the length of the slope separating the cliff from the tunnel. If they could reach them, they may have a chance.

He pulled her into a sitting position. "Can you walk? Run?"

"My head's exploding."

"Can you move?"

"I…think so."

He sniffed the air. "Gasoline? They must have shot up the gas tank. He bent over and looked under the chassis. Leaking like a sieve. He turned back to Mallory. "We need a diversion. Are you ready?"

"Whatever…" she mumbled.

He opened the driver's door and searched for the cigarette lighter. Finding it, he punched it in. Realizing he had lost his radio communication, he waved his hand in the air and signaled, knowing his agents would understand. "Get ready," he said pushing Mallory in front of him. "When the fire starts, run like hell."

She nodded.

He heard the lighter pop out. He reached in and retrieved it. Gunfire rained down from above. He tossed the lighter under the chassis into the pooling gas. A flame erupted.

"Now!" he yelled, pushing her forward. Shots rang out from above. Mallory took off at a run, stumbling towards the trees, McKenzie on her heels. The VW went up in flames, lighting the cliff in a display of combustible might. They ran through the trees as fast as they could. A second later, the VW exploded, throwing debris and burning metal in a hundred foot radius.

Coulomb shielded his eyes from the flame and the intensity of the heat, as bullets rained onto the roadway and into the tunnel opening. It could only be the CIA. The professor's protection was much better than anticipated.

He hurried and opened the Mercedes' trunk, pulling out an AK-47. Staying in the shadows, he worked his way towards the tunnel entrance. The gunfire had slowed, only an occasional flurry of shots aimed in his direction. Several orange bursts could be seen on the hill above the road. During the commotion, Wallace and the driver were pinned behind a rock outside the tunnel.

"Shelby, can you hear me?" he yelled.

"We're pinned," Wallace yelled back. "Throw 'em a couple of rounds. We'll break for the tunnel."

Securing the assault rifle, Coulomb pulled away from the wall and emptied the magazine, spraying the area where he'd seen the orange tracers. A second later, one man dove into the tunnel. There should have been two. A crumpled form lay on the ground outside, vague and immobile. Retreating back towards the Mercedes, he met the beam of Esra's flashlight. Coulomb felt relief.

Wallace's face was just as happy. "Nice to still be kickin'," he muttered.

CHAPTER 25

McKenzie rubbed his weary eyes, unable to come to grips with the chaos of the last several hours. Mallory sat across from him still wearing her wine-soaked blouse. To him and his men, she looked like shit, but relieved, he was grateful she was alive.

He raised his voice. "What the hell were you thinking? You came close to getting killed, not to mention endangering me and my men, and blowing up the whole fucking surveillance operation."

Her voice hoarse. "Sorry."

McKenzie glared. "SORRY, simply SORRY! Is that all you have to say? We told you we'd put all our resources into finding this Katie, didn't we?"

"Yes."

"Then why the fucking disobedience?"

"Information."

"Information? We're all looking for information, everyone, the whole bullshit world is looking for information. Why'd you think you could get it so easily?" He was beginning to think she was a nutcase. And he was beginning to think he wanted to get to know her better. He discarded his stirred emotions. Right or wrong, this woman had no problem defying authority.

"What was so goddamn urgent that you had to go and meet Coulomb himself?" he asked.

"I told you, Katie."

"Bad move."

"It worked," she protested. "I *know* where she is."

He smirked. "Where, smartass."

"I overheard Wallace tell Coulomb she's held in the electrical gallery at the dam."

He looked stunned. "Tepecik Dam, in Turkey?"

"Tom Haley and the dam, remember? Now Katie is held prisoner there. That's where we go, Turkey."

"Whoa—hold on *kemosabe*. Who said we? Aren't you getting ahead of yourself again?"

She didn't waver. "I'm aware of my mistakes, but now that we've gone beyond that, don't you think we could all work together?"

"Gone beyond *that*," he exploded. "I don't think so. As far as you are concerned, you're out of here and will be on the next flight back to the States. Do I make myself clear?"

Frankfurt, Germany

Late afternoon and Mallory found herself sitting in the International lounge waiting for her Lufthansa flight to Philadelphia. After McKenzie had read her the writ, she was whisked to the airport and popped on the first plane to Frankfurt. Obviously, McKenzie was determined to get her out of his hair. To think she was so close, now being treated like a child and sent home.

The fact that she'd risked her life for the information didn't seem to register. In retrospect though, she risked everyone else's life, including Lane's. She wouldn't be here now if it wasn't for him. But Katie still needed her. She took a deep breath trying to calm her frantic mind. She felt like a hamster running inside the wheel, round and round ending up nowhere—helpless and inconsequential.

Was she inconsequential? *Cram that shit*, she thought. She again remembered another part of Coulomb's conversation, something about *e-mailing the bastard* as if they were pen pals.

She walked over to a vendor and bought a bottle of water. A thought had been gnawing at her since she discovered the notepad at Tom's house with the irrationals embedded in the drawing of Angels Landing. Tom Haley didn't scribble things down for the fun of it. They had to have significance. Three of the irrationals were seen on the water feature except the $\pi^2/6$, which was deleted—and floating down the Virgin River on Tom's drawing.

Deleted? Why hadn't she thought of this before? It now clicked, made sense —or so she assumed it did. The dossier that McKenzie had shown her a couple of days ago described the three Möbius players—Coulomb, Meadowlark and Wallace. But was there a fourth—Esra Sahin? Four players—four irrational numbers. Yes, in that order—Paul Coulomb, Harry Meadowlark, Shelby Wallace, and Esra Sahin. And the water feature two months ago had them popping up as π, $\pi^2/6$, e and $\sqrt{2}$. They had to be calling cards. She couldn't stop analyzing—Harry Meadowlark, aka $\pi^2/6$, now missing from the water feature and missing from Möbius' inner circle. She could kick herself for not asking McKenzie to show her a picture of Meadowlark—she was convinced he was the same man in the museum photo with Katie. Maybe that explained the $\pi^2/6$ floating down the river sketched on the notepad away from the other irrationals. That aside, why had he defected? What did he know?

But there was *something else* going on here other than the IFC and Katie and a hydroelectric dam. Mallory could feel it, almost taste it. Now her very cogent senses were beginning to emerge after a hiatus smothered by near death. *Concentrate!* That day at Zion, listening to Tom Haley's desperate plea right before the helicopter arrived—he himself said he *knew too much.* Reason enough his house was ransacked.

Whatever it was—*he had known it all.*

Her mind switched back to what she had overheard on the *Lune Corbeau.* Wallace had spoken of a SAT phone. Could a satellite phone be located by GPS, like locating a cell phone using triangulation?

She had three hours until her flight. Finding a small area with free Wi-Fi, she sat down and began to google GPS and SAT phones. It didn't take long to find software that could pinpoint a satellite phone's location. But she didn't have a number. Further searching gave her the name of a company called GPS-INTERNATIONAL-LOCATOR. There she discovered a phone number wasn't necessary, only the approximate location.

Feeling the excitement, she pulled up the webpage and followed on screen instructions. First, they wanted a credit card number for a 30-day free trial. No problem. She drew out her Visa and typed the requested information. Once approved, she pulled up Google Earth and zoomed onto the desired location after she checked Wikipedia for the location of Tepecik Dam in Turkey.

Checking her data, she hit the enter key. A few moments later, the map sprung to life with several pinpoint bubbles, each one a SAT phone location based upon when last used. She painstakingly checked the map and found two bubbles near the Tepecik Dam, a very rural and rugged area. After a few more entries, the two phone numbers scrolled on the screen. She checked the country codes for the two numbers and found that they were for two different satellite phone providers. One number, an 8821 code, was for a company based in the United Arab Emirates—the other, an 8816 code, was for a larger international network. Which one would Meadowlark be using? Why not try both.

She dialed the first one, making sure she used the correct protocol for calling international numbers. She waited, the cluster of periodic high-pitched beats filled her ear. No answer. She hung up, a bit of depression seeping in. Shaking it off, she dialed the other number. It took a few seconds before the sound of ringing and more high-pitched beats. Finally, an answering machine came on. In English, the generic recording asked that a number be left.

Mallory began, "My name is Mallory Lowe, a friend of Katie Haley. If you know of her, she has been kidnapped. I know where she is. Please call or email me." She proceeded to give her number and e-mail.

It wasn't more than fifteen minutes later that her heart skipped a beat when her iPhone pinged. She saw the subject line on the received e-mail: iatbp16449@gmail.com.

Had she called the right number? Then her eyes turned to the numeric, 16449. "Goddamn", she murmured. She should have registered this immediately. She did the calculation on her calculator. The display spit out the four decimal places for $\pi^2/6$:

$$1.6449$$

Her pulse flew off the charts. Did she need more evidence? What about the iatbp? That had to be an acronym of some type. Could it be this simple? She wrote it down on the sheet of paper in large capital letters and stared at it long and hard. Her face broke into a wide smile.

I AM THE BASEL PROBLEM.

CHAPTER 26

Roman Ruin
Above Eshai, Turkey

S ari stood inside the stone hut, the flickering flashlight beam searching. He spotted what appeared to be a rope curled in a corner. Walking over, he picked it up, half-buried in the dirt floor. It was an electrical cord, like those used for a computer. It looked like they just missed Meadowlark.

He realized they now had the advantage. Coming up short was not the end of the story. It was just the beginning. Those on the run usually made mistakes, especially when in a hurry. All indications showed they had cleared out in a very short time. Footprints were everywhere. He could see where equipment rested on the dirt floor, table leg imprints, square and rectangular impressions. The electrical cord confirmed electronics. No doubt a portable generator was used for power. Other items were discarded, empty plastic water bottles and cigarette butts scattered among the old Roman walls, indications of Meadowlark and his associates.

He ducked his head and walked back out into the open. The sky was clear, but the sweltering sun produced a heat haze that obscured the dam far below. He understood why Meadowlark had picked this place—high on a hill, great visibility for miles in all directions. Even though there were only a few paths to the ruins on rocky four-wheel drive tracks, there were multiple avenues of escape.

It was fortunate Katie Haley was cooperative earlier this morning, even though it took a double dose of scopolamine. Her babbling led them to the ruin, an old stone fortification. During her interrogation, she was pressed on their location. The woman was strong, protective of both. Maybe he should triple the dose next time and see what fluttered from her trembling lips.

He lifted a pair of binoculars to his eyes and gazed at the green expanse of water behind the dam, mostly hidden by the steep cliffs of the gorge. At the far end, the reservoir spread out upon the plain to the north where the gorge vanished onto the steppe. There he spotted the village where he grew up. He swore he could see the house where he lived, but knew it was too far away to distinguish in the haze. It was there that he learned the lessons of life. His father, a martial arts master, had taught him how to compensate for his small size and lack of brawn. Quick maneuvers would always keep him above the fray. Develop your reflexes, his father swore, be aggressive—like a mongoose on the cobra. Stay alert—stay alive. The lessons served him well. His father was wise, patient, a teacher with a rough touch that instilled a winning nature. If it wasn't for his father, he was convinced he would have never developed the mental and physical abilities that he now possessed. There was so much more he yearned to learn from his father—now gone, replaced by an emptiness that could never be filled.

CHAPTER 27

Somewhere over Serbia

M allory slept restlessly during her flight to Istanbul, knowing quite well once she got there she would hole up in the airport terminal overnight, since her flight to Diyarbakir was at 6:20 a.m. Sleep did not come easy; she was troubled and guilt-ridden. Soon, McKenzie would be notified that she had not arrived in Philadelphia. They'd try to figure out how she had escaped their surveillance. It was a risk she took without reservation. Once the Philadelphia flight had been announced, she stole away to the woman's restroom until an hour after the plane had departed, then she worked her way into a crowd that was disembarking from a Stuttgart flight. Her hope was if the CIA were watching her, they would have left right after the flight embarked, and if they were still there, they may have missed her in the crowd.

Her anxiety at being detained by the CIA was overridden by the prospect that things could be changing. She had e-mailed the iatbp16449@gmail.com address right before leaving Frankfurt, but there was no immediate reply. A few minutes before boarding for Diyarbakir, that all changed. Frankly, she couldn't believe her luck. Scrolling down the screen, she read the thread:

Subject: Katie Haley
July 20, 5:55 A.M.

> Find Café Kazan in Eshai. Order some Rize tea and ask for six lumps of sugar. Drive careful coming to Eshai. The roads are rough.

July 19, at 4:01 P.M. Mallory Lowe wrote:

> Harry Meadowlark,

> I recently found out Katie Haley has been kidnapped and held prisoner and I know where. I saw them murder Tom Haley. I need your help. Respond a.s.a.p., as I am on my way to Eshai now and will be there tomorrow.

McKenzie's order to stay away from the operation and let them do their work was now out the window. Once she got to Istanbul, she would call him. He deserved to know where she was. Reclining in her seat, she closed her eyes. Sleep overtook her but offered little in serenity; it only brought nightmares of getting killed by Möbius. If not by them, the CIA, with Lane being the first in line to have her head.

CHAPTER 28

M cKenzie ran his hand through his hair, trying to coax some mystical powers of understanding into his brain. How could an intelligent, attractive woman make his life so miserable? How did she avoid the flight, the one he was assured she had taken? For several minutes, he stared at the wall—once again the woman from hell had ignored his orders. She seemed to be playing with him, making it impossible to follow Amistad's directive.

Mallory Lowe had a death wish, that was all there was to it. After they discovered she hadn't made the connection to Philadelphia, they checked the other flights out of Frankfurt. Sure enough, she had booked Lufthansa to Istanbul and from there would catch a Pegasus flight to Diyarbakir. She was headed to the dam no doubt, to find Katie.

While contemplating his dilemma, the phone rang. He picked it up and couldn't believe his ears.

He calmed himself. "I am honored to get a call from the expert of malfeasance."

"I don't blame you," Mallory offered, "but give me the benefit of the doubt."

"Is it just me, or do I get the impression that you love to pull the strings."

"Only when I get motivated. I could hardly get on that plane to Philadelphia knowing I contacted Harry Meadowlark."

"You what?"

He listened intently as she revisited her connecting the irrational numbers to the four Möbius players, the one missing being Meadowlark.

"I'm on my way to see him now."

The tightness in McKenzie's throat began to spread throughout. "You could have called when you were in Frankfurt, goddammit. Where are you now?"

"Istanbul. I'll be in Eshai tomorrow morning."

"Do me a favor. Hold off on that meeting until we can get down there."

There was a pause. "How long will that take?"

"Damn, do you think we're that efficient? It will be tomorrow sometime; depends how fast I can scrounge up transportation. I have to call Zurich. Tomorrow morning, call this number again and tell me exactly where you are. If I don't answer, leave a message. We'll find you. You will hold off?"

"I'll see what I can do."

"That doesn't sound convincing."

"Lane, I have to. Please understand. And for what it's worth, I think Meadowlark's disappearance is bigger than we think. When I meet with him, I hope to know more." The line went dead.

Why did he let this woman control everything and get away with it? And why had he made no effort to lock her up? For months they'd researched the connection between Möbius and the IFC. They were desperate to uncover the illegalities that bound them together. It seemed unbelievable that the top brass disregarded Möbius' associate, Harry Meadowlark—now renegade associate— possibly the one man who had the answers.

With that thought, how could he be so pissed off at Mallory? Who was the fool here? Wasn't she the one pointing them in the right direction? Wasn't she the one who told them about Katie Haley? Isn't she the one who thinks she knows where Meadowlark is? If he is in Turkey, what the hell else is going on between Möbius and him?

Yet, he owed her—Amistad owed her. Maybe Amistad would back off on this ethic board bullshit. McKenzie promised they would find Katie, and yet they hadn't done anything about it. In an ideal world, they would have already been halfway routing out the corruption within the IFC, if it existed, and putting Coulomb and his thugs behind bars.

They best get off their asses before Mallory Lowe made them fools again. And if she thinks there *is something else* going on because of Meadowlark's defection, then he'd better listen. So far, she's beating them to the punch.

CHAPTER 29

Eshai, Turkey

A fter spending the night in the Istanbul airport, Mallory took the early morning flight to Diyarbakir after making a quick call to McKenzie. Three hours later, she drove into Eshai, a small village off the beaten path. The further away from Diyarbakir, the closer she got to a thousand years in the past. The village sat three hundred feet above the lower Tepecik River gorge. The only access was by a narrow dirt road that crossed the river on a bridge that seemed to be made of reinforced rust. The road climbed abruptly through a steeply winding cut in the gorge's volcanic layer, then leveled off on a massive plateau. To the north the gorge deepened, the sandstone layers giving way to a much deeper chasm composed of Pre-Cambrian granite. Unusual rock formations the locals called *fairy spires* rimmed the area west of the village. Seven kilometers upstream, the dam controlled the formerly wild Tepecik River, now lazily flowing below Eshai, tamed and shamed.

Another hot and intolerable day was building. In the center of the village, a cluster of mud and stone huts lined the road, topped with ruddy clay-tiled and corrugated metal roofs. A few women sat on colorful rugs, assortments of fruits and vegetables for sale—corn, peppers, carrots, figs and apricots along with buckets of milled wheat. Most of the women wore headscarves, even the few Assyrian Christians she read about in one of the travel brochures she picked up at the Diyarbakir airport. Most of the townsfolk were Kurds and a smattering of Arabs with Syrian lineage.

She spotted a wooden sign attached to one of the stone buildings. In washed out letters, she made out the name Café Kazan. Two men sat out front on plastic chairs, locked in a game of backgammon. She parked the rented Ford along the side of the road, wrapped a gray scarf around her head and walked toward the café. The two men barely noticed her, one raising a wandering eye as she approached, and just as quickly, returning his interest back to the game. It was a relief to see she did not raise suspicion. Possibly Katie was a known figure here, so foreign-looking women didn't raise many flags.

The door to the café was open. She walked across the threshold and entered a modest room, dim except for a lone window along one wall. There were only four tables with two chairs each. No one else was inside. Finding the nearest table, she sat down, readjusting the scarf. She looked around the café, the walls whitewashed, featureless; the floor chipped and cracked concrete; the tables and chairs modern plastic. The tablecloths were orange-plaid vinyl. The only pleasing attribute she could detect was the sweet aromatic smell of warmed tea drifting from a stacked set of kettles sitting on hotplates. The calm was shattered by a door bursting open. A short man, early thirties wearing a dirty white apron, moved her way. He had high cheekbones, brown hair, unshaven. With a bored look, he said something in Turkish, maybe Kurdish.

Not understanding, she responded with her order. "*Rize* tea please, and six lumps of sugar."

The man's expression remained the same. He turned and walked to the counter removing a small kettle that rested on top of a larger one. He slowly poured tea into a tulip-shaped teacup and finished it off with some hot water from the lower kettle. He returned and placed a saucer and teacup in front of Mallory along with a small plate with only six lumps of brown sugar. He disappeared quickly through the back door.

Mallory tossed a cube into her tea and stirred. She took a sip and nodded. *Damn good tea.* But now what? She sat pinching the teacup handle, her mind awash in the realization she may again be on a fool's errand. She checked her watch. She'd only been in the village a short while, so why did she feel defeated already? Maybe it was taking Meadowlark longer than planned. Maybe she should go ask the man who delivered her tea. Maybe that might put everyone on edge. There must be a reason for this cloak and dagger pretense. She would wait it out. Like she had a choice; there was nowhere else she had to go.

The isolation fed her fears. Another fifteen minutes passed. *Dammit, something happen, please!* As if on cue, the tea server opened the door, softly this time, and motioned to her. "Come, please, this way," he said in very understandable English.

Now, she was faced with the reality of her situation—follow the man and pray that she hadn't walked into a cult of killers bent on raping and eliminating the evidence.

He took her into the back room, which was little more than a closet lined with shelves. Along one wall, magazines and newspapers were stacked three feet high. She caught a glimpse of an aging Turkish copy of Playboy. At first surprising, until she remembered Turkey was secular.

The room had a door leading into a narrow courtyard. Mallory tried hard to contain the apprehension building with each step. Next to a stone wall, the man bent down and lifted a u-shaped piece of rebar, welded to a rectangular steel hatch cover. He waved her over. Rotating the door open, he pointed into a man-size shaft that ran straight down. The top of a wooden ladder could be seen just below the surface. Now, this was not in the bargain. "I'm not going down there."

"Please, —is okay," he said, showing his pearly teeth.

"No way," she protested. "Where is Harry Meadowlark? I came to see him."

The man freaked out. He put his fingers to his lips and whispered, "Shhh—" His eyes darted around.

Mallory drew in a rushed breath and stepped back when the head of a man poked above the shaft. Her heart was surely going to jump out of her chest.

"Sorry, but there is no other way," he said, looking up at her.

She stared at the handsome man with the short black beard. He seemed non-threatening.

"I am Ismet." His eyes glistened. "Katie and I, we—" He couldn't finish.

In that instance, she felt relief, like a thousand pains had been numbed. Someone saying Katie's name in this strange place had to be a victory. In a subtle, self-conscious way, he acted as if he and Katie were more than just acquaintances. She recognized something else—his eyes pleading.

With the help of Ismet's flashlight, Mallory eased herself down the ladder, a good ten feet. She reached the bottom and stood on solid ground. Her heart fluttered as the steel cover above was closed, the rectangular view of sun-drenched sky now a memory. Another one of her phobias on display. If it wasn't fear of heights, it was fear of closed, tight spaces. Acrophobia to claustrophobia —wonderful.

As darkness filled the room, coolness swept over her, a damp caress of stale air that gave her chills. In the dark, her eyes adjusted to the light from a sole incandescent attached to the low ceiling of carved rock. She was in a cave of sorts, yet it was not natural; a low-ceiling corridor that extended in both directions.

Ismet turned on an electric lantern, illuminating the space further. It was, indeed, a tunnel, carved out of the volcanic stone.

"Where are we?" she asked.

"Hittite tunnels. Been here for thousands of years. They were once underground cities. Centuries later, Christians used them to escape and hide from the Romans."

"And they're still in use?"

"Used for storage and stables by the people in this village. In Nevsehir Province, hundreds of underground cities. Some are tourist attractions."

"Where is Harry Meadowlark?"

He ignored her question. "Katie, I must know about Katie."

Mallory was frustrated. "Once I meet Harry Meadowlark."

Ismet frowned. "This way."

Mallory followed Ismet in silence down the tunnel. Several lone incandescent bulbs strung along the ceiling cast shadows on the ancient walls. Soon, their only light was Ismet's lantern. The cross-tunnels created a labyrinth of confusion. They negotiated a series of low steps, the tunnel narrowing and falling with frequent twists—an endless maze. The passageway came to an end; a large round stone blocked further access. Mallory knew she'd never find her way out.

Giving Ismet a worried look, he explained, "Centuries ago, these stone doors were rolled into place to protect the villagers from enemies. At that time, very effective."

He leaned his head near the large circular stone and said something she didn't understand. A muffled reply came from the other side. A moment later, the large stone rolled to their left, scraping along on the ground until it disappeared into a slot cut into the wall. They were greeted by a man with an assault rifle. Another man held a flashlight, the beam shining into Mallory's eyes. A few words were exchanged. She caught the name Alev as the man with the rifle. She followed Ismet down the corridor, listening to the huge stone door being rolled back in place. The other men did not follow.

At the far end of the passageway, the feeble source of light began to intensify. The closer she got, she saw it was natural—from sunlight, not flashlights or incandescent bulbs. They were coming out into daylight. The warmth in the air mitigated evenly as outside heat took control. Leaving the confines of the tunnel was welcome.

The passage turned a corner and the bright light of day greeted her. Mallory clasped her chest as her heart rose into her throat. She found herself in an alcove the size of a two-car garage. Across the way, the sun shined brightly on a burnt-umber cliff. Birds darted about, screeching and circling their nests built into crevasses in the face. She moved a little closer and stopped. She was high above, in an alcove in full view above the lower Tepecik River gorge.

"Not too close," Ismet said, coming up alongside her. "Long way down."

She moved back a step.

A gritty voice from behind startled her. "And there's not much river to soften your blow."

She whirled and saw him in shadow, sitting on a rock outcrop. The butt of a gun poked out of his waistband.

Harry Meadowlark.

Striking a match, he lit the cigarette clamped between his lips. The flame highlighted his deeply-lined face. He was five-foot-seven at best; unkempt thinning gray hair combed back and tied in a short ponytail. He took a deep drag and eyed her with a prying curiosity, giving her a once over like she'd never been scrutinized so closely before. With a nod, he spoke. "Not exactly what I imagined."

She felt violated like she was probed and examined under a microscope, picked apart and dissected. Who the hell did this enigma think he was? "I'm not sure that's a compliment."

"Trust me, it's a compliment."

Her nose itched from the fragrant Turkish smoke. Reaching into her fanny pack, she pulled out the wrinkled photograph. She handed it to him.

Harry took it and nodded somberly. "Tom took this picture. He was fiddling around with a new digital camera." A melancholy haze fell over his expression. "Katie and Tom were having a hard time then. You can see it in her eyes."

"Your e-mail address. I don't suppose it's the same one used by you and Paul Coulomb?"

Meadowlark raised an eyebrow. "I have several accounts. How'd you know about us being pen pals?'

"Same place I heard about Katie, snooping around."

"That can get you killed."

"It almost did." She gazed at a gold chain hanging around his neck. Moving closer, she stared long and hard. She couldn't believe what she saw.

Noticing her interest, Harry fumbled with the pendant, a gold cutout of a $\pi^2/6$. "So you know about *The Basel Problem* and Euler?"

"Of course, it was an ingenious solution, using the Taylor expansion of the sine function to come up with this extraordinary sum.

"You know it well."

"Does the $\pi^2/6$ mean something to you?"

"In a vindictive sort of way. At one time, I felt it embellished the renegade in me. It still does, but on a whole different level." His eyes strayed from the photograph back to her. "Listen lady, you're quite famous in the Haley circles."

Surprise filled her face. "You know of me?"

He didn't answer. He slid off the rock, tossed the cigarette down, ground it out with his foot, and handed the photograph back. He walked over and stood inches away from the edge. Defiantly, he looked out across the gorge not concerned with the danger of falling. "How'd Tom die?"

She stared at Meadowlark, picturing the last time she saw Tom Haley. "In a similar situation in Utah, standing on the edge of a cliff. He was being harassed by a helicopter. They killed him."

Harry didn't flinch. He kept his eyes trained across the gorge, never once looking down. "Bastards. Tom and I were both colleagues at OU a few years way before you showed up, back when Katie was a mere child. I got him the job at Möbius as a consultant while he was with UNLV. I thought he would be okay leaving this mess. Obviously, I miscalculated." He stepped away from the gorge and stared at Mallory.

Looking on anxiously, Ismet moved closer. "Where's Katie?"

The sound of an explosion ended their conversation.

CHAPTER 30

Katie Haley tugged on the chain cuffed to her wrist, a futile attempt to pull free. The opposite end was wrapped around a concrete column and secured with a padlock. With only three feet of lead, her movement was severely restricted. She walked around the column like a dog on a leash, inspecting the small room. She knew where she was, a prisoner deep within the guts of Tepecik Dam's power plant. Large conduits penetrated one wall, traversing horizontally and disappearing in the distance. Signs in Turkish indicated: DANGER, HIGH VOLTAGE. The electrical gallery separated her from the generator hall. For the last month she had studied the hydroelectric plans. Harry had gone over the intricate blueprints with Ismet and her many times, insisting on a complete picture of every nook and cranny of their objective. This knowledge provided an understanding of the incredible technical sophistication of the impenetrable space.

A further complication clouded her mind. Not only did she fear her abductors, she feared Harry's operation itself. It was scheduled for tomorrow night. Even with her missing, the rest of the team would carry through with the plan. That was the agreement. There would be no delay.

She stopped pacing in a circle. Her body ached and her pulse clamored like a freight train. There was no way Ismet or Harry would know where she was. The feeling of isolation and claustrophobia was mounting, overwhelming her senses. A low, methodic hum sent a chilling, haunting shiver down her spine; the generators were cranking out 60,000 KW, each protected by forty-five feet of concrete, the only protection from the tremendous hydrostatic pressures of the reservoir.

It was no secret she was being held for ransom. They wanted Harry. She winced at the methods they might use to extract information—drugs, torture—even rape. And if they didn't kill her by tomorrow night, her death would be at the hands of the operation.

She thought back to the last time she saw Harry. It was only a day or two ago. She was with him at the ruin on the hill. They had talked…a lot of things to discuss.

There was kindness…

"How about a cookie?" Harry had said, waving her over and pointing at a bag on the table. "Turkish, but passable."

Katie eyed the cookie bag. She remembered as a young girl, maybe six or seven years old, Harry often treated her to goodies and attention, like a favorite uncle. She reached over and gave him a hug. Why could she hug her father's good friend, but not her father?

There was conflict…

"Why in the hell did I ever introduce you to Ismet?" Harry had said, "Out of all the stupid things I've done in my life, that may be one of my greatest mistakes."

"Why do you say that?"

"Because you wouldn't be tied up in this mess, that's why."

Irritated, she had snapped back. "I disagree. The best thing you ever did was introduce me to Ismet. My stint in the Peace Corps taught me about compassion. Did you expect me to just walk away and go home after learning what the dam did to Ismet and the rest of his Assyrian community? What about their way of life—robbed, taken over by corporate greed. Remember you were part of that. And now this talk of a Phase Two, the construction of pipelines to siphon off water for other purposes. Tell me about not wanting to help Ismet fight back, will you?"

Meadowlark shook his head. "My mistakes go back farther. We wouldn't be having this conversation if I never hired your father."

"You hired him because he's an expert in hydrology."

"Fuck the hydrology. We're on a different path now. At least your father is away from all of this."

"Maybe so." She wondered—did she really care? After all, she seldom talked to him.

And seldom was there resolution…

"You almost got killed in Istanbul," Harry said. " We can do this without you. I want you away from here."

"What are you talking about? I've got a job to do. I've done my part in helping with the supplies and logistics. I'm part of the team."

"When this all started, I knew Tom was treading on thin ice. I'm not sure why, but I have my theories. Anyway, they were entangling him in their same sick schemes. He was glad I bailed. Tom decided to stay a little longer. I think I know why, but the bottom line: he had asked me to keep you away from him. I told him I would keep an eye on you until he got safely out of the picture."

"Why didn't he tell me, talk to me about this?"

"Because he didn't want them to know where you were. They have ears. In reality, this is my fight. This is Ismet's fight. I told Tom I'd send you back when the time came. Dammit, the time has come. Don't make me renege."

"I won't go until the job is finished."

"It doesn't take a genius to see your affection for Ismet. If he feels the same, he wouldn't want you within a thousand miles of this place. Face it, this isn't your fight."

"It's not affection; I love him."

"I don't give a rat's ass about that! I want you gone."

"Why shouldn't I help finish it? I'm as much a part of this as everyone else."

"That's the point, dammit." He stopped short; his face hardened. *"Your father's an old friend; he left and that makes me happy. You are my responsibility, and if you left too, I would be doubly happy."*

The sound of a key being inserted into the door brought her back to reality. She watched the door open and two men crowd the doorway.

One man entered, walking towards her, his face coming out of shadow. As he neared, the light emphasized his features, especially his hesitant brown eyes. But it was his baby-smooth face that rallied her memory.

Sari stopped in front of Katie. The room was silent except for the residual hum of the generators. He didn't look at her directly, allowing his eyes to roam the room. But he could smell her, beyond the sweat and grime. The scent of a female was alluring, yet in a different sense—like a hound after the fox. After a moment, he gathered his composure and turned her direction. He felt a shiver ripple down his spine as his eyes fell over the rest of her body—fine hair, attractive face, swollen breasts. He'd never had a woman before, never…ever. Even when he and Ismet were friends, Ismet had no problem talking to women, Muslim or Christian, it didn't matter. He was the shy one; the one who looked like a ten year old. How could he ever have the confidence to interact with chatty and giggly girls? That was then, and now he was beyond the desire. He would deny Ismet the pleasure of his lover…and then kill them both.

He calmed his nerves. "Where is Harry Meadowlark?"

She didn't respond.

His hand slapped across her face. She crumbled to the floor. Her vision floated in and out of focus, the pain searing her cheek as if it had been hot-ironed. She stared at the floor, dazed.

Sari bent down, grabbed her by the hair and yanked her head level. He glared viciously at his prisoner. "Why protect your friends, you, a nice American girl? Where are they? Tell us, we let you go. You go home." He tightened his grip and pulled her closer. "I give you opportunity—now."

"I—I don't know where they are."

Sari reared back and punched her solid in the jaw. She fell backwards, hitting her head on the concrete column. A trickle of blood ran from her nose. Again, he yanked her up and drew her face close to his. "Where is Harry Meadowlark?"

The pain intensified. She touched her swelling jaw, feeling the sticky blood. "I don't know."

Sari's pale baby-face flushed red. Nowhere had he ever felt such power. Now, he reveled in it. "Is he with your boyfriend?"

Fear coursed through her. "I don't know…"

"It is good to have boyfriends, girlfriends. Where would we be without them? They are always there for us when we are in need."

Katie turned away.

"Is he a responsible boyfriend? Is he good enough to come to the rescue?"

"I don't know what you mean," she said in pain.

Sari's smile evaporated. "You have very little time to come to your senses. If you do not tell us what we need to know, you will die." He motioned to the man standing in the doorway. "Bring the needle."

CHAPTER 31

Coulomb walked near the roulette table in the Palace Casino and headed for the open staircase. He spotted Marotte on the far side at a Blackjack table, with a diminished chip pile. Coulomb had distaste for this casino. It reminded him of the glitz at Reno and Las Vegas, a mosaic of bright lights, obnoxious slot machines, and flowery carpets. To him, it was tasteless, without class, unlike the magnificent Casino de Monte-Carlo along the Riviera.

Marotte did not see Coulomb passing by. The attorney was busy, engrossed in the game. He was a gambler, as was Harry Meadowlark, a very sophisticated and calculating gambler. Maybe that was their connection, but Marotte was also a boozer. Surprisingly, today he played without a drink in front of him. He looked serious, carefully scrutinizing every card that was dealt from the double-deck game. His eyes were watery, his face lined with stress.

The row of noisy slot machines interrupted Coulomb's thoughts of Harry Meadowlark and probability. Harry excelled in games of chance, especially Blackjack. He was a natural, gravitating to the only casino game that offered a skilled player the opportunity to win. Mathematics taught him that the risk changed with every card dealt. He loved to work out different card-counting schemes, those that provided the highest reward in every situation and to put his theories into action, calculating the standard deviation, working out the variance probabilities and executing the optimum betting strategies. It was all a game, and he loved winning.

Gazing around the casino for Shelby Wallace, he continued to reminisce, plunging back to his Berkeley days when he and Harry spent many a weekend at Lake Tahoe. A little carousing, drinking, womanizing and gambling was a nice break from the drudgery of grad school. Harry was an excellent card counter, as was Coulomb, but he also mixed this skill with a little bit of *in-your-face* risk management. During one particular session at a full table, the dealer had inadvertently dealt through more than three-fifths of a single deck because the other players had all asked for hits, depleting the deck beyond the house rules. Of course, the dealer had to finish the play. Harry sat at third base and when it came his turn to hit or stand, he had a five and a four for a nine total. His card counting accuracy was seldom off. He knew there were a large number of ten cards left, eight out of thirteen cards remaining. In the jargon of professional card counters, a very rich deck indeed. If he was to draw, he had a sixty-two percent chance of drawing a ten. The dealer had a six up. He would rather have the dealer have the higher percentage of busting, so let him draw. Harry stood on nine. The dealer turned over his bottom card. It was an eight for a total of fourteen. He drew a card, a ten for a bust.

His gamble paid off. The other players at the table sat in amazement when Meadowlark's cards were turned over for a nine total. The dealer looked stunned. Harry collected his money with a grin.

"Paul, over here." The familiar voice shook his thoughts back to the present. It came from his left as he approached the top of the stairs. Seeing Wallace at a corner table in the mid-level bar, he strode over and sat down.

"Any info?" Coulomb asked.

"Our lawyer friend has stumbled," Shelby boasted.

"We had the little man tailed this morning. Little past ten, he entered the Vontobel bank over on St. Alban-Anlage, withdrew something from a safety deposit box. Now, 'bout ten forty-five, he went to the UBS on Clarapatz and entered the safety deposit box vault. He deposited whatever he took from Vontobel."

"Strange enough."

"That ain't the kicker. We did some diggin'. The safety deposit box at Vontobel belongs to none other than our old friend Harry."

Coulomb's eyes reflected the dazzling lights, fresh and vigorous. "I guess a little chat with Vincent is in order."

CHAPTER 32

Eshai, Turkey

Nevzat Sari stood on the bluff, binoculars aimed at the rugged terrain of *fairy spires* and hoodoos on the northern side of Eshai. He could make out a Land Rover in a small opening surrounded by a stand of Syrian junipers. The carpet of green amid volcanic spires gave the impression of a miniature forest in the arid landscape. The view was clear, the sky cloudless, sun blazing. A lone sentinel could be seen pacing back and forth on an outcropping of rock above the vehicle. This had to be their escape route—and now he had them.

Today, he expected payback. Ismet was now in his sights, along with an unknown woman. They would soon be dead, and Meadowlark would be captive along with the Haley girl. He remembered what Coulomb demanded. *Do not harm the traitor; he must be taken alive. As for the others, they are of no use.*

Sari thought of his father. Ismet would be the first to die.

He lowered the binoculars and wiped his brow. He waved a hand to one of his men stationed on another rise a couple hundred meters away. Soon, he would signal the others and all would be ready.

Today was hot, and it was about to get hotter.

Mallory's instinct made her duck. Ismet pulled the gun from his waist and rushed to the tunnel opening only to be forced back by an incredible burst of smoke and dust. Alev emerged, bleeding and coated with dust. Blood oozed from his forehead and arms. He sputtered something in another language.

"Diğer?" Ismet asked.

Alev only shook his head.

"Quick!" Harry screamed. He pulled Mallory up and towards the far side of the alcove where a narrow ledge extended out along the cliff face. "This way."

Mallory hesitated, reluctant to follow. *No chains*, she said to herself, wanting the security measure that Angels Landing offered. "You want me to follow out there?" she asked incredulously.

"Ten meters only to the other tunnel," Ismet coaxed.

Forcing herself to look straight ahead, she watched Meadowlark traverse the ledge and disappear into a man-size opening cut into the cliff face. Sucking in a deep breath, she scooted out onto the ledge, heart pounding. She could do this; she had before. Ignoring the exposure, she kept focused, one step after another. A moment later, she reached the opening. Crouching, she entered. The ceiling was much lower than the last tunnel. Ismet and Alev were right behind her. Stooping low, she followed Meadowlark and his flashlight, keeping a fierce pace through the curves and dips. After a minute, they stopped and took a breath.

"We are not safe in Eshai," Ismet said. "I don't think we have many friends left."

"Move it," Meadowlark barked, taking off at a swift run. "We've got a job to do."

Mallory didn't hesitate; she had to extricate herself from this rock-covered tomb. If the explosion was the mark of Möbius, as it appeared, their tentacles certainly spread far and wide.

After what seemed like a half mile, Meadowlark came upon a set of chiseled steps cut into a narrow fissure. He stepped halfway up, cusped his hands around his mouth, and let out a shrill whistle.

A second later, a return whistle responded. Ismet slipped up the stairs. He yelled back down, "That was Yusuf. Come!"

A moment later, Mallory found herself standing outside and breathing in the hot, stifling air once again—rejuvenated.

Sari was pleased with what he saw. Several people had materialized next to the rust-colored Land Rover. He kept the binoculars focused on one individual—and one individual only—Ismet. He now had the bastard in sight. A surge of adrenaline shot through his body as he signaled his men to be alert. Next to Ismet, he recognized Meadowlark. Besides them, there was the woman from the café and two other men, both armed with automatic rifles.

The heat of the day was beginning to take its toll. He knew Meadowlark and the others would leave the area knowing they could not go back through the tunnels. He was pleased. His men had done their job—flushing them out into the open.

"Do not kill anyone yet. Keep them trapped; the older man must be taken alive," Sari said in Turkish over the radio to his men. "When I give the signal, fire at the vehicle: make it no use. We push them to the gorge. There, we take them."

"What happened back there?" Mallory sputtered.

"You've just involved yourself in our little ruckus," Meadowlark said with a leer. "Now it's become a real family affair."

Mallory took a step forward. "What's going on?"

He ignored her. "What do you know about Katie?" The lines on his sun-drenched face deepened.

Mallory decided it best to get to the point. As fast as things were moving, keeping the information bottled up now made no sense. "She's being held prisoner."

"Fuckin' A, Sherlock. That's old news."

"At the dam."

"The dam!" Meadowlark shrieked. "You got to be kidding?"

The raised voice got Ismet's attention.

Mallory's back hurt from the tunnel's low ceiling and her patience was fraying. "Dammit, you owe me now. Every time I turn around, someone's trying to kill me." She held her gaze on Meadowlark. "Your name has turned up quite a lot the last few days, so you tell me, what's going on?"

Meadowlark gave an icy grin. "Real simple lady, the river is about to be set free."

She didn't flinch, knowing he was talking in poetic symbolism, but she needed confirmation. "In plain English, please."

"THE-DAM-WILL-BE-BLOWN-UP. Tomorrow at this time, the restrained waters behind it will be rushing down into the Tigris, just as God intended. Early morning, the river will no longer suffer the indignity that has been thrust upon it."

Tom had been right; the dam was to be destroyed. It didn't surprise her.

"Katie in the dam?" Ismet asked, panicked.

"She's held in the electrical gallery," Mallory said.

Meadowlark raised his voice. "Who said?"

"Paul Coulomb; it's a long story."

"Try me," Meadowlark snapped.

CHAPTER 33

Somewhere over Bulgaria

McKenzie wanted a drink—something to loosen the vice that had his head in a grip. Vodka and tonic sounded nice. Flushing the numbing desire of alcohol from his mind, he settled back in the seat of the C-12 Huron he'd wrangled from the embassy in Zurich. Joined by Neal and two other CIA operatives, he figured they were four hours away from touching down. The U.S. government had secured permission from Turkish authorities to land at a NATO training facility twenty-seven miles from Diyarbakir. From there, they would only be twenty minutes away from their final destination.

"I just heard from the navigator," Neal said, taking the seat across the aisle. "There's been some activity in Eshai. The Diyarbakir police were alerted to an explosion beneath the village."

"What kind of explosion?"

"Limited details, from what I gather. The village is riddled with underground passages, a series of interconnecting tunnels from ancient times."

"Great, just what we need, more chaos. What are the chances Mallory isn't involved?"

Neal pretended to hide a smirk. "That's like saying bacon doesn't come from hogs."

"Neal, you're getting too philosophical."

CHAPTER 34

Eshai

The frenzy of gunfire sent Mallory and the others sprinting for cover behind the nearest stone spire. Tires exploded with a bang, and bullets rattled as they tore into the Land Rover.

"Everyone down," Meadowlark yelled.

"They have us trapped," Ismet said.

"Your phone?" Mallory ventured, pointing.

Meadowlark reached down and patted the phone clipped to his belt. "What superhuman are you gonna call, Superman?"

"No, someone who can help."

Meadowlark shot her a doubting look. "Lady, we don't need the police or Turkish military, if that's who you have in mind."

"Do you have another option? If you haven't noticed, they're shooting to kill."

Meadowlark chewed his lip. "Who the fuck can give us a hand with all this crap? If it ain't Superman, who, then?"

"The CIA."

"CIA—you crazy?"

"No crazier than all of us caught up in this mess. I don't understand this vendetta against the dam, but I do know Katie is held prisoner and if I understand you correctly, the dam is set to be blown to pieces."

"What's your fucking point?"

"As I see it, we have two problems: One, Möbius wants us dead; two, get Katie out before the dam blows."

"I will not let her die," Ismet vowed.

Several rounds slammed into the surrounding rocks, a signal that their attackers planned to keep them pinned.

"Let me try to get them," Mallory said. "They're aware of most of what's going on and are on their way. Let them know our location. Be a shame if they arrived too late."

"Sun will be down by then, putting us in worse shape. They can see in the dark, we can't." Meadowlark handed her the phone with a disdainful eye. "You have peculiar connections, lady. Make the call."

Mallory dialed the number. A recording came on, just as McKenzie had cautioned. She gave the GPS coordinates and told of their situation. "When will the explosions be detonated."

Meadowlark kept his voice low. "Tomorrow—four in the morning."

Mallory exhaled. "Not much time to get Katie."

A volley of gunfire tore into the spire that shielded them.

"That came from a different direction," Meadowlark shouted. "After dark, it will be easy to move in and pick us off, one by one. We'll spread out and head south."

Sari waited until near darkness had cloaked the *fairy spires*. The waxing moon wouldn't be rising for another two hours. Until then, they had the eyes. He looked through the night-vision binoculars and made out sporadic movement. The group was working their way towards the southeast. What other choice did they have? He would be doing the same thing in their situation.

Earlier, he had instructed his men to move in from opposite directions and separate Meadowlark from the rest of the group. Once he was isolated, he would be taken captive.

The rest would be eliminated.

Mallory kept low to the ground and under cover of vegetation. She waited her turn to dash to the next protected spot. Heart pounding, she brushed at the sweat dripping into her eyes. She anxiously looked for Meadowlark. He and Alev had hustled ahead, marking a path where they thought the best cover could be found. It was a risk to move from behind the spire, but they realized if they stayed put, they would be at the mercy of the gunmen. Every remnant of common sense told her they were being pushed into a box—a deadly game of hide-and-seek.

She rose and looked behind. Ismet and Yusuf were nowhere to be seen. Maybe, just maybe, Meadowlark's plan would work.

Piercing gunfire disturbed the night. Where were the shots coming from? In the blackness, she had no idea where they were aimed, nor had she any knowledge if anyone had been hit. It was obvious the gunmen were searching; a laser red dot would appear on a juniper branch, bounce around and disappear. The dancing movement of the blood-red dots unsettled her nerves. They were probing, looking for movement. It took all her self-control to keep from screaming from fright. If she did, she would certainly draw fire. These killers were methodic and skilled.

Another combination of rounds exploded into the tree next to her. She dove, head first, under the tree branches, slamming hard into the ground. Her head buried into the soft earth, sand and crud mixing with her saliva. A fusillade of rounds flared, the reports getting louder by the minute. It took all her self-control to keep her sanity. She quickly reviewed her options: make a break for it—or stay put and hope they missed. The headlights from a distant vehicle slashed across the bush tops in front of her, erratic shots erupted, and the whine of engines grew louder. She pulled back into the shadows to escape the lights. Two vehicles were bearing down, cutting her off from Meadowlark and Alev. Moving to her right, the headlights disappeared.

A rustle behind her caught her off guard. She whirled just as Ismet appeared, breathless.

"They are behind us," he said.

She looked at him. He held an assault rifle. "Where's Yusuf?"

"Dead."

Ismet drew out his pistol and handed it over.

She accepted it reluctantly. There should be a tear for Yusuf, the violence of the last several days awakening an inner numbness.

Mallory and Ismet crouched behind a small mound and watched the two vehicles close in on Meadowlark and Alev.

"Give us some cover," Meadowlark yelled through the dimness. "We're stranded. There's a clearing."

"When I start shooting, take off towards us," Ismet yelled. He glanced at Mallory. "Wait until you see Harry and Alev, then follow. I'll catch up."

"You sure?" Mallory moaned.

"Do as I say."

She nervously nodded.

"Now!" Ismet yelled. Squeezing the trigger, he let loose, firing at the vehicles with all he had. One of the headlights went out.

Out of the corner of her eye, she saw two blurred figures running her direction. She waited until they were closer. They had made it across the open area. Taking a deep breath, she took off after them.

A moment later, she and the other two disappeared into a thick grove of junipers. They stayed put until the gunfire ceased, then the footfall of someone running their direction. It was Ismet.

"Let's get the hell out of here," Meadowlark said, waving everyone forward.

Sari was enraged. He bent down and examined the top of the mound where the distracting gunfire had come from. He poked into the dirt, finding spent casings. They had just missed whoever had shot at them. He thought about Ismet. It could have been him here, firing away, causing them to lose sight of Meadowlark. And now, they all had escaped back into the spires.

There was still time. "Spread out," he ordered. "We can still push them towards the gorge. Once the moon shows itself, we will lose our advantage."

Readjusting his night goggles, he clamped onto his AK-47 and followed his men into the hunt.

He would get the bastard Ismet.

CHAPTER 35

Once they landed at the NATO facility, McKenzie and his men boarded a Bell OH-58 Kiowa for the flight to Eshai. Mallory's description of their situation kept him on edge. Visions of gunfire having them pinned down troubled him the entire flight. Mallory had rolled the dice; unfortunately, he had to live with the consequences. What they would find once they arrived was unknown.

He glanced at the instrument panel on the helicopter and estimated they were eighteen minutes away from the GPS coordinates Mallory had left on the recording. "We need to approach from the south," he told the pilot. "That will take us up the river west of Eshai."

"Anymore communications from those on the ground?" the pilot asked, adjusting the pitch control, putting the chopper into an initial descent.

"Haven't been able to raise them." He sucked a deep breath. "We're their only hope."

The pilot nodded.

McKenzie looked across at Neal and the other three agents. Their expressions hardened. The reality of dropping into unknown territory did not sit well, yet their training was evident. They all knew their jobs. They were equipped and ready. Donned in camouflage, night-vision goggles, and H&K 416 assault rifles, McKenzie reflected on simpler times when being in the CIA didn't equate itself with being militarized. Back then there was no camouflage, just suits and ties, *à la James Bond* without the swizzle sticks and vodka martinis. What happened to all that Cold War stuff?

He shrugged off his philosophical musings, adjusted his goggles, and readied himself. The window of opportunity was upon them, and if it was still open, it was closing fast.

Mallory followed Ismet and Meadowlark, wielding flashlights, their only way to penetrate deeper into the *fairy spires* without stumbling over volcanic rocks or stepping into rodent burrows. She moved briskly, still holding Ismet's pistol. It felt the same as the Beretta that McKenzie had given her in Nevada, but still…a gun was a gun. Christ, why was she carrying a gun anyway? She wasn't trained for this kind of crap. What had turned from a search for Katie had become a deadly nightmare. At least the vehicles could not reach them. The intermittent stands of junipers, spires, and hoodoos gave them protection. The terrain became rougher, and the smell of gunpowder dissipated the closer they got to the gorge.

Meadowlark insisted he knew the area like the back of his hand. It was questionable whether their assailants were as familiar. He was confident in his plan, or so she hoped; otherwise, they were going to end up with their backs against the gorge surrounded by their pursuers. She had to trust him, but another question raised its ugly head.

Why was Katie involved with these men?

If Meadowlark and Ismet were intent on blowing up a major asset held by Möbius, from all accounts, Katie was involved as an accessory. The implication she could be considered a terrorist frightened the hell out of Mallory. Katie's relationship with Ismet was deeper than she thought.

Now Mallory herself was involved with the two men who would be responsible for the dam's demise. If the gunmen didn't finish her off, would Turkish authorities jail her and throw away the key? Spending the rest of her life in a Turkish prison was too frightening to consider. In what had become a continuing nightmare, she was caught up in a hopeless loop of changing circumstances. What was it that drove Meadowlark to want to destroy a dam he had worked to develop and build? Why the change of heart? These questions deserved an answer, but first, they had to get Katie out of harm's way.

Meadowlark stopped, the flashlight out in front, beams penetrating the gloom of air over space. They were at the edge of the gorge. Mallory could feel the tension. The emptiness ahead was not only horizontal, but vertical as well—a cold, hollow feeling of blackness. She backed away, her leg muscles slow to process commands. A shapeless glow rose above the hills to the south. "The moon will rise in an hour." Meadowlark said. "That could help us a little, but no time to wait." He turned and motioned Ismet. "The cache box is ten minutes to the west. You can get there faster than the rest of us. We'll wait until you return."

Ismet nodded.

"A cache box?" Mallory asked.

"In this business; one must be prepared. We've been on the run from Möbius for over a month. The cache box provides another safety net—rappelling gear. If we can reach the river, we can elude these maniacs."

Ismet disappeared into the night without a word.

Meadowlark turned his attention to Mallory. "Thanks—for back there."

Mallory nodded; surprised the man would acknowledge the help.

"Alev, find a high spot and keep your ears and eyes alert," Meadowlark ordered. "When Ismet gets back, we get the hell out of here."

Alev trotted off.

"Now lady, we talk."

Her voice was calm and clear as she spoke of her relationship with Tom Haley and how she saw him die. Her saga continued with Tom's involvement with the CIA and her close encounters with Möbius.

Meadowlark came close to interrupting, but thought better of it.

Mallory took notice. "What's wrong?" she asked.

"Nothing, not a damn thing."

"I don't buy that. It's about Tom. I could tell the way you wanted to interject, so tell me."

Meadowlark hesitated. "I've known Tom a long time. We were friends before your dissertation days."

"Did you know Tom was involved with the CIA?"

Meadowlark leaned back. "I suspected Tom was more than just a consultant for the dam. On more than one occasion, he harassed me to no end to leave. I think we both sensed the shit was ready to hit the fan. He said he would leave, too. Unfortunately, he stayed longer than I imagined—and he learned things he shouldn't have. That was a clear sign he had other irons in the fire. When I approached him on his extracurricular activities, he got defensive. When he did leave after I had, I never thought Möbius suspected him." He lowered his eyes. "That's a hard pill to swallow."

"What about Katie; isn't she just as important as Tom?" Mallory demanded.

"Don't lecture me, lady," he said, shaking off any guilt. "She was involved with Ismet, and I couldn't convince either one of them that she didn't belong in this operation. Ismet was protesting the dam's construction way before Katie showed up. Hard for me to tell them both to cool their hormones." His face turned to rage. "Don't think it's not killing me knowing she's held prisoner at the dam."

"Then why destroy it?"

He remained silent.

She wanted to slug him, knowing he was holding back information. "What about the dam and the IFC?"

Meadowlark sat on a rock and pulled at his ponytail. "The original intent of the dam was to control flood waters, provide irrigation and hydro-power. During the design and construction, the project became a personal endeavor. I had the opportunity to make this dam the most efficient from a water manager's perspective. The computational software and multiple sensors integrated into the infrastructure, reservoir, and hydrological basin have the ability to regulate storage and flow like no other dam. Climate change, evaporation, morphing hydrology, storm surge, temperature, silt density, saturation, all these parameters are considered for optimum water usage. Every single drop is utilized to its fullest. No other storage project in the world comes close to this state-of-the-art control. I designed the system. He wiped at the corner of his eye. It's my baby, but now—I will destroy it.

Mallory moved over and studied the man. A brilliant man with two PhD's. This ageing hippie hiding the genius that he possessed was nothing short of fascinating.

He continued. "After construction, I learned of another, unpublicized use for the dam."

"Which was?" she asked.

"Salability. Who's going to pay the most for a reservoir full of water?"

Mallory remembered her conversation with McKenzie. "How would that work?"

"Behind closed doors, the IFC financed and the government of Turkey granted Möbius permits to construct a pipeline to the Gulf of Alexandretta in the Mediterranean. Cyprus has already contracted for over thirty percent of the water. Another future pipeline would supply water to Israel and Jordan. The Jordan River is running dry as we speak. It's all behind the scenes, political stuff. Lots of corruption. To Möbius, there are huge profits to be made."

"And so that will dry up water for farmers."

Meadowlark nodded. "That's why Ismet and his people are desperate to destroy this fiasco. The dam uprooted them for what? Not even the promised irrigation will hold. They're basically fucked without any legal recourse."

Mallory looked him in the eye. "Why do you care?"

"The same reason I left Möbius. I couldn't support that—that and other things they had up their sleeve."

"What do you mean, other things?"

Meadowlark waved her off. He wasn't going to answer.

"Let me get this straight. You're going to blow up the dam, which in the eyes of the world will be a terrorist act. How will that help the Assyrians?"

"The Assyrians then can resume their historical and cultural way of life."

She kept her eyes on Meadowlark, a man whose mysteries increased with every word. There had to be more. "What about Paul Coulomb?"

"Smart—and stupid at the same time."

"Shelby Wallace?"

"Not so smart, plenty of stupid."

"Esra Sahin?"

He raised an eyebrow. "You met her?"

"I can't say it was enjoyable."

Meadowlark stared out across the gorge, the glow above the hills brighter. His face showed a melancholy side she hadn't yet seen. "Yes, good old Esra. She came to Möbius a few years back. She's not dumb; dug herself out from under a pretty shitty upbringing, lived in an orphanage. Tough as nails, hard to believe the good-looking bitch could scratch your eyes out. Hell, worse than that, she ended up pummeling another girl who was bullying her in the orphanage. Didn't quite kill her, but…gouged out an eye." He stood and walked a few feet toward the gorge.

Mallory recalled earlier when he stood on the edge, solitary, in another dimension. "That doesn't surprise me."

"One tough bitch. Still, we fooled around before she started to believe in the bullshit Paul was proposing. It was at the same time Möbius was reaching an apogee of success. We had gained a foothold in the world of private water utilities and futures, betting on where the next shortage would occur. We were damn good at it. When a crisis hit, we were there, ready and willing to invest millions to solve the problem. We had solutions, new sources, water treatment facilities, engineering and distribution systems, aquifer management, all legal and seen as a true model in the eyes of the U.N. and the IFC."

Mallory followed his gaze across the gorge.

"What the hell did she see in me? Even that asshole Paul couldn't garner her attention. He was the handsome bachelor, the man with a million women. I, the scraggly one, the unkempt fading dissident with the roadmap face." He sighed.

He glanced back at Mallory, hesitated, and turned back to the gorge. His face shone, sort of a strange luminescence. "I asked her on several occasions why she would make love to me and not Paul. 'He has many lovers,' she would say every time. Like a fool, I would let her suck every ounce of tension from me." His smile grew wry. "Her dark eyes and red lips would entice me. I was the lamb led to slaughter. Eventually, she drifted away. It was okay at that point. All she wanted was the big man on campus. Dammit to hell, she didn't love me, she just liked to fuck and make Paul jealous."

He picked up a rock and flung it hard into the gorge.

CHAPTER 36

A rustle of brush caught Mallory's attention. Fearful that they may have been found, she dropped to one knee, the gun aimed at the unknown. Alev shrilled a bird call from the top of the rock where he was stationed. The moon had just cleared the hills and the welcome luminosity showed him pointing to the west. She lowered the gun. Ismet emerged from behind a juniper carrying an aluminum box. He laid it down, unlocked it, and pulled out two climbing ropes, carabiners and nylon slings.

Meadowlark knelt and picked up a sling. He handed it to Mallory. "Ever rappel before?"

She looked out over the black chasm. "Tried it once on a whim; scared the living crap out of me. Obviously, I have no other choice." Grabbing and stepping into it, she fastened it snug around her legs and hips with a carabiner.

Meadowlark looked over, impressed. "Once," he said with a flicker in his eye.

"I can fix a rappel sling but don't ask me to enjoy heights."

There was a gunshot—Alev cried out, toppling from his perch.

A second shot echoed, shards flew off the boulder where she had sat earlier. She dashed behind one of the smaller spires. Meadowlark and Ismet followed, guns drawn.

"Christ!" Meadowlark yelled.

Ismet moved to the other side of the spire, frantically looking for Alev, only to see him on the ground, unmoving.

Mallory crunched low and a wave of sickness engulfed her. To her immediate right, a steep, deepening fissure ran fifteen or twenty feet towards the cliff edge. She thought about ducking into it for better protection, but it was filled with loose debris. Hot air rushed up from below, a reminder of her tenuous location at the edge. A sudden misstep and she could slip off into the abyss.

A burst of fire raked down on them, rock fragments flying in all directions.

She aimed the gun into the darkness where she thought the gunfire had originated. She pulled the trigger. Nothing! She pulled it again. Nothing! The magazine was empty.

And then silence.

"They're moving closer," Ismet uttered.

Meadowlark checked the magazine on his gun. To his dismay, only a few rounds left and no spare. The assailants were on one side—the black, gaping gorge on the other.

Under assault again, but this time no place to run.

Sari moved quietly with his men, their semi-circular approach hemmed in Meadowlark and the others on all sides. The rising moon had made it easier to negotiate the rough terrain—even though it helped his enemies.

It was fortunate one of his men spotted the sentinel on the rock; otherwise they may have missed where Ismet and the others had escaped. The lower gorge had become Ismet's last stand. Soon he would see the Assyrian beg for his life before he planted the final bullet between the bastard's eyes.

He smiled. His quest was about to reach its glory.

Off in the distance, a faint *thwap-thwap* could be heard, growing stronger.

"Hurry, give me your SAT phone," Mallory yelled. Meadowlark handed it over. A quick dial of numbers, a voice answered.

"Mallory, is that you?" McKenzie asked.

"Tell me, you're on the way."

"We're coming up river now."

With relief, Mallory read off their coordinates from the phone and warned of the attackers and their location.

"How many?" he asked.

"Five or six."

"You should see us any minute." The line went dead.

"No time to dawdle," Meadowlark barked. "We're better off over the edge waiting for your CIA buddies." With Ismet's help, he knotted the two ropes together, looped it around the trunk of a stout juniper, and tossed both ends over the precipice.

"There's enough rope to reach a lower bench. Ismet, you go first, then the lady."

"But—"

"No dissent. I'll go last, now move it."

Ismet didn't argue. He clamped onto the rope and disappeared over the edge.

"You next," he ordered, clipping a carabiner to the rope and Mallory's sling. "Ready, go."

She had hated that feeling of relying on rope friction to save one from sure death. But bullets raining down on her forced her decision. She had no time to fear heights, or fear falling. No time to analyze. No time to allow her pounding heart to get the best of her. She wrapped the rope behind her back and held her breath, then backed up to the edge, remembering *never to look down*. The first push was the most unnerving moment of rappelling—a full reliance on rope and hardware. What could go wrong? Trust it. Trust it all. Trust the hardware, trust your ability, and trust those that talked you into such a crazy thing in the first place. Meadowlark's voice rattled in her brain. She leaned back out over the edge into the daunting darkness, letting her full weight stretch the rope and her imagination. After a breathless moment, she bounced down the cliff, reaching the ledge with Ismet. Helping her unclip from the rope, they both looked up, watching Meadowlark advance down the face. There was still another hundred and fifty-feet to go from where they stood to the river.

Gunfire rattled again, bits and pieces of sandstone spiraling above them. Mallory crouched with Ismet against the cliff face. Above and to her left, an assailant leveled a rifle for another shot. The gun resonated, fragments of sandstone peppering them. There was no room to maneuver, in fact, barely enough cover for one. The angle of the sniper seemed to be perfect, their only hope the darkness. The moonlight had not yet penetrated below the rim where they huddled. Still, another random shot or two and they would be dead.

Where was Meadowlark? Then she saw him, hanging on rappel. He was visible, the moonlight squarely on him. Yet, they hadn't fired at him. Why?

Another gunshot—rock shrapnel flew, hitting her in the face—and another. Ismet moaned in pain, bent over holding his shoulder.

Sari heard the whine of rotors, and then he spotted the helicopter racing up the gorge. From the chopper, a continuous clatter of weapon fire erupted. The buzzing of orange tracers raced their direction, the bullets slamming close to his position. The chopper disappeared behind the spires. His mind rushed through scenarios—Turkish military—the police—the CIA? His imagination went wild. One thing was certain—whoever fired at them would be back.

The gunman again aimed into the shadows where Mallory and Ismet crouched. A round struck the rock above, narrowly missing her head. She glanced at Ismet, who still gripped his shoulder.

And then another shot, but no ricocheting bullets. She heard the gunman scream and saw him nose-dive over the cliff, careening and cartwheeling. Seconds later, he slammed into the scree of rocks at river's edge.

Mallory focused skyward. Meadowlark eased the pistol back into his waist. She could see him shake his head as he continued rappelling. She reached over to help Ismet.

"Let me look," she said, staring at the reddening spot.

"I'm okay," he said, grimacing

She leaned in and pulled back the blood-encrusted sleeve of his shirt, exposing a gash. She gently tore the ripped sleeve off his arm, then wrapped it around the wound, tying it off. "That should slow the bleeding."

Above, a cacophony of voices stirred, growing louder. And then one, two, three figures materialized on the edge, all carrying rifles. From where they huddled, they had no protection. Meadowlark fumbled with his pistol and it fell from his hands, crashing onto the rocks below. The figures raised their weapons and aimed, not at Meadowlark, but at them. Ismet stood and moved in front of Mallory. Their eyes connected. He was attempting to shield her, but it wouldn't make any difference. They were sitting ducks. Soon, they all would be dead.

Faraway gunfire echoed across the gorge. Mallory wrenched her head around, staring at their executioners, but they were no longer bent on finishing her and Ismet off. In a panic, they began shooting indiscriminately the other direction. One gunman clasped his chest in agony and collapsed. The two others disappeared beyond her view, gunfire seeming to come from all directions.

Mallory heard voices speaking in English. They were low, but were gaining in strength. She kept her eyes trained along the cliff edge. The gunfire continued another minute.

Then, an eerie silence.

Every muscle tensed, she kept her eyes riveted on the rim of the gorge. Now, she could make out two figures. Ismet raised his gun, but Mallory pulled his arm back down. It may have been wishful thinking or a suppressed intuition that was long in coming. She yelled, "We're down here."

McKenzie's voice echoed from above. "Everyone okay?"

She never thought a voice could be so welcome.

CHAPTER 37

McKenzie observed one of his agents clean and dress the wound on Ismet. Both were sitting in the open doorway of the helicopter, the light from two portable lanterns bathing the area with a militarist glow. The bullet had grazed Ismet, taking a chunk of flesh in the process. Fortunately, it wasn't serious. Once their barrage of gunfire confused the attackers, they found a clearing where they were able to land. From there they spread out and counterattacked, killing two and forcing the others to flee. The area was now secure.

He saw Mallory sitting on a rock away from the activity. He walked over and slid next to her. They sat there for a long time without talking. It was an awkward moment.

Finally, he spoke. "Why risk your life?"

She hesitated. "I've asked myself that a thousand times the last few days. I keep coming up with the same answer."

"Which is?"

"A deadly habit of procrastination…and a nagging hypothesis."

His brows rose.

Mallory tried to smile, instead stared at the night sky, the moisture in her eyes glimmering in the moonlight. "Many years ago, my younger sister Britt planned to come for a visit when I was working on my masters. She was living in Shawnee, had a job as a bank teller. I told her to come the next day, I was too busy—grad projects and all, you know, important things. The next day, there were developing thunderstorms. The smell…the humidity, darkening skies, black as night I can tell you. Then the rains…and the wind. My ears popped, dust everywhere, flying debris. Half a mile away you could see it, spinning and touching down, coming from the south, destroying everything in its path."

She paused and shook her head. "You never forget the massive sound, like a freight train barreling down and nowhere to go. I ducked into the shelter—but the tornado never came any nearer. I wasn't surprised, hell, this was Oklahoma for Pete's sakes. I did a quick weather check; the activity was worse to the east."

McKenzie could see her throat tightening in the moonlight.

"That's where Britt was, fifty miles away. Several tornadoes spawned in her area. Later, I found out Britt's house was destroyed, nothing left, nothing but a foundation."

She turned and gave him a grief-stricken look, tears emerging. "Her body was found a mile away. If I would have allowed her to come the day before, then maybe…she would still be alive."

McKenzie lowered his head. "I'm sorry, wasn't my place to ask."

"Please, don't apologize. I don't know myself how this crazy mind of mine works anymore."

He sat there, regretful. What did he know of other people's motivations, their guilt, aspirations, and feelings? Now he understood her fear of losing Katie Haley. At this moment though, he had true feelings for Mallory. For the longest time, he sat there looking at her. He wanted nothing more than to reach over and hug her and kiss her tears away.

But what was this about a hypothesis? But then, he heard a commotion. The man they all wanted, arguing and moving in their direction. McKenzie couldn't help but ponder his expression. His timeworn face seemed to indicate a level of suspicion—the same opinion McKenzie had of him. He acknowledged Meadowlark's presence as Neal joined the group.

"I take it I'm the winner of the popularity contest." Meadowlark grinned cynically. "What's the prize?"

"We need information. You're our only connection to Möbius—and the IFC," McKenzie said.

Meadowlark cocked an eyebrow. "What do you know?"

"Not enough, but you do," McKenzie said.

"It's pretty simple. I have a list of all the names of the IFC criminals that have crawled into bed with Paul Coulomb and that bitch Esra."

"We want that list."

"I'm sure you do. I'm pretty positive your analysts will be able to hack into my many computer files and find the names, but that…is for later."

"Later?" McKenzie asked. "Later than what?"

Mallory jumped in, wiping an eye. "Katie's still in danger, and time is not on our side." Her glare at Meadowlark was extreme. "You tell him—and tell him straight."

Meadowlark sighed. "We do have a problem." He brushed his dirty hands through his dirty hair. "Katie is indeed held captive in the dam."

"How do you propose we get her out?" Neal asked.

"That's not the problem," Meadowlark said. "Right now, we're up against the clock. He looked at his watch. We only have a little less than four hours."

McKenzie squinted. "Four hours 'till what?"

Mallory didn't hesitate. "The dam blows up."

He wasn't sure he heard correctly. "Blows up? Seriously?" He caught Mallory's *I told you so* look.

"We cannot stop it!" Ismet said. He favored the shoulder wrapped in a large gauze bandage.

"And who the hell are you?" McKenzie asked, standing.

"I am Ismet. My people are Assyrian. They took our land, destroyed our villages. We have to get Katie," he finished, lips quivering.

"Why don't we just disarm the explosives?" Neal asked. "Grab the woman, piece of cake. I worked demolition in the army."

"Over my dead body," Meadowlark said, irritably. "We risked our lives rigging them."

"And kill innocent people," McKenzie asked sharply. "Man, what the hell are you thinking?" He looked at his watch. "Four hours, is that what I heard?"

"You heard me. The explosives are set deep within the dam for maximum damage," Meadowlark explained. "We don't expect full-fledged destruction at first. After the explosion, the penstock will go through a process called cavitation; large chunks of concrete will be propelled through the inlet, battering and enlarging it under the pressure of four hundred head of water." His voice rose. "The guts of the dam will be obliterated, followed by the power plant, and eventually, the structural capacity to hold back the water. That gives time to evacuate downstream."

"How sure are you of that?" McKenzie asked.

"One hundred percent."

McKenzie's eyes flared. "A hundred percent; nothing's a hundred percent except getting killed. Are you insane?"

Meadowlark shook a finger. "Don't lecture me. I was involved all through the design and construction of this dam. The planned explosion will result in a progressive failure."

McKenzie couldn't believe what he was hearing. "That still doesn't answer my question. Where are the explosives placed?"

"Next to the penstock," a panicked Ismet snapped.

Meadowlark approached Ismet, his fists balled. "Ismet, that's enough."

McKenzie jumped between the two men, gazing at the aging hippy. "Cool your jets." Meadowlark slowly relaxed his fists.

"How did Katie get involved in this?" Mallory asked.

"She wasn't part of it originally, but—" Meadowlark hesitated, his eyes on Ismet. "She was to be long gone by now, somehow love got in the way."

He turned to see Ismet rubbing at his eyes. *Now, the dots connect.*

Meadowlark continued, "Yes, I too have a reason for seeing she doesn't die. Tom Haley was a friend—a good friend. I owe him; I owe Katie, but at this stage—" He then looked Mallory's direction.

Mallory's breathing rasped. "I won't sit back and do nothing."

"There may be another way to get her out—notify Turkish authorities about the explosives," McKenzie said. "I would think they would order the dam evacuated."

"Are you crazy," Meadowlark shrieked. "This is Southeastern Turkey. By the time they get their shit together the dam will be history."

"We can't give up now; we just can't," Mallory implored.

Meadowlark lit a cigarette and took a long, revered drag. "There is an exploratory tunnel chiseled through the south abutment, used for the geological study. During construction they built a secondary tunnel for maintenance of the main penstock. Both intercept near the powerhouse. The maintenance tunnel is also accessed from inside the powerhouse. Problem is, there's a steel door that's locked from inside."

"That doesn't help us much," Mallory said.

McKenzie looked briefly at Mallory and Ismet, their faces a study in anguish and sweat. He brought his eyes back to Meadowlark. "Where there's a will, there's a way."

Meadowlark nodded, pacing back and forth. In the moonlight, the man's pony-tail shone silver. Was he coming around, realizing they had to try and get her out, exploding dam or not? He took a final drag of the cigarette and tossed it aside. "They want me, so I'll surrender."

McKenzie rolled his eyes. "You'll what?"

Meadowlark raised a hand. "They want me for other reasons. They will not harm me until they have what I have."

"What do you have?"

Meadowlark shook his head. "No time for that. Just understand that I am safe until they get what I have. We will drive to the powerhouse with one or two of your men hidden in the back of the vehicle. I will turn myself in at the guardhouse which is located near the powerhouse. During my surrender, the guard's attentions will be on me. That will give your men the opportunity to sneak into the powerhouse without being spotted. There is a door off to the side that can be accessed without being observed. From the inside, the door to the maintenance tunnel can be unlocked. Once Katie is located in the electrical gallery, she can be whisked out through the tunnel."

"Only one problem," McKenzie said. "One or two men aren't enough if we plan to free her."

Meadowlark didn't look concerned. "Then others come up through the tunnel. Once your men are inside, they let the others in through the locked door to the tunnel."

He looked over the other faces, solemn but willing. His eyes strayed back to Mallory. "You will stay here."

"The hell I will."

"Now listen, I—"

"No, you listen. I need to be there when we get Katie. She knows me, and we don't know how she'll react."

"True, but—"

"She's got a point," Neal said.

McKenzie turned from Neal to Mallory. "Against my better judgement, but we do need bodies." *Amistad will have me crucified.* He looked at Meadowlark. "Let's move!"

CHAPTER 38

Tepecik Dam

Katie struggled to remember. How long had she been here? The room was only blackness, except when someone entered to administer the drug. She felt the IV port taped to the back of her hand. Why hadn't she ripped it out? She had the answer—they'd put it back in.

With each passing hour, her strength diminished. Her eyelids were heavy, and her mouth was dry. She was deathly thirsty. A dream, that's all it was, a dream that would reignite other dreams and blurred memories that had no timeframe.

But this was no dream.

She had been so hostile to her father's earlier attempts to reconcile. It was her decision to reject him. Sure, he wasn't there for her after her mother passed away. She was only twelve, and he ignored her. In retrospect, she'd been selfish. For God's sake, he was hurting too. His wife had died; someone he had loved as much as her. How did she expect him to act? He had brought Mallory into the fold to help her cope. Who helped him?

What a fool.

She brushed at the tears, recalling the last time she spoke to him.

"Katie, I know we've had our disagreements, but I don't have a good feeling about your involvement with Ismet."

"Why do you care? You haven't shown an interest in my life for, what? It seems forever.," she snapped.

"Listen to me, Katie. I know I've been distant and unavailable. After your mother died, I was depressed, isolated. I didn't stay involved. It was as if I thought you could raise yourself. For that I am sorry, truly sorry, but I can't change what happened; I can only hope to do better in the future."

"Well, I survived, no thanks to you. The only good memories I have of those years were with Mallory. She treated me like I existed, like a sister."

"Katie, I'm sorry. Let me make things better. Please come home; we'll start over."

"Why? I've got a new life here. Ismet is good to me, and Harry is close by. Shouldn't that satisfy your concerns?"

"I know you have feelings for this young man—but going to Turkey is the worst thing to do at this time. Ismet has been recruited by Harry. You could be implicated."

"Don't worry about me. I'm a big girl and can take care of myself. You saw to that."

Sweat poured from every pore as she shook the memory away. This was reality, no dream.

Maybe she would never see her father again...to apologize. Maybe she wouldn't survive.

CHAPTER 39

Tepecik Dam

cKenzie and Neal squeezed into the back of the aging Citroën. Meadowlark drove, negotiating the steep road down into the gorge heading for the powerhouse. They were fortunate to have the beat-up hatchback with bald tires and a leaky oil pan. It was the only transportation they were able to scramble up when the Land Rover was destroyed. The twisting and narrow gravel track with curves and drop-offs took Meadowlark's complete concentration. Deep inside the gorge, the setting moon gave no light and the crystal-clear sky exploded with stars.

"If you're one hundred percent sure the dam won't flood people downstream, how sure are you this plan will work?" McKenzie asked.

"Fifty-fifty. Ten percent me, it's up to you and your team to make up for the other forty percent to have an even chance."

Horseshit calculation, but then he didn't try to figure out why Meadowlark would give himself up so easily. Surely, he knew the risks. There must be a reason Möbius wanted him alive. It sure would be worthwhile to know why—but Meadowlark was not in the mood to elaborate.

McKenzie checked his watch. They had two and a half hours to extract Katie before the dam blew. He held his breath, knowing a rush into the enemy camp provided either a slim hope for success, or a massive failure. Limited time and crazy odds had him leaning toward the latter possibility. Their only option: roll the dice and pray they didn't crap out too soon.

"We're coming up to the checkpoint," Meadowlark said. "I'll stop in the shadows on the right, that way you'll be able to crawl out the back without being seen."

As they approached, Meadowlark described what he saw. "There is a chain link fence running from the river to the guard shack. It continues up a steep hill disappearing into blackness. An entrance gate wide enough to allow vehicles through is closed. I see a guard coming out of the shack next to the gate. He's waving for me to stop." Meadowlark pulled slightly off the road into shadow.

"Good luck," McKenzie whispered.

Meadowlark grunted, opened the door, and stepped out.

At the same time, McKenzie pushed the hatchback partially open. He slid out; Neal followed, carrying a set of bolt cutters. They slithered down into cover of a drainage ditch. He felt for the security of his Beretta, strapped to his waist shafted with a suppressor.

Meadowlark approached the guard and said in English. "I'm Harry Meadowlark. Your boss is looking for me."

Curious, the guard shot a glance at the vehicle and examined Meadowlark thoroughly. McKenzie heard him yell something back to another guard who strode out of the shack and walked over. He carried a flashlight. As he approached, he beamed it on Meadowlark's face. Both guard's faces broke into wide smiles.

Meadowlark raised his hands in a sign of surrender. He was frisked top to bottom. Finished, the guard ushered him through the gate.

Now, hidden behind a large bush, McKenzie could see the guard with the flashlight approach the Citroën. "Stay low," he whispered to Neal. The guard walked around, examining the vehicle inside and out, stooping down to check the undercarriage. Satisfied, he chuckled to himself and murmured something in Turkish. He headed back toward the guard shack. McKenzie surmised his comment related to the vehicle, something to the effect of, *what a piece of junk.*

He moved along the drainage towards the chain link fence, his head well below the view of the guard building. The ditch flattened. Still in the shadow, he could see Meadowlark being led to the powerhouse. He sniffed; the smell of moisture carried in the air and the roar of water shooting from the turbines imitated a powerful waterfall.

Reaching the fence, he motioned to Neal. The younger agent gripped the bolt cutters and snipped a few links, the cutter smoothly taking care of business, the sound of the discharged water masking the noise of the snips. Removing the links, they ducked through the cutout and hustled toward the large storage area on the south side of the powerhouse. McKenzie crouched behind a row of steel drums, his heart pounding. He'd been in situations like this in the past, but this operation was thrust upon them—without the luxury of planning.

McKenzie eyed the powerhouse. Beyond, the magnificent grandeur of the dam emerged—a gray, massive wall of concrete, four hundred and eighty feet high and eight hundred feet long at the crest. It caught the waning rays of the moon. McKenzie looked in awe, recollecting the statistics Meadowlark had thrown out. An engineering marvel—*one of the highest double curvature thin-shell concrete arch dams in the world, thirteen feet wide at the crest and fifty-seven feet at the base.* Up close, and from the bottom, the dam demanded reverence.

The powerhouse was separated by a rectangular concrete elevator core. A bridge spanned from the core to crest. Meadowlark indicated it was one of two ways to reach the top of the dam—the other, a series of catwalks and stairs that clung to the steep granite cliffs only in case of elevator malfunction. McKenzie looked up and behind him, a series of lights following the stairs path up the face of the cliff.

He turned his attention back to the task at hand. He saw two doors—just as Meadowlark had described. The man-door that they would use to enter was at the left side. Thirty feet to the right was an overhead door that covered an exterior elevator for hauling oil drums and other equipment down to the lower level. Further right wrapped another fence, enclosing a row of transformers and circuit breakers. Draped gracefully from a series of insulators high above the transformers, high voltage lines connected to the first of several steel transmission towers that worked their way up and out of the gorge. He thought about what Ismet had said about the Assyrians and the possibility they would lose the water that was stored. That begged a second question: who gained from the sale of the electricity? Certainly not the Assyrians who had their land and villages buried under three hundred feet of water.

Mallory couldn't believe she was underground again, confined in a shallow tunnel, surrounded by millions of tons of rock. And she couldn't believe she convinced McKenzie that she should come. She remembered him saying something about a man named Amistad who would surely fire him when he found out. But she was adamant—once they found Katie, a familiar face other than Ismet's might be a necessity. He agreed.

Hidden on a rock shelf above the gravel road a quarter of a mile from the guard shack, the entrance was well camouflaged, if not forgotten by the operators of the dam. Less than five feet in height and four feet wide, the wormhole made her yearn for the Hittite tunnels she had negotiated hours earlier. There was only one tunnel, not the multiple tunnels that created a maze of confusion.

McKenzie had given Mallory a .9mm Beretta, knowing she had admirably handled a similar one in Nevada. She readily accepted it. It was gratifying how packing heat could add to one's comfort level in dark places. It was a feeling she hoped she'd never get used to.

They didn't anticipate being in the tunnel long. Once they reached the metal door to the powerhouse, they hoped it would only be a short time before it was unlocked.

Ismet came to a stop where the tunnel ended. He shined the flashlight up a ledge six feet above the floor. There, Mallory saw another hole edging into blackness.

"That is the maintenance tunnel for the penstock." He reached around and found a handhold and pulled himself up, using a rocky protrusion for a foothold. After a few seconds, he was standing on the ledge. He reached down and helped Mallory.

She beamed her flashlight back down the hole. The passageway they came from was well disguised, hardly noticeable.

Ismet flashed the light to the left. "That is the way to penstock. It's where explosives are hidden." He swung the light back around and continued in the other direction.

The claustrophobia of the tunnel became unnerving, and with the thought of the explosives back in her mind she was close to making a hasty retreat. She shivered, even though it wasn't cold. Shaking it off, she followed Ismet. The tunnel narrowed and sloped upward. The air was stifling, dank, and suffocating. Cut through granite, the dampness was surprising. She touched the side of the wall and her fingers came back wet. The moisture didn't enhance her comfort level, knowing there was several hundred-feet of static water pressure behind them.

They entered a larger space. "We are here," Ismet said, beaming his flashlight ahead, the glint of metal reflected a set of stairs.

Mallory angled her flashlight up the stairs, the grated treads ending at a landing eight feet above from where they stood. A gray metal door reflected the beam. She could sense a small vibration. "Are those the generators I feel?"

"Yes, there are six. Listen, they hum." Ismet climbed the stairs and tried the door handle. "Locked. We wait." He pressed his ear against the door.

What was it about freedom fighters that intrigued Katie? Mallory had to know. "Are you in love with Katie?"

Ismet glanced back at her. In the residual light, she could see the pain on his face. He didn't answer directly. "Do you know about my people? Assyrians are one of the oldest ethnic groups in the world. We have been through genocides, massacres, wars." There was a brief silence. "Katie always listened, wanting to learn about our struggles, wanting to help." He hesitated. "She's the only woman I've ever loved."

Mallory didn't know if she should pursue it, but there was one other question she had to ask. She remembered Meadowlark hanging precariously from the rope during their rappel, yet he did not seem to draw fire. "Can you answer this for me, Ismet? During the rappel, they never once aimed their weapons at Harry Meadowlark. Why not?"

Ismet rubbed at his shoulder, favoring the bandaged wound. "Möbius wants him alive."

"Why?"

"He didn't tell you? Then, I don't think—"

"Don't stonewall me, Ismet," Mallory growled. She stood and shined her flashlight directly in his eyes. "If we are to get Katie out unharmed, I have to know the facts. Harry surrendered without much discussion. Why do they want him alive?"

Ismet sat down on the landing. "Without Harry, it's dead."

Mallory cocked her head. "What's dead?"

"*Socrates.*"

"*Socrates*, what's that?"

"It is bigger than destroying this dam, *something deadly.*"

Mallory's ears stung from the revelation. This *something deadly* was now reverberating like a Chinese gong between her ears. "Why Harry?"

"He has the *final key.*"

CHAPTER 40

Coulomb rubbed his eyes to expel the fatigue that had taken control. He would spend the night at his corporate office, as there was too much at stake to be away. A good night's rest would have been a welcome pleasure with Valencia, rubbing and massaging. Unfortunately, she was back in Spain.

How had he allowed things to get so screwed up and out of control? He picked up a glass of Van Winkle Special Reserve from his desk and downed it in one gulp. For the first time in his life, the special buzz the whiskey offered was absent. He reached for the bottle and poured another shot.

Was he not the smart one, the one with the vision to turn a small company into a world behemoth? He knew where to leverage his assets, chase the financing, and align the investors with promises of high returns, and—he knew how to produce results. After thirty years, the outcomes were remarkable, sustainable, and nefariously unbelievable. So how the hell did they end up at this point, teetering on the edge?

Maybe if he had recognized Harry's increasing indecisiveness, he could have kept him in the fold. He knew the man well, but through the years he must have missed something deep and disturbing inside. Compassion—did Harry finally gain some? Morality—he never showed any before. They had been competitors yes, but they knew each other's strengths and weaknesses. They would feed off each other, adding different perspectives to every new situation—but never once would they step back from not declaring victory, even if it meant rubbing someone else in the dirt.

Harry was from a lower middle class family, never had many things. Coulomb, the opposite, fully endowed with any and everything he ever wanted. But each lifestyle had a lesson. Rich or poor, it all boiled down to survival. What Harry had missed in life because of a lack of wealth and stature, he made up by shrewd negotiation, reasoning, and smart maneuvers. Coulomb learned well from this. It was refreshing to see how the other side could adjust—claw and fight back to succeed.

But now Harry had fled for reasons still debated. Who would have expected there would be a limit to everything, a point where friends and accomplices would become bitter enemies intent on destroying one another? Coulomb felt a little sorry for his former friend. Why did it have to end this way? It was a shame Harry would not be here with him to celebrate the joy of success in the most important undertaking Möbius had ever attempted.

He yawned, now thinking of his other colleague Shelby, who was not, in fact, the most intelligent person he knew. But there was one helpful trait that stood out—manners, exhibited in an unusual, faux way. Maybe it was a Southern thing, dissimilar to what the French were known to possess—brusque behavior. He kind of liked that. Shelby had a second trait more beneficial—obedience, unlike what Meadowlark possessed. He knew damn well when someone erected a roadblock to Möbius' success, he could certainly count on Shelby to knock it down; and when the phone rang, he was hard-pressed to believe that he wasn't receiving good news, as it was Shelby Wallace.

"Damndest thing," Wallace exclaimed. "Marotte shook us."

"How'd he do that?"

"He was leaving the casino. Saw me. Next thing, he's gone. Disappeared, as if the lil' bastard knew we were on to him."

"Find him, Shelby—find him, now!" Coulomb slammed the phone down into the cradle hard, frustrated.

CHAPTER 41

Tepecik Dam

McKenzie studied the south side of the powerhouse—a concrete and steel structure one hundred feet wide by two hundred and fifty feet long and sixty feet high. Inside, six French-made generators provided a combined capacity of five hundred and forty megawatts of electrical power. He could easily hear the hum of the transformers indicating a steady discharge of power. He placed the small set of night-vision binoculars against his eyes and scrutinized the building closer. Just as he had anticipated, there was a video camera in the far upper left corner with a view of the area in front of the man-door. Getting a closer look, it was automated, having the ability to adjust its field of vision at any disturbance it detected. Meadowlark had warned about the possibility, but he didn't have any up-to-date knowledge of the security since he hadn't been in the powerhouse for over a year. Somehow, McKenzie had to make the camera swivel away from the door.

He handed the binoculars to Neal. "Take a look."

Neal scrutinized the building and surrounding area. "That's a problem."

But was it insurmountable? First, they had to get to the far corner of the powerhouse without being seen. The only option that made sense would be a path that went through the transformer sub-station and high voltage. The mere thought of being only feet or inches away from disaster tightened around his neck like a noose. The good news: going through the sub-station avoided the camera. The constant transformer humming would probably keep the camera from spotting their movement if it was sound sensitive.

"Only choice is to go through the sub-station," McKenzie sighed.

"You can't be serious. There's a heck of a lot of KV's whistling through those transformers. One false move and kapow! We'll be deep-fried."

"Concern noted. Any other ideas?"

Neal shook his head.

McKenzie scanned the storage area closer. By keeping to the shadows, they would have easy access. The chain link fence had two rows of barbed wire at the top. At least he didn't see any razor wire. "Let's go," he said, not giving Neal time to object.

He moved slowly toward the enclosure, hidden by shadows. The camera itself was shielded by the transformers, so if it happened to swing their direction, he doubted they would be noticed. Neal followed, his shuffle now in defensive mode.

Nearing the fence, McKenzie studied the enclosure in detail—roughly ten feet tall, including the barbed wire. Taking a deep breath, he clamped onto the links and climbed the fence. As he suspected, the transformers shielded him from the camera. Steadying himself, he pulled up straight and carefully overstepped the barbed wire and scrambled down the other side. Grudgingly, the younger agent followed, taking a wary approach. A moment later, he stood next to McKenzie.

Keeping next to the fence, they crept towards the powerhouse at the maximum distance from the transformers. He swore he could feel the electrified air. A glance at Neal confirmed; the younger agent's hair was frizzed out, clown-like. At the far end, he climbed the fence again and dropped down, still in shadow and out of sight of the surveillance camera. Neal followed; glad to be away from the electrical hum.

The clamor of the maintenance door opening brought McKenzie to his knees. A man stepped out and lit a cigarette, the door closing behind. Dressed in coveralls, his bald head sparkled under the mercury vapor lamp above the door. He estimated between six to eight guards were stationed in and around the dam and powerhouse. Counting the two guards at the entrance and two or three patrolling the top of the dam, it left a possibility of three or four inside the powerhouse. *Hell, just a walk in the park.*

The man finished his cigarette and flicked the butt a good thirty-feet. As it hit the ground, the whirl of the camera caught McKenzie's attention. The man looked up as the camera spun, looked back down, spat a wad on the gravel and wiped his mouth. He turned, opened the door, and disappeared inside.

The sensitivity of the camera's sensors surprised McKenzie, although it gave him an idea. From their vantage point they couldn't see the guard shack. The only obstacle was the camera. Looking around on the ground, he picked up a small stone. "If this works, be ready to beeline it."

Taking aim, he tossed it out towards the steel drums. It hit the ground, barely making any noise. The camera whirled, the field of vision pulling away from the door. They didn't waste any time. With a sprint, they rushed towards the door, McKenzie opened it and they ducked inside.

Nevzat Sari hung the phone back up on the wall. His silken baby-face contorted a mixture of anger and bewilderment. He was worried. Drugging Meadowlark seemed risky but their only option to get him to talk. How ironic, he thought. After all that had transpired, the gunfight earlier, losing two men in the process—and then Meadowlark showing up out of the blue, alone. His surrender didn't make any sense—any logical sense at all. He kept his gaze on Coulomb's former associate, hands bound behind his back sitting in a chair in the control room. Was Coulomb's threat to have Katie Haley killed the catalyst for Meadowlark's appearance? In Sari's mind, history never would have indicated such a move. There had to be an ulterior motive, something they were missing. Harry would not have given up without a plan.

Three guards stood at the door, assault rifles trained on their captive. "Double the watch around the powerhouse," Sari ordered one of the guards. The man nodded and left. Turning his attention back to Meadowlark, he said in monotone. "I am skeptical of your visit."

"It makes perfect sense why I am here," Meadowlark responded.

"Tell me."

"Katie Haley. You have me now. Release her."

Sari glared at Meadowlark, his face unambiguous. "Why would she be here?"

"Don't fuck with me, Sari."

Sari feigned a surprised look. "Oh, you know of me. Let me guess, is it that *piç kurusu*, that *son of a bitch* Ismet, spreading rumors?" His smile disappeared, replaced with a flushed anger.

"Your distasteful reputation comes from several sources."

Sari stroked his glossy black hair and paced around Meadowlark, stopping behind him. "We do have the woman. I assure you she will not be released. Unfortunately, her usefulness has diminished."

Meadowlark craned his neck attempting to see Sari. "If she's harmed, that scumbag Paul will not get what he wants from me."

Sari reached down, grabbed Meadowlark by his ponytail and yanked. His head snapped, pummeling the back of the chair. Leaning in, Sari said, "Don't be so sure of that. After we are finished with you, you will beg us to slit your throat."

"Go fuck yourself."

Sari coiled back and slapped him across the face. Meadowlark did not show fear, his face tightly wound.

"Bring the needle," he yelled to one of the guards.

McKenzie held his Beretta out front. They found themselves in a room with a table and chairs, a wall clock, several sheets of paper tacked to the wall, a Turkish calendar displaying the wrong month, and a row of lockers along the far wall. A closed door penetrated the wall at the opposite end.

"This must be the break room," McKenzie said. He moved to the door. Cracking it open, he gazed out onto an eight foot wide mezzanine that gave way to a cavernous hall, two and a half times as long as it was wide. A heavy dose of ozone attacked his nose, given off by the electric generators running at high capacity. Their incessant drone filled the space, the steel-framed ceiling a generous distance above. His eyes swept back and forth, attempting to see if there was anyone moving around.

"I don't see anyone," he whispered to Neal. "Follow me."

McKenzie stepped out onto the mezzanine crouching low. He knew well-enough to keep out of sight of anyone who might be looking up from the floor below. He crept towards the stairs, edging his head over the landing. Signaling Neal, they moved silently down the stairs to the main level. The first room on their left was the oil pump room. Feeling a raw nerve, he surveyed the hallway. Not surprising, another door. It was open, and through it, he saw a pair of booted feet, the toes pointed away from him. He stooped lower. It was the man they had seen earlier taking a smoke break. He was busy adjusting something on one of the large pumps. A few seconds later, he pushed a switch and the pump sprang to life. Satisfied, he turned and headed out the door and into the generator hall.

McKenzie stepped into the hallway and entered the room. A row of man-size pumps on concrete pedestals lined the wall separating the room from the generator hall. Meadowlark had explained that the pumps fed lubricants to the generators and turbine via a pipe tunnel. Between two of the pumps, he spotted the hatch—a checkerboard steel plate that covered the entrance to the pipe tunnel. This would be their access point.

His mind raced. They had to work fast. "Stay here and keep your eyes peeled," he said. He took the bolt cutters and rushed over to oil storage room, dimly-lit, with several barrels resting in the middle of the room on pallets. On closer inspection, he could see the open-walled elevator next to the exterior wall. Next to the elevator was the door to the maintenance tunnel.

He examined the steel door. It was paddle locked. He knocked quietly two times. Ready to try again, the signal came back—three knocks. Attacking the lock with the cutters, he leveraged, gritting his teeth. The lock snapped. Ripping it from the latches, he pulled the door open.

Ismet and Mallory stood on the stair landing, relief on their faces having been rescued from their subterranean world.

"Quick," McKenzie said. "We haven't much time."

Once Mallory stepped across the threshold; a rush of warm air flew past her face, driving the dank tunnel into a distant memory. She drew a deep breath and shuddered, a ripple flowing from her shoulders to her feet. There was greater reason to be afraid here than in the tunnel, but there was no time to ponder and self-analyze the situation. If there were snags along the way, *make them manageable.* And then the room began to spin, and she felt herself drifting away. Maybe it was the sudden change in temperature, or the growing hum of generators playing with her mind, or the immense exhaustion setting in. Groggily, she sensed that Katie was nearby, and the mission would succeed beyond expectations. She began to feel giddy. She heard Tom's voice— *find Katie, tell her I love her.*

"Are you okay," McKenzie said, staring at Mallory.

"Yes—yes, I'm fine," she said, snapping out of the trance. She wiped the sweat from her brow and looked at McKenzie. "Need to adjust to the heat." Deeply, she wondered if she was okay.

Considering the circumstances, she couldn't imagine having someone other than McKenzie leading the operation. Fighting an impossible clock, the pace and professionalism of the hastily planned operation gave her encouragement. She felt better. Who else would she rather be with in a dangerous situation. The high temperature of the powerhouse was now forgotten.

"We've only seen one maintenance man, no guards, but that doesn't mean they aren't here," McKenzie said. "Odds are they're around. Neal will keep in contact. With any luck, Katie is still in the electrical gallery." He scanned the faces.

"What about Harry?" Ismet asked.

"At the moment, he's not our priority," McKenzie said.

Ismet nodded.

McKenzie and Ismet disappeared into the pipe tunnel. Mallory and Neal lowered the hatch cover level then moved into the hallway. She glanced into a cavernous room that dwarfed any large room she had ever been in. The humming generators sounded like giant bumblebees, but these weren't zipping from nectar to nectar. The generators were shielded behind a legion of self-standing electrical switches and control equipment.

"Let's set up shop here. It might be a good place to observe any activity," Neal said.

Mallory agreed in theory, but deep within she was scared to death.

Neal took up a spot on the east side, concealed behind a large self-standing control box fixated with dials and flashing red lights. Mallory stationed herself along the west side next to a set of stairs that serviced an upper-level catwalk. From Meadowlark's description, the control room was below the catwalk about halfway down the hall. If anyone exited the room, she could tell where they were headed. From her vantage point, she could see Neal, who gave a thumbs-up. Even with the generator hum, she swore she could hear the pounding of her heart echoing loudly in the high space. She wanted to be with McKenzie looking for Katie, but consented to Ismet's wish because it made sense. If she rushed in and showed her face, how would Katie react? It was a situation that no one could forecast; after all, what kind of interrogation had Katie been subjected to? McKenzie explained different methods of prisoner interrogations and torture. Ismet would be a reassuring face, Mallory a confusing one.

She peered out from behind the stair. There, at the far end of the hall, a man leisurely walked her way, a rifle slung over his shoulder. *One of the guards.* If he passed the stair she hid behind, she would be seen. She spotted Neal and raised a hand. Her wave caught his attention. Pointing down the hall, she played a game of charades. Neal nodded an understanding that someone was headed their direction.

She noticed a large trash container along the west side, ten or fifteen yards away. That would be a better place to hide. A glance at the catwalk above didn't reveal movement. Meadowlark's lecture indicated an assortment of auxiliary equipment rooms opened off the catwalk. Despite no sign of guards, she couldn't rule out any personnel above her.

She placed a finger on her lips and held her breath. She made her move, dashing behind the trash container.

CHAPTER 42

McKenzie glanced at his watch. Time was running out. He felt entombed in the pipe tunnel—a claustrophobic subterranean concrete hallway thankfully lit by an even spacing of cage-protected lights mounted to the walls. Overhead pipes ran the length seven feet above the five foot wide tunnel. It was an industrial tomb, no doubt, and if the lights went out…

He moved briskly. His senses began to transition from the constant hum of the generators to a mounting vibration. Off to their left, another tunnel emerged.

"That services the first turbine," Ismet remarked impatiently.

"Stay here, I'll look." He could see the man was on edge. He didn't blame him. He'd be anxious too, if he was in the Assyrian's shoes, knowing that the life or death of someone close to you, someone you deeply loved, hung in the balance. Even though he didn't know Katie Haley, he could relate to Ismet's emotional rollercoaster. He felt certain Mallory Lowe would create a similar emotional undercurrent.

He shuddered.

Every minute was critical.

He moved along the service tunnel for twenty feet until it ended at a metal landing and a short set of stairs heading down. The vibration was now a droning, repetitive shudder. McKenzie saw the metal stair railings and treads dancing fiercely, caught in the natural frequency emitted by the turbine. Grabbing a rail, he stepped onto the landing and raced down the short flight of stairs. There in front, a stout vertical steel shaft rose from below and disappeared into a large circular steel cover and into the generator above. Below, the hidden fans of the turbine whirled at a high revolution. Even with the mechanical whine and wicked vibration, he could sense the thousands of gallons of high-pressure water rushing through the turbine, spinning the shaft at a furious pace.

A feeling of insignificance settled upon him. To be surrounded by the powerful forces of nature harnessed by man and the crushing force of over four hundred feet of hydrostatic pressure morphing into electricity was dazzling. Engineering aside, he had to consider the explosives—waiting to be detonated. That overrode everything else. But what if Meadowlark had not been totally truthful about the timing? Could it blow sooner? If he was crazy enough to destroy such a valuable piece of infrastructure, how could he be trusted in the first place?

He'd seen enough. Backtracking, he found Ismet impatiently waiting where he left him. They moved with speed down the tunnel, checking out the next two turbine service areas.

McKenzie again glanced at his wristwatch. Time was moving too fast. They had to hurry if they were to find Katie in time. On the wall to McKenzie's left, they found an opening covered with a metal grill.

Ismet stopped and beamed his flashlight through the grill. "Utility chase to the electrical gallery."

McKenzie looked. "Meadowlark said it was a thirty foot crawl, another grill at the other end through the floor above. I'll do a quick check of the other turbines. You remove the grill. I'll be quick."

Ismet gave him an anxious look. "Hurry."

He nodded—hopeful Ismet would keep it together. This was not the time to have his accomplice go off course emotionally. He turned down the tunnel and accelerated his pace. He lowered his guard, letting his arm hang loose at his side and off the butt of the Beretta. Once he was sure no one else was present, they would scramble through the utility chase and locate Katie.

A loud noise broke the silence. A man appeared some forty feet away. There was surprise written all over his face. Banging a toolbox he was carrying into the wall, he yelled something incoherent, his eyes settling on the pistol holstered on McKenzie's belt. Dropping the toolbox, he fled.

McKenzie took off at a sprint after him. The man had no place to go other than the stairs to the last turbine. At the far end, he saw him fishing for a key from many dangling from his belt. McKenzie realized where he was from the blueprints Meadowlark showed them only a couple hours earlier. He was at the penstock control room. If the maintenance man got inside, he'd likely be able communicate with the main control room alerting the guards. At that moment, the man found the key and inserted it into the lock.

"Stop!" McKenzie yelled, pointing his Beretta.

The man was too fast, already inside. McKenzie reached the door. It was locked. Aiming the Beretta, he stepped back and pumped two rounds into the lock. With one leg, he wound up and kicked the door open. Ten feet straight ahead, he saw the man drop the phone from his ear. His sweat-covered face magnified his panic. McKenzie raced over, aiming the Beretta at the man's head, grabbed the phone and listened. Turkish gibberish came from the other end. The man turned to run, but McKenzie swung the Beretta, connecting solid against the man's temple. He dropped like a swatted fly.

Sari popped the cap off the hypodermic just as the control operator rushed in from the adjacent room. "We have trouble in the penstock control room, intruders!"

Dropping the needle, Sari's eyes brimmed with rage. "Sound the alarm. Secure the building."

Within a few seconds, the alarm sounded in a series of sharp shrills. He pulled the Makarov pistol from his waistband and shoved the muzzle against Meadowlark's temple. "Your friends have arrived. What is their plan?"

Meadowlark stayed mute. He stared at Sari vengefully.

Sari pulled a walkie-talkie off the wall and clipped it to his waistband. "Keep him covered," he said, nodding to the guard in the room. Fleeing, he ran across the generator hall towards the electrical gallery. His only thoughts now were with the girl, Katie Haley. Sari knew Ismet would be anxious to rescue his damsel. Encouraged, he felt an overwhelming joy. A grin creased his face. *This is good, so good.*

Talk about having the bastard delivered to him on a silver platter.

The pulsating alarm shook Mallory to the core. *What the hell*—she could only guess that something went wrong. But her first concern was the guard coming down the aisle. She peered around the trash bin. He was out of sight. Gathering her wits, she scrambled back toward the stair, the siren still blasting. She saw Neal, hand signaling from behind a control panel. He moved her direction, threading his way between self-standing electrical panels.

"What happened?" Mallory asked.

"I don't know, but this place should be swarming with guards."

"What about the others?"

"Lane contacted me. Said they had a problem with a maintenance man. He wants us back in the pump room. We must keep it secure, so they can have an avenue to flee after they find Katie. Otherwise, we're screwed."

Mallory gritted her teeth. She was deeply agitated.

The loud pop and the twang of a bullet ricocheted off the stair stringer. She recoiled. On impulse, she slipped underneath the stairs. They had been spotted. Her eyes caught the figure above on the mezzanine, a gun in his hands readying another shot.

A shot came, but not from the gunman. She poked her head out for a closer look. The lifeless guard hung over the handrail. She glanced at Neal, gun drawn. He tucked the gun back in his waist and spoke, his earpiece vibrated. "Lane, do you copy?"

There was no response.

"Lane, do you copy?" he asked again.

Her thoughts of Lane were lost in the sound of stomping feet coming down the aisles from the opposite end of the generator hall. In the dim light, she made out two guards, each carrying what appeared to be assault rifles. She staggered backwards, reeling from the sight of their firepower. Her sweaty hand pulled out the Beretta. It felt like a lead weight shaking in her hand. This was not part of the plan.

A barrage of bullets screamed, slamming into the equipment and pinging off the stairs. She looked for Neal, but he was gone. Panicked, she turned to make a dash for the pump room when she saw Neal at the far end of the room near the control panel. Several pops came from his gun. He'd spotted movement as well.

She spun around and sprinted down the hall. An indistinct figure dashed behind a generator. She rubbed her eyes and then caught movement on the catwalk above their position. The sound of voices echoed down. She watched as three men scurried behind the railing toward Neal. He was a sitting duck.

"Neal, the catwalk!" she screamed. "I'll cover you."

He waved an understanding.

I'll cover you, she thought. Did she really say that! She taught math, not armed conflict. Faking it, she triggered several rounds at the movement, ducked back behind the stairs and breathed fitfully. Her heart pumped like never, the adrenalin sprinting through her veins.

A salvo of bullets pinged into the metal treads and the concrete floor surrounding her—the response that she expected. She checked her back. The stair gave adequate protection from those on the catwalk. With her attention anxiously skipping from the aisle to the catwalk, she waited—and prayed for this nightmare to be over.

By the time McKenzie caught up with Ismet, he had finished prying the grill loose from the chase.

"What happened?" Ismet's voice was strained.

"We had company. Before I could silence him, he alerted those upstairs."

Tension etched Ismet's face. His eyes wavered, first searching the utility chase and then back along the tunnel towards the pump room. Perspiration beaded his forehead.

"Let's go get her while we still have a chance," McKenzie said.

Ismet didn't hesitate. He jumped up and shimmied into the chase, his flashlight illuminating the narrow space. McKenzie stuck the Beretta in the holster and followed. Warm air blew across his face. He knew they were in a precarious spot, waiting to be caught—or killed. If Neal and Mallory had the pump room secured, there was a slim chance of getting out alive.

Sari unlocked the door to the electrical gallery. Redoubling his concentration, he entered, his Makarov out front. Immediately, he felt the stifling heat of the electrical bus ducts overhead. He swore he could see the heat radiating. The alarms kept pulsating, muted by the concrete wall separating the generator hall and the electrical gallery.

He could hear gunfire coming from the generator hall. Let his men handle the intruders. His task was to make sure they didn't find the girl—not just yet. Ismet had his heart set on freeing her and now she would draw him in. He imagined the scenario: Ismet watching his lover die. The anguish would be devastating. After Ismet begged for her life, he would shoot her and watch him agonize and grieve. And then he would shoot the bastard through his broken heart. He couldn't imagine a more satisfying ending.

He walked under the ducts, checking each nook and cranny. He sidestepped a large air handler mounted on a concrete pedestal. Circling, he hustled behind a large piece of metal ductwork where a door was hidden. He inserted the key and opened it slowly. Visible through the gap, he saw the woman on the floor, shackled to a concrete column.

Shoving the Makarov back in his waistband, he eased inside. Here the sound of the alarm and intermittent gunfire was muffled, the concrete walls buffering out the noise. He walked over to the woman, her head bowed as if she was sleeping. He felt a warm rage build. He kicked her. Her head jerked. She looked up with hollow eyes. Her spirit had submitted long ago. He kept staring. There was no pity. In his world, she was a pawn, an inferior, and would be dead soon.

Where was Ismet? Certainly, the gunfire had to be a diversion, a distraction to provide cover for the bastard in his quest to reach his lover. He went back to the door. He would leave it closed, but unlocked—just in case. Agitated, he grumbled. *Where the hell are you Ismet?*

Ismet pushed the grill open and exited the chase. McKenzie crawled out and accidentally kicked the grill, listening to the scrape and clang on the concrete. He caught Ismet's bulging eyes. "Fuck," slipped from McKenzie's lips. On edge, he looked along the length of the long, narrow room. The good news: the gallery appeared empty.

Meadowlark told them he thought Katie would be held in a storage room midway down the gallery. They moved cautiously. The heat was suffocating. And if there were guards watching Katie, how did they manage the heat?

After a minute, they heard the whining of motors and fans coming from the air handler. Oversized metal ducts attached to both ends, diminishing in size as it fed a system of louvers with fresh air. But it didn't seem to be doing the job. It was stifling as hell. Trying to regain focus, he wiped another round of sweat from his face.

He took a deep breath and squeezed between the air handler and the wall. Sure enough, as Meadowlark had described, there was the door. It was closed and there was no sign of any guards. He signaled Ismet. McKenzie saw relief in the Assyrian's eyes, yet it was tempered by apprehension. What would they find behind the door?

He grabbed the handle and surprisingly, it turned. Opening it a few inches, he peered through the crack. There, in the middle of the room, someone was splayed on the floor. He had barely swung the door fully open before Ismet rushed past him into the room. He bent down next to Katie.

"Katie, it's me!" he cried. He lifted her head and gazed into her glazed eyes.

McKenzie eyed Katie for the first time. She appeared drugged. He noticed her hands behind her, shackled to the column with a chain.

Ismet kept talking to reassure her, caressing her face. McKenzie knew he had forgotten the danger. They had to get her free, and then get the hell out of here. He reached down and examined her hands. They were clasped with a pair of ordinary looking handcuffs looped through a locked chain encircling the concrete column.

"Ismet, help me get her to stand."

Ismet nodded.

McKenzie noticed an IV taped in crook of her elbow. He carefully peeled the tape away and withdrew the port. Standing, he reached under her arms and slowly lifted her to her feet. He was relieved to see that she was starting to comprehend. Her eyes fell on Ismet.

"I want...to go home," she murmured.

Ismet pulled her close and encircled her fragile body with his arms. "Stay strong," he reassured.

McKenzie pulled her hands away from her body. Reaching for his Beretta with the suppressor, he placed the barrel against the end of the small chain that attached to each cuff. "Don't move." Taking aim, he triggered a shot. A muted pop echoed in the room. Reaching down, he freed her from the chain. "Let's move, now."

The door banged shut.

Sari appeared, eyes blazing, his Makarov pointed at them.

"Such a pity—now more prisoners."

CHAPTER 43

Basel

Coulomb, dozing in his office, clamped his fingers around the phone on the first ring. "Shelby, is that you?"

"We got 'em. Found him ready to board an early morning train for Zurich. He's as nervous as a twit pie. I think he'll talk."

"Get his ass over here." He hung up. Never had he felt so tense. He looked at his hands and found himself trembling.

Thirty minutes later, Marotte walked into Coulomb's sixth floor office, followed by Wallace. He looked worn out, a mirthless mask covering his face.

"Vincent, sit down," Coulomb said.

Nervous, Marotte took a seat, fidgeting with his fingers.

"You understand why you're here, don't you Vincent?" Coulomb asked. Wallace poured a tumbler full of whiskey and handed it to the attorney.

Marotte took the offering and downed it in two gulps. "I-I 'm not sure."

"Shelby tells me you were trying to leave Basel quite suddenly."

"Well, I—"

Coulomb zeroed in. "Don't jack us around, Vincent."

Marotte's face turned pale.

"We're waiting for an explanation," Coulomb said.

"I-I have a problem. I gamble—" He stared at the ceiling. "I'm on a losing streak, can't shake it. The money I borrowed, no—no, I lie—I took it from the firm. Be assured, I plan to return it. If they find out, I'll be fired, maybe go to jail. It's just a short term loan, I promise."

"Why were you leaving in such a hurry?" Coulomb asked.

"I need to clear my head, change my luck." He bent over, rubbing the tumbler raw.

Coulomb traded glances with Shelby. This was totally unexpected and not what he expected to hear. "Talk to me Vincent, and I may be able to help you."

Marotte's eyes widened. "What do you need? I'll do it, anything." He took a deep breath.

"Forget the indiscretions with your law firm for now," Coulomb continued. "You are aware of the dissolution of our relationship with Harry Meadowlark. Since he is no longer involved in the affairs of Möbius, it is of the utmost importance clients cease contact with him immediately."

Wallace took the tumbler, poured another shot, and handed it to Marotte.

Marotte took another gulp. "Oh, of course. Attorney-client relations—we have stringent rules. I would never do anything that would compromise our relationship. Möbius is our most valued."

Coulomb gazed at him steadily. "Then, what were you doing removing something from a safety deposit box in Harry Meadowlark's name?"

"Well, I—"

"I am at a loss as to why one of our attorneys is dealing with a defector behind our back."

Marotte drained the remaining whiskey, choking as it went down. "There—there's no impropriety here," he said, beads of sweat popping up on his forehead. "Mr. Meadowlark signed the box over to me. Check my signature on the register."

"Vincent," Coulomb snapped. "Why would he sign over his box to you? Is there something inside, something valuable?"

Marotte wiped more sweat from his forehead. "It was a gift—for me, just for me."

"Just for you?"

"Yes, for me—to use when the time was right." Marotte's voice shrilled. "It—it could be worth a lot of money."

"What is it, Vincent?"

Marotte looked from Coulomb to Wallace and back to Coulomb. "It's—it's the key."

Coulomb couldn't believe his good fortune. He glanced at Wallace, back at Marotte, and steadied his stare. A slow grin emerged on his face. "What kind of key, Vincent?"

Marotte hesitated, unsure of his words. Finally, he submitted. "It's Mr. Meadowlark's notebook. It's the key to optimum betting, adjusting your bet amount based upon the card count, you know, finding the ten-rich decks. Mr. Meadowlark devised a system that has a higher winning expectation than any other card-counting system I've seen, better than Hi-Opt II, better than KO, and even better than the Wong Halves level three system." Marotte wiped more sweat from his brow.

Coulomb's elation had turned to dead weight.

"Card-counting?" Wallace scoffed.

Marotte continued. "Blackjack. Mr. Meadowlark's method is the best and much simpler, although I haven't finished testing it."

Coulomb regained his composure. "So…what did you deposit in the other safety deposit box, the one at UBS?"

"The notebook." He looked meekly between Coulomb and Wallace. "It's the key, it's priceless, worth a lot of money—the casinos money someday."

CHAPTER 44

Tepecik Dam

The lights in the generator hall flickered out. A series of emergency lights came on, providing opacity amongst the cavernous shadows. Mallory had to escape her predicament—or die trying. Nausea hit her straight on, turning her anxiety into a bottomless pit of fear.

Suddenly, a spotlight came alive somewhere on the catwalk. The beam bounced around the hall, then settled on the stair. Frantic, she moved out of its glare. Rounds ripped into the exposed stairway, pinning her into a tight ball. She was trapped.

And then the fusillade ended. Broken by the constant whine of the generators, it was deathly quiet. A clink of metal came from the direction of the control room, loud; something heavy drew her attention. The operator of the spotlight swung the beam towards the racket. She bolted from under the stairs and cowered behind the trash bin providing her better protection. She heard the shuffle of footfall. A cacophony of automatic gunfire ripped from her side of the hall. The spotlight went dead. Peeking around, she caught a shadow fluttering like a flag across the nearest generator.

"Lady, you okay?" The voice sounded familiar.

Mallory relaxed her grip on the Beretta. "Harry?"

"Don't shoot."

The next moment, Meadowlark slid next to her. He was wheezing.

She searched his face, dimly lit by the emergency lighting. "Did you shoot out the light?"

He nodded.

She cast her eyes at him, all curious. "I never thought I'd see you again."

He took a deep breath, steadying himself. "You and me both, lady."

"Where'd they have you?"

"Tied up in the control room. The guard wasn't looking. I managed to unravel my bound hands. Don't exactly remember how, but I cold-cocked him with my fist." He flexed his fingers. "Damn, it still hurts."

Mallory noticed the rifle. "How'd you get that?"

"The guard's. I see you found your way inside."

"Fine, until they spotted us."

"What about Katie?"

"I can only hope," she said loosely. *I can only hope.* She slumped against the bin.

"Listen lady, you and your people need to get the hell out of here. There's only an hour left before this place blows to smithereens."

"Not without Katie."

He peered at her bluntly. "If they do get her out, we should all have our fucking heads examined."

McKenzie watched the man move from shadow into the room. He studied his movements, the way he waved the gun, the smoothness of his face, his effeminate mannerisms.

"Guns, on the floor," Sari commanded, stopping a few feet away. "And back away, slowly."

He bent over and laid the Beretta down. Ismet followed.

Sari stepped over and picked up Ismet's gun, stuffing it into his trouser waistband. He kicked the Beretta into the shadows. His eyes wandered from Katie to Ismet, then trailed back to McKenzie.

"You, I do not know. CIA, I would guess, from our little conflict a few hours ago."

McKenzie stayed silent.

"Oh, how is the saying—cat got your tongue?"

"Only long enough to figure you out."

Sari waved the Makarov. "Too late; I have you figured out." He looked at Ismet. "Where did you find such a joker? I thought you knew better than to associate with such morons."

"You have me," Ismet said. "Let these two go."

"Oh, you know me so well." He laughed playfully. "But we have things to do."

"This is no game," Ismet said loudly.

"Do not be so sure. This *is* a game, a game of life—and death."

McKenzie didn't like the tone of the conversation. Obviously, there was something between the two. Sari looked like a pantywaist, but proved he was a killer. That was confirmed earlier.

"Let her go," Ismet pleaded.

"Bastard!" Sari blasted. He pointed the gun at Ismet. "Now, you will make restitution."

McKenzie watched, helpless to do anything. The man was incensed, filled with a growing rage, his baby-like face had transformed into a killer's guise, savage eyes atop a vein-popping neck.

"Just as you have taken from me, I will take from you." Sari turned the gun on Katie.

Ismet leapt to shield Katie but the gunshot stopped him cold, the bullet whistling past his head.

McKenzie knew the next bullet would find someone and subsequently all three of them would be dead. He had to do something. It was now, or never.

He took a step forward. "Killing her will not solve your problem."

Sari bounced the gun between Ismet and McKenzie. "The only problems I have are the three of you."

"Don't believe it." McKenzie pointed at his watch. "In exactly forty-two minutes, this dam will be history. The explosives are well hidden, and the timer is ticking."

"Why would I believe such a thing?" Sari asked.

"You have Meadowlark; why don't you ask him?"

There was a hesitant look in Sari's eyes. Ismet seemed to understand.

"That has been the plan," Ismet broke in. "The clock is counting down."

Sari's eyes wavered. "You are lying. There is no way to sabotage the dam."

"Why don't you ask Ismet where the explosives are located?" McKenzie said.

"Let her go and I will tell you where," Ismet said. "Semtex, plastic explosives, you know what I talk about?"

He noticed the confusion in Sari's eyes. Just a slight distraction is all McKenzie needed.

Ismet took a step to the side. Sari took the bait and swung the Makarov in Ismet's direction. McKenzie didn't hesitate, rushing headlong toward Sari. But the Turk, small and nimble, anticipated the move, spun on his right foot like a matador, and with his free leg thrust a groin kick. Sensing Sari's martial arts skill, McKenzie deflected the kick and came back with an uppercut with his right elbow. Sari countered with a straight right arm, pivoted three hundred sixty degrees, and swung the barrel of his gun hard into McKenzie's temple. He dropped to the floor—blackness ensued.

"Don't get heroic," Sari said, swinging the barrel back as Ismet moved ready to pounce. "Now, you and the woman—out the door."

He forced Ismet and Katie out of the storage room. Reaching the door to the crest elevator, he punched the button and waited. He should have put a bullet in the CIA man; what was he thinking? He started to return when the soft whine of the elevator car increased and then the ding of a bell. The door opened. He didn't have time. He kept his attention riveted on his two prisoners.

"Inside," he demanded. He was going to savor every minute of their shortened lives, especially the part where Ismet watched his lover die. By the time the CIA man became a factor, if he were still alive, it would be too late.

McKenzie felt the side of his head where he took the blow. He had an excruciating headache. At least he wasn't bleeding. He pushed up on one knee and tried to focus. He had to admit, Sari's martial arts techniques were a stage above the Jujitsu he had learned in training. Struggling to his feet, he stumbled over to the door and leaned against the jamb. Head throbbing, he had to stay alert. Off in the distance, he heard the ding of a bell—*the elevator*.

Without a gun, what could he do? And then he remembered. His gun may still be somewhere in the room. He turned a circle, blurred eyes searching. He spotted the Beretta in a far corner and felt relief. He picked it up and felt the comforting weight in his hand. His head was on fire—headache and all. He left the storage room and raced towards the elevator. He pushed the button and it lit. Good, the elevator was on its way down. He could only hope he was in time. "Neal, do you have a copy?" he said adjusting the earpiece.

Mallory followed Meadowlark, crouched behind a large spool of sheet metal on a wooden pallet. Another two pallets lay nearby, filled with an assortment of steel plates and boxes of hardware. Thirty-feet away, cut in the west wall was a door. If they made a break for it, there was a good possibility they would attract gunfire—not a pleasant scenario.

"That's the door to the testing laboratory," Meadowlark said. "If we can get inside, there's a louver through which we may be able to escape. From there it's a concealed path behind a retaining wall to the penstock discharge, and then a ramble down river and away from here. If that doesn't work, we're fucked."

"That's assuming a lot," Mallory said. She didn't like the plan, not knowing about Katie and the others. There had to be a better way. They had very little weaponry compared to those who wanted them dead. Weapons or not, she wasn't trained in this kind of thing. The odds were against them.

Meadowlark leaned against the back of the spool. "If we get out of this, someone will have to tell Katie about Tom."

"I guess it's me."

Meadowlark's prying eyes kept her pinned.

"What's your problem?" she asked.

"*You,*" he said.

She recoiled.

"Why did Tom convince you to come?" He looked at her with analytical eyes. "Come to think of it, you and Katie do have a resemblance."

"Our eyes are similar; we've been told that. What difference does that make?"

"With Tom dead, she doesn't have anybody else, no other family that I'm aware of. She may just have *you.* Hell, she might even have the urge to track down her DNA, see what she's made of. You too, lady; what's in your genes that keeps you boring into danger?"

"What are you talking about?"

"Think about it. Why'd Tom drag you into this mess? Why you?"

Now, she was at a loss for words. What did Meadowlark know? He and Tom were good friends. Her mind muddled, she peeked over the top of the steel spool, aware she might be shot at. Just another risk. The strain was getting to her.

The movement was unexpected, a dull reflection off to her left on the catwalk. Something caught the nearest rays from one of the emergency lights. Mallory lowered her head just as an outburst of bullets pounded into the steel spool.

"What the hell you doing?" Meadowlark screamed. "They've seen you. Now they know we're here."

"What the hell are you going to do to get us out of here?" she shot back.

"All right, all right. We'll have to cover each other. I just checked the magazine on this weapon, maybe twenty rounds. You make a run for the door. "You up for it?"

"Not on your life."

"If that's the case, we stay here and fight to the finish, like *Custer's Last Stand.*" His eyes were lit with a pissed-off, unpredictable glow.

She looked away. How much longer? He seemed crazed and her head was aching, her body trembling all over. There was too much gunfire, too much chaos, too much…*too much*. Her mind shifted back to the others. Had they found Katie? Not knowing was agonizing. A glance at her watch confirmed time was running out.

But even with the immediate danger, she had to analyze things. Harry Meadowlark was the prime suspect—if only she could figure him out. He had left Möbius for unknown reasons, planned the destruction of a dam his company had built, and now had surrendered to the enemy to help them rescue Katie. But what really seemed to matter was what Ismet had told her in the tunnel.

"*Socrates*, tell me about it." she demanded.

Meadowlark twisted uneasy. He was visibly shaken. "Ismet has a big fucking mouth."

"It's your turn to talk. What's *Socrates*? You owe it to me. What's going on?"

"You already know everything."

She watched his face in the meager light. He looked uncomfortable.

"What about this *final* key?"

"That son of a bitch told you way too much."

Agitated, Mallory pressed on. "Look around, are we in a position to argue? If I'm going to die here, I goddamn want to know why."

"Lady, if you die here, it's your own damn fault."

She grabbed his arm and pulled him close. She let his eyes feel the wrath of her own. "The key—what about it?"

Meadowlark's face contorted. "It's hidden, right under Paul's fucking nose! It's a mystery why he can't find it. It was his idea; a key for each of us, a thoughtful security measure on his part—or so he thought. He has the other three keys, but they won't do any good unless he gets the fourth."

"And without the fourth key, *your* key, *Socrates* or whatever the hell doesn't happen. Is that right?"

"Yes, does that make you feel better? Now let's move on from the fucking key and find a way out of here." He pulled away from her grasp.

She didn't let up. "Where's the key, and what's it for?"

"You too! Christ, everyone wants the fucking key."

"Where is it?"

"You and Paul, mathematicians," he snickered. "All he has to do is use his head. He can't figure it out. I doubt you could, either."

"What is this, some kind of game between you two?"

"Yes, yes it is, always has been. Way back to our time at Berkeley we would always try to outdo the other. It was…our nature. Of course, I would usually win; but nevertheless, he did provide good competition. Now, I think he's lost it. For once, I wish he'd use his fucking head."

Her mind was in the crossfire. Why would he make this a game? None of this made any sense. It sounded as if Meadowlark wanted Coulomb to find this so-called key and was pissed he wasn't up to the challenge.

All through the generator hall, the emergency lights snuffed out. Mallory let out a gasp. They were killing the lights, whatever meager illumination they had grew dimmer. Then, it was totally dark, only a sliver of light came from the hallway that led to the pump room…and that was impossible to get to without being shredded by bullets. She wanted answers, but the desperation of their situation took precedence,

"We must move—now," he said. "They have night-vision. Stay here, we're dead. Reach the wall and feel your way along it. You'll find the door."

And then he was gone.

Mallory waited a few seconds after she heard Meadowlark shuffle off. The gunfire had ceased. Now it was her turn. With only the sound of her deep breathing, she blindly paced off close to twenty steps in the general direction with her arms reaching out front. Feeling along the wall, she worked to her left.

Nothing. Where was the door? Was she going the wrong way? Blind as a bat, her eyes didn't register anything. Panic reappeared—and then it skyrocketed as gunfire erupted.

She dove to the floor, not sure what to do. Sporadic gunfire continued, echoing throughout the immense hall. Tracers could be seen coming from the catwalk, and intermittent shots from the hallway to the pump room. Was Neal keeping them busy? At least she wasn't being targeted—yet. Crawling along the floor, she kept searching for the door, scratching, feeling her way along the wall like a blind woman reading braille. Even in the dark she kept her eyes wide open, on alert for any red laser dot that would find her and snuff her out.

She was close to giving up when her hand found the door. Fumbling around, she located the latch. She hesitated. *This may be the easy way out.* On the surface, odds were overwhelmingly stacked against her. Below the surface, she was committed to Katie. That would not be accomplished if she bailed.

With a sense of duty, she slid down, hoping that they hadn't spotted her with their night vision. For the next few seconds of eternity, she tried to figure out how the hell she had gotten into such a mess. She was shaken and fearful for her life, but her memory hadn't failed her yet. Wasn't she close to the electrical control equipment that provided Neal his protection? All she had to do was creep to her right before a bullet would find her. Crawling and shimmying her way, she could see a halo of light coming from the direction of the pump room.

No sense stretching the inevitable. She jumped up and rushed into the hallway. Several rounds slammed into the wall. An arm reached out and grabbed her as she flew by, pulling her to safety.

"I thought for sure I lost you," Neal said, releasing his grip. He triggered a couple of rounds into the dark. Spinning around, he yanked the empty magazine out and reached into his pocket for a fresh one. "Last one," he said, frustrated.

Mallory caught her breath. "What about the others; are they back?"

"Lane just made contact. Ismet and Katie were taken to the top of the dam, both now prisoners. He's going after them."

Mallory felt emptiness like none other. What would it take to have just a little bit of luck? It was as if their goal line kept shifting, getting insurmountable, like Coulomb's irrationals, those never-ending, non-repeating numbers marching to infinity.

"We have our own problem," Neal yelled. "The explosives, remember? My watch says we only have thirty minutes."

Mallory's felt defeated. But this didn't need to be; *deep down*, it didn't need to be.

"How do I get to the top of the dam?" she yelled.

Neal kept his eyes on the corridor leading to the generator hall. "You're not going; too risky."

"The hell I'm not. How do I get there?"

He shot a glance at Mallory. "The fastest way is the elevator, but stay behind me."

Mallory clutched the Beretta tight and raced after Neal.

CHAPTER 45

Heat still radiated from the high granite cliffs, still cooler than the stifling electrical gallery. Katie stumbled as she was pushed onto the crest of the dam. What was happening? She could hear voices. She remembered the needle and the cruel face that held it. The same man, barking orders—the man named Sari. Muscles aching and head still throbbing, she took slow, painful steps. The pain was intense, but there was a difference now; her mind no longer was swimming in circles, going in and out of consciousness. It was stabilizing. She took a wary breath and even with the discomfort, the night air was a welcome change. And the drugs, yes, the drugs…wearing off, her mind clearing. There was much to process.

"Here," Sari barked as they neared the west parapet. "Turn slowly. I want to see the lovers' faces."

"Kill us; it won't stop it," Ismet said, standing next to Katie. "Four o'clock is near."

"Your threat too late."

Katie started to recognize her surroundings—the mechanized penstock gate, the valve that controlled the water to the turbines. Directly below, several hundred feet were the explosives. Four o'clock—that was the plan.

"The dam will be destroyed," she said weakly.

Sari's wild brown eyes fell on Katie. "Oh, so your lover has come to her senses."

"Möbius will blame you once it blows," Ismet said.

Sari shook his head, his baby-face smile shone in the crest lights. "Lies! Do not insult me."

"Let her go."

Sari's smile twisted. "No. I have other plans."

"You have me; let her go!" Ismet raged.

Sari's smile disappeared. "We will play a little game first."

A vengeful expression forged on Sari's face. Now he was in power and would force Ismet to watch... *wretched, pitiless bastard.* Oh, how he had waited for this moment, this time, this one place to avenge his beloved father's death.

He glared at Katie...*wretched, pitiless bitch.* "You will now perform for your lover." He waved the gun and pointed at the parapet. "Get up on it!"

Katie had recovered enough from the effects of the drugs to feel the fear that was sweeping through her every fiber. The man was mad, deranged. She shook her head in contempt.

Ismet rushed Sari, but Sari anticipated it, firing a single shot. Ismet buckled over clutching his right arm. Blood trickled through his fingers.

Another guard appeared from the control tower but was waved back.

Katie turned to help Ismet. Sari shoved her back.

"Up on it!"

The pain in Katie's head was relentless. She again reached for Ismet. Sari fired another shot, striking Ismet. He stumbled and fell to the pavement, clutching his ankle, his face contorted with pain.

"The wall, bitch—now!"

Reeling with terror, Katie stretched her arm over the parapet, reluctant to take her eyes off Ismet. When she did, they floated out over the dam and settled on the pump house far below. With tears streaming down her cheeks, she pulled herself up onto the narrow parapet, trembling. Her thoughts were milky, bungled, compacted. A slight breeze flowed up the dam face, warm and sultry. She could hardly hear Sari's voice commanding.

"Now...stand up, *bitch*. Give us a dance; your lover is watching."

Dizziness and confusion took over. Maybe the drugs were returning, giving her much needed relief.

With trembling knees, she slowly stood up. Her pulse jackhammered, rearranging her equilibrium. She stared straight down the near-vertical face of the dam. The breeze intensified, ripping the tears from her face, misting them into the dark void. Her eyes rolled skyward, and she began to wobble...

McKenzie held his Beretta firmly with both hands. He didn't know who would be meeting him once the door opened. There were only two stops on the elevator, 1 and 2, and they were over four hundred feet apart. After a few seconds, the 2 lit up and there was a ding. He kept the Beretta pointed at the door.

The elevator door grated open.

Just as he stepped out, a guard twirled on the bridge, his assault rifle leveled. McKenzie pumped off a round. The man clutched his chest gasping. He fell over, lung-shot, unable to breath, blood frothing from his mouth. McKenzie steadied the pistol. A row of high lights followed the curve of the dam as it stretched away from his view. There had to be at least three or four guards patrolling the top, according to Meadowlark. One was dead. Where were the others?

He picked up the guard's weapon and dashed across the bridge onto the dam. The crest was roughly twenty-five-feet wide at this point. He gazed along the crest, only seeing about a quarter of the way to the far side.

Where the hell are they?

He cupped his ear and held his breath. They had nowhere else to go. Sure enough, voices ahead. As he moved forward, the voices grew louder. A gunshot echoed. *Oh Jesus!* And then—another gunshot popped. Slowly, he looked over the parapet, fearful of what he might find. The full curvature of the dam came into view. About a quarter of the way across, he saw a large gantry crane and a control tower. But what he saw across the way scared the hell out of him.

There was Katie on the parapet, walking the plank.

The first thing Mallory and Neal saw when they exited the elevator was the man sprawled out on the bridge face down, dead. Shaking, her emotions spun out of control—colliding, crashing like a particle accelerator gone mad. With Lane a few minutes ahead of them, she hoped the next body she found would not be his. And what about Katie?

"You stay here," Neal ordered, "while I check out the area behind the control tower." Circling to the other side of the dam, he raced quickly to the tower.

Mallory watched Neal disappear behind the structure. She kept creeping forward, following the curve of the parapet towards the center of the crest, knowingly disobeying Neal's direct order.

McKenzie tried to figure out his next move. He didn't want to put Katie in further danger than he was witnessing. One thing he couldn't do was stand pat. He took off at a run following the curvature of the dam. The starry night disappeared as he closed in on the brightly lit steel framework over the penstock crane pit. His eyes swept the area from the control tower to the west parapet looking for guards, hoping he wouldn't be spotted. It would behoove Möbius to have security in place not only in the powerhouse but high along the crest. So far, there was none. He looked around and spotted a small pickup parked next to the tower. He knelt to catch his breath. Voices carried from somewhere on the other side. He crept to the front of the pickup and looked beyond the bumper to where he thought he had seen Katie. One of the small spillway buildings blocked his view. If he was to get closer, he would be seen by whoever was behind the gantry crane. He didn't have time to analyze. He had to get to where Sari had control of Katie.

Rising, he rushed headlong toward the voices, startling the two guards. He pumped two rounds dropping one guard; the remaining guard disappeared behind a concrete wall.

He didn't have time to readjust. The guard reared above the wall and started shooting, an assault weapon spraying bullets his direction. Ducking back behind a building, he had adequate protection, but had to get to Katie and Ismet. He felt the sweat trickle down his back.

Suddenly, the guard made a run across the crest. McKenzie didn't wait; he pointed and pressed off several rounds. The man jerked in stride and fell lifeless. Taking advantage of the opportunity, McKenzie rushed to within thirty yards of Katie. Sari came into view. He tightened his viewpoint, keeping the Beretta aimed. The Turk stared back, pulled Katie off the parapet, and held her in front in a chokehold. The muzzle of the Makarov was pressed against her temple.

"Drop it, or I will kill her!" he demanded, glaring at McKenzie.

McKenzie surveyed the scene. Ismet lay on the ground behind them. He was still alive, crawling slowly. He was glad Katie was off the parapet; in her distraught state, no telling the outcome.

"You kill her. I kill you, simple as that," McKenzie yelled back.

"You are a fool. You will soon be surrounded by my men. Drop the gun!"

Damn if he didn't have a point. Right now, he was in a Mexican standoff. His eyes kept floating to Ismet who was on his knees now, pushing himself up, slowly rising to his feet. He had to time this perfectly. If he lowered his gun, Sari would certainly shoot. Ismet seemed ready to rush Sari, even in his injured state.

Timing…is everything.

Sari didn't notice Ismet's movement. McKenzie lowered his gun slightly, and just as he anticipated, Sari rotated his. At the same instant, Ismet crashed into Sari, knocking him off balance. Katie went flying, striking the concrete as Sari triggered a shot. It sailed wide, hitting the corner of the building. McKenzie backed away, fragments of concrete peppering his face. He squinted, working his eyelids, teardrops struggling to wash out the debris. Blinking wildly, he saw a blurred Sari and Ismet entwined and rolling on the ground. McKenzie raised his pistol. He dare not fire; his vision was one large distortion. He kept rubbing his eyes, globules of tears slowly dislodging the particles.

Sari recognized McKenzie's dilemma. He fired, but not at McKenzie. Ismet's head exploded with a violent reverberation that rang out all along the crest of the dam.

Katie cried out, a painful shrill echoing throughout the canyon.

Sari laughed out loud as he walked in McKenzie's direction, sensing an opening. Eyes blind and in pain, McKenzie raised his gun, but it was too late. Sari kicked it from his hand and pressed the barrel into the side of his head.

"You die too, moron."

McKenzie heard a gunshot. He jerked at the sound. He was still alive. Sari's androgynous face froze and twisted into the epitome of disbelief. The Turk stared into space and pitched forward, slamming his head onto the hard concrete.

McKenzie tried to regain his composure, tears finally washing the last painful fragments from his eyes. Mallory in a blur, a gun clutched tightly in both hands, came into view.

Mallory couldn't control her pulse. Her hands shook, and she struggled for a breath. She walked slowly, the Beretta still pointed at Sari who lay dead. His smooth baby-face was plastered on the concrete; his outstretched hand still held the Makarov. She looked at the gun in her own hand, as if it had magically materialized, then handed it to McKenzie.

He took it with a grateful acceptance.

Neal ran onto the dam crest from underneath the crane gantry. He caught up with McKenzie and lowered his gun.

A few feet away, Mallory saw Katie, Ismet's bloody head cradled in her arms. She rocked ever so slightly, gently, like a mother caressing her baby, back and forth. The scene was gray and white, the pole-high lights barely adding depth and clarity to the two forms. Tears streamed down Katie's cheeks mixing with the blood on her hands. Mallory stood transfixed, wanting to rush over and wrap Katie in an embrace. She felt tears form in her own eyes, matching those visible on Katie's cheeks; her Katie, the young girl from so long ago. Now was not the time.

McKenzie saw the pickup and ran over to it, turned the key—nothing. He turned it again and it roared to life.

"We need to get the hell out of here. Now, before the dam blows!"

Mallory heard his urgency. Together with Neal, they placed Katie into the truck. There was no resistance. Her eyes were vacant and dazed as Mallory joined her in the back seat. A moment later, McKenzie gunned the pickup and raced across the crest, nearly running over another guard. The pickup crashed through the entrance gate and climbed the switchback away from the mayhem, fishtailing up the road chiseled in the cliff face.

Mallory craned her neck to take one last look, when a loud, muffled boom echoed throughout the gorge. McKenzie stopped the pickup. She hopped out and wiggled up to the edge of the cliff to look down onto the once placid reservoir, now awash with a turbulent slashing of waves and smoke rising from bubble bursts next to the dam. McKenzie and Neal crowded next to her. They watched in awe as a whirlpool formed behind the dam, swirling, a maelstrom in the making. The lights along the crest flickered out right after reflecting every new forming swirl, black as night, silvery as metal, like a black hole determined to draw in the nighttime stars.

Mallory thought about what Meadowlark had said—it would be a slow, weakening process. She could only hope he was right, wondering if he had escaped.

By the time they reached the top of the gorge, the immense panorama of the Milky Way appeared, stretching into a welcome arc across the sky. No one spoke. Mallory looked at Katie, whose eyes were red and swollen. It was obvious she didn't recognize Mallory. Why should she?

She had just experienced hell.

C oulomb had to think logically. Just like one of the axioms of arithmetic: if a = b and b = c, then a = c. Simple and to the point. It followed with Harry. If he was saying one thing, it usually meant another, and then one could infer what he really meant. Maybe his hints were small talk. *Its right under your ever-loving egotistical ass*, he had mocked.

Coulomb walked briskly over to his desk. A smile crept across his face. Of course, both he and Harry were mathematicians first; both had shared a common goal of a successful Möbius. Just as it was three centuries ago, he and Harry were each playing out a logical drama, both assuming the role of one of the Bernoulli brothers. *It's you and me bro...* Harry played the part of Johann very well: jealous, egotistical, overachieving anything Jakob has done. But Jakob never submitted, and neither would Coulomb. He would never give in. In fact, he would have the last laugh.

His eyes glowed with the certainty of a man possessed. It was right under his nose—it had to be. Why hadn't he thought of this before? Where else would Harry conceive of a hiding place except in the theater of his mind? And it was there, the Bernoulli brothers Jakob and Johann, still competing head to head after all these centuries.

CHAPTER 47

Over Northern Turkey

I t had been less than thirty minutes since the C-12 Huron took off from the NATO training center and set course for Basel. Mallory accepted the can of Coca-Cola from the airman and moved past McKenzie and Neal to the back row where Katie sat stone-faced, wrapped in a blanket. How would she process Ismet's death? How would she react when she heard about her father? That would have to wait.

She sat down next to Katie, pausing for a few moments. "How're you doing?" she asked gently. She knew the feeling of having a loved one taken from you tragically, of never being able to finish telling them everything you wanted them to know.

Katie faced her, battered and overwhelmed, blood still on her clothes. "I didn't know it was you. Why would you be here?"

She handed Katie the Coke. "Your favorite; maybe this will help."

Katie clasped the can in her hands. "You remembered?"

"Always."

Katie's mouth twitched. "Glad you're here."

"Your father asked me to come," she managed to say.

"You've seen him?"

"He asked me to find you."

Katie nodded. "I know he's been worried. I don't blame him. I guess I would like to see him and apologize."

Mallory returned a somber nod, knowing Katie would never have the chance.

"Who are these people?" Katie asked.

Mallory looked to the front of the cabin. "They're American agents—CIA."

Katie blinked. "I think I'd like to get some sleep."

"Let me get you a wet cloth to wash up a bit."

"No, I'm fine," she said, rubbing her blood-stained arms. "I'll wash up later. I just need to close my eyes."

Mallory stood and walked slowly to a seat in the front of the plane next to McKenzie. She glanced at Neal, sleeping in a seat across the aisle, then back to McKenzie. It was close to two o'clock in the afternoon and none of them had had any sleep for what seemed to be an eternity.

"How'd it go?" he whispered.

"She has a lot of strength. I didn't tell her about her father."

McKenzie nodded.

She sat down, having every reason to believe that the last ounce of fortitude she could muster in finding Katie alive had come to an end. But there was a little bit of tail-between-her-legs that was likely to take center stage.

"I went crashing into your world half-baked, unconscious of what my meddling would do to your operation," she said, placing a hand on McKenzie's arm. "You had every reason to send me away. If and when we get back to the States—if you throw me in jail, I'd understand. I can deal with that, but I want *you* to know…thank you, thank you for saving Katie's life."

McKenzie gazed into her eyes. "I don't think I've ever met anyone more in-your-face, impulsive, and determined in my life. But I don't think jail is justified. You were instrumental. Meadowlark did tell us there are corrupt IFC members. He has their names."

She shook her head. "I wonder if he got out.

"Don't we all."

"I hate to add to your burden, but there's a connection between Tom Haley's murder and Meadowlark's defection.

He grimaced uneasily. "I'm afraid to hear it."

"Ismet told me about a big operation Möbius is planning. Meadowlark affirmed it. It's code-named *Socrates*. I still remember Ismet telling me it was something *deadly*."

"What the hell is it?"

"I couldn't get it out of Meadowlark, but I don't think it's a workshop on ancient Greek philosophical teachings. What I did get out of him is this: there are four keys that are needed to put this *Socrates* into motion." She continued to fill him in on the four irrational numbers and how she believed each one was a calling card for the four major players. "Coulomb has control of three of the keys; he needs the fourth—the one Meadowlark has hidden."

"If what you say is true, we need to find it before Coulomb does."

"Meadowlark is playing a game with Coulomb. In fact, he said he's disappointed Coulomb is not up to the challenge."

"What kind of game?

Mallory shook her head. "I don't think it's as simple as tic-tac-toe. Listen, if we don't get some sleep, we'll never be able to figure it out," she said, touching her dried lips.

McKenzie stared at her, fighting the urge. He succumbed, leaned in, and kissed her on the cheek, then sat back and closed his eyes.

A euphoric shiver rippled down her body, a brief pause of her beating heart. She levered her seat back, tried to forget about something called *Socrates*. For now, she smiled and dreamt of a kiss that lingered.

Coulomb stormed into David Wyss's office at the Basel Museum of Mathematics and Science and tossed a sign on his desk. "Put it on the front door. This museum is now closed!" He headed for the exhibit area.

Wyss looked at the sign. "Closed, what do you mean? What's the reason?"

Coulomb turned in midstride. "Send everyone home." He strode out the door, followed by Wallace. Wyss reluctantly trailed after them, sign in hand. "Why are we closed?"

Coulomb didn't answer. His pulse raced with excitement as he walked through the exhibits, a display of historical virtuosity at every doorway. He strolled over to the Bernoulli display, the wax figure of Johann standing behind his brother Jakob. The Bernoullis, like himself and Meadowlark—always challenging one another, a constant game of competition, always in search of one-upmanship.

Wallace strode next to Coulomb. "I see a common thread between these brothers and you and Harry. Ya'll have behaved as if in some sort of sibling rivalry. I know what motivates you. Harry, I'm not so sure."

"You know him as well as I do. You must have an inclination?"

Wallace looked at Coulomb then back at the exhibit. "I think he found morality. *Socrates* drove him into exile."

Coulomb nodded. "Maybe, but his defection may well be his downfall." He turned and hurried toward the next exhibit.

Wallace filed after him. "Could this be the spot?"

Coulomb looked at the descriptive board that explained *The Basel Problem*. It appalled him to think this exhibit still took space in the museum—Meadowlark's prized mathematical problem. If it wasn't an integral part of the mathematical history of Basel, he would have had it removed long ago. Maybe later, it could be emphasized as a lesser historical episode.

"Touching, isn't it?" he remarked. "While we all picked our favorite irrationals, symbols that signify the never-ending string of Möbius successes, Harry chose this one, $\pi^2/6$. We should have recognized at that moment that he was the black sheep."

Wallace stared stoically at the placard. "And now we live with it."

Coulomb muttered under his breath, "And Euler may be hiding what we are looking for." He moved over in front of the Euler diorama. Once he gave the order, he knew the curator would be livid.

"Shelby, be so kind as to remove Mr. Euler's head."

Wallace stepped over the display rope and moved to the sitting figure. He reached around the mathematician's neck and ripped the laced jabot away from the shirt.

Wyss darted over, his face aghast. "What, you can't be serious! These wax figures took months to make at extreme cost. I won't let you destroy it."

Coulomb stepped in front of Wyss restraining him. "We will do as we damn well please. Do you forget, David, who pays the bills?"

"But, the display—"

Coulomb released his grip, staring firmly at the curator without contempt. "Shelby, you may continue."

Wyss' anguished face turned red with shock.

Grabbing the wax head with both hands, Wallace twisted it sideways until it snapped loose from the steel framed body. Examining the interface and inside the head, he looked at Coulomb. "Nothing here."

"Check everywhere," Coulomb said. "Examine his clothes, wig, the frame—don't give up, it's here!"

Wyss could only stand by stunned, watching Wallace tear into the wax figure of probably the greatest mathematician the world had ever known. The head was discarded, the crème-colored silken shirt ripped from the steel frame, wax hands tossed aside, shoes and trouser pockets searched and dropped in a pile. After a grueling five minutes, the unparalleled Leonhard Euler lay on the floor, a waste pile of wax, fabric, and metal.

Wallace frowned at Coulomb and shook his head. There was no key.

Fuming, Coulomb directed Wallace to tear into the Bernoulli brothers. Maybe Harry's bizarre twist of humor was meant to sidetrack him. Maybe it was Harry's fierce competition with him, like the Bernoulli's, that required he hide it amongst the two.

Wyss could not help himself. He lifted a leg over the exhibit rope to stop Wallace when Coulomb shouted, "Back off, David!"

Whirling at the powerful voice, Wyss stared in fear. Coulomb held the Glock, pointed straight at him. Retracting his leg, he slunk away. Wallace continued his demolition, working his way through every nook and cranny of the Bernoulli wax figures, body parts and stuffing tossed haphazardly on the floor, like the remains of the Scarecrow from *The Wizard of Oz*. Again, he looked over at the Frenchman. "Nothing here."

"Do not miss anything." Coulomb raged.

Wallace immediately tore into the bookcase, flipping through the old leather-bound volumes, chucking them at will onto the floor. Not finding it, he pushed the bookcase over to see what was behind.

Nothing.

The enraged look on Coulomb's face said it all. He looked between the two displays, the heaped piles of shredded wax effigies. Then he remembered another thing that Meadowlark's e-mail said. *This is child's play.* He looked back at the Euler diorama and spied the two wax children playing under the desk. With the slaughterous expression of a Nazi medical experimenter, he stepped over the exhibit rope and tore into the wax figures himself. He gouged their eyes and gutted their torsos, dismembered arms and legs, wildly shredding any resemblance of what they once were. He left the discarded pieces in an appalling pile —still, nothing.

Fifteen minutes ago it didn't matter whether Meadowlark was dead or alive. It mattered now. Time was the enemy if *Socrates* did not commence within the next forty-eight hours.

CHAPTER 49

Basel

A t 6:04 in the evening Mallory woke from a well-needed sleep as the C-12 Huron touched down. She and Katie were whisked off to CIA *Operations*. After a shower and a fresh change of clothes, compliments of the U.S. government, Mallory joined McKenzie, grateful for the coffee and the splendid view of Basel. Across the Rhine, the last rays of the setting sun glinted off the mix of old and *avant-garde* architecture. She was exhausted and overwhelmed by the frenzied activity of the last thirty-six hours.

She was hopeful Katie could get a good night's sleep. The upcoming days and weeks would be difficult. McKenzie was anxious for any information Katie could provide about Meadowlark and her captors. It wouldn't be easy. Coulomb and Meadowlark were on everyone's mind.

"You and Katie will be debriefed tomorrow and sent back home. I have you to thank for the direction we have taken against Möbius. We have a strong case going forward."

Mallory hesitated. "And this *Socrates*, what are you going to do about it?"

"I'm not sure. We don't have a timeline on when this *Socrates* thing is to happen. Hell, we don't even know what it is. We're at a disadvantage unless we get new information."

"Maybe I can help."

McKenzie looked at her, stunned. "You've got to be kidding. You're officially done. Why would you want to submit yourself further?"

"I can't get *Socrates* out of my mind. Why would Meadowlark challenge Coulomb to find this key? Both are math guys and so am I. I'm intrigued. This can't be just a game, can it?"

"You've convinced me he sees it that way." He took another sip of coffee. "If this missing key unlocks the mechanism that starts this so-called *Socrates*, where the hell would Meadowlark hide it?"

Mallory rubbed her blood-red eyes. "I can only guess."

"Try me."

"Meadowlark wears a pendant around his neck prominently displaying the answer to *The Basel Problem*, the number $\pi^2/6$. That points to Basel and maybe the museum."

McKenzie appeared to wake up. "Where would Meadowlark hide it—a display, some back office, where would you start?"

"*The Basel Problem* exhibit, that's where I'd begin."

He checked his watch. He gave her a crooked grin. "I can't ask you to involve yourself any further. You've done more than enough."

She leaned back, knowing full well that Lane was right. Katie was safe; she had accomplished her goal. But she knew better. Mathematicians were inquisitive, always energized when looking for answers. She couldn't quit now. Leaning forward, she said, "Maybe I could be an observer—not really involved, just offering advice."

McKenzie smiled. "Amistad would kill me."

Mallory's eyes drifted around. "After all this? Are you kidding?"

He shook his head. "Well, here we go again. Are you up for a little nighttime breaking and entering?"

Could he be serious? There was a flame flickering in his eyes. There didn't seem to be any let-up to the rollercoaster that had defined the last several days. She visualized the exhibit she had seen days earlier extolling *The Basel Problem*. She remembered the wax figure of Leonhard Euler in the diorama and the details of the infinite series of inverse squares that sums to $\pi^2/6$. "Do you have a tape measure?"

"What the hell for?"

"Just a hunch. Do you have one?"

He nodded. "I think we have one around here someplace."

Katie pinned her ear to the door. She heard the entire conversation—the mention of a key. Hadn't Ismet talked about keys? With Mallory and the CIA man leaving shortly, there would be only the one agent, Neal, who was sleeping, and another agent manning surveillance in one the back rooms. This would give her the opportunity to slip away without being seen. During the flight back, she envisioned Paul Coulomb suffering the same fate he had inflicted on Ismet. Her rage gave her motivation to find and kill him. She heard the voices fade with the sound of the front door opening and closing. They were gone.

A few seconds later, she checked the well-lit front room full of an array of electronic equipment. In the next room, a lone agent sat at a monitor, his back to her. Quietly, she headed for the door. She glimpsed someone's cell phone lying on the table. Grabbing it, she shoved it into her pocket. Exiting the door, she hurried down the hall.

After walking fifteen minutes, she crossed Oberer Rheinweg and headed west. She had a friend in Basel. She would give her a call, maybe spend the night. Then tomorrow, she would plan her revenge. She would not sit idly by and let Paul Coulomb get away with destroying her life.

Off the sidewalk, she found a bench between the street and the placid Rhine. She took the phone out of her pocket and began to dial when she stopped short. As horrible as her life had been recently, she couldn't forgot Harry. Mallory told her it was Harry who surrendered in order to allow the CIA access to the dam and her rescue.

Was Harry alive or dead? She had no idea if he'd been able to get away from the dam. How could she go on planning to do what she must when she was forgetting about the one man who may have been instrumental in saving her life? Harry had told her on numerous occasions that if she was ever in need of help, call him. He always carried his SAT phone. If he was still alive, she needed to know.

Remembering his number, she punched it into the phone and waited. It was ringing. She gasped when he answered.

"I usually don't answer unknown numbers, but under the circumstances, speak," the voice demanded.

"Harry, thank God you're alive." Her heart was beating out of control.

"Katie, I'm ecstatic to hear your voice."

She kept the phone pressed against her ear. He sounded genuinely relieved. His voice did not carry the bitterness and causticity it normally did.

For a moment there was silence. "Sorry, I was checking the GPS. *Sonofabitch,* you're in Basel."

"Since earlier this evening."

"Did the others make it?"

"Yes, except—" She couldn't finish the sentence as she began to sob.

"Are you alone?" he asked.

"Yes."

"Stay where you are. I'll be there in twenty minutes."

CHAPTER 50

Paul Coulomb was enraged. The dam had been destroyed and Sari and many guards were dead.

The traitorous bastard Harry had pulled it off.

Coulomb's investors believed they were hung out to dry. He would need to move slowly with precision. He had invited them all on a midnight cruise set for tomorrow night. He sat back in his chair, stared across the nighttime lake, and rubbed his temples. Losing the dam and a pipeline project wouldn't be the end of the world. When *Socrates* was achieved, he envisioned a multitude of opportunities in investing in European water utilities, possibly less risky for his investor's billions. That should calm their fears.

On the other hand, the international community would demand answers—how did this happen—why did this happen—who was responsible? He felt confident the IFC would be shielded for the time being. Shelby had been in communication with the Turkish Ministry of Water Development, the organization in charge of investigating the incident. Reason enough, he smiled, that corruption of high officials was necessary. It looked promising that they would be able to deflect the blame to the Kurdish Worker's Party, the PKK. The insurgent group had been carrying out attacks across Turkey for years.

Without the dam, he must focus on more pressing matters. He still had to locate Harry's key. Marotte, the museum, where else would the bastard hide it? Now, months of painstaking preparation were at risk.

Just as Coulomb let his thoughts simmer with possibilities, the door to his office opened. Esra walked in. He rotated his head, finding his thoughts shifting away from urgency to desire. The multi-colored lights of the console colored her cheeks with a pleasing iridescence. It changed his troubled mood. She really never was Harry's lover. That was just a test to get his attention. As much as he desired it, he had forestalled making love to her. She understood his reluctance. But the time was upon them. Once Harry was eliminated, she would be dominated.

She moved over and slid next to him, her dark eyes pulling him in. "The key will be found."

"Esra, my dear, you are so optimistic. I do not know what I would do without you."

She smiled. "And when it is found..." She brushed the tip of her finger with her tongue.

A tingle shimmied down his torso. "And when Harry is no longer amongst the living..."

"...you need faith—just a little bit of faith."

CHAPTER 51

M allory stood in front of the Museum of Mathematics and Science. On the door was a cardboard sign, in German, French, and English:

Museum Closed Until Further Notice
For Exhibit Refurbishing

Had she underestimated Coulomb? *Had he already gone through the displays?*

"It's closed at this hour anyway; why the worry?" McKenzie asked.

"We may be too late."

After slipping through an alleyway on the east side, they located the back door. McKenzie picked the lock after he rendered the security system useless by disengaging the main telephone line into the building. They ducked inside, securing the door.

"Impressive. You guys are jacks-of-all-trades," she whispered.

"We train in a lot of dishonest skills."

Flashlights glowing, they took a short hallway to a set of stairs. "If I recall, the large exhibit room is up a flight," she said. "Although, things look quite different entering from the alley."

Climbing the stairs, they kept the flashlight beams pointed low, not wanting to telegraph suspicious activity out any windows and alerting the police. The only other light in the museum filtered in from an array of skylights above, a dim glimmer from Basel's nightscape. Reaching the exhibit room, Mallory followed the path and backtracked through each archway separating the exhibits. Coming around a sharp corner, she encountered a display about Daniel Bernoulli, Johann's son, and a placard explaining his famous mathematical principal of hydrodynamics. She missed this exhibit on her earlier visit. Passing through another archway, her flashlight illuminated the placard describing *The Basel Problem.*

McKenzie waved his flashlight around. Beyond the sign, they saw the heap of rubble on the floor.

She gasped.

"Someone got here first," McKenzie said.

"That used to be a wax figure of Euler."

"Who?"

"Leonhard Euler, a famous mathematician."

McKenzie's face displayed dismay. "We're screwed."

Mallory pointed her flashlight further to the left, raking the Euler diorama. It looked like a tornado had hit: a pile of dismantled wax figures—arms, legs thrown about, overturned bookshelf—books and folios scattered about. She stood quietly, gathering her thoughts, the beam bouncing back and forth between the two wrecked displays. Coulomb had been here, it had his signature. What was it with this deranged man, destroying something of importance and value? And what was it with Harry Meadowlark, this whole insidious affair a game, a theatrical drama played upon the stage of intellectual competition? What was he trying to prove?

McKenzie shook his head. "From the carnage, we're too late."

Both Coulomb and Meadowlark had immense egos. But, from what she knew of them, having met them both, their egos were exclusively independent. Still, the question remained: Did Coulomb find the key?

McKenzie touched her arm. "I need to get back to *Operations* and warn higher ups about a catastrophe called *Socrates.* This is serious."

Mallory's scrutinized the two displays, her mind shifting into overdrive. "Maybe Coulomb doesn't have it."

Katie's eyes roamed up and down the pathway that paralleled Oberer Rheinweg, anxiously waiting for Harry. At this late hour, the street traffic was unusually brisk, automobile fumes mingling with the moist air flowing across the Rhine. She checked her watch. It had been eighteen minutes since she last spoke with him. Harry didn't say how he would find her, but she knew he worked like clockwork, punctual as the church bell at twelve noon. Across the street a black Audi pulled into an empty parking space that miraculously had appeared. The driver exited in a hurry, weaving through traffic, not waiting for it to clear, then sprinted across the street. Katie recognized him and allowed herself to relax.

"Thank God you're okay," she said, pulling back from their warm embrace. He looked scruffy, beat up, the amber light of a nearby streetlamp accentuating his deeply-lined face. He wore a light jacket and a pair of dirty trousers that looked like he had slept in them. "How'd you get out of Turkey?"

"I know pilots in low places."

"I see you've got wheels already."

"I used to live here, remember? Still have a few connections." He looked around suspiciously, watching nighttime strollers and traffic with a keen eye. "Does anyone know you're here?"

She shook her head. "I don't think so."

Harry clasped her shoulders and looked at her straight on. "What happened?" His voice was gentle and even.

Tears flowed. "Ismet…gone…killed."

Harry pulled her close and held her for several moments. Katie sobbed, the tears wet on his shoulder.

"If I could bring him back, I would do it in an instant. But you know me, Katie. I'm not much good at those kinds of things."

She wiped her tears. "I don't expect you to. This is my burden. I'll handle it my way."

"I don't like the way you said that."

"Why not?" She pulled away abruptly, exposing teeth like a mad dog. "Paul Coulomb will pay even if I die trying."

"No one said Paul doesn't deserve what's coming to him. He's an A-1 scumbag. Let me take care of him. I have him in my sights." He stood back and stared at her. "Look at you; you aren't prepared to fight a man of Paul's wealth and power. I promise; he'll get his just reward. "

Katie frowned. "You're right, I'm not prepared." she said, knowing she didn't have a plan.

Harry's eyes darted up and down the street.

"I have to tell you something. I heard Mallory say she thinks she knows where it is."

Meadowlark's eyes flared. "Where what is?"

"A key, I heard about a key."

Meadowlark's interest peaked. "Where?"

"The museum, about a half an hour ago, she and the CIA man."

"What! I have to stop them."

Katie grabbed his arm. "Not without me." She clasped tight.

"I don't have time to babysit!"

He started to whirl away, but she didn't let go. He half-dragged her back to the car. She didn't remember him being so strong. "I'm not letting you out of my sight, again."

Harry acquiesced. "But you stay outside. The shit's about to hit the fan."

Katie agreed and released her grip.

Mallory moved over to *The Basel Problem* placard, beaming her flashlight on the series of inverse squares.

$$1 + 1/2^2 + 1/3^2 + 1/4^2 + 1/5^2 + 1/6^2 + \ldots + 1/k^2 + \ldots = \pi^2/6$$

McKenzie looked closer at the display. "Is there something here that we should recognize?"

"I don't know, but what I would ask is why does the museum keep this exhibit so prominently displayed? Recall the dynamic water irrationals at their headquarters. They eliminated the $\pi^2/6$. Why not here, or at least, minimize this part of Basel's mathematical history? Franz told me he heard the curator arguing over the phone. It was about this exhibit. To them, Meadowlark is a traitor. Why allow an exhibit that represents his calling card, the chain around his neck? They don't want any reference to him left within the company." Her eyes kept wandering over to the two dioramas with the heap of destroyed wax figures, skeletal steel supports thrown helter-skelter, and the clutter of books battered and torn. Her thoughts focused, allowing a small smile. *They didn't look in the right place.*

She stepped back—then her eyes fell on the archways at both ends of the display. On her first visit to the museum, she had observed these openings as architectural dressing designed to enhance the exhibits—providing the feel of walking on an eighteenth century village street, narrow and medieval, even the floor had tile reminiscent of cobblestone.

She stepped over to the archway on her left and measured the distance across the opening at the floor level with the tape measure.

McKenzie looked on. "So that's why you needed the tape measure?" he asked, puzzled.

"Here, give me a hand. We need to measure the arch height."

He didn't question, helping stretch the tape up to the bottom of the arch.

"Three meters exactly," she said, reading the measure. The bottom width is two and a half meters across." Now, let me run some numbers." She pulled out her iPhone and opened a calculator app. After a couple of more measurements and number punching, she said, "Checks out. The shape of this arch is pretty close to the equation of a parabola."

He scratched his head. "Where you headed with this?"

"I'm not sure, but the other day I noticed one of these openings didn't seem as wide. I noticed the layout of the cobblestone tiles were slightly different in the arch opening." She stared at the archway at the other side of the exhibit. "Here, it was this one." She stepped over and measured the opening at the floor. "This one is different, it measures two-point-three meters, that's point-two meters less than the other archway."

"Construction error?"

"I don't think so." Taking a few more measurements, Mallory worked her calculator, sweat beginning to glisten on her forehead. With a notepad and pencil from her pocket, she scribbled down the equations and drew a rough sketch.

"This archway mathematically approaches the curve of the parabola, but the legs depart. It's not a true parabola, it's an inverted catenary."

"What's a catenary?"

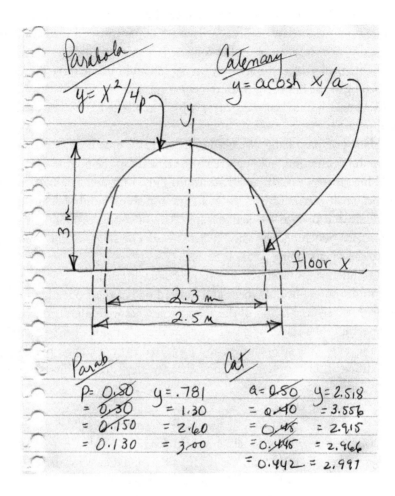

"It's the shape of the curve a hanging chain makes when strung between two points, like the Gateway Arch in St. Louis, which is an inverted catenary. Its equation consists of a hyperbolic cosine."

"A what?"

She regressed. "Not important; don't worry about the math. This is just two geometric curves, two arches with different door widths." She then remembered her foray at Zion, the catenary chain and the Knife-Ridge. She froze.

"You okay?"

"Uh, yea, just thought about something else." She shook her head. Let's verify the rest of the archways.

After a few minutes, they returned to the display next to *The Basel Problem*, an exhibit on Infinite Series.

"Here's what we know: there are two archways that are catenary, the two that sandwich this exhibit on Infinite Series. All other archways are parabolic."

"So, what's the point? These archways use lengths, heights, and numbers. Hell, this is a math museum. No surprise."

She stared at McKenzie with her green eyes, more vibrant the more she thought. "The Bernoulli brothers, Johann and Jakob, we're right back with them. Johann solved the equation for the catenary around seventeen hundred. He beat Jakob to the solution. This could be the first clue that Meadowlark left for Coulomb. Meadowlark is channeling Johann, complete with the insults."

"Are you saying both Meadowlark and Coulomb are actors in a three hundred years historical drama?"

Mallory nodded. "Meadowlark certainly is. He's fixated on Johann, and Johann was a teacher for the younger Euler, the man who solved *The Basel Problem*. Viola! Another inner channeling."

"So, the key is in this exhibit?"

"Coulomb hasn't been here, nothing is destroyed." If Meadowlark hid the key here, it is a brilliant deception, although we have one clue already." She walked through the exhibit, checking the different placards. She came across the first one, explaining the Taylor series and uses it had in mathematics. "This series is used in hundreds of applications, especially when representing complicated functions—in other words like calculating trigonometric, hyperbolic, exponential functions on a calculator—things that are time consuming by hand. Very useful."

With a frazzled expression, McKenzie said, "Where's the *key?*"

She shook her head. And then her eyes fell on the placard explaining the Harmonic Series: Convergence or Divergence? Below the title in large black letters was the famous series:

$$1 + 1/2 + 1/3 + 1/4 + 1/5 + 1/6 + \ldots + 1/k + \ldots = \infty$$

"You're staring at that math thing like it means something important," McKenzie said.

"These *math things*, as you so eloquently noted, either converge to a particular numerical value, or diverge, they head off into the sunset straight towards infinity. Their use may seem inconsequential, but they're the backbone of the higher mathematics that has shaped our technical and social fabric."

"Social fabric?"

"Finance, nothing as social as money. Think compound interest. Where'd that all come from?" Compound interest is a function of the series for finding the constant e." She walked to the other side of the display, continuing to stare at the placard. "This famous series is called the Harmonic, something the Bernoulli brothers worked on. Interesting, it's displayed as prominently as *The Basel Problem*."

His head was spinning.

"It's sometimes called the psychotic series because of its counterintuitive nature: as each consecutive term on the left approach zero, the sum on the right diverges to infinity."

"Are you telling me all those small terms added together, getting smaller and smaller, really will add up to infinity? Hard to believe."

"They don't add up to infinity, nothing ever does. They approach infinity." Mallory felt a rush of energy.

"The *key*—yes, or no?"

She didn't hear McKenzie. Moving closer, goose bumps popped. The infinity sign was a three-dimensional black metal twisted Möbius Strip attached to the top of a gold-plated plaque screwed to the placard.

Take a close look. See anything unusual?"

"Looks like a figure eight on its side, but it has a twist like a Möbius strip."

"The infinity symbol was devised by John Wallis, an Englishman. Later, it was named by Jakob Bernoulli, a *lemniscus*, which in Latin means ribbon. And here we are, back with Jakob Bernoulli, who in Meadowlark's world, is his nemesis Coulomb. Every chance he gets, he inserts the company's identity, just like the fountain at their headquarters. This infinity symbol had to be mounted on a gold plaque. It couldn't have been stamped in indiscreet black on the placard like the rest of the verbiage. No, it had to stand out and glorify Coulomb and his self-importance."

What was Meadowlark's intent here? Mallory tipped her head, reflecting. She glanced over at McKenzie who could see she was absorbed.

"A penny for your thoughts?" he asked.

She had never been one to get caught up in evasive riddles, but Meadowlark obviously enjoyed them. Didn't he tell her *the key was right under Coulomb's nose?* She bent down for a closer look. "I need a screwdriver."

He pulled out his pocket-knife, popped a blade, and began to remove the screws holding the plaque. After a moment, it pulled free. Lifting it away from the placard, Mallory reached into a small kerf beneath, a quarter of an inch deep, and withdrew something, bright and shiny with a black plastic handle. She locked eyes with McKenzie and they traded smiles.

"I'll take that."

Mallory spun around at the familiar voice a mere fifteen feet away. She stared in disbelief. A ghostly apparition would have been easier to believe in.

Meadowlark stared back, his troubled face deeply-lined in the murky shadows, downright cadaverous.

CHAPTER 52

McKenzie's flashlight beam underscored the gun in Meadowlark's hand.

"The light, turn it off," Meadowlark barked. "I like low-light ambiance. It's quite romantic."

McKenzie complied, questioning Meadowlark's allegiance. He was beginning to think they've been had by the former Möbius associate—or was he still involved? "You're quite resourceful. How the hell did you get here?" he asked.

"I'd ask you the same question, but I already know." His eyes strayed to the key gripped in Mallory's hand.

"For some odd reason, I'm not surprised to see you, although pointing a gun at us seems out of character," Mallory said.

"No hard feelings, lady. By the way, thanks for getting Katie out safely."

McKenzie caught Mallory's rising eyebrows, *how did he know she was safe?* "We wondered whether you'd made it out yourself. Should we concern ourselves with your motives?"

"That's a topic for future discussion." Meadowlark wagged the gun at McKenzie. "Your shoulder holster, slowly remove your weapon and place it on the floor."

McKenzie reached around and slid his Beretta out, holding the butt delicately by his fingers. He bent over and set it on the floor along with the flashlight.

"Why the museum for a hiding place?" Mallory asked.

Meadowlark took a few paces to his right. "Why not? Mathematicians love to solve puzzles. You lady, you must have an appreciation for the lives of those who went before, creating extraordinary mathematics. Sometimes, those same mathematicians live within ourselves."

"Let me guess," Mallory said. The Bernoulli's are obvious. I would guess Johann is your alter ego."

Meadowlark nodded. "Yes, he is a dynamic character, but there's another."

"Of course, Euler." She stared at the pendant hanging about his neck. "The $\pi^2/6$. Why did you adopt it as your irrational calling card?"

"It's a beautiful piece of mathematics," Meadowlark said. "Squares to circles. Extraordinary to say the least, and such a surprising solution. Now, the key, please."

Mallory ignored the request. "Quite the interesting hiding place."

"The arched openings were my design. They turned out well, don't you think? They were my one and only contribution to this museum. Paul thought I should have been an architect. Tsk, tsk, if he only knew.

"Why the game?" Mallory asked. "Doesn't seem much fun if people die."

"Oh, it's a game for sure, but the outcome has never been in doubt. The winner will be me. Rotten, I admit, but the other participant is the bigger scumbag." He paused and gave her a crazy grin. "You seem to have more smarts than Paul. I'm impressed you found the key. I won't ask again." He held out his hand.

The sound of creaking floorboards roused everyone's attention. McKenzie's eyes swung toward the sound. A blurred shadow fluttered from the walkway to the back wall. His muscles tightened.

The noise was deafening. The bullet tore into the placard inches from where Mallory stood. McKenzie darted to her side, yanking her down as two more rounds whizzed above their heads and slammed into the wall beyond. He spotted Meadowlark hidden by one of the arches pointing his gun toward the shadow. He pumped several rounds, and was gone.

McKenzie found his Beretta, readied for a shot, but the shadow had vanished. "Quick, this way. To the exit."

In less than a second, Mallory was racing down the exhibit path. McKenzie kept after her, thankful for the cover of near darkness.

Mallory kept running. Her eyes never lost sight of the lit green exit sign, a pictogram of a man running. Sufficient light from the skylights provided enough visibility to keep from stumbling into exhibits and partition walls. Entering the hallway under the running man, the light diminished. Feeling her way along the walls, she turned a ninety-degree corner and abruptly ran into a closed double door. Feeling boxed in, she fumbled down the wall until she found the panic bar. Pushing the door open, she emerged into the anteroom. A moment later, McKenzie rushed in.

"We can't lock them out," he yelled.

She scanned the room. Diffused light came from a window. Compared to the rest of the museum, it was almost daylight. Noticing a computer monitor behind the counter, she grabbed the electrical cord and ripped it out of the socket and wall plug. She tossed it to McKenzie, who threaded it through the door handles and pulled it tight, securing it with a square knot.

She crossed over to the front door and tried the latch. Frantically searching, she couldn't find the lock button. She recoiled in fear; it was one of those archaic double-sided locks. *Damn, isn't this a code violation?*

Taking control of her senses, she studied the window on the right side of the door. It had a network of steel sash bars dividing the glass panes into squares. She glanced around the room, looking for anything that might work as a battering ram.

"If we can break through the window, we may be able to get out." She pointed to the counter. "What about that chair?"

He shook his head. "Too dainty."

She spotted a dark form moving off his left, deep in another hallway near the west end of the anteroom. "Behind you, the hallway!" she yelled.

McKenzie jumped out of the way as a flurry of rounds ripped into the anteroom, peppering the wall beyond and splintering the top of the wooden counter. Kneeling behind it, he triggered off several shots.

She spotted a self-standing lamp next to the brochure rack. Her face glistening with sweat, she picked it up and with the heavy tripod base pointed away, thrust it into the window. A few panes shattered, but the metal sash bars remained. She had to get those out to open a hole large enough. Again, she wound up and stabbed the lance-like spear. Three, four times, she kept punishing the window.

The double doors rocked back and forth on their hinges. The electric cord stretched and strained. Her eyes drifted to the doors, then returned to the task at hand. She clutched the lamppost tightly and flung it as hard as she could. A couple of steel sash bars bent outward. With an abrupt crack, the wood jamb and sill ripped away. She dropped the lamppost and wrung the bars loose enough to make a small escape route.

Sirens blared.

McKenzie fired another shot

"Over here!" she yelled.

He fired another three times into the hallway, retreated to his right, and rushed to the window. Mallory was halfway out, hanging onto one of the bent sash bars. He stuffed the Beretta into his shoulder holster and pushed her through, forcing her to rely on the remaining bars for support. "When you hit the sidewalk, run like hell. The key must be secure."

"But what about you?" she protested.

"Do as I say!"

Not exactly what she had in mind. She knew he didn't have any choice. Lowering herself down, she analyzed the distance. But she couldn't let go. How many times had he come to her rescue—and now, she was bailing in his time of need. She looked back up into his eyes. Even in the dim light and the bullets flying, she could see the blueness, still soft, still hopeful.

"Please, pull me back up," she strained. "I can't leave you here."

"The key, get it to operations. That's an order" He reached down and pried her fingers loose. She dropped the last seven feet. She hit the sidewalk hard and buckled over. "Now hustle," he yelled, then vanished from the window.

McKenzie whirled around just as he heard the double click from an automatic. An empty mag. A large man burst from the hallway and slammed into him with a savage agility. His rib cage flared with pain as both bodies flew across the room. The glint of metal in the man's right hand glowed. The man stabbed. McKenzie caught the blow with his outstretched hand. The man kept the pressure on, forcing him to fall. His head snapped backward and slammed against the wall, his senses flickering on and off. On the edge of losing consciousness, he swore he saw the double doors fly open.

Mallory heard the siren before the first police car came into view. She looked back up at the broken window, but no McKenzie. She had the key and it was the most important thing she possessed. Damn, how she wished he wasn't so stubborn; *same as me*, she thought. But now, it was her turn to come to the rescue. It must not end up in the wrong hands. She had to get back to *Operations*.

She sprinted up Freiestrasse to the first cross street. More sirens closed in from the opposite direction. Turning down the street at a quick pace, she slalomed past a couple of pedestrians, ran another half-a-block, and ducked into a doorway shaded by a cloth awning. Sirens blared. She stuck her head out and looked both ways along the street.

She hurried down the sidewalk away from the sirens. The quiet allowed her to hear the footsteps. Before she could react, she was shoved from behind. Tripping, she fell to the sidewalk.

Looking up, a man stood alone. She stared at the figure that stared down at her.

"Well...lordy, lordy...have mercy. What the hell we got here?" he drawled.

Where had she heard that voice?

He moved closer, his face lit by a nearby streetlamp.

It was Shelby Wallace.

Katie sat in the passenger seat of the Audi two blocks away from the museum. A few pedestrians ambled along the walks on each side of the street, taking in the late evening. Twenty-five minutes had passed since Harry left. She should have followed. She reached for the door handle, an approaching siren screaming louder, fraying her nerves. She held her breath and felt her pulse skyrocket as the police car raced by on Freiestrasse, the ear shattering, high-low shriek fading as fast as it had arrived. It was headed in the direction of the museum.

Her mind raced as well. Something bad had happened. So why was she sitting idly? She slid over onto the driver's seat and turned on the ignition. Looking across the street, she swore she saw a woman being forced into the back of an idling vehicle that wasn't there a few seconds earlier. Were her eyes deceiving her, or did the woman resemble Mallory? Within seconds, the black sedan sped away from the curb.

Katie panicked. She placed the Audi in gear and pulled out into the street, cranking the wheel tightly and making a U-turn. Thoughts of following the car swirled in her head, but she had to think! She pulled next to the curb, shaking.

A pounding on the front hood startled her. She looked up. It was Harry, his face twisted and lined with pain. He was holding his wrist, his fingers bloody.

He pulled open the door and slid into the passenger seat. "The professor lady, did you see her?"

Katie stared at Meadowlark with uncertainty. "I—I thought I saw her forced into a car."

Meadowlark pulled his jacket off and with a handkerchief from his pocket, wrapped it around his wound and tied it with one hand. Katie noticed the gun stuffed in his waistband.

"What happened?"

"Just a scratch.

Katie felt otherwise. "You need some medical attention. We need to find a hospital."

"No time," he barked.

Sweat poured from his forehead. Determination clouded his eyes. "We won't be going to a hospital. Now put this thing in gear and drive."

Katie hesitated. This was not what she had in mind. With Mallory abducted, she had no choice but to go back to CIA operations and ask for help and get Harry to a doctor.

"You need to have that wrist looked at," she said.

Meadowlark leaned in and spoke forcibly. "You either drive me, or I will toss you from this vehicle and drive myself. You want justice for Ismet—for the professor lady, do as I say."

Katie's world tightened around her. For Mallory's sake, she had no choice.

CHAPTER 53

Near St. Erhard, Switzerland

I t was a crazy, crazy, crazy, shapeless and heartless truth that bordered on insanity. By all accounts, Katie had let her emotions get the best of her. Every thought of Ismet brought tears like floods. He was dead. And she should be dead. And she wished she was dead, but her one chance to get even was on the horizon—isn't that what she wanted first?

Mallory, like a sister, who helped with her escape, was in danger. She had lost Ismet; she couldn't bear losing Mallory, too.

She tightened the grip on the steering wheel. Air whistling through the open sunroof drowned out the whine of the engine. As they whizzed by cultivated fields and sleepy towns, she listened as Meadowlark gave her directions. His desertion from Möbius' inner circle created suspicion. She vaguely remembered Mallory and the CIA man discussing something ominous on the flight from Turkey when they thought she was asleep. *Socrates*, they called it. What it meant, they didn't say. But now, it was beginning to make sense. The key that had everyone's attention was about to be delivered to Paul Coulomb.

If Meadowlark knew where Mallory was, that was enough to convince her to take him there. She drove like she was in a trance, her foot heavy on the accelerator, her attention to traffic and highway signage non-existent. Like a robot, she took verbal directions from Harry, who sat next to her with a blood-soaked arm. Leaving Basel, they took the A2 motorway towards Lucerne. A few kilometers north, he asked her to get rid of the cell phone for fear they could be traced. She complied by throwing it out the car window. For the life of her, she couldn't reason why. Harry only raised an eyebrow.

Twenty-eight kilometers northwest of Lucerne, Meadowlark directed her to exit at the small town of St. Erhard. Finding a truck stop with a small restaurant attached, they parked behind.

"Why are we stopping?" Katie asked.

"Food, that's what. We need something to eat before we continue."

"But aren't we in a hurry? They have Mallory. We don't have time."

Meadowlark opened the door and pointed at the building. "I'm thinking there's a bathroom in there. I need to clean the blood off my arm and while I'm there, I'll purchase a box of gauze. Truckers are always cutting themselves. Once that is done, I will meet you in the restaurant. I would guess the food is as good as anywhere else, especially at this hour. Go find a table. I'll be there shortly. Order me a coffee." Taking care not to use his right arm, he crawled out, disappearing around the building.

Katie sat for a moment, realizing he was right about food. She was hungry. Stepping out of the car, she walked around to the front and entered the restaurant, finding a wooden booth near the door. The restaurant was empty, except for a truck driver sitting at a table near the kitchen, eating a plate of sausages and potatoes. She sat down and ordered two cups of café au lait. Just as the waitress returned, Harry appeared. He slid into the booth and handed Katie a rust-colored wool sweater. "They sell everything at these places. You might need this where we're going. It gets a little chilly in the mountains." He ordered a bowl of Muesli, a plate of eggs, sausage and potatoes. Katie did the same.

The waitress returned with their meals and they ate without a word. It was not that Harry had nothing to say; he seemed to be contemplating. Katie was sure of it. Something had stirred his blood as to the chain of events now unfolding, and it was as if he was relishing the challenge.

Katie broke the silence. "Why aren't we concerned about getting to wherever we're going immediately?"

Harry finished chewing a mouthful and washed it down with a drink of the cream-covered coffee. "Trust me; Paul won't try anything until nighttime."

"Why not?"

"Think about it. Indians preferred attacks with the cover of darkness. Just like them, it's his best window of opportunity—and ours," he said.

Her mind still racing, Katie didn't like just sitting, biding their time. "But we need to get Mallory now. They'll kill her."

"Paul won't touch her until he is assured his plan has been set in motion. That's the way he is; I know that as fact." He looked over at her full plate. "Eat up. It may be the last meal you have for a long while."

Thirty minutes later, they were back on the A2, speeding for the north side of Lucerne. Turning north onto the A14, then the A4, she gunned the Audi towards the town of Arth. Traffic was almost non-existent with daylight creeping closer. Katie followed Harry's orders, taking the exit to Arth, but instead of going into town, they followed a less travelled country road for another quarter of a mile. At the first switchback, the road began an earnest climb up the back slope of *Die Wandung*, past pasturelands and herds of dairy cattle. Katie rolled her window down to take in the welcome mountain air. She needed to clear her head. The sweet aroma of freshly cut hay and bouncing headlights on cud-chewing cows provided an iconic Swiss mountainside. After another eighth of a mile, they came to a sign that read *Kein Übertreten*: No Trespassing.

"Turn here," Harry motioned, pointing towards the narrow track off to her left. "We take that road."

Katie gazed at his dashboard-lit face. The wrinkles were muted along with the anger that had abated. It was as if he was in a state of bliss, at peace, a place that she never thought he would find.

"What are the chances we won't be caught?" she asked.

"There's always a chance. I don't think Paul would have a reason to have it guarded now. This road was used to bring equipment and materials up when they built the upper terminal of Paul's aerial tramway. It's mostly forgotten since it's on private land."

As the Audi climbed the deserted road up the slope, the pastures gave way to a forest of firs and pine. Katie slowed as the road narrowed with tight switchbacks. She eased the Audi over the incessant water bumps once constructed to funnel snowmelt and rain across the road. Negotiating a steep switchback, the Audi's headlights bounced off a chain link fence and pad-locked gate strung perpendicular to the road.

"Stop here," Harry said.

It was obvious they couldn't go any further.

"Damn, I was afraid of that," he said, exiting the Audi and slamming the door.

Katie opened her door and stepped out, feeling the mountain chill. She pulled on the sweater Meadowlark had bought. "What do we do now?"

"The only thing we can do—walk." He retrieved a flashlight, a small leather case, and a pair of binoculars from the glove compartment. "Let's go."

They climbed the fence and continued on foot, circling beneath the northeastern flank of *Die Wandung*. After several miles, they walked out of the forest onto a mountain glade. Ahead, a stone building stood at the edge of the clearing.

"We'll rest here," Harry said.

From all appearances, the dilapidated structure had been vacant for years. The windows and front door were long gone, obviously ripped out for booty at some point in time. What was once the wooden deck now, a pile of decomposing timbers.

Katie was exhausted. They had walked most of the night along the abandoned road. The sun broke the eastern sky and a few cumulus clouds streamed by. She found a sheltered spot on a patch of meadow grass next to the structure and curled up into a ball. It didn't take long for her to be lost in sleep.

CHAPTER 54

McKenzie sat in the chair rubbing at the walnut-size knot on the back of his head."

It ached like it had never ached before. Prior to getting bashed into the wall and losing consciousness, he remembered staring at the large man's mug—thick black eyebrows, straight jaw, and homicidal eyes. Now that his vision had cleared, a question remained: what happened after being knocked unconscious?

He waited patiently in the small room of the police station for the inspector to return. He glanced at the wall clock. His vision was still blurred; he couldn't read the time. He recalled being taken to a hospital, released, and brought to the station. All a fog, but for some god-awful reason he was still alive. When given the opportunity to make a telephone call, he contacted Neal, sharing his situation. With any luck, Neal would be able to get the Swiss FIS to take responsibility for the breaking and entering.

The door opened and Inspector Guy Schenker entered. He was a short man with slit eyes and graying hair. He wore a white shirt with an open collar and a slack red tie.

"I just got off the phone with the FIS out of Zurich," he said in perfect English. "They verify your story that this was a joint operation between the FIS and your CIA. Just the same, this is a serious matter for our jurisdiction.

"You have my statement."

"Your statement is rather vague."

"I don't remember much after my head was bashed."

The inspector seemed agitated. "Look at it from my perspective. All I see is a major incident at the museum, criminal intent if you wish. Now our department is caught up in some wild international surveillance operation and I'm left out to dry. A little clarification is all I'm asking for."

"I can only tell you what I already have. In a day or so, I'm sure you will receive a better explanation from the FIS."

"What about the dead man, can you tell me who he is?"

"Dead man?" McKenzie straightened up. "I was unaware that there was a dead man in the museum."

Inspector Schenker leaned over the table. "Oh, he was quite dead. A large man, in fact slumped over your feet when we arrived. You, of course, were somewhat delirious."

McKenzie remembered being attacked with the knife after the man ran out of ammo. "How was he killed?" Did Meadowlark save his life? He could sort of remember seeing the double doors fly open but he had no idea who had come through. The thought that the man was dead stirred a question of his own.

"Shot; bullet to the back."

"I didn't shoot him."

"We'll determine that with ballistics. For the time being, we will keep your gun."

He didn't argue. He desperately wanted out. The whereabouts of Mallory concerned him—as did Meadowlark, the joker in the deck. It made absolutely no sense to divulge that there were others in the museum.

The phone rang and the inspector picked it up from a small table in the corner. Listening intently, he acknowledged with a "*Danke*" and placed it back in the cradle. "You are free to go."

McKenzie stood, thanked the inspector, then left and met Neal in the lobby. "Thanks for getting me cleared," he said.

"Sorry to give bad news, but both women are missing."

"Both?"

Neal nodded.

McKenzie rubbed the back of his head. He didn't have time for this headache.

A gentle squeeze on Katie's shoulder roused her from a deep slumber. Groggily, she opened her eyes. Rubbing the sleep from them, she squinted at the crystal blue sky. The few clouds had dissipated. Her feet were in sunshine but the rest of her remained in the contracted shadows of the crumbling chateau, telling her the sun was high in the sky. "What time is it?" she asked.

Harry was standing over her. "Little past two."

Katie jumped up and brushed the grass from her sweater. "Past two, we need to get going!" she exclaimed.

"Calm down," Harry said. "We're on schedule."

She picked up a water bottle and took a welcome drink.

They started up the road as it wound across the glade, reentering a dense thicket of fir. It continued its steady climb upward until it reached a crest sloping down the other side. Straight ahead the trees thinned, allowing the afternoon sunlight to filter through.

Meadowlark slowed his pace and whispered, "From here on out, we must be quiet. I guarantee there will be at least one, maybe two guards."

A few yards further, the road emerged from the forest to a view like none other. It took her breath away. Nestled on the edge of a cliff, the gleaming structure cantilevered precariously in a feat of gravity-defying legerdemain. Enclosed by glass on three sides, the structure's massive arrow-shaped roof shot out above an encompassing deck like an eagle about to take flight. Two rows of deeply slanted cables rose from the darkness of the shadowed cliff and split the deck, coming up beneath the nib of the roof and disappearing inside.

"What is that?" she asked.

"Paul's very expensive toy. It's the upper terminal for his aerial tramway. Let's get comfortable," Meadowlark said. "We'll wait 'till dark; that's when he will be coming up."

Katie looked at him strangely. "How can you be so sure?"

Meadowlark smacked his lips. "I know how the bastard operates."

"I hope Mallory will be okay. She said my father wanted her to come."

"Meadowlark took a step towards her, throwing his arms in the air. " Oh Christ, this can't wait."

She straightened. "What can't wait?"

"This was to be the lady's job. But since we're here—and she isn't—you need to know."

His voice had trailed off. She could sense the tension building. There was sadness stenciled across his face.

"I should have told you in Basel."

Told me what?"

Meadowlark's face was distraught. "Your friend Mallory was with Tom … your dad…"

"Harry, what is it?"

"Katie…your father. He was killed."

She sat speechless. There didn't seem to be a normal reaction, only a stoic, endless stare.

"You don't deserve this, your father…Ismet."

After a long silence, she asked quietly. "How did it happen?"

He lowered his head. "Not sure. Your lady friend didn't give details. Only that Möbius was involved."

Katie slowly drifted away. She wanted to cry, but the tears wouldn't come. Harry's words continued to resonate, creating an endless stream of emotions. Loneliness settled over her like she'd never felt before.

She stared at the upper terminal, as she cowered in the meadow like a rabbit with a hawk's talons ripping her innards.

CHAPTER 55

Basel

I t had been five hours since McKenzie walked out of the police station and barely four since he agreed there was a high likelihood Mallory, and maybe even Katie, were being brought to Coulomb's lakeside retreat. Meadowlark's whereabouts was also a mystery. After he and Neal reached Operations, it was discovered one of their agents was missing a cell phone. They tracked the phone through GPS, pinpointing its location fifteen kilometers northwest of Lucerne. The only rational hypothesis, Katie snatched it when she slipped out. They decided not to call it, but use it as a GPS tracking device instead. Regrouping, they gathered short-range radios, ear mics, and other necessary equipment. McKenzie secured another 9mm Beretta and thrust it satisfactorily into his shoulder holster, making sure he had a couple of spare magazines.

Ten minutes later, the GPS signal for the cell phone disappeared. If the abductors had found the phone, something sinister was likely. He didn't want to entertain that thought.

McKenzie and Neal sped down the A2 motorway to Coulomb's retreat, one hundred and twenty kilometers to the southeast. Once they reached the village of Vetsch, McKenzie commandeered a Zodiac tied up to one of the town's docks. It took about forty minutes to motor around the promontory that separated the town from Coulomb's mansion. Neal stayed behind to wait for agents from the Swiss FIS.

McKenzie reached the point just as the sun slipped below the horizon. From where he hunkered in the stern three hundred yards away, he could make out the dock lights bouncing rays off the hull of the *Lune Corbeau*. Deck lights indicated the multi-million dollar yacht might be going on a cruise.

Darkness descending would assure enough cover. Silently, he paddled away from his hiding place, keeping careful not to be seen by the indirect glow of the lights. Gliding under the end of the dock, he tied the Zodiac up to a wooden brace. Crouching behind a piling, the ramble of footsteps reverberated overhead. Voices were heard, mostly in German, but a few sentences of English were recognized.

"Recheck the ice," one voice said clearly.

Footsteps resounded, coming down the ramp from the *Lune Corbeau* to the dock.

McKenzie looked towards the shore. There had to be a place he could hide without being seen. To his right, he spotted some rocks and vegetation. He untied the Zodiac and maneuvered it further underneath the dock by leveraging off the braces. After ten or twelve feet, he could go no further.

The voices and activity accelerated. He climbed out of the Zodiac onto a horizontal brace, and then shimmied beneath the dock until he found dry land. He moved behind a rock wall and scanned the area. He found a path leading up onto the terrace. Silently, he crept along hedgerows and planting beds that lined the path as it curved up towards the house. Sticking his head above a glossy-leafed shrub, he glassed the house with binoculars, spotting a man dressed in a suit and tie near the front door pressing his ear, obviously adjusting a small hearing device. *Very CIA-like*, thought McKenzie. He felt his own earpiece and spoke softly. No response. He knew it was a moot point to communicate directly with Neal, who was on the other side of the promontory. He needed line-of-sight communication. Turning his attention to the parking lot, he caught another well-dressed man walking past a parked Mercedes. After the other night, he understood Coulomb's need for extra security.

McKenzie scrutinized the facade of the large, extravagant mansion. Now and then, he caught a fleeting shadow cross a window at the third level—Coulomb's office, he realized, recalling the architectural drawings the CIA had obtained.

He looked up the road that curved down to the parking area. Another vehicle was parked part way up, the driver standing beside it. He, too, was well dressed, ably keeping an eye on the winding road exiting the trees. Tonight, security seemed excessive. To his rationale, something must be happening inside the house, probably involving Mallory and/or Katie.

Paul Coulomb was on the cusp of corporate history.

It was one of those tranquil moments when a rare evening mist hovered over the lake, sprinkling the evergreens and broad-leafs with a gentle touch of dew. Outside air drifted through the open window, feeling crisp and invigorating to his lungs. Everything had finally fallen into place.

It was a grand time to be alive.

His fingers flipped the key over in his hand, like a gambler manipulating a chip, rolling it from knuckle to knuckle. In conjunction with three other keys, all four embedded with critical signal detection software, the time was now. Bits and Bytes. Zeroes and Ones. On and Off. Simple switches placed in the right combination, in the right order, in the right sequence—and the world would succumb.

He stared across the desk at the professor, her hands bound, helpless. It had been mere chance she was caught with the key. He felt euphoric, almost giddy— except for one thing. A tinge of regret swept through him as his eyes pawed over her lovely features, her chestnut locks curled in a mess. *Such a darling. Too bad she has to die.*

Placing the key on his desk, he leaned back. "You impress me. As fellow mathematicians, it's unfortunate we are on different sides of the equation. I could have used someone like you in my organization."

"It would never work," Mallory spat. "I'm not into killing."

A smile flickered. "Oh my, we have such moralistic convictions, don't we?"

"Go to hell."

He ignored her remark and tapped the desk. "Speaking of killing, I almost eliminated you a few days ago. That would have been a terrible mistake. If I had succeeded, I would not be sitting here now enjoying our little conversation." He chuckled.

Mallory seethed. "You're a cold-blooded bastard."

"You are in no position to lecture," Esra said coolly, rising from a chair behind the professor. "Someone about to die should have respect, a little control."

"How do you look yourself in the mirror and not gag?"

Esra slapped the professor hard across the mouth.

Coulomb waved her back. "Esra, my dear, let us be the best hosts we can in this exhilarating situation." He turned his attention back to the professor. "I am sure you cherish your life, so I have a proposition."

"Shove it," she said, still reeling from the sting to her cheek.

"Oh, please, hear me out," Coulomb said, his smile widening. "It's very simple. Your life for Harry's. Tell us where he is?"

He was sure he saw the professor flinch. She knew something—something about Harry. Maybe he shouldn't kill her just yet.

"What's the point?" she asked. "You have the key."

He stroked the key, innocently lying on the desk. "That I do. But there are matters that need to be resolved." He gazed over at Esra. "You would very much like to see him again, wouldn't you, my dear?"

"Harry and I have some issues." Her voice was controlled, but her hands were curled into fists.

Coulomb was thrilled with the way things had turned out. Harry had played his game and lost. Would he attempt to get the key back before the sequence initiated? If that was the case, he didn't have much time. Better yet, let a new game begin. The professor must know of Harry's whereabouts. Guilt was written all over her face. Once she squealed, Esra would enjoy killing her.

He locked eyes with Esra. And when Harry was found, he too would be history. A dead Harry would please her immensely. She never was his lover, only a pleaser. And Harry was undeserving. Now, things were about to change. She smiled a sensuous, soon-to-be smile. Who was he to deny her the pleasure to satisfy? Why not let her fantasies become reality.

"Professor, Esra and I are hosting a moonlight cruise this evening, so we must apologize for wanting to proceed with the sequencing immediately. We regret not inviting you to the soiree on the lake. I do believe you would have declined. But not all is lost. I have a consolation prize for you." He punched a button on the phone. "We have a special guest here. She informed me she would love nothing more than to experience a breathtaking ride up the mountain. Prepare the tram."

McKenzie saw the large entry door open. The individual who emerged brought an accelerated heart rate. It was Mallory, hands tied behind her back, pushed down the path by the man in the suit. Immediately two more individuals appeared in the doorway—Paul Coulomb and Esra Sahin. They trailed Mallory and the other man across the terrace toward the tramway terminal.

The master himself and his right hand woman.

His pulse was now pounding, seeing the scene unfold before him. Where was the third cog, Shelby Wallace? Didn't he possess a key, just as Esra did, all necessary for *Socrates*? No doubt Coulomb now controlled Meadowlark's key, and that could only mean one thing once Wallace appeared.

Four keys secure—*Socrates* was about to be put into motion.

CHAPTER 56

Mallory was escorted into the lower terminal, her stomach in a knot. She let out a shivery breath on seeing the bright red cabin suspended by cables. Once she was taken up the mountain, she would not be coming back down alive. The reality was ingrained in her head, knowing they would finish the job this time. That summed up the habit of killers.

Esra pointed a gun at Mallory. "Get in," she hissed.

Mallory didn't move. Esra nodded to the guard who immediately shoved Mallory in the back with the broad side of his gun. Maneuvered into a corner, she swore she saw the merciless choreographing behind Coulomb's eyes as he and Esra entered. She already had imagined her fate. They were going to push her out of the cabin. She hoped to God they would shoot her first.

"What a beautiful evening for a ride to the top," Coulomb remarked, directing his comment at Mallory. He smiled briefly then took his place at the helm. "Most aerial trams are controlled by operators at both upper and lower terminals. This one is different, a state of the art design. I can control it from here. There are two cabins. When we leave this terminal to go up, the other one comes down. Simple and convenient."

He flicked a switch. The door slid closed and the electric motor inside the terminal hummed to life. He pulled a lever and the large deflection sheave was put in motion, moving the cabin forward. Once outside the terminal, the car picked up speed and gained height quickly.

Mallory found it hard to breathe. She stared out the window watching the normally large conifers on the steep slope decrease in size, becoming dots in the subdued light. Dusk was settling in, with just enough residual light to still see a large rock field below. The car zipped up the mountain, soaring past the first intermediate tower crossing the jagged landscape. She yanked at the tightly bound cord that restrained her hands. Her heart pounded so loudly she swore all could hear it.

A minute later, they rolled past the second intermediate tower and ascended into a steep pitch. In full view, the near-vertical thousand-foot-high conglomerate cliff came into view, the notorious *Die Wandung*. There it was: the sheer face of death, a vertical peril that sent an uncontrollable terror gushing through her veins. Pushed out here would be the same as being pushed over *Die Wandung*.

Acrophobia be damned didn't seem to register here. Oh how she wished she could hug Kato one last time with his watchful eyes and comforting purr.

The thin red glow of the setting sun still blanketed the upper portions of the cliff, reflecting the upper terminal like a signal at sea. In the immensity of the precipice, her life was insignificant, registered clearly on Möbius' *accident* list. For some odd reason, she thought of the several climbers who had died attempting to climb the vertical face. It was their fate, and now hers. She realized she should mentally prepare for the inevitable—people live, people die.

"By acquiring *Die Wandung*, I have been instrumental in saving lives," Coulomb remarked.

Mallory wasn't sure she heard correctly. She was too scared to ponder his words.

"I remember my time at Berkeley. A favorite excursion was to travel to Yosemite and watch the climbers going up El Capitan. We would station ourselves across the road and catch the activity, sharing a picnic lunch and a beer or two. Such sadists we were, repugnant doctoral students anxious to catch a climber's mistake. It was great diversion. On one trip, an unfortunate climber fell to his death on the Muir Wall. From all indications, a piece of protection pulled loose, triggering a rock fall that severed his lead rope. He fell nine hundred feet." He shook his head as if he cared. "What a tragedy."

Mallory's eyes bounced between Coulomb and the darkening cliff. Sweat soaked the back of her neck. Her world was about to end. She wanted to get on her knees and desperately plead for her life.

Whose ass can I kiss to save mine?

Grasping her sanity, she felt her inner strength take over. She couldn't believe her weaknesses had reared. This wasn't like her. She shook her head in shame.

What was she thinking? Katie was safe, that's all that mattered.

Möbius can go to hell.

Coulomb glanced out the window at the massive face of the cliff, now a black mass creeping closer to the tram. He spun away from the helm, reached over and grabbed the latch to the door. The door slid open effortlessly.

Esra shoved the gun barrel into Mallory's back, forcing her to move toward the opening. Mallory resisted, but the barrel dug deeper. She tripped, falling to her knees. Esra kept pressure, pushing Mallory closer to the door opening. She leaned to her right and wedged her shoulder against the side, her head hanging over the threshold, inches out the opening. It was deathly silent except for the rush of air whistling past, icy upon her face. She closed her eyes to keep from seeing the ominous blackness below and prayed a bullet to the head would come fast.

Coulomb's voice broke the terror. "Information has value, and you have information. Tell us about your adventures in Turkey. You and your CIA friends have caused us a great deal of trouble, not to mention expense. And Harry—you were with him. So, where is he at this moment? That is a critical piece of information which may save your misguided life. Think about these questions and answer *truthfully.*"

Esra pulled Mallory back by her collar. The door slid closed. At that moment, she grasped she had a short reprieve. She tried to unscramble her brain; her pending death was not immediate, but how long—a minute, five, twenty, an hour? She looked up and saw the deck of the upper terminal close in on both sides and the mechanized world of drive sheaves and counter weights appear.

She focused on Esra, her face a savage smile. Her eyes stung Mallory, her stare predatory and bloodthirsty. If there was a way to survive, Mallory had to find it.

CHAPTER 57

L isten!" Harry whispered, placing a finger to his lips.

Katie heard the motorized drone coming from the terminal. Her swollen eyes fell upon the cables threading up from the valley below, beginning to shimmer with the last sunrays of the day. She swore she saw movement, a minute undulation of the top cable out of the corner of her eye. She caught the tramway climbing steadily.

"Just as I suspected. Paul is coming to sequence, as I doubt he's coming for a sunset view."

Katie shook the thoughts of her father's death from her mind. Her voice was feeble. "Is Mallory with him?"

"I would bet yes. Paul has a need to flaunt his wealth and power and parade his massive ego in front of his victims."

Katie kept her eyes glued on the tram as it approached the terminal sliding between the two arms of the deck. It vanished from view beneath the roof. The motorized hum ceased.

Meadowlark motioned up the slope where the observation deck was located. Taking in the scene with binoculars, he strained to see with the meager light. "There's our guard," he said, "just as I thought."

Katie had to stay strong. She had to keep her thoughts controlled away from her personal heartbreaks. "What's our plan?" she said, biting her quivering lip.

"There's no 'our plan.' Once the guard is out of the way, I get the drop on Paul. For you and me both, I want to see the bastard's eyes one last time before—" He didn't elaborate further. He pulled out his gun, a .40 cal. Smith, unsnapped the leather case, and withdrew a short steel silencer. He lined it up with the barrel and screwed it on.

Katie considered what she was observing. This was a Harry she never knew existed.

"I'm going to work my way around to the other side of the observation deck. By the time I get there, it'll be dark. It should be easy to take out the guard."

"What about me? I'm not staying here. You need my help."

He gave her a cold glare. "You won't move. Ismet lost his life because of me. I refuse to let you join him. You stay away from the terminal. I guarantee in very short time the professor lady will be safe, and you'll have the revenge you want, and that's a dead Paul! Wait 'till I call you, understand?"

She hesitated, wanting to strike him for his insolence, but before she could analyze her options, he was gone, slipping into the forest and disappearing into the mounting darkness.

McKenzie craned his neck to glimpse the miniscule tram disappearing into the arrow-like structure that jutted out over the darkened cliff. Simultaneously he saw the downward tram slide into the lower terminal. His first thought was to take that to the top, but there was a little problem—he wasn't invited. Unless those on top were expecting someone else, they would pick him off the minute the doors opened. Worst yet, they'd stop the tram halfway up and keep him suspended forever, like a lobster in a restaurant tank next to be the main course.

He knew he couldn't sit idly by. Every second lost was a second closer to whatever doom was in store for Mallory. Should he attempt to reach Neal and have the FIS storm in? He shook the thought from his head. Most hostage situations turned out bad when the authorities rushed in. That would have to be a last resort.

He looked back at the terminal. The man with the gun was no longer there. A line of vehicles, headlights beaming, came down the winding road. He glassed the car parade, counting one, two, three…nine, ten, eleven as they approached—three Mercedes, two limos, a Jaguar XE, a Porsche Panamera 4S, a couple of BMW 650i's, an Audi A8 and what appeared to be a Rolls.

The vehicles parked, doors opened, and the visitors poured out. A cadre of servers carrying trays of champagne streamed out of the mansion and dispersed onto the multi-leveled terrace. McKenzie skulked deeper into the bushes hoping to keep hidden.

Another man left the house walking towards the parking area. McKenzie kept the binoculars trained on him. Shelby Wallace had shown his face.

The Alabaman strode over and stationed himself by a set of steps rising from the lot. He greeted the guests as they arrived, offering small talk in what appeared to be a personal welcome. The guests moved to the terrace, accepting champagne from the servers. McKenzie was now cut off from the path that led to the tram terminal by the swarming guests. He kept a count: roughly fifty individuals had converged on the upper terrace above his location. He recognized Khalid Al-Firaih and Omar Baeshan, two Saudi billionaire businessmen; Donald Bromley, a leading bond broker from Chicago; Bruno and Pauline Metzier of pharmaceutical fame; Hui Kuang from the Ying Consortium. The CIA had detailed information on all of them. There were a few others that had made the list—people of interest associated with Möbius, but it was the last fellow shaking hands with Wallace that piqued his interest—Jim Romano of the IFC. Short, with a thin face and round eyes, he looked every inch the weasel McKenzie had envisioned. If only they had gotten additional information from Meadowlark, they'd have plenty of evidence to blow the case wide open.

McKenzie kept his eyes pinned on Wallace, now working the crowd, chatting with guests. He was working his way toward the terminal, but like a good host, he mingled and socialized. McKenzie's heart started to palpitate. If Wallace was on his way to join the others on top, he might be able to hitchhike. The opportunity was now. He had to get to the terminal first.

Glancing back at the crowd, he noticed everyone was casually dressed. Certainly, he could blend in, wearing jeans and a black short-sleeve, tails out. Without hesitation, he hid the binoculars and slid out from behind the bushes. Meeting a server, he snatched a glass of champagne, and with a smile, sauntered further onto the terrace, posing as one of the guests, smiling, laughing, and truly enjoying the affair. People smiled back and exchanged pleasantries, as if they knew him. All the while he kept an unwavering eye on the Southerner, still entertaining.

Nobody seemed to pay him much attention. Reaching the far end, he spotted one of two stone paths that led to the lower terminal. It followed the slope of the hill down and then climbed the other side, settling on a flat area a few yards from the main terminal door. He turned back for one last look at

Wallace, still deep in conversation with two guests. With an air of confidence, he pitched the champagne glass into a nearby bush and stepped onto the path.

A voice rang out in English. "You don't like Salon 1995?"

McKenzie stopped dead in his tracks.

Pauline Metzier stood composed, leaning to one side, a cigarette dangling from her elevated right hand and a glass of champagne in the other. Wearing a low-cut blouse and tight Roberto Cavalli jeans, her eyes scrutinized McKenzie's body. She took a drag and blew smoke over her shoulder. "The champagne you just tossed, if my memory serves me, goes for over two hundred Euros a bottle."

He didn't know whether to feel exposed or play along. He decided to play along. "I've had better."

"Do tell." she said, angling closer like a she-wolf on the prowl. "I doubt that would insult our host, but it might not help if you are looking for favors."

He moved back onto the terrace. "What favors would I want?"

"What everyone here wants?" She tossed the cigarette down and ground it into the stone pavers with her stiletto toe. "Money, isn't that what drives people?"

He felt a trickle of sweat run down the back of his neck. He glanced back up at Wallace still engrossed on the upper terrace. Somehow he had to get away from this woman without blowing his cover.

Pauline took another step forward. "I don't believe I've seen you before," she said. "What's your connection with this farce of a gathering?"

Christ, he had to think fast! Out of the corner of his eye, Wallace was seen shaking Donald Bromley's hand and patting him on the back. "Financing, bond issuance," he said, looking back at Pauline.

Pauline lifted her champagne glass and drained it. "What's your name?"

He thought fast. "Porter, Doug Porter." He could see she noticed his eyes flitting back from Wallace and Bromley. "I work for Don Bromley."

She twisted her lips and gave him a seductive smile. "Problem is, affairs like this bring out the worst in people. Everyone trying to impress, showing their weaknesses, highlighting their insecurities. Gather all these individuals in one place, and you have the largest group of assholes the world has ever seen." She stepped closer. Eyeing the bush where McKenzie had hurled his champagne glass, she tossed hers. "On second thought, you're absolutely right, this stuff is crap. Oh, and your name is not Doug Porter."

He felt naked, vulnerable. He thought about reaching for his Beretta holstered in the small of his back. He nervously kept one eye directed Wallace's direction and the other on Pauline.

With a sensuous glance, she nestled against him, pressing her body close. "Whatever you have in mind, you'd better hurry. Don't let me detain you." She turned, her heels clicking on the stone path as she moved away.

With relief, McKenzie took one last look at Wallace before racing to the terminal.

CHAPTER 58

Mallory braced herself for the unknown. Led to the lower level beneath the platform, she watched Coulomb place his index finger on an indented cradle on a wall-mounted pad. Within seconds, the biometric scanner flashed green, the steel door slid open. Forced by gunpoint inside the windowless concrete bunker, she was tied to a chair strategically placed in the middle of the large room. She faced a crescent-shaped electronic console with keyboards, banks of switches and a continuous row of flat screen monitors. The plain concrete walls and high-voltage components wafted a certain olfactory atmosphere. She sensed the intricacy of the equipment, the heat-generating circuity and components casting warmth that in any other situation would be a pleasant caress. In front of the state of the art equipment was a large LCD screen suspended from the ceiling displaying an immense high-definition map of Europe highlighting several cities. The entire scene looked straight out of mission control Houston.

This had to be the portal to *Socrates*.

She looked at the cities, each with a glowing red dot. The realization hit her like a sledgehammer. She felt numbness in her throat, as if the revelation had been wedged there, choking every breath she took. It was what the map represented that made it hard to breath.

The cold, hammer-forged barrel of the Glock 26 stroked Mallory's cheek causing sweat to glaze her face. She could feel Esra's hot breath torch the back of her neck, the sensation of hot and cold messing with her sanity. Esra's words put it all in perspective: "Enjoy the show—it will be your last."

Mallory knew not to inflame her in any way. She remained stoic as Esra stepped in front, her smile a sadistic smirk, a torturous expression of evil. She walked over to the console where Coulomb was seated working through some unknown computer protocol.

Mallory watched him type commands and check each location on the map against a monitor in front of him. She spoke forcibly. "Socrates was convicted by a jury of Athenians for refusing to idolize the gods recognized by the state. The law stipulated that he must drink from a cup of Hemlock—self-inflicted suicide. The display map, those cities—am I on the right track?"

Coulomb whirled in his chair, surprised by Mallory's deduction. Eager to boast, he answered. "You are a most intelligent woman, professor. Your observation and conclusion deserve a detailed and exhaustive explanation, which I am thrilled to share. What you are witnessing is a remote hookup by a geostationary satellite to water treatment facilities in each of these cities. Unbeknownst to others, we have modified the storage tanks to accept our commands."

So that was it, water distribution facilities to be poisoned? She kept her eyes glued to the screen.

"This was not, how would you say— a walk in the park, I can assure you." He smiled, gloating. "Our work was not easy. Retrofitting these municipal storage tanks under the cover of darkness took two years to complete. We had to recruit corrupt water managers, engineers from many European countries to achieve our goals. It was difficult, but because of an amazing human quality— there are people who will do almost anything for money, even sell their soul. We had to find tanks that were accessible without elaborate security measures. Europe has taken steps to safeguard many things from terrorist attacks—mass transit, public spaces, their military—but alas, their utility infrastructure is somewhat lacking. We have taken advantage of that. Tanks that we identified are very large, thirty to forty meters in diameter, massive, above ground. They are either steel or concrete structures, most with a slight dome shaped roof. In the center of these roofs, there is an air vent. Easily modified, I must admit. Beneath each air vent, we have installed a series of containers invisible to authorities, impossible to detect. Water from these tanks is used for human consumption: drinking, cooking, and bathing. Once the signal from the satellite has been received, the containers beneath the vent will be dropped into the water. Their protective coating will dissolve immediately."

Mallory couldn't believe what she was hearing. She yanked on her bound hands, not expecting them to come free. The cords only tightened further, like a Chinese finger trap, the harder she pulled, the tighter the restraint.

Coulomb's smile widened. "These containers are filled with a derivative of Sarin, one of the deadliest nerve agents known to man. The compound formulated by our very own Bruno Metzier. You do remember old Bruno. I believe we all enjoyed a lavish meal and cruise the other evening."

Mallory shuddered. How could she forget that? Now Bruno Metzier and his pharmaceuticals made crazy sense.

"Anyway, we call it Sarin-TX. It is tasteless and colorless, even odorless, soluble in water and easily transmitted through municipal piping. Once the victim comes in contact with it, through drinking or bathing, he or she will immediately experience blurriness, confusion, rapid breathing, convulsions, paralysis—and eventual death." Coulomb rolled his eyes in a display of faux feelings of sorrow.

Unfathomable someone could kill innocent people. Genocides and ethnic strife, she understood the horrors of past atrocities. But corporate cleansing? How could evil like this be viable in this day and age? She struggled with her restraints.

Coulomb pointed at the map. He was in his zone, immersed in the power he now had at his fingertips—exhilarating! "These red dots represent fifty-three water storage tanks in a multitude of municipal systems, mainly medium-size cities. All together, they supply water for an estimated fifteen million people."

He swiveled in the chair and pushed a few buttons on the console. A monitor flickered on with a close-up view of a large round structure with a dome-shaped roof taken at a slightly high angle. A small window in the lower left-hand corner scrolled open.

Lyon Municipal Water Works

Tank No. 2

Tank Inside diameter = 62 meters

Water height = 12 meters

Capacity-30.0 mil. lit.

"You are looking at one of the water distribution tanks. Each location has been fitted with the video feed you are now seeing, the cameras hidden and well protected.

Now if you will excuse me." He activated all the other monitors, each displaying an image of a large water tank, filtered with a greenish blush.

Mallory was unable to speak. This was beyond the pale—an insidious scheme to kill tens of thousands, maybe hundreds of thousands, and for what? She knew she was going to die anyway, so why should she care about *Socrates*? Yet, she did. Wanting to know *why* was an ingrained driving force, just like finding the solution to some stubborn differential equation.

"*Why* do you want to kill? *Why*, for what purpose?"

"Oh, it's a very simple calculation," he said, keeping his back to her. "Freshwater is an endangered species. Over one-sixth of this planet has inadequate water for survival and it is only getting worse. *I am* the only one that can fix the problem."

What! Now she knew he was blabbing beyond the borders of sanity. "By killing? Where in the world does that equate to solving the fresh water shortage?"

"Oh, don't be so harsh. It's so perfect. Yes, it will take time, but great deeds never happen overnight." He stood and moved in her direction. "This is only one step toward water dominance. By sacrificing a few victims, these poor defenseless water districts will have no choice but to turn their failed and insecure public water systems over to private enterprise. When they look at Möbius, they will see an uncompromised water utility, unparalleled in security. We are the experts. Our reputation as an honest and efficient water manager is above all others."

Mallory shook her head attempting to rid the visual Coulomb had created. She had heard enough. The scheme sounded preposterous, unworkable, and to kill thousands to test his capabilities… this was beyond insane, this was shear lunacy.

"Oh, the blame game will surface. We know how these things work. Any of the scores of world terrorist organizations will want to take responsibility. Terrorist organizations always do, especially ISIS or Al-Qaeda. They love the notoriety. It's enough to make your head spin, is it not?" He laughed uncontrollably.

"You're mad!" she screamed.

Coulomb stared hard at Mallory. His eyes were a wild blaze. "Don't you see? Only we can save the day, we'll be the only ones able to provide clean water in these cities' desperate time of need. Our present utilities won't suffer the problem of tainted supplies. We have uncompromising security. Water administrators will see that, making it easy to enter into contracts appointing Möbius operator and savior. We have proven abilities, and they will trust us to prevent this tragedy from happening again. And as time goes on, we will be entrenched. It would take an act of God to dislodge our dominance."

The hairs stood straight up on the back of Mallory's neck. "You are a sick …sick man."

"This is but one phase," he continued, ignoring her. "Other operations are in progress. Tepecik Dam was one; fortunately, losing it doesn't slow us down. We will rebuild, and soon we will have the capacity to deliver water to other thirsty nations. In essence, we will have control— all the control. Möbius will be the world's foremost freshwater provider…a force to be reckoned with."

"What makes you think you can get away with this."

"We have uncompromised references. The World Bank has great faith in Möbius. We do the best for the impoverished. They like the way we do business." Coulomb continued to work the keyboard, completing the hookup procedures. "We've worked many years networking and cultivating our allies. The only obstacle remaining is sequencing."

Coulomb reached into his pocket and produced the signal detection keys, placing them with a flourish on the console. Mallory remembered each of the four being associated with a constant and a key, π, e, $\sqrt{2}$ and $\pi^2/6$. Now that Coulomb possessed Meadowlark's key, there was nothing anyone could do to prevent him from carrying out his nightmarish plan.

She felt a shiver race down her spine and reach the very core of her being.

Coulomb pushed another sequence of buttons. *Yes, the contracts will be ours*, he contemplated, and all the power and billions of Euros that go with it. He felt elated. The success of *Socrates* would more than make up for the loss of the dam. "We can now sequence!" he cried out in a vociferous voice filled with emotion. He pulled a handkerchief from his pocket and patted at the lines of sweat beading upon his forehead. Never had he ever imagined the euphoria he was now experiencing. For the first time, he was on the cusp of unabated achievement —something that would live on in the annals of history.

He gazed at the controls. On the right side of the keyboard, four key slots stared back at him, waiting for the four independent signal detection keys. His hand was shaking as he picked up the first key, the red one, signifying π in all its might and glory. He took his time and slid it into the slot. "We are on our way," he celebrated, taking a deep and vigorous breath. He continued with e and $\sqrt{2}$, green and yellow, inserting them. His eyes grew wide with delight. He paused when he picked up the last key, $\pi^2/6$, the black one. Without this one, the greatest strategy in capitalistic subjugation would never come to fruition. No way in hell would he ever absolve the man who came close to sabotaging his finest achievement.

He inserted Meadowlark's key and leaned back. A row of four amber lights on the front of the monitor flicked on and off, eventually staying lit from left to right. One by one, he turned each key. They were engaged, the engine had been started.

Now to put it in gear.

Reaching over, he flipped a column of switches. He stood and allowed himself a long, pleasant stretch, arching his back with a sigh. He gazed at Esra, and in that moment, he felt a glorious future closing in on them. He accepted her ravenous smile, and without hesitation, turned back to the console and pushed a button below the bank of switches. Almost instantaneously, on the upper left hand corner of the large screen, four columns of alphanumeric figures flashed by in a blistering sequence of on and off...on and off...on and off...

Coulomb held his breath. The moment of truth was upon him. The first column froze, the word plastered on the screen:

SEQUENCED

He felt his heart skip a beat like it had never skipped before. He steadied himself, pupils raged red reflecting the remaining alphanumeric columns. The second column came to a standstill:

SEQUENCED

He could almost feel himself weep. And the third:

SEQUENCED

And the fourth:

SEQUENCED

The operation had commenced. If he was a believer, he would have felt as if the hand of God was on his side.

Instantly, the red dots on the large screen locating each of the fifty-three cities flashed one at a time, He nodded confidently to Esra as they turned a steady green, beginning with Bonn, Wiesbaden, Mannheim, Utrecht and working on down from Northern to Southern Europe. Coulomb's eyes widened when the city of Chambéry flashed. Never before had he experienced such a fleshy tremble of relief. His parent's deaths avenged. Justice served on a grand scale, forcing Chambéry to its knees.

Finding his thoughts to be floating over the top of the world, he turned and faced Mallory. "You have had the greatest opportunity to witness history, but the question remains: what to do with you?"

McKenzie took off at a jog, hoping to avoid detection. The path cut sharply through a glade of English yews, and then wound steeply up the opposite side. Near the top, he stopped and surveyed the upper terrace. The guests were filtering down towards the dock, awaiting access to the *Lune Corbeau*. He caught a glimpse of Wallace, waving goodbye as he headed in his direction.

He scanned the back of the terminal and found a door at the top of a set of steps. He took off at a run, leapt over a low hedge, then raced up the stairs. Catching his breath, he kept his eyes peeled for any terminal personnel. Time was slipping away. He ducked inside, sprinting along a catwalk that wrapped around the machinery and massive counterweights.

He pulled his Beretta out, keeping his ears and eyes alert. He turned the corner and drew back. Standing near the tram was an armed guard. With the clock ticking, what were his options? Plan A: take the man out and wait for Wallace to show up. Take Wallace hostage and use him as bait to free Mallory. Plan B: stowaway on top of the car as Wallace takes it to the upper terminal. Surprise all three Möbius thugs, free Mallory and be a hero for the rest of his life.

Who was he kidding? Plan B was the fantasy option and would take a miracle to pull off, probably get him killed in the process. Plan A was his only sane option—take the guard out now.

He looked over to the guard's position. Dammit, the man was gone. Fighting to suppress his panic, he caught the shadow of him stepping through another door at the front of the terminal. No guard, no plan A. He didn't need someone prodding him in the back to tell him what to do now. Plan B, the fantasy option now made sense, except for the part about getting killed.

Another obstacle suddenly surfaced. What about security cameras? As sophisticated as Coulomb was, he surely would have a video feed from the terminal building. Could be he'd already been captured on camera. With tensions rising, he surveyed the area. No cameras that he could see. It was now or never. He sprinted past the motor, rounded the large overhead cable sheave, and vaulted up a metal stair that led to an upper catwalk. He crawled over the railing and stepped out onto the top of the tram. The carriage arm was wide enough to huddle against, hidden from anyone who may come through the door. He could only hope it worked.

Hadn't he seen this stunt before? Wasn't it *Where Eagles Dare*, Richard Burton and Clint Eastwood riding on top of a tram, defying the Germans in WWII? Of course, they were successful, but that was the movies.

He couldn't believe he would try the same thing.

Mallory again yanked sharply on her bound hands. The chair bounced crazily across the floor. With a sinister grin, Esra pulled back on the barrel of the Glock, chambering a round.

"Go ahead, bitch. Do it!" Mallory goaded. Esra pointed the gun at her, her finger tightening on the trigger—

McKenzie heard words spoken, mixed conversation in English and German, and the clink as the terminal door opened. Over the top of the carriage he saw the guard return, followed by Wallace. Ducking back down, he waited patiently, hoping he would not be seen.

The door to the tram car slid open. The car bounced slightly as Wallace entered and the swish of the door closing. The electric motor hummed to life and the tram lurched forward. McKenzie stared out ahead, the cool air whooshing past his face. He held tight to the carriage arm, feeling his heart pound rhythmically with the cable sliding smoothly over the rollers. Grateful for the increasing darkness, he didn't dare look down.

CHAPTER 59

Mallory was stuck in the region between awareness and sound mind when she heard the voice: "Everyone freeze! This gun is loaded and the operator will find pleasure in pulling the trigger."

She looked up, stunned. Harry Meadowlark stood in the doorway, a gun aimed at Coulomb. There were bloodstains on the sleeve of his right arm, which hung limp at his side.

Mallory cringed. Esra's gun was still pointed at her, surprised that she hadn't pulled the trigger.

"The second you shoot the lady is the second I drop your lover-to-be," Meadowlark swore to Esra. "I suggest you lay your weapon down."

Esra's face filled with rage and hate. After a few seconds, she lowered the gun.

"Place it on the console, slow and easy," Meadowlark ordered. "Then back away. That goes for you *too,* Paul."

As if in slow motion, they both complied. Meadowlark moved further into the room and strode over to Mallory.

"The keys," she yelled. "They've been sequenced. Do something!"

"I can see that." Meadowlark didn't seem concerned.

Mallory stared at him. She didn't understand how he could remain so calm. Did the catastrophe occurring across Europe have no meaning for him? She remembered the game he was playing with Coulomb. Was it still in play?

"Welcome, Harry," Coulomb said with calmness. "You can see you have lost at your own game."

Meadowlark walked over to the console and picked up Esra's gun, then shoved it in his waistband. "I guess that's a matter of opinion." Stepping back, he switched the gun to his right hand, grimacing in pain. He bent down and untied Mallory.

Mallory rubbed at her swollen wrists. She stood and rushed to the console, frantically looking for an off button.

"I'm afraid Paul is right," Meadowlark said. "There is nothing we can do now."

Was Meadowlark going to sit idly by? "Stop this game!" Mallory pleaded. "People will die."

"And so will you," Esra mocked.

Meadowlark gave her a skeptical look. "Esra, now that's not showing compassion." She bared her teeth in a contained rage.

Meadowlark bit off his next words. "But I do know about honesty and trust, something that is counter to your character. And should we talk about your skill as a lover? Paul may get a kick out of that."

Esra's face tensed. For a moment, Mallory thought she would rush Meadowlark, and beat the living hell out of him if he didn't shoot her first.

"There never was anything between the two of us, if you are insinuating I loved you," Esra spat.

"You played me for a while," Meadowlark said with evident satisfaction. "We all make mistakes; I've made mine. Now, your sights have been set on the kingpin himself." He shifted his stare to Coulomb. "What about it Paul? Are you ready to indulge with the two-timer here, or are you still in lust with the Spanish whore?"

Mallory saw Coulomb's face boil with anger. He took a step towards Meadowlark but held up, looking into the barrel of the gun.

A tell-tale vibration shimmied across the room. She heard the hum and saw Meadowlark perk his ears. She realized what was happening—the tram had started again.

"There is no escape, Harry," Coulomb said calmly. "You may hold the cards now, but you will not leave here alive."

A cool, upslope breeze caught Katie off guard as she huddled near the upper terminal. She was beginning to chill. Meadowlark had been gone for over forty minutes and staying here was no longer an option. She had the binoculars and the flashlight that he had left, but what she needed was a weapon. The moon had just begun to clear the mountains to the east and the cliff-defying terminal was once again birthing shadows. Now, it would be difficult to get closer without being seen.

Hidden along the edge of the clearing, she darted behind a thicket of trees and shrubs on the lower slope below the observation deck. Reaching a small knoll, she swore her hammering heartbeat would warn others of her approach. No matter how much she tried to convince herself that Harry and Mallory were safe and the bunker under his control, her gut told her otherwise.

Nothing ever came easy—she knew this first hand. What did she have to guide her from here on out—a misguided ideology—naivety—stupidity—love—all of the above? She could feel the tears once again well in her eyes. Through her mind's disarray, she pictured Ismet. Could she still see his face, the deep hazel eyes, square jaw, neat beard, the muscular body with the gentle touch, gone? She tried hard to visualize her father. *God, why can't I see him?* Had she forgotten his fatherly face just as easily as she had ignored him? She let the tears cascade with the realization that she would never again feel his presence or hear his comforting words.

She couldn't stay here and lose Mallory, too. She zeroed in on the observation deck, above on a hillock to her left. Rising up, she raced up reaching a waist-high stone wall that encircled the timber structure. She pressed her back against the wall and caught her breath, wondering if someone was on the other side.

Was the sentry that Harry saw still here? Crawling along on all fours, she found an opening. The moon was now behind a copse of trees drowning out the rays. She stuck her head inside and surveyed the darkened space. Eye level with the concrete floor, she didn't see nor hear anything. Yet, there was something there. Across the floor at the edge of another opening, she saw an object—oblong, like a pile of rocks, something that shouldn't be here. Curiosity growing, she crept cat-like across the deck.

Her heart leapt out of her chest when she glimpsed an arm extending from the darkness where the light of the moon had found an avenue through the trees. The sight of the body went to the pit of her stomach. She prayed it wasn't Harry. She pulled out the flashlight and turned it on, masking it with her hand to keep the beam directed down. Shedding her fears, she looked closer. The body was a man, a dead one. It was the sentry. She took a reassuring breath. The spill of the flashlight revealed the cause of death—a near perfect bullet hole to the center of the man's head. Blood pooled on the concrete where the bullet had exited. The man still gripped an assault rifle tightly in his right hand. She was surprised Harry hadn't taken the weapon.

She beamed her light along the sentry's body, checking for other weapons, maybe a handgun. Nothing, except a sheath looped on his belt carrying a folding knife. Reaching over, she felt queasy prying the dead man's fingers from around the stock. She stood, holding the assault rifle against her shoulder steadying it with both hands. She stared at the terminal, now fully bathed in the light of the moon. There was no movement, but that didn't mean there were no other lookouts.

A monotonous hum broke the silence. The cables were in motion. The upper tram slid out of the enclosure and drifted into the dark abyss where the moon rays hadn't penetrated. If no one was aboard, it could mean only one thing.

Someone was coming up.

Mallory watched the screen, enumerated with flashing red dots, Le Havre, Lyon, Toulouse, Bilbao, Verona, each turning green, north to south. The poisoning continued. She turned her attention to Meadowlark. Why was he so calm? This was no longer a game.

Meadowlark's attention remained on Coulomb. "For Christ's sake Paul, do you think you will get away with the killing of thousands of innocent people? And Möbius to the rescue; you can't be serious?" He moved in front of the console, the gun barrel wagging at the Frenchman. "Don't make me puke. You're nothing but a delirious, egocentric fool."

Coulomb stared at Meadowlark's gun, ignoring his banter. "The deed is done."

"Yes, it is," Meadowlark said, somewhat submissive. He tipped his head, listening. The sound of spinning wheels and sliding cables could be heard through the concrete ceiling. "I assume that other stooge, our friend Shelby is on his way. Not the brightest crayon in the box, but his appearance can be problematic."

Mallory couldn't take it. She had to do something. Looking around, she spotted a telephone receiver cradled at the end of the console. Rushing over, she picked it up, contemplating the buttons on the belly. She had no clue as to what to dial to get an outside line. She stared at Meadowlark for help. He ignored her.

"Tell me Harry, why are you here?" Coulomb asked. "Don't get me wrong, I am happy you decided to join in the fun. Did you think you could stop the sequence, or did you wish to see your genius programing at work?"

"As a matter of fact, neither. But now that you mention it, I have to admit, I have embedded a beautiful piece of coding in those keys, a complex version of the Lisp programming language modified exclusively for this application. Who would have thought a code developed in 1958 would have the ultimate sophistication to function impeccably. It has a paradigm I developed, unknown to any other soul on this planet. The internal functions cannot be manipulated. It is unbreakable. Quite clever, if I say so myself. Still, I have to give you credit Paul, it was your idea after all, a way to make sure all four of us were on the same page. If even one key was missing, the sequence wouldn't work. There is absolutely no way in hell any one would be able to get into the lines of code and modify it. At your reasoning, that was to insure a shared accountability."

Coulomb let out a long sigh. "And what caused you to take on this Judas affliction—a change of heart, moralistic evaluation, the fear of success? What would cause such a dramatic shift? And why come here, to watch your work succeed and destroy your new found goodness?"

Meadowlark stared at Esra and then turned his attention back to Coulomb. "I actually wanted to see the face of a murderer and the bitch that drools over him."

In that moment, Esra rushed Meadowlark, who spun the gun away from Coulomb. But it was enough of a diversion. Coulomb lashed out with his hand, striking down on Meadowlark's bloodied arm. The gun dropped, clattered off the top of the console and onto the floor. Coulomb lunged at Meadowlark, kicking the gun away. Meadowlark grabbed him by the throat and began to squeeze. Coulomb's face turned red. Thrashing about, they twisted in a circular dance, the Frenchman pounding Meadowlark's midsection.

Immediately, Mallory lunged for the gun, only to find hands clawing across her face—needle-sharp fingernails gashing into her forehead. The fingernails dug deep. Mallory grabbed Esra's hands, trying to push them aside. At the same time, Esra cocked her elbow and slammed backwards, catching Mallory in the side of the jaw.

She went down on her knees, gasping. Blood streamed into her eyes from the vicious nail cuts. She raised her head in time to see Esra seize the elusive gun and point it at her.

But the bullets never came. Esra bared her teeth and spun the barrel away from Mallory and triggered off a shot, catching Meadowlark squarely in the chest. His hands released Coulomb's neck. The impact flung him back several feet, and he collapsed in a heap.

Esra swung the gun back to Mallory, ready to finish the job.

"No, not yet," Coulomb said, rubbing his neck and breathing heavily. He straightened up slowly. "We need her a little longer. She still has information."

Mallory dashed over and crouched next to Meadowlark. He lay on his back, blood draining from the wound. His eyes were open and his mouth twitched as if he wanted to say something. His words were garbled, a bare whisper.

She cradled his head in her arms and pulled him closer. "It's okay," she comforted.

He fought for another breath, clinching her arm. His voice was weak. "Get out…now…the clock ticks…" His lips quivered and his eyes rolled around in agony.

Esra rushed over and pushed Mallory out of the way. With a methodic, savage look, she leveled the gun at Meadowlark and shot him in the head.

This was beyond the shroud of anything Mallory had ever witnessed. Her awareness blurred like black ocean waves washing the numbness completely over her.

McKenzie held tightly onto the carriage arm, the crisp air whistling by in a sea of near blackness, save for the fading lights from Coulomb's terrace party. He dare not think about slipping from the top of the tram, knowing he was hundreds of feet above the ground. The only sound other than the shrill of air came from the smooth rumble of the haulage cable through the sheaves of the second intermediate tower.

The pitch of the ascent changed, the increased inclination rocked the car back and forth. Sliding forward, he tightened his grip on the carriage arm with both hands and straightened his legs out, hoping his feet would catch something. One heel snagged a seam at the edge of the car's roof. He took a deep, cool breath. Heart racing like mad, he hoped to hell Wallace hadn't heard anything.

Straight ahead, a massive black escarpment appeared, blacker than the night. *Die Wandung* loomed like a one-eyed menace from the depths of hell, the one-eye being the pinpoint of light from the upper terminal. He watched the light grow and the arrow-like roof come into focus. Nearing the top, the moon rose above the ridge to the east, bathing the terminal in a silvery sheen.

Knowing someone might be waiting for Wallace, he moved to the horizontal portion of the carriage arm, taking care not to make any noise. Feeling secure and hidden, he waited as the tram glided into the terminal, the interior lights brightly turning night to day. The sound of sliding cables ceased and the tram came to a stop.

He gripped the Beretta with a steady hand. The car door slid open, the sound echoing through the high space of the terminal. He could hear Wallace, the crisp *click* of his dress boots on the concrete floor. Gradually, the sounds of his footfalls ceased.

McKenzie raised his head and surveyed the space. It was bright as day from the overhead halogens; fortunately, no guards were seen.He took a steady breath and noticed there was no catwalk similar to the lower terminal. He lowered himself along the side, catching the door handle with his foot. A second later, he was on the platform. Nary a sound had been made. Finding a hidden spot behind a wall enclosure near the back of the terminal, he whispered, "Neal, do you copy." His earpiece vibrated.

Neal responded. "Loud and clear. Where are you? We were worried."

"We finally have good line-of-sight radio contact now. I'm at the upper terminal—it's a long story. They have Mallory here somewhere. What's your situation?"

"We've closed in on the compound—two of our men and a contingent of FIS. We didn't want to move in unless we heard from you. We can get a helicopter up there in fifteen minutes. You can't do it alone."

"Give me thirty minutes, okay?

A short pause. "Be careful," Neal said. "Copy and out."

McKenzie half-smiled. Hugging the wall, he extended his head around the corner—nothing, nobody, nil. He could see a set of stairs thirty feet away disappearing below the floor. He moved swiftly, pausing behind a steel column.

In the tensed silence, his eyes zipped around. The stairs led to a lower level surrounded by a railing. He saw a steel door in the concrete wall. An exterior light flooded the space. Beside the right jamb, a small security panel was seen.

Katie waited impatiently. It had been several minutes since the tram car docked. Hidden behind a wide-trunked fir, she watched with petrified fascination as Shelby Wallace walked rapidly around the corner of the terminal ducking out of sight. She was more surprised to see the CIA man creeping after him, his gun in full view.

McKenzie shuffled down the stairs and moved next to the door. He placed an ear against it. Sure enough, voices could be heard coming from inside. They were garbled and incoherent. His nose twitched. The air smelled of ozone and electrified equipment. He turned his head and spotted an opening a couple of feet above and to his left—a duct, venting the heat from the array of electronic equipment.

McKenzie's nerves went haywire at the sensation of a gun thrust into his back.

"Don't think 'bout it," Wallace said, snatching McKenzie's Beretta from his hand and plucking the ear piece out of his ear.

McKenzie swore silently.

"Hands high," Wallace demanded.

He held them over his head as he looked out of the corner of his eye at Wallace, placing his finger into the groove of the wall-mounted pad. Seconds later, the door rolled silently open.

"Inside," Wallace demanded.

A wave of dread swept over McKenzie as he was led into the bunker. His anxiety was met with reality when he spotted a body on the floor. He took a closer look. The body lay on its side, blood all around. It was Meadowlark. Next to him was a kneeling Mallory.

CHAPTER 60

Mallory didn't know whether to rejoice or cry. She locked eyes with McKenzie, reading his vigilant facial expression. She understood—*don't give up, stay alert.* After the shock of Meadowlark's savage murder, her brain was close to mush. Seeing McKenzie, she felt a rekindling of purpose. She glanced up at the screen and saw that there were only two cities left awaiting the satellite instruction. Once they turned green, it would be done, all fifty-plus cities with water supplies tainted with a deadly poison. She looked at McKenzie and mouthed, *we've got to do something.*

Coulomb stared at McKenzie. "Well look here. The CIA man to the rescue, although a bit late to save the day." He broke into laughter.

Wallace joined in. "Now that you mention it, he does look familiar."

"Where did you find him?" Coulomb asked.

The Southerner kept the gun firmly planted in McKenzie's back. "Ridin' the top of the tram. He's a brave soul; alerted me with his scratchin'."

"How about this, everyone's here, except the Haley woman," Coulomb remarked. "Did she return home to attend to her dead father's affairs?"

In her topsy-turvy state, Mallory had totally forgotten about Katie.

"For Christ's sakes, you bastards killed everyone that girl has feelings for." McKenzie yelled.

"Y'all diggin' your own graves," Wallace warned. He leaned back and swung the butt of his gun into McKenzie's left temple hard, launching him into the console with a thud. Furious, Mallory bent down helping him into a sitting position. His eyes were dazed.

Esra kept her gun pointed at them both. "Why do we wait? We do not need them now." Her finger kept pressure on the trigger.

"Patience, my dear; in due time."

Wallace forced them into chairs, binding their hands behind their backs.

Coulomb looked down at them like a triumphant dictator after a coup. "Esra and I have some entertaining to attend to, but don't worry, we'll be back in a couple of hours. In the meantime, Shelby will keep you company. I'm sure your study of the wall map will be enlightening." He gazed up at the large screen, and a broad smile emerged. "Well, look at that, everyone, Granada and Catania have come through. The screen is as green as the flowing vineyards in the Rhone Valley. When we return, another trip on the tram will be special. It will be a rare moonlight ride." His smile turned to a degenerate smirk.

Katie froze. It happened so fast. Could she have helped? In despair, she caught herself from crying out. Back resting against the tree, she slid down, scared. She didn't know what to do. For a couple of minutes, she just sat there, unable to think rationally. From all indications, the CIA man was now captive, probably Harry as well. And Mallory, what about her? Her father, God how she needed him. The night turned dark and cold. The emptiness that surrounded her now was greater than any she had experienced before.

She stood up and felt the weight of the rifle. She wouldn't let this nightmare continue. She took a step out in the open right as the door slid open. Two people emerged. Quickly, she retreated.

Her blood boiled. The man was Paul Coulomb, the one responsible for the deaths of her loved ones. Gritting her teeth, she stepped out from behind the tree, pointed the assault rifle and pressed the trigger.

It didn't respond.

Dammit, the safety was on!

Fumbling along the right side, she found the safety and pushed it down. Leveling the weapon again, she crooked her finger over the trigger and aimed.

They were gone, hidden by the walls of the terminal.

Feeling the weight of defeat, she dashed down the slope onto the concrete floor of the terminal. Cautiously, she approached. Her pounding pulse would not let up. Gathering courage, she took a frenzied breath. She heard a high-pitched whoosh, the mechanized hum of a taut cable sliding between sheaves.

She whirled, staring helplessly as the tram bucked and disappeared into the gaping darkness, shielded from the moon rays by the dramatic face of rock known as *Die Wandung*.

Mallory kept working her hands back and forth, trying to loosen the cord that bound her. She turned her head and glanced at McKenzie, still groggy from the blow to his head. The extent of the blunt trauma was unknown. His head drooped. An uncertain silence filled the air.

Their chairs were set in the middle of the bunker, well away from the console. Meadowlark's body lay on the floor between her and the door. She tried to remain calm after attempting to make sense of what he said—*get out now...the clock ticks*.

Wallace sat, picking at his fingernails with a pocketknife. He stared at his captives and remarked with a chuckle. "As they say in my neck of the woods, you two seem to have gotten the 'short end of the stick.'" He winked and continued picking.

"Listen, why don't you untie us from these chairs and take us away from here?" Mallory pleaded. "None of us are safe."

Wallace folded his knife and pocketed it. "Now, why'd I do that? Don't you feel safe in here, concrete bunker and all? Ya'll get fresh air soon enough. I suspect, 'bout a thousand feet of fresh air." He broke into laughter.

Just then, an overpowering alarm went off, a steady, incessant shrill that brought Wallace to his feet. A large digital timer appeared on the upper left-hand corner of the screen; a countdown had begun.

1:59...1:58...1:57...

Wallace stared blankly at the screen. "What the hell?" he drawled. He bent over the console and looked up and down the array of buttons and lights, frantically searching for something to push.

The ear-piercing alarm continued.

Mallory furiously worked her wrists back and forth. Was this the *clock ticks* Meadowlark had warned about?

1:49…1:48…1:47…

She saw shock etched on Wallace's face.

"All outa kilter, what the fucks happen'n—" he kept blabbering as he jabbed buttons, attempting to gain control of the situation. He spun around to another monitor, hands poised over the keyboard. The timer kept rolling off seconds. "Dammit," he screamed. "This damn thang won't respond." His eyes were ablaze and his face covered with perspiration. He was in absolute panic attack, totally confused.

Time was not on their side. The head-jarring alarm was creating chaos with Mallory's nerves as well, but it only made her more determined. She struggled to loosen the restraints, a thin, string-like cord that cut into her wrists. She took a deep breath. A countdown could only end with one thing, something bad. She knew Meadowlark was clever. He already blew up a dam, and the game he was playing with Coulomb—now it could only mean one thing. No wonder he wasn't concerned. Another yank, she felt the cord loosen.

1:21…1:20…1:19…

Wallace kept attacking the keyboard, his eyes flitting back and forth between the console and the screen. In a fit of frustration, he picked up the keyboard and flung it across the room.Meadowlark's last words kept resonating in Mallory's head—get out…now…the clock ticks… Out of the corner of her eye, the countdown continued. "We have to get out of here!" Mallory screamed. "This place is not safe."

1:11…1:10…1:09…

Wallace turned pale. "Jeeebeezy Christ, I don't know what to do!"

Mallory pleaded. "Get us out. We all have to leave—now!"

Katie stood next to the door and examined the wall-mounted pad with the top groove. This was the security system—something to maybe place a finger into, a fingerprint security code. She suddenly remembered the dead sentry above on the observation deck.

Wallace gave Mallory a hostile look. "Whad'ya know about this? He dashed over and gripped Mallory by the shoulders, shaking her hysterically. "Whad'ya mean we must leave?"

Mallory felt nauseated from the abusive shaking. She tightened her muscles. "This place is a ticking time bomb. It's going to explode."

"Explode, what the fuck?"

"Yes, yes it is. We must get out!"

Wallace wound up and slapped her hard across the face. Mallory absorbed the blow and shot him a hateful look.

McKenzie roused. "Leave her alone," he mumbled

"Shut the fuck up!" Wallace reached over and grabbed the legs of McKenzie's chair, flipping it. He went down, landing hard against the concrete floor. He didn't move.

Wallace turned back and stared at the screen, a frantic look of terror on his face.

0:58...0:57...0:56...

He rushed back to the console, desperately pushing buttons, flipping switches, anything.

"Abort the system!" Mallory yelled.

"I can't, goddamn it! Wallace whirled and faced Mallory. His eyes flew wild around the room as if in a hallucination.

Mallory yanked like hell on her restraints.

0:44...0:43...0:42...

Out of breath from the quick run up the steps to the observation deck, Katie knelt down beside the dead guard. What was she thinking? He wouldn't have had the security clearance to enter the bunker. Or would he? There was only one way to find out.

Gathering her strength, she reached down and snapped open the sheath on his belt and pulled out a folding knife. Trembling, she held it in her hand for a moment, contemplating the thought. Inside her wildest imagination, she never would have considered such an act, but did she have a choice?

She opened a blade, splayed the man's cold fingers flat against the concrete slab. Her heart thumped in her chest as she gritted her teeth, located the knuckle joint on his index finger. Her stomach lurched in a moment of revulsion. Turning away, she sliced the blade back and forth. The sound—ripping, tearing cartilage, the sundering of the final piece of bone. With a final saw, the blade scratched into the concrete, the last bit of tendon and skin snapped like a rubber band. In a daze, bile in her throat, she latched onto the assault rifle with one hand, macabrely held the finger in the other, and scrambled down to the bunker. Yelling could be heard from inside above a consistent pulsating alarm. She aligned the lifeless digit onto the groove located on top of the wall pad and held her breath.

A green light flashed. Instantly, the door swooshed opened.

She rushed in.

Mallory pulled harder, almost pulling a hand free…almost. Just as she felt the cord give, she heard the door open between the blasts of the alarm. The first thing she thought of was Coulomb and Esra returning to take her and McKenzie for the last ride of their lives. *My God, Katie!*

Wallace stiffened.

Katie stared at Meadowlark's bloody body. In shock, she held the assault rifle limply in her hands.

Wallace reached for the gun beneath his jacket.

"Katie!" Mallory yelled.

Katie was unable to escape her stupor.

Pulling with all her might, Mallory's raw wrists popped loose. Unrestrained, she rushed Wallace and slammed into him just as he fired at Katie. The bullet flew past, cratering the concrete to the left of the door. Wallace kept his balance and flung Mallory off.

He turned the gun in her direction.

Katie winced at the sound of the gunshot, drowning out the persistent screeching of the alarm.

Gathering her senses, she saw Wallace level the gun at Mallory. Without hesitating, she raised the assault rifle and pulled the trigger, and then again…

and again… A quick burst of bullets plowed into Wallace, hurling him off his feet. The weapon recoiled out of her grasp falling to the floor.

Mallory regained her composure. Wallace lay next to the blood-smudged console on his back, chest soaked in blood, but it was the countdown that grabbed her attention.

0:27…0:26…0:25…

She rushed over to where McKenzie lay prone on the floor. She lifted him into a sitting position. "Can you move?" she asked.

He nodded, too weak to speak

After unravelling his restraints, Mallory helped him to the door. Katie came over and lent a hand. Mallory glanced back at the screen.

0:19…0:18…0:17…

"Quick!" she yelled. "Out now."

Understanding the urgency, they each wrapped an arm around McKenzie, half-dragging him up the stairs. He found his feet and they broke into a trot up the path towards the observation deck.

Mallory sensed time had run out. At that moment, an earth-shattering explosion shattered the moonlit night just as they reached the observation deck and dove behind the walls.

Coulomb tried to steady the tram, bouncing erratically, whipped by the thrashing cables. A split second earlier, a loud boom echoed across the mountain. In that instant, his eyes caught the terrified expression on Esra's face. He gazed up toward the terminal, now a luminous fireball spitting chunks of debris out over *Die Wandung*.

Hysterical, he searched the levers of the lopping car, thinking he could stop what was happening. "No!" he screamed, his lips quivering and his eyes bulging. The veins in his forehead popped like a hideous creature from some distant planet, as he frantically worked the controls. Up the mountain, the arrow-shaped roof was now engulfed in the inferno, the intense heat melting structural steel like candle wax. Horror flashed through his mind as he stared at the cables, his lifeline consumed in flames.

The tram took another downward bounce, undulating with deep, unforgiving amplitude. A sudden jerk sent Coulomb slamming into the side of the car. He crouched into the corner, weeping. Esra looked on in pure shock. The cables severed, and there was nothing but the sensation of weightlessness as the car plunged a thousand feet into the cavernous darkness below.

CHAPTER 61

Lake Lucerne

The early morning sky framed the smoldering apex of *Die Wandung,* and the stench of the massive fireball could still be detected in Vetsch. Wisps of black smoke swirled upward and arced over Lake Lucerne. The incinerated remnants of the upper terminal were an indistinguishable concrete crater filled with blackened and twisted sheaves, cables, and warped structural steel.

Far below, throngs of boats, full of gawkers and sightseers, had converged from across the lake, angling to get a glimpse of the unfathomable tragedy that occurred the night before. On shore, Coulomb's retreat was awash with local law enforcement, agents from the FIS, and the CIA. Officials were interrogating guests from the midnight cruise that never took place. One by one they were interviewed, scrutinized, and compelled to elaborate on their association with Paul Coulomb and Möbius. As questions continued, most would be found to be innocent investors, naïve business partners. A few would later be charged with serious offenses—two such individuals being Jim Romano of the International Financial Corporation, and Bruno Metzier, a pharmaceutical titan from Basel. Talk surfaced that his wife Pauline was actually smiling during her interrogation, feeling a sense of liberation.

What had happened on *Die Wandung* that led to the disaster was too complex to be plausible; a far-fetched tale that could only happen in the movies.

A concise narrative detailing the incredible drama was delivered by an automated e-mail to the world's largest news outlets precisely fifteen minutes after the upper terminal exploded. Penned by Harry Meadowlark, a former official of the international corporation Möbius, the e-mail indicted Möbius and issued a step-by-step blueprint of its horrific plan, *Socrates*, described in minute detail. Meadowlark outlined his involvement and control over the termination of the evil scheme. He explained how over the last two years, Möbius constructed the command center in the bunker. Meadowlark headed the project using sophisticated computer and communication hardware that he alone had designed. During this period, he covertly installed the explosives to detonate soon after the keys were sequenced. Activation could only be achieved by the complex programming embedded in the four signal detection keys. Like some sophisticated science fiction movie that placed general relativity, wormholes, and binary code in the lexicon of the general public, π, e, $\sqrt{2}$, and $\pi^2/6$ became just as common—irrational numbers that reached a historic level of recognition, bumping mathematics and math education into the pop culture of the day.

Meadowlark's genius computer coding eliminated the possibility of Sarin-TX from ever entering the water tanks across Europe, thus preventing the deaths of tens of thousands. Posthumously, he earned hero status and was awarded the highest civilian honors from several European countries.

Harry had planned well.

He had won the game.

CHAPTER 62

10 Days Later
Springdale, Utah

Mallory sat on the stone patio overlooking the Virgin River as it snaked its way from Zion National Park through the small town of Springdale. It was late afternoon, and she sipped a glass of ice-cold water at her hotel as she imagined the river tumbling down rugged Zion Canyon and eventually settling into a peaceful meander.

There was something about water, the elixir of all life, whether here on this earth or on planets yet discovered. The reality of a homicidal controller of the planet's life blood now extinguished brought relief. Water, without it nothing would exist—a necessity—a human right? But what would it take for the world to realize the true worth of water, and to honor it, cleanse it and…save it. Water should never…ever…run uphill to money.

She remembered the quote by Benjamin Franklin: *When the well is dry, we know the worth of water.*

What was true then, was true now more than ever.

As a mathematician, she understood the self-evident process of reasoning, that numerical processes are undeniable. Plug in the variables and get the solution. But what about emotional trauma? How would one go about processing that in terms of axioms and postulates? She realized there was no debate here. There were no set-rules that one could follow.

A wisp of courage was all she needed.

She took another sip and relaxed. She'd moved past her acrophobia by running headlong into it. Earlier that morning, she had traversed the Knife-Ridge of Angels Landing once again, brushing away her fears of that fateful day three weeks earlier. She couldn't leave the stunning views and Tom's murder side by side, locked in her mind forever.

She had to reconquer.

Katie understood completely. There was no argument; in fact, she implored Mallory to spread Tom's ashes for her over his favorite national park. It made sense. Mallory accepted Katie's reasons not to come. It was hard enough to lose your father in such a brutal manner, but to see where he died would be too much of a burden.

Mallory resisted at first, but recognized the honor. The Park Service issued the special use permit in three days. All she had to do was negotiate the heart-stopping Knife-Ridge. This time she conquered her fears, hardly noticing the twelve hundred foot drop-off. After what she had experienced the last few weeks, Angels Landing was a walk in the park. Standing near the very location where Tom had been murdered, she felt an unexplainable calmness. Inches from nothing but air, she stared out over the natural beauty that was Zion. She recalled Harry Meadowlark taunting the edge of the lower Tepecik River gorge with his daredevil stance, with not an ounce of fear. He would teeter on the brink as if he was daring gravity to take him. Even a sudden breeze could rattle one's balance, but Meadowlark didn't seem to worry over the risk. Watching him precariously close to the edge, Mallory wondered if there was not an ounce of fear in the man. Did he trust himself to not make a mistake, or did he use some inner embodiment to test his courage? He lived and died by his games, his rules. She imagined there was *reason for everything*, a philosophical statement that she didn't understand.

Smiling broadly, she removed the lid from the scattering tube and gently shook out the ashes into the air, and then watched them churn with the warm breeze, eventually becoming one with the heavenly beauty of Zion. Fellow hikers stood behind her, gazing at the scene with reverence and understanding. She felt a peace she had never felt before.

A voice from the corner of the patio brought her out of reflection. "Just the person I want to see."

Mallory looked up and saw McKenzie, dressed in plaid Bermuda shorts and a striped blue shirt. He had the welcoming smile of a man who had not a care in the world. His grin widened as he walked her way. She rushed up, pulled him tight, and kissed him on the lips. "That's for coming out of this alive," she said, examining his left side temple. A small scar remained where Wallace had pummeled him with the barrel of the gun. "How's the head?"

"Maybe I should put myself in danger more often if that's the reward."

"You could be damaged goods." She grinned.

"A minor concussion. I should be fine except for the scar."

"It adds to your rugged good looks."

"Truthfully, I want to avoid ruggedness for a while."

"Can I get you anything, glass of cold water, lemonade, juice?"

"Tonic water later with a splash of vodka sounds good, but now, how about a walk?"

She led him across the patio and down a short path that looped to the banks of the Virgin River, edged by willows and cottonwoods. The gentle rush of the river, more like a creek, flowed over sandstone cobbles, providing a soothing babble over clear pool-drops.

"What's the latest?" she asked as they neared a bench and sat.

He reached down and picked up a small stick and began to snap it in two, tossing a piece at a time into the current. "The arrests continue with Möbius insiders and associates. Even with all the inner circle dead, there were plenty of others involved in creating *Socrates*. Imagine if one private utility had control of that much useable water in the world."

"That's disturbing."

"The other hot-button item is the IFC. Governments are now waiting to see how far the corruption has infiltrated the World Bank. It may take years to unravel. In the meantime, I believe Katie Haley is out of the woods."

"That's good for Katie, but with the IFC under the microscope, that creates problems for developing countries."

"Obviously," he said, throwing the last bit of stick into the water.

"I heard Harry Meadowlark had planned his retaliation two years before he went AWOL."

"He was the brains behind the programming. Coulomb didn't think anything of his work with the sophisticated bunker computers. All that time, he never realized Harry was rigging explosives right under his nose."

She thought about Meadowlark's preparation to pull off such a feat, and to pull it off with a caveat. He would make Coulomb work for his success, although Harry knew it would never come to pass. Brilliant. Coulomb's *Socrates* was usurped by Meadowlark's game playing ingenuity.

"By the way," McKenzie said, "Neal gives his regards.

"He doing well?"

"He says he misses the chaos you create."

Mallory raised a brow. "Oh, really?"

McKenzie smiled. "Said he misses having you around."

"Tell him likewise."

"How's Katie coping?"

"Quite well. Better than expected—for both of us. I'm going to see her tomorrow." Her eyes stayed on Lane. "Thanks for everything. I apologize for putting you and your men at risk, I should have never—"

McKenzie crisscrossed his hands above his head signaling a timeout. "Hold on, you saved my skin just as well, so no more of this apologizing stuff. But if you do owe me anything, you owe me an explanation."

"I'd love to. What do you want to know?"

He slid over on the bench, brushing against her. "Above the Tepecik River gorge, you mentioned a *hypothesis*. What did you mean by that?"

She tilted her head and smiled. "Imagine a woman who has cancer, months to live. She gives birth to a stillborn. Imagine a couple who adopt a baby, less than twenty-four hours later from the same hospital. Now imagine in your wildest dreams that the stillborn was, in fact, not stillborn, but a live, healthy baby. What would the odds be that this baby was the adopted child? Would you say it was possible, or just a far-fetched story?

"Quite the story, but who, why?"

"It's just a crazy idea I've had in the back of my mind since—well, since right before my mother passed away."

McKenzie rolled his eyes. "Are you serious?"

"Do I have any evidence?" She shook her head. "My mother was dying of pancreatic cancer. Dad was going through tough times with the farm. Even at the age of thirteen, I could see they were concerned about another mouth to feed. You could see the stress that could bring."

"And you're saying your parents lied to you, and Katie could be a sister?"

"Just a wild hypothesis, with not a shred of evidence; only that the Haley's did adopt a child at the same hospital that my mother delivered the stillborn."

"Simple, compare your DNA. You'd know one way or the other."

"What—and *ruin* my *hypothesis*? Now, let's talk serious. What are your plans, Mr. McKenzie?"

"I mentioned a splash of vodka. Maybe we could find a place for dinner before I head to Nellis and hitch a flight back to Langley."

Mallory gave him a surprised look, and then her eyes zoomed up to the incredible cliffs overlooking Springdale. "Take a look around. I could show you Zion without the drama. Are you that important that you have to be back at work so soon?"

"Well, I—"

"Spend the night here; I've got room."

He blushed. "That's taking a big risk."

Mallory's lips twisted into a devilish grin. "I like risks, and I'm spontaneous. You ought to know that by now."

CHAPTER 63

Mallory drove slowly down the lane, and then turned onto the gravel driveway to Tom Haley's house. After saying goodbye to Lane at Nellis and promising they would get together soon, she fought the traffic through Las Vegas and headed for Mountain Springs. She gazed at the barren hillsides, scoured by the late July sun, interrupted occasionally by high cirrus clouds trailing across the deep blue sky. It felt like an eternity since she'd been here. She braked slightly, as a roadrunner, a lizard in its beak, scurried across her path. With a steady grip on the steering wheel, she pulled up in front of the house, letting out the breath she didn't know she held.

She swallowed hard and got out of the car. The rustic wooden door to the house was open. She remembered the last time she was here, and it wasn't a pleasant experience. Taking a breath, she rang the doorbell. A voice echoed. "Come in."

She stepped inside and saw Katie splayed on the floor of the study, rifling through a box full of papers. Seeing Mallory, she rose and rushed over, giving her a long hug.

Katie leaned back, smiling. "Boy, you've certainly been busy the last couple of days."

Mallory glanced around the house. Her pulse accelerated, knowing she didn't want to share the terror she experienced here recently. "Everything went beautifully at Zion. Tom is flying high as we speak."

Katie wiped a tear and smiled at the same time. "Thanks a million."

"The house looks good. It's strange how quiet—" Mallory stumbled on the last word. "Sorry, I didn't mean it that way."

"Hey, no need to apologize. I feel a renewed sense of calm here. She picked up a sheet of paper from a pile on the floor and handed it to Mallory. "I found this in his stuff."

It was a photograph of Harry Meadowlark together with Tom Haley at the museum. They stood in front of one of the arches. "They both look peaceful, don't they?"

Katie nodded. "They do. Have you considered if we had known Harry's plans, things might have turned out differently?"

"He was the game player; one way or the other he would have won."

"I've given a lot of thought about it these last couple of weeks. One thing keeps coming front and center."

"What's that?" Mallory asked.

"If dad hadn't found you right before—" She paused. "—I try to imagine what would have happened."

"I think it was destiny."

"Fate, destiny. You could have been killed six times over."

A genuine smile. "You would've done the same for me."

Katie changed the subject. "How about a glass of wine? We have some catching up to do."

Mallory agreed.

Katie went into the kitchen and poured two glasses of some unknown red. They retreated to the patio out back and sat under a pergola that provided shade from the afternoon sun. The temperature was around ninety, cooler than normal for this time of year.

"You seem to be getting things under control," Mallory said.

"Have you and Kato made up?"

"For the time being. He watches me like a hawk."

Katie smiled and took a sip of wine.

"Katie, I'm so sorry. No one deserves what you've been through."

"She shook her head in disagreement. "I used Ismet as an excuse to estrange myself from my father. I took advantage of the situation." She turned to Mallory, her eyes reddened. "Did I love Ismet? I loved him, but maybe in a different way."

"Katie, you did what you thought was right."

"What I did was wrong. I was a terrorist, set on destroying that dam. It's only a matter of time before I'm extradited to Turkey to face charges."

"Don't get to thinking your future is a Turkish prison. Remember, the Turkish government has problems of their own with corruption and the IFC. Lane assured me the U.S. government will fight any extradition, in fact, you were working as an inside operative, just like your dad."

"That's a far reach."

"And you were good at your job. It was you who helped us survive the terminal explosion."

After a long moment, Katie asked, "Tell me, did you really risk your life because my father asked you—or, am I missing something?"

"Katie, you mean a lot to me."

Katie rubbed the side of her glass. "I don't mean to pry, but…did Britt's memory ever enter into your decision?"

Mallory considered what Katie had asked her. She remained silent, not sure how to answer.

Katie continued. "It's no secret you've continued to blame yourself for Britt's death, not so much by words, but by actions. It's as if you have a need to punish yourself for what happened."

Mallory's face fell in shadow. "Some things in life you never get over."

"I should have the same guilt, God knows I should. For years I brushed away my father's attempts at reconciliation until it was too late. But this last week, I've come to a conclusion. I've vowed not to blame myself. That would be self-defeating. The whole Möbius affair was a combination of bad choices made by both *me* and *my father*. No one's perfect. Stop beating yourself up for all the things you thought you should have done for Britt when she was alive, but didn't."

"The past can dig you a grave."

"Or offer you a way home. Now, it's my turn to help. Remember the things you did for her when she was alive. You helped raise her. Your mother was fighting cancer, and your father passed on a few years later. You were under a tremendous burden, but you were there for Britt, helping her through school, in life, and when the farm was in foreclosure. That was an awful lot of pressure."

Mallory gazed at Katie, examining eyes that held a persuasive truth. "You know too much."

"Don't let the circumstances of her death trump all that. She loved you; never forget that. We've been like sisters, but I'm not Britt, never was, nor would

I ever want to replace her. You were there for her, and you were there for me. That's what counts."

Mallory swore she could hear Britt talking. The voice was as clear now as it was so many years ago, same inflection and same innocent tone. She recalled Britt when she was in high school, looking at her with those deep-set brown eyes, asking a question on pre-calculus. *Please explain the relationship of the unit circle to the trigonometric functions, I'm having a hard time absorbing all this, but you have a way of making this stuff fun and easy.*

She felt herself move swiftly forward a few years, in a trance, to the days when she had become Katie's best friend, her protector, her *older sister*, someone who was always there to listen to and share the problems of every young girl. Could this be the same young woman she mentored so long ago, the rebellious teenager that evolved into a head-strong adult? Back then Mallory was the rudder, stabilizing Katie's concerns and fears, providing guidance when dealing with peers and a sometimes impassive Tom.

She stared at Katie for a long time. Many remarked how their sharply defined cheeks and deep-set eyes were alike, although Katie had brown, just like Britt's, and Mallory sported that mysterious green. But did that prove anything? As she continued to gaze, she envisioned looking into a mirror. She remembered what Harry Meadowlark had said in the powerhouse below the dam, when they were in danger and on the cusp of being killed—something about Katie having the *urge to track down her DNA*, and what about Mallory herself, *what's in your DNA?* What a strange thought. *What would a foray into the world of DNA analysis be like?* She pictured the mathematics of the double-helix, the sinusoidal x and y components of intertwined space curves—*arc length... curvature ...torsion...arc length...curvature...torsion.* Her relationship with Katie was much simpler, based upon the human bond of love, unencumbered by complex mathematics. Why screw it up now.

She couldn't alter the past, but she could change the way she remembered it. She felt Britt's presence standing in a spectral background behind Katie. Her sister's voice was soft, an eternal smile upon her face.

Mallory, you're my sister. I love you, but it's time to move on. Stop carrying the weight.

AUTHOR'S NOTE

I hope the reader comes away from this novel with a sense of urgency about the importance that water plays in the survival of all life on this planet, especially the human species and its dependence on clean, potable water. Those who have never had to grapple with a water shortage may find it difficult to understand the critical nature of this most precious resource. Sure, almost seventy percent of the earth is covered by water but only one percent is useable, and that amount is diminishing. Without clean water, everything will suffer—agriculture, sanitation, wildlife conservation, even efforts to eradicate hunger. The powerful corporate structure that has emerged in the last several decades suggests that we should be suspicious of motive. All who have a stake in the survival of life, whether they worry about themselves, their children and grandchildren, should not remain silent. We must accept our role in resisting those who support the historical claim that "water flows uphill to money."

ABOUT THE AUTHOR

Lee Lindauer has a MS degree in Structural Engineering and spent over twenty-five years as principal of a consulting engineering firm he founded in Western Colorado. Using his knowledge as an engineer and passion for the world, he constructs problem-solving scenarios in authentic technical and natural settings. He is a member of the International Thriller Writers. He and his wife Teri divide their time between home base Grand Junction, Colorado and Mesquite, Nevada. Visit the author's website at www.leelindauer.com

CPSIA information can be obtained
at www.ICGtesting.com
Printed in the USA
FSHW01n1638070718
50213FS